✓ **NORTHUM**

You should return this book on or before the ~~~~~~ stamped
below unless an~

D0714644

S

ICE AT STONEWYLDE

Also by Kit Berry from Gollancz:

Magus of Stonewylde
Moondance of Stonewylde
Solstice at Stonewylde
Shadows at Stonewylde

SOLSTICE
at
STONEWYLDE

The Third Novel of Stonewylde

KIT BERRY

Copyright © Kit Berry 2007, 2011

All rights reserved

The right of Kit Berry to be identified as the author of this work
has been asserted by her in accordance with the
Copyright, Designs and Patents Act 1988.

First published in Great Britain in 2011 by Gollancz
An imprint of the Orion Publishing Group
Orion House, 5 Upper St Martin's Lane, London WC2H 9EA
An Hachette UK Company

A CIP catalogue record for this book is available
from the British Library

ISBN 978 0 575 09887 9

1 3 5 7 9 10 8 6 4 2

Typeset by Input Data Services Ltd, Bridgwater, Somerset

Printed in Great Britain by Clays Ltd, St Ives plc

The Orion Publishing Group's policy is to use papers that
are natural, renewable and recyclable products and
made from wood grown in sustainable forests. The logging
and manufacturing processes are expected to conform to
the environmental regulations of the country of origin.

www.stonewylde.com
www.orionbooks.co.uk

The Stonewylde Series
is dedicated to the memories of
Jean Guy, my best owl aunt
and
Debbie Gilbrook, my dearest friend.

Ghostly wreaths of mist clung to the great stones, shrouding the sinister images painted all over them. Black crows with outstretched wings and gaping beaks, leering white skulls, grinning Jack o' Lanterns; the emblems of Samhain loomed ominously from all directions. Two old women, grimy shawls clutched tightly around them, entered the Stone Circle. Black feathers and white bones hung from the elder branches that arched over the entrance to the sacred space, brushing their whiskery faces as they shuffled beneath the archway. It was silent and eerie inside the Circle and the sisters surveyed the menacing scene with grim approval.

A labyrinth delineated by smooth black stones was laid out on the soft earth. The ancient cursal pattern filled the arena and the path it marked out led to the centre where a great pyre had been built. The women hobbled across to the old cauldron squatting balefully on the Altar Stone, surrounded by boughs of yew. A great black crow painted on the stone behind the altar hovered threateningly above them, its wings splayed as if it were about to enfold them both. The crones lit their cracked clay pipes and puffed contentedly at the stinking smoke, undaunted by the dark and sinister atmosphere of the Stone Circle. They both took a swig of cloudy liquid from an old glass bottle and smacked their lips with satisfaction.

''Twill be strange, sister, both our boys here with us tomorrow.'

'Aye, blessed be that Magus fetched our Jackdaw home, his banishment over. My own dear son back again.'

'Things'll change now Magus brung him back to deal with the brat.

Dark Angel didn't want the boy up on Mooncliffe at Hunter's Moon, but tomorrow, sister, 'tis Samhain! With both our sons to help, the boy will be taken.'

'Aye, Magus must have a clear path to the moongazy maiden. He needs her magic, like his father afore him with that Raven!'

They cackled hoarsely at this and took another swig.

'Moongazy as they come but didn't save her, did it? Nought but a pile o' ash under the Yew! Old Heggy got it wrong there.'

They spat in unison, then knocked their pipes against the stone.

'Work to be done now, sister, and best get on with it. We need to be ready for tomorrow night, when the Angel comes a-walking in the Stone Labyrinth.'

'Aye, when the Dark Angel comes looking for his own at Samhain.'

1

Magus strode purposefully along the Tudor gallery to the rooms at the end. He had much to do, with the festival so close, and no time to waste today.

'You're not still in bed!' he said irritably. He stood with Miranda in the girl's bedroom gazing down at Sylvie as she lay against the pillows, white and exhausted. She pointedly looked away, refusing to meet his eyes or answer him.

'You should be up and about by now, young lady,' he continued. 'A week in bed is more than enough. Don't you agree, Miranda?'

'I'm not sure she's quite ready yet,' said her mother tentatively. 'She's still a bit weak – look at the shadows under her eyes.'

'Rubbish!' said Magus firmly. 'Remember that I know best in these matters. I've warned you that Sylvie's prone to malingering and attention-seeking. It's Samhain tomorrow and she should be preparing for the festival along with everyone else. This is all for show – she's absolutely fine. Leave us, Miranda. I want to speak with her alone.'

Reluctantly Miranda left the room and Sylvie struggled to sit up. She stared hard at him, her eyes pools of icy water in her white face.

'It's not for show,' she said in a small voice.

'You're being pathetic, Sylvie,' he said tersely. 'All you did was stand on a rock for a few hours. I don't understand why you're making such a fuss over nothing.'

'I'm not making a fuss over nothing! How could you be so cruel? You had no right to do that to me and I won't go up there next month. I'll never let you take my moon magic again.'

Magus's lips tightened into a hard, white line and he sat down on the bed next to her. He leant forward and pushed his face close to hers, black eyes glittering.

'You'll do exactly as I tell you,' he said in a voice of steel. 'Everyone else does and you're no exception. You know full well why you were brought to Stonewylde and what I need from you. You'll go to Mooncliffe every month for as long as I want you to.'

Sylvie closed her eyes, trying to summon the strength to stand up to him.

'I won't,' she whispered. 'I'll leave Stonewylde rather than go on that rock again.'

He chuckled at this and reaching out, gently stroked the hair back from her face. She flinched at his touch but was unable to move away.

'No, no, Sylvie – you won't leave Stonewylde. You're only fifteen and far too young to be all alone in that big wide world out there, especially given your allergies. The Outside World could kill you. And your mother's expecting my baby and she'll never leave – you wouldn't abandon them here, surely, wondering how they'd cope with my anger and displeasure. To say nothing of what I'd do to your sweetheart Yul. You'll stay here for their sakes and you'll do exactly as I want.'

Sylvie stared at him helplessly through a mist of tears. She had no energy to fight. He continued to brush the hair off her forehead and the feel of his sure fingers made her skin crawl.

'Is Yul alright?' she whispered, vaguely recalling his dramatic arrival at the moonrise but with no idea of what'd happened to him after that.

'No, not really,' he laughed. He stood up and looked down at her with a pitiless smile. 'And by the time I've finished with him, he'll never be alright again.'

'I hate you,' she whispered, even more softly. 'I really hate you.'

Magus laughed again and then called her mother back in. He put his arm around Miranda, his other hand resting proprietorially on her swollen belly.

'Sylvie's to get up now. She's not ill, she's just wallowing in self-pity. She's far too keen on playing the martyr and expecting us all to run around after her. Get her out of bed now and make her eat. Do you understand me, Miranda?'

'Yes, Magus, whatever you say. You know best.'

He smiled and gently patted her stomach.

'Yes, I do, so make sure she's ready for Samhain. That's an order, Miranda. I want her down in the Village tomorrow taking part in the festival. This attention-seeking behaviour stops right now.'

The Village Green was alive with activity as Nightwing trotted along the cobbles. Magus reined the horse in, holding the black stallion in check as he surveyed the scene before him. The Green Labyrinth was almost complete. Scorched lines marked the pattern on the grass, which was picked out further with white pebbles interspersed with tiny candles in coloured glass jars. In the centre of the enormous seven-coiled labyrinth the Villagers had built a large wicker dome, and many people were still busy adding the finishing touches. This labyrinth would be the spiritual focus for tomorrow's events.

Magus swung the horse around and urged him towards the open doors of the Great Barn. Peering in, he nodded with satisfaction at the preparations taking place. The ancient building was decorated in the same manner as the Stone Circle, with black birds, pale skulls and bright Jack o' Lanterns. Twigs of elder and slips of yew hung around the walls and rafters, tokens of the trees sacred to Samhain. The elder was the crone's tree, the waning and dark face of the Triple Moon Goddess and thought to guard the gates to the Otherworld and the dark mysteries of the dead. The yew was the tree of death and regeneration.

Emblems of death were everywhere and Magus smiled grimly. Death was exactly what he had in mind for the ashen-faced boy lying in the byre. Yul had led a charmed life thanks to that meddling old crone, but maybe this Samhain her binding spell could be side-stepped. Maybe, at last, the Dark Angel himself would intervene to break her spell of protection over the upstart Villager who'd caused him so much trouble this year.

Magus wheeled Nightwing around and trotted down one of the lanes that radiated away from the Village Green like spokes of a web. He'd already visited three of the families involved, and had one more call to make this morning. Maizie saw the tall figure of Magus through a window and hurriedly opened her door. She'd been worried sick since receiving a message after the Hunter's Moon informing her that he was keeping Yul up at the Hall for a few days, following an incident with Sylvie at Mooncliffe. The implication was that her son had committed a serious misdemeanour. Maizie's heart had sunk at this news, and she now greeted Magus with some trepidation. He dwarfed the cottage parlour, his head brushing the beams as he gazed down at the anxious woman before him.

Despite having borne seven children and enduring a brute of a husband, he still recognised the spark that had so attracted him all those years ago. Those dark curls and slanted grey eyes, the rosy cheeks that burned now with emotion, just as they'd once done for entirely different reasons. Her dimples were the same, and her proud chin. He shook his head to dispel the memories and sat down in an armchair, indicating that she too should sit. A little girl came running in from the kitchen, freezing when she saw the grand figure of the master of Stonewylde seated unexpectedly in her home.

'Blessings!' he smiled, holding out a welcoming hand to her. Shyly she approached and he lifted her onto his lap. He gazed down at her pointed little face and gently ruffled her mass of black curls.

'She's so like you, Maizie,' he said, his dark eyes soft. 'Not in Nursery yet? Or do you like to keep her at home with you?'

'She won't be two till Imbolc, sir,' replied Maizie. 'Time enough then for Nursery.'

'Nearly two years? Doesn't time fly?'

'Like a crow, straight and true. Have you come to tell me, sir, what's happened to Yul?'

'No, Maizie. I wished to speak to you about your husband. I think—'

'But what about my boy, sir? When will he be coming home?'

'I'm keeping him at the Hall for a little longer.'

'I don't wish to be disrespectful, sir, but last time you had Yul up at the Hall you nearly killed him. Whatever he's done, surely he don't deserve that?'

Magus looked deep into her eyes and remembered how he'd once felt about this woman, only a girl then. There'd been women and girls aplenty, but she'd always been different. She was by his side all through that long year when he'd worked himself to the bone, struggling to rescue Stonewylde from the slough of neglect that was the legacy of his father, uncle and grandfather. Three bad masters in a row, and the very fabric of Stonewylde almost torn apart by their laziness and greed. It was a daunting task for the young, idealistic man, who'd put his burgeoning career in the Outside World on hold to return home and put things to rights.

Maizie had been his saviour that year, her vivacity, prettiness and uncomplicated sense of fun the only light in those dark days of endless labour and exhaustion. She'd been a complete contrast to the smart, sophisticated women he'd left behind in London – Maizie was pure Stonewylde, just when he'd discovered his obsessive love for the vast country estate. She'd sparkled brightly, his one ray of sunlight right up until the fateful Winter Solstice when everything had fallen apart so cataclysmically in the Stone Circle. He sighed and smiled sadly at her.

'Now, Maizie, you must trust me on this. We both know that Yul is wilful, disobedient and a complete troublemaker. That's why poor Alwyn had such a difficult time with him over the years. It can't have been easy bringing up a son as rebellious as Yul.'

Maizie regarded him steadily, also remembering the past. She'd once loved this man so desperately and she was sure that part of her always would. She took a deep breath.

'We both know, sir, that Yul is no son of Alwyn's. Now that the man's ill and not likely to recover, we can speak openly. After all this time, surely you can acknowledge the boy as your own.'

There was silence in the small parlour. Magus's black eyes glittered dangerously. He tapped his whip against his boot, mouth tight with displeasure.

'I thought we'd agreed never to discuss this? The matter was dealt with years ago. You were already pregnant at that Moon Fullness up at Mooncliffe and if I'd realised, I'd never have taken you up there that night, nor carried on with you all summer and autumn. I don't make love to women already pregnant by another man. You deceived me, Maizie, and you even admitted it just before your handfasting to Alwyn.'

She gave him a hard stare, then looked away, her cheeks burning fiercely.

'I was *not* pregnant and you know it! Anything I admitted was because 'twas forced out of me. I'd never lain with anyone other than you, not till after Yul was born. You and I both know that night of the Blue Moon was my first time, and we both know right enough why you've denied Yul all these years. But Mother Heggy's a mad old biddy and you should never have taken heed of her foolish words.'

'It was nothing to do with that, Maizie.'

'You know 'twas! You were happy enough about me carrying your baby up until then! But because of that stupid rant, you condemned me to years of misery with Alwyn, and condemned your own son to suffering beyond belief!'

'You're wrong, Maizie. I—'

'No I'm not! All these long years I've kept quiet! All these years I've held my tongue and stood by silently, scared silly of Alwyn and his fists. And of you. You know how I've tried to talk to you about it, asked you to put the terrible wrongs right, but always it were the same limping excuse from you – Alwyn. But he's not around no more and at last I can speak plain. Any fool can see Yul's yours.'

'Yul's nothing like me! He has dark hair and grey eyes.'

'Yes, that's from me. But he has *your* build and height, *your* way o' moving and riding, *your* hands and fingernails, *your* eyebrows and cheekbones – I could go on forever. He's clever like you, determined, quick-witted and so strong-willed. He won't be told what to do unless he wants to do it – and he has your temper.'

'Maizie, that describes you too. You're strong-minded and bright – it's what I loved about you. All those qualities are from you. And anyway, Yul was born eight months after the Blue Moon up at Mooncliffe. That was our first time together so you must've conceived before then.'

'No! He came a month early! 'Tis not that unusual! Would I have been up in the cold and dark at the Stone Circle for the Winter Solstice if he'd been due then? I thought I'd another month to go! I was as shocked as anyone when he were born during the ceremony, in the middle of that eclipse, with me squatting on the earth while everyone looked on and Mother Heggy capering about and laying him on the Altar Stone all bloody and screaming. Not the best way of birthing your first child, and not expected neither!'

She stared angrily at Magus, her nostrils flaring and grey eyes flashing. He was reminded forcibly of the boy who now lay like death up in the byre; this was how Yul looked when he was angry. He knew Yul would've been a worthy son, someone to groom as his heir, as the future magus. The boy had courage, pride and was a natural leader. He was tough and intelligent and passionate about Stonewylde. But Magus'd been haunted by Mother Heggy's prophecies ever since Yul's birth. If he acknowledged Yul as his own, he risked their coming true. *Conceived under a blue moon, born under a red one, the fruit of his passion. This child would one day rise up with the folk behind him to overthrow him at the place of bones and death.*

Magus had woken in the middle of many a night in cold, sweating panic, haunted by the thought of a child of his growing up at Stonewylde, whose destiny was to destroy him. It was like something from a Greek tragedy and must never be given any credence whatsoever. How could such a beautiful act of love-making with a young girl who'd captured his heart, result in such horror? Maizie had seemed to be his destiny, his true love. Despite the differences in their upbringing, he'd recognised something in her that called to his soul, and in his naivety had thought that love would overcome all. With a pretty, intelligent Village girl by his side, he'd bring Stonewylde back to a golden age of happiness and prosperity. That was his plan and he'd intended to announce it that Imbolc after the baby's birth, when he would crown Maizie as his Bright Maiden and be handfasted with her. But the terrible events of the Winter Solstice had put paid to that idea. So he told himself that the baby coming a month early was proof of just how wrong a man could be to ever put his trust in a happy-ever-after future with any woman.

Magus shook his head and once more denied Yul's paternity, hoping as always to thus negate the prophecy. He looked across at the pretty woman before him, his face implacable.

'I'm sorry, Maizie, but you're wrong and I'll be very displeased if you continue to make these false allegations. Yul will remain at the Hall whilst I investigate his latest insubordination. I'll deal with him as I see fit. I'm the magus and it isn't for you to question the punishment I choose to administer, so keep your remarks to yourself. I'll hear no more about this and you'd do well to remember your place.'

'I'm sorry, sir,' she said, lowering her eyes, although her anger remained palpable. She was still so attractive; he'd always pre-ferred women with spirit and Maizie was certainly one of those. She'd never gone soft and fawning, never given in to him and lost her independence. She'd endured the life to which he'd consigned her with stoicism, her pride never allowing her to become anything less than the woman he'd fallen in love with all those years ago. He glanced down at the tiny girl sitting silently in his lap listening to everything being said, and his heart twinged with remorse. She gazed up at him with enormous green eyes that seemed to search his soul. Eyes that looked inside him and knew exactly what dark truths he tried to conceal.

'Bad man,' she said clearly. 'Bad, bad man.'

'Leveret, come here!' said Maizie sharply. Magus handed the child over to her mother, who clasped her tightly.

'Anyway ... I came here to speak to you about Alwyn. You know there's been no improvement since the stroke? He's still alive but can do nothing for himself and he's not aware of anything. He's shrunk to skin and bones and has to be fed through tubes. I wanted to ask if you'd agree to Alwyn entering the Stone Labyrinth this Samhain for the Dance of Death. I think he should, but as his nearest relative it's your decision. You know the custom – permission can only be granted by the closest member of the family.'

She took a deep breath to calm herself. If there was one thing Maizie had learnt from living with Alwyn all those years, it was self control. She nodded.

'Yes, I agree he should go. Let the Dark Angel decide – 'tis the best way.'

'Good,' he said, smiling briskly. 'I'll arrange for it to be done. Well, I must be off.'

They both rose and he gazed down at her. She stood before him, Leveret on her hip, and his dark eyes softened at the pair of them. He took one of the woman's hands.

'Maizie, let's not spoil things between us now, not after all this time and all that's happened. You know that you've always been special to me. You were such a lovely girl and you're a fine woman. I wish that—'

She frowned at him and removed her hand from his.

'Thank you for calling on me, sir. Samhain Blessings to you.'

By mid-morning the next day the heavy mist had lifted, although the day remained overcast and grey. Children ran around the Village excitedly, desperate to get on with the festivities. Every fire in the Village had been extinguished and everyone must fast until the feast in the evening. The trees encircling the Green had already shed their leaves, victims of a wild and gusty storm that had raged the day after the full moon, and had now taken on their skeletal winter appearance. The remains of the messy rooks' nests had blown away too in the south-westerly gales and now only the great yew remained clothed in glossy dark-green, its slips looking like the barbs of a bird's feathers. It was the last day of the pagan year, the day for ending the old. It was the day of death.

In the morning the Samhain drama prepared by the youngsters was performed in the Great Barn. It was a spectacular event, full of dance and music with everyone masked and costumed. Sylvie hadn't taken part; she was feeling far too weak and she'd missed all the rehearsals anyway. Magus noticed her absence and at midday he left the festivities to fetch her from the Hall. She sat now in the jolting cart beside her mother, huddled miserably in her black cloak. This was her first time outside since the night of the Hunter's Moon over a week ago.

Sylvie hadn't wanted to come today, but Magus had stormed into their rooms and insisted that she go to the Village immediately to take part in the afternoon and evening ceremonies. He'd been furious when she'd refused. Miranda hadn't batted an eyelid when he'd slapped Sylvie hard, shouting at her and throwing clothes at her to put on. Her mother had merely looked on as he dragged her, crying and struggling, out of the rooms and downstairs. He'd bundled her roughly towards the waiting horse and cart, his one concession to her weakness.

'Behave yourself, girl!' he'd hissed menacingly into her face, dumping her on the seat in the back of the cart. 'I told you yesterday you'd take part in the festival and so you shall. There's nothing wrong with you so snap out of it and stop being pathetic!'

Shivering in her cloak, she tried to stifle the sobs that escaped every so often. She felt ill and weak, but a dull anger burned inside her. It was only when Sylvie realised it was Tom at the reins that she managed to pull herself together. As soon as Magus had ridden on ahead, she leant forward and whispered to the ostler.

'Tom, do you have any news of Yul? Is he alright?'

The old man turned and gazed down at her in consternation. He was unsure how honest to be for this poor girl looked little better than the boy, but she deserved the truth.

'I'm not to speak of it, but I reckon you won't spread the word and get me into trouble. So no, miss, Yul's not alright at all. He's alive, and that's a miracle in itself, but he's in a bad way. He can't stand nor barely sit up and he can't take no food. I done what I can, and Mother Heggy's sent potions. But ... well, 'tis not looking good for the lad.'

'What did they do to him?' she whispered, closing her eyes in anguish at the thought of Yul suffering. 'Was he whipped again?'

'No, miss! He were brung up to the Hall like this the day after the Moon Fullness. That Jackdaw carried him into the byre like a brace o' rabbits slung over his shoulders. They done nothing to him since, but I reckon Yul's been poisoned. His eyes aren't right and he don't know who he is or nothing.'

Miranda pulled her back onto the seat.

'What are you whispering about, Sylvie? Don't talk with the servants like that. You know Magus wouldn't like it.'

Sylvie glared at her. Even under Clip's hypnosis, she couldn't understand how her mother could behave like this.

'All you ever think about is Magus! He always comes first, before anyone or anything. How could you have let him hit me, Mum? *You've* never hit me and you've always said it was wrong. Do you really love him so much that I don't matter now? Don't you care about me any more?'

Miranda looked away uncomfortably.

'Of course I do. But Magus is right – you can't just take to your bed for half the month. If you insist on dancing on that cliff, you'll have to put up with feeling tired afterwards and get on with it. And anyway, Sylvie, Magus didn't hit you. It was just a little slap.'

'That's not true! He did hit me, he was rough with me and it really hurt, especially when I feel so ill. Why do you *always* take his side?'

'Because he knows best. He says I've been too soft with you all these years and that's why you're so weak and quick to take to your bed. He says you've got no backbone and you enjoy being an invalid and I think maybe he's right. We have to obey him, you know that. Please don't be difficult, darling – it makes life so unpleasant and I don't want him to get angry. I must think of the baby, after all.'

Sylvie turned her back on her mother, seething with outrage. When they reached the Village, Tom helped them out of the cart and Sylvie managed to whisper to him again.

'If you get the chance, tell Yul I love him. Please, Tom?'

'Aye, miss, I'll do that.'

Sylvie stood shivering at the entrance to the Green Labyrinth marked out on the Village Green, waiting her turn to go in. Her face was so white and thin that she hardly needed a skull mask and she pulled the thick black cloak tightly around her, trying to keep warm. The atmosphere on the Green today frightened her, all the more because of her dreadful weakness. Everything in the Village today spoke of death and darkness, and this emphasis on mortality and morbidity terrified her. It was so different from the joyous maypole dancing at Beltane or the holiday fun of the Summer Solstice.

Everyone wore a hooded black robe or cloak and many wore skull masks. A thin line of smoke trickled from the wicker dome in the centre of the labyrinth, but the cottages seemed strangely lifeless without their habitual plumes of smoke. It was quiet too, despite the many people thronging around the cobbles. Sylvie wanted very much to cling to Miranda, who stood nearby, but that was out of the question given Miranda's earlier remarks. Her mother had made it very clear where her priorities now lay. Sylvie felt abandoned – and very vulnerable.

A man in a crow mask stood at the arch of elder branches,

identical to the one up at the Stone Circle. He allowed young people to enter the sacred space nine at a time, one by one. As Sylvie's group waited he reminded them of the labyrinth's significance. This was a pilgrimage and a moment of deep meditation. The walk through the labyrinth was symbolic, representing the journey towards death. When they entered the dome in the centre they entered the Otherworld, the Realm of the Dead, where they shed their past life and lay reflecting on all they'd left behind. Then, reborn from the dark womb, they began a new life, a new journey starting afresh as they retraced their steps and followed the path back out of the maze. This, said the crow man solemnly, was also symbolic of the death of this year and the birth of the new one. A time of endings and beginnings.

Sylvie watched the youngsters already in there. They walked very slowly, guided by the white pebbles as they followed the symmetrical, tortuously curved path. They walked with heads bowed, making sure they kept distance between each other until they reached the entrance to the dome. Sylvie really didn't want to enter the labyrinth; the whole thing was macabre and absolutely terrified her. She swayed on her feet at the entrance thinking she might at any moment faint. She'd barely eaten all week and couldn't shake off the overwhelming exhaustion that smothered her. She'd been on a drip for the first few days and her arm was still bruised, but she was still unable to eat normally. Her legs were shaky and her stomach felt hollow.

She surveyed the great coiled labyrinth ahead and felt panic well up inside. There was nothing on the path to hold on to – what if she collapsed in there? What if she never came out again? Nobody at Stonewylde cared for her apart from Yul and, if Tom was right, he was in mortal danger himself. She could die inside that wicker dome in the darkness and nobody would realise until it was too late.

As her fears and terrors spiralled out of control, she grabbed hold of the archway and gulped in air, trying to fight the waves of dizziness. She wanted to cry at Magus' harshness towards her. This was all his fault; he'd put her through the terrible ordeal again up at Mooncliffe and she couldn't help being slow to recover after being forced to feed him her moon magic. She'd never be able to take this every month. She looked across to the wicker dome in the centre and hoped desperately she'd make it that far without passing out.

'This is a very solemn journey,' continued the crow man, 'and not one to be undertaken lightly. As you walk towards your death, take stock of the past year and all your achievements and failures. While you're inside the Otherworld, in the dome, confront your weaknesses and your innermost desires. Clear your minds and savour the darkness and the special drink. When you emerge, newly born, remove your death mask and look to the New Year ahead with a bright face. As you walk back along the path, think hard on what you hope to achieve this coming year, what you can do for Stonewylde, for our community. You'll be given a slip of yew as you finish the journey to remind you of your rebirth and your resolutions. May the Dance of the Green Labyrinth at Samhain be sacred to you all.'

As the gate opened and the group began to move forward, Sylvie glanced across the Green and saw the tall black-robed figure of Magus staring intently at her. His face was impassive but his dark eyes burned into her. She shuddered and stepped under the arch of elder, the black feathers brushing her white face.

'Pull your mask down!' hissed the crow man, bundling her in and blocking the exit behind her.

2

Yul's eyes stared straight up at the cobwebbed ceiling of the stone byre. They were enormous and glassy, his pupils so dilated that the grey irises had all but disappeared. His face and lips were ashen and his heartbeat slow. His hands were as pale as his face as he lay unmoving and cold amongst the scattering of mouldy straw that littered the stone floor.

Earlier in the day Magus and Jackdaw had looked in on him. Magus had been pleased to see the boy was now at least conscious, if not in good health. Unbeknown to him, Mother Heggy's remedies and Tom's care had dragged Yul from the brink of death, where he'd hovered since the night of the Hunter's Moon. The hallucinogenic substances in the cakes he'd been fed were grown and harvested on the estate, and fairly harmless if only taken occasionally and in small doses. But Yul had been forced to swallow a huge quantity and they'd proved almost fatal. A week later he still lay in the straw, covered only by an old horse blanket. He was alarmingly thin and wasted, his cheekbones and chin sharp and pointed, the hollows of his cheeks and eye-sockets deep and shadowed. His black hair was lank and matted, his eyes strange. The bruises where Magus had hit him so hard around the face up on the clifftop were stark against his grey-tinged skin. All traces of the tanned and healthy Village lad were gone, and this skeletal wraith had taken his place.

When they'd come in and shut the door, Yul had clumsily tried to cover his face. The harsh light was blinding. Jackdaw stood cracking his knuckles as he looked down at the still figure, and Magus sat on a straw bale, also surveying the boy.

'Can I work him over a bit, sir, now he's finally woken up?'

Magus hesitated.

'It's tempting, but I think not. He still looks very fragile and I want him with us for the ceremony tonight at Samhain. Sorry to disappoint you, Jackdaw. Just see if he can stand, would you?'

Jackdaw bent and hauled the boy to his feet as if he were a marionette. Yul crumpled immediately, falling first against Jackdaw and then onto the floor in a boneless heap.

'Nah, he can't.'

'Oh well. Go and get him some food from the kitchen, something light. We'll see if that does the trick.'

With Jackdaw gone, Magus dragged Yul over to another bale and propped him upright. The boy was cleaner than Magus had thought he'd be, and he wondered if Tom had been showing him any misguided kindness. But he was in a terrible state nevertheless; limp and passive, enormous eyes staring blankly from his skeletal face, his head lolling weakly.

'Cat got your tongue?'

Yul looked at the silver Magus cat and nodded slowly. The cat had played with him for so long, chasing him all over the floor of the byre, in and out of the straw, tormenting and teasing him. He knew it was easier to play dead than try to escape.

'Do you realise it's Samhain today?'

There was no reaction and Magus sighed in disgust; this was no fun.

'Well, just in case anything's reaching your addled brain, you'll be joining me up in the Stone Circle tonight, for the Dance of Death. You know what that means.'

Yul gazed at him vacantly and Magus sighed again.

'Oh dear, oh dear. Looks like we have a new Village idiot.'

Jackdaw returned with a tray of food.

'Bloody hell! That sour-faced old cow in the kitchen hasn't changed much since I left Stonewylde. Marigold gave me a right tongue-lashing, and she's got no right to do that, even if she were my mother-in-law. You'll have to speak to her, sir. I ain't putting up with that, not from a woman. Tempted to ram her tea-towel down her bloody throat.'

'Just be patient, Jackdaw,' said Magus. 'Things will be alright eventually but it'll take time. You're still not a popular person around here, so just go easy.'

The huge, bald man put the tray down on a bale with a grunt of annoyance.

'Here's the grub then, Guv.'

'Good.'

They looked at each other.

'Well feed him then!'

'What – me, sir?'

'Yes, you!'

With another grunt, Jackdaw sat heavily on the bale and started to shovel food into Yul's mouth. Yul gagged and vomited repeatedly, unable to stomach the food crammed so relentlessly into his mouth. Magus stood up in revulsion and waved his henchman away.

'Goddess, that's disgusting! Enough, Jackdaw. We'll try again later.'

The men had stomped out of the byre, snapping off the electric light and locking the door behind them. But now as Yul lay on the stone floor in the cold gloom, the weak afternoon light filtering through gaps under the door, he could make out the tray of food. His vomit was spread in a small, splattered pool on the flagstones. A ray of light stirred suddenly in his brain and he blinked, then carefully sat up, the room spinning around him. He realised where he was, but this time there was no Alwyn, no excruciating pain in his back. He had vague recollections from the past days of Jackdaw leaning over him, slapping his face and shouting at him, but he wasn't sure if that was a memory or a dream.

Yul saw the jug by the door. On his hands and knees he crawled over very slowly, hoping it contained water. He drank deeply and splashed his face, then crawled back to the meagre remains of congealed food on the tray. Avoiding the mess on the floor, he ate what little food was left. He felt queasy but, eating slowly and carefully, managed to keep it down. Trembling with weakness and the aftermath of the poisons still in his body, he lay back against a bale and tried to think. His mind was a kaleidoscope of images and he didn't know which were real and which imagined. In the murky light, Yul closed his eyes and tried to make sense of the chaos in his head.

Behind the mask and under the hooded cloak, Sylvie felt private and sheltered. Despite her misgivings about this bizarre experience, she did as instructed and reflected on the past year. So much had happened and her life had been turned upside down. She thought of her joy when she'd first come to Stonewylde and believed she'd found paradise. And she thought of the reality now. Magus' words rang in her ears – *You know full well why you were brought to Stonewylde and what I need from you*. As she shuffled along the convoluted path of the Green Labyrinth, careful to keep within the white stones that marked the way, Sylvie felt a surge of rebellion rising up. She understood exactly how Yul felt and why he defied Magus, even though he knew he'd be punished. She would not obey that man, nor would she serve him. Being forced to give her magic to him wasn't why she'd been brought to Stonewylde at all.

Sylvie didn't understand the elemental powers at work in this special place; the moon magic spirals up at Hare Stone, the Earth Magic in the Stone Circle, the green magic in the Village Green. Nor did she understand the evil that stalked Quarrycleave and the coiled malignance at Mooncliffe. But she knew she wasn't here to serve Magus' needs. She must dance at Hare Stone at the rising of the full moon, just as Yul must stand on the Altar Stone at sunrise and sunset. Together they seemed necessary to both ground and release the energies that worked so powerfully here. They were both crucial to the very fabric of Stonewylde.

And she must be with Yul. She loved him; they belonged

together and their souls and destinies were linked, but if Magus had his way they'd be kept apart forever. If Magus had his way, Yul would be treated so badly that eventually he'd die. And she'd become Magus' vessel, used every month to feed his hunger for moon magic, then confined to her bed, too weak to move, when he'd taken his fill. She couldn't live like that and would never meekly obey him or accept his cruelty towards Yul. She'd rather not exist at all than exist on those terms.

Tom was back at the stables again with the cart. He knew that Magus was down in the Village and took the opportunity to visit Yul. He was delighted to find the boy sitting up and aware of who and where he was. The stench of vomit was strong, but Tom couldn't risk cleaning it up.

''Tis good to see you back in the land of the living, Yul,' he said, going over and tousling the boy's matted hair.

'I'm glad to be here,' said Yul, the words sounding strange to him. He hadn't spoken for a week. 'Could I have some more water please, Tom? I'm so thirsty.'

Tom quickly refilled the jug from the tap outside and helped him to drink, cradling the fragile boy as he struggled to sit upright and hold the heavy pottery vessel.

'I daren't stay long,' Tom said hurriedly. 'I'm not meant to be in here at all and that brute Jackdaw's still about somewhere. Look, I've some more of Mother Heggy's remedy here. Can you drink it now?'

Yul put the little bottle to his lips and swallowed the draught, fighting the nausea that rose instantly.

'I just saw your sweetheart,' Tom said, trying to hide the pity he felt for the boy. Yul looked up desperately, his eyes huge in his bruised face.

'Is she alright? Was she ill? I don't even know what day it is. Is it long since the Moon Fullness?'

'Aye, 'twas a week ago and you been on this floor all that time. 'Tis why you're so weak. But your young lady is fine. She's been ill too, they say, but she's down at the Village right now in the

Green Labyrinth and she had a message for you. She said she loves you.'

Yul closed his eyes, relief sweeping through him. Knowing Sylvie was alright was the best medicine of all.

Sylvie reached the centre of the labyrinth, her legs shaky from the walk. It was the first time she'd been out of bed in a week and she was horrified at her own frailty. She felt as weak as she'd done months before, in the London hospital, and this stiffened her resolve to fight Magus. Nobody had the right to deliberately steal her health.

Inside the dome it was very dark with only a little light filtering through the densely woven wicker. The smoke from the small fire, the only one that burned at Stonewylde today, hurt her eyes and throat at first, but she became accustomed to it quite quickly. A robed adult in a skull mask pointed for her to sit cross-legged on a mat with the others, in a circle round the fire. Real bones and many black feathers hung from the low ceiling of the dome. Once all nine of the group were seated, the figure began to chant in time to the drums played softly by another crow-masked person.

'Enter the darkness of the tomb, the darkness of the womb.'

A tray of small, white bowls was passed around, looking like babies' skulls full of blood.

'Drink of the blood of death and the blood of rebirth.'

They each took off their masks and gingerly sipped the deep crimson liquid. It was a sweet, aromatic elderberry wine made from the fruits of the tree of death, and laced with something that made their heads spin. Being so weak already, Sylvie was particularly affected. One by one they lay back on the mats and let their minds drift away, whilst above them the black feathers and white bones moved gently in the swirling smoke. Sylvie's head jostled with strange images – a black raven, white rocks, a chevroned serpent, a circle of hares. Everything seemed fantastical and dream-like, significant and yet not making sense.

But too soon the robed figure commanded them to stand and

they obeyed, unsteady on their feet. Sylvie found it very difficult to stand, her legs buckling and the world tilting alarmingly. She wanted to cry with frustration at her weakness, and vowed once more that she'd never let Magus do this to her again.

''Tis time to leave the Otherworld. As you leave this womb you'll be reborn. 'Tis the beginning of a new life, a new start, so as you walk, think on your resolutions for the year ahead. Farewell.'

One by one they left the dome, blinking in the afternoon light and inhaling the fresh air in gulps. This journey was uplifting, a real new beginning, and Sylvie focused on the coming year and what she wanted: to join Yul in the fight against Magus and never give in, whatever the outcome, and to be as brave and strong in her defiance as Yul was. She thought too of Mother Heggy and her wisdom. The old woman knew something of what lay ahead and Sylvie must take heed of her advice.

She walked slowly and unsteadily, her eyes fixed to the ground, guided by the white pebbles in the grey fading light as she thought carefully about her resolutions. She must stay at Stonewylde; despite her threat to Magus yesterday, leaving here wasn't an option. As he'd reminded her, the Outside World could kill her. Having spent months at Stonewylde, she may find her allergies were even worse should she return to the pollution and allergens, the chemicals and additives. More, she had to be with Yul and he'd never leave Stonewylde. He was a part of the place, his very bones the rocks and his skin the earth. His soul was rooted here and he could never abandon it even if he wanted to, and therefore neither could she. She'd stay at Stonewylde for ever until her bones too became the rocks and her skin the earth. Her body would become part of the substance of Stonewylde for eternity. She knew this with sudden, piercing certainty. Shuffling along the path of the labyrinth, her body cloaked in black and her face masked with death, Sylvie realised the full impact of where her thoughts had led. She'd fight Magus to the very end. And she'd rather die here than live under his dominion.

The exit of the labyrinth was ahead. Sylvie was handed a slip of yew and then she was out. She staggered along the edge of the Green, free of the guiding path of the labyrinth, and made her way not over to the Barn with the others but into the cavernous gloom under the great yew tree itself. She drew strength from the strange atmosphere in the dark, natural dome under the branches. She cast her mind back to her birthday, the Summer Solstice, when she and Yul had had their first kiss in this magical place. She'd thought at the time that nothing else in the world mattered compared to that moment of perfect joy, but she realised now that she'd been mistaken. Many other things mattered a great deal.

She sat for a while on the bare earth littered with dead, brown barbs of yew and thought hard of Yul, trying to reach him. She felt the cold and smelled a foul stench. She sensed pain and a body so weak and poisoned that it barely functioned. Sylvie hung her head in sorrow, sending her love to him wherever he was, hoping desperately that he'd find the strength to fight back.

Just after Tom left the byre, Clip arrived. He was heading to the dolmen where he liked to spend Samhain night but felt a twinge of conscience as he remembered Yul and his plight. He'd called in briefly during the week and had realised there was nothing he could do for the boy who lay there like a corpse. Clip knew from experience how it was when the soul was away on a journey to other realms. The body left behind was an empty shell and there was nothing to be done until the soul returned.

Unlocking the door, he wrinkled his nose and peered into the gloom. He'd hoped that Magus had released the boy by now but then saw him sitting up, propped against a bale in the near darkness.

'Ah, there you are,' said Clip. 'You've come back from your journey then. How are you?'

'You were there that night,' said Yul slowly, his tongue awkward. 'You know what he did to me and how powerful those cakes were.'

Clip frowned.

'I can barely see you in this murk. What's that disgusting smell?'

'I was sick. There's a light somewhere.'

Clip located the switch outside, and in the glaring electric light his face dropped at the sight before him. He realised it was now over a week since Jackdaw had been sent to collect the boy from the cliff top and the time had flown by. He looked at Yul and was deeply shocked. The boy was a living corpse; face white and skeletal, eyes sunk in his head. His pupils were still dilated and stared darkly from deep sockets.

Clip felt a sharp twist of guilt; he should never have been a part of causing this boy or Sylvie to suffer. Why did he always allow Magus to over-ride him? Why did he never find the courage to stick to what he knew was right? He stood there indecisively, wanting to get Yul out but frightened of Magus' reaction if he did so. He was also terrified of Jackdaw. The man was so intimidating and there was something about the way he looked at Clip with such contempt that made him feel uncomfortable and inadequate.

'Is there anything I can get you?'

'Food please – I'm very hungry.'

While Clip was gone, having locked the door behind him, Yul reflected on his predicament. His mind was suddenly and completely clear; maybe vomiting had finally flushed his system. He didn't know what had been happening during the past week, but knew he must escape from this prison before Jackdaw and Magus set to work on him. He shuddered to think what they had in store. Perhaps Tom would help him escape – or even Clip. He'd recognised the look of guilt on the man's face; maybe he could be persuaded to help.

Clip returned from the kitchens with a plate of sandwiches. He watched in revolted fascination as the boy devoured them, only to be racked by excruciating pain the moment he'd finished. He doubled over, clutching his stomach in agony. Clip stood back in case he was sick again but after a while the danger seemed to have passed. Yul realised he should've eaten only a little and very slowly.

'I'm feeling a bit better so can I go home now, sir?' asked Yul casually.

Clip stared at him in consternation.

'Well . . . you're hardly in any fit state to leave.'

'But my mother will be so worried about me. You're the master here really and you could help me get home.'

'I'd like to,' said Clip hesitantly, 'but I think Magus wants you here a bit longer. If . . .'

'Too bloody right he does!' said a deep voice.

They both jumped in fright as Jackdaw's powerful bulk filled the doorway. He was unshaven and the stubble glistened greasily on his jaw and head. His massive arms and chest were exposed by the leather waistcoat he wore, even in this cool weather. His bulbous muscles, covered in writhing tattoos, bunched menacingly. He came inside and sauntered over to where Yul sat.

'Nice try, kid, but we all know Magus has something in mind for you. The last thing you'll be doing is going home.'

'Er, I think I'd better be leaving,' said Clip, edging towards the door.

'Sounds good to me,' said Jackdaw rudely. 'Here, did you bring him food?'

'Yes, yes I did. He was very hungry.'

'Oh, what a shame! You should've waited for me. I'd have enjoyed feeding him again.'

Jackdaw lowered his bulk onto a bale, watching Yul closely. His bright blue eyes gleamed; the boy seemed much better now. Clip sidled away and out of the byre, closing the door behind him. Jackdaw smiled, revealing a gold tooth, and Yul eyed him warily, remembering the humiliation he'd endured at Quarrycleave.

'Just you and me now, mate,' said Jackdaw. 'Are you thinking of old times? Because I am.'

Yul nodded and stared down at the stone floor, too frightened to speak and knowing whatever he said would only make things worse. Jackdaw chuckled, then cracked his knuckles and spat into the corner.

'It's good to be back but it's a pity I ain't got longer with you. No, don't look like that, my son! You know you missed me too. It were fun back in the summer, weren't it? Happy days at ol' Quarrycleave and now they're here again.'

Jackdaw fished in the breast pocket of his waistcoat and pulled out a pack of cigarettes and lighter. He lit a cigarette and inhaled deeply. He examined the glowing tip speculatively, and glanced down at the quaking boy at his feet.

'You still look a bit dopey to me, Yul me old mate. After that long sleep I reckon you need waking up good and proper. Yeah? Let's get that shirt off, then.'

When the all young people had been through the Green Labyrinth, the candles along the path were lit and the adults began their journeys. The afternoon wore on, the light continuing to fade from the sky. Sylvie sat alone outside the Barn wrapped in her black cloak, shivering and watching the amazing spectacle on the Green. The entire labyrinth was ringed with glowing lanterns forming a great circle of light in the dusk. Hundreds of tiny candles in coloured glass jars twinkled amongst the white pebbles. The paths of the labyrinth were scattered with silent figures in black hooded robes, their faces turned to skulls, shuffling slowly towards or away from the wicker tomb in the centre. She shuddered at the macabre sight, and then looked up and gasped.

The leafless trees surrounding the Green were clotted with birds, not only rooks from the rookery in the chestnut trees, but also crows, jackdaws and hundreds of starlings too. They were all perched in the bare branches watching the Dance of the Green Labyrinth taking place below. It reminded her of the funeral.

'Incredible, isn't it?' said a mellow voice next to her, making her start. Magus sat down close beside her on the bench and she began to tremble more violently.

'Sylvie,' he said quietly, 'I'm sorry. I've treated you badly and

27

I want to make amends. You genuinely struggled with the walk around the labyrinth and I can see I've been unfair.'

He paused and looked at her but she stared straight ahead, watching the silent black figures. Birds were still alighting on the branches to swell their numbers even further.

'I don't blame you for being angry, but I'm going to show you over the next month that I'm not such a terrible person. I've let my love of Stonewylde blind me to how hard I've been on you. The only thing that matters to me – the only thing in the world – is Stonewylde. This place is my whole life. Can you imagine what it's like to be the magus here? The responsibility of it? Apart from the spiritual guardianship of the place, there are so many people dependent on me.'

He sighed heavily and sat back, stretching out his long legs while Sylvie remained huddled in the corner. His voice was silky and gentle.

'And lately . . . for some reason I'm no longer getting the same energy from the Stone Circle. I used to come away from the ceremonies buzzing with it and it helped me in the weeks ahead as I struggled to get through all the work. When that power started to ebb, I became so exhausted. And then that night up at Mooncliffe, I found that you were able to channel moon energy into the great rock! It seemed as if the Goddess herself had intervened just when I needed it most by sending you here to help me. I know that this has been done before because I was told my mother had the ability to channel the energy as well.'

Sylvie retreated deeper inside herself. He put a gentle arm around her hunched shoulders and pulled her close to him. He turned her face with a finger under her chin to make her look into his eyes. They glowed dark and bright and she knew he'd been soaking himself in his stolen moon magic. He oozed it from every pore. He exuded power and energy and it was like a magnet, even to someone who hated him. He smiled at her and she thought again how very attractive he was, despite being so cruel. There was something beautifully vicious about him. He squeezed her tightly and kissed her forehead.

'I'm so pleased you and your mother came to live here. I was delighted to heal you when you were so sick, and now, in return, I'm grateful for your gift to me of moon magic. It's the New Year tomorrow. Could we start again as friends? And that which I've forced you to give, can you think about giving freely? I need your moon magic, Sylvie, I need it so desperately. If I'm going to run Stonewylde as it should be run, I need the energy only you can give me. I can get Clip to use his hypnosis to help alleviate the discomfort for you.'

She remained silent but he continued undaunted.

'Sylvie, if you do this for Stonewylde, I'll be in your debt forever. Nobody else has your gift, nobody else can do what you can. Please share it with me. You'd be like a queen here and you could have anything you wanted.'

She sat stiffly despite his arm holding her so close.

'There're only two things I want,' she replied shakily, scared at how he made it all sound so simple. Scared that she wouldn't be strong enough to resist the full assault of his charm and persuasion. 'I want you to leave Yul alone and I want you to allow us to be friends.'

His face tightened and his voice changed.

'Sylvie, we've been through this so many times. We had a deal, didn't we? I'd lay off Yul if you stopped seeing him. And who broke that deal? You've brought suffering on him by not keeping your side of the bargain, so this is your fault and it's too late now for any more deals. The boy has pushed it too far this time.'

'What do you mean? What have you done to him?'

'I've done nothing to him yet.'

'But yesterday you said . . .'

'I was just winding you up, Sylvie. It's not difficult. You made me angry, threatening to leave Stonewylde, and I retaliated.'

'So where is he?'

'He's been around. You're the one who's been out of action, not him. He's actually taking part in a ceremony tonight up at the Stone Circle. Alwyn will be there too, and it'll be good for the son to go with the father.'

29

'So he's alright then?' she asked eagerly, her eyes wide with hope. 'I'd heard he was really ill.'

'I don't know who told you that, but I can assure you he's alive and kicking.'

'And he's taking part in a ceremony tonight? Oh, that's such a relief! Is he here now?'

'No, he should be in the hospital wing with his father by now. Alwyn's a very sick man and he hasn't got much longer.'

'So can I—'

'Sylvie, I don't want to talk about Yul now. In the morning, in the New Year, we'll discuss this. Things will be very different then. And now I really must go. It looks like most of the folk have performed their Dance of the Green Labyrinth and we need to move across to the Playing Fields to light the Samhain Bonfire and start cooking the food. Come with me, Sylvie – lean on my arm and you can stand by my side and help me. I want your role in the community to be acknowledged and you can start by assisting me this evening. Everyone will know how special you are, and what a fine thing you're doing every month for me. And for Stonewylde.'

He spoke as if she'd already agreed to everything, but Sylvie felt too tired to argue now. It was easier to let it go and let him think what he liked. She remembered her resolution made in the labyrinth. She'd never give in to him but for the moment, she'd use his strength and support to get through the evening and gather herself ready to fight him in the future.

It was some time since Jackdaw had left the byre and Yul was huddled up alone in the darkness. His mind was now completely clear, although in many ways he wished he were still in a stupor. At least then he wouldn't be able to feel the awful pain that Jackdaw had inflicted so casually, just for a bit of fun to while away the time. He didn't dare try to imagine what further torture Magus had in mind for him. He hugged his knees and closed his eyes, shivering in the cold byre and desperate for more food. He wished with all his heart that he'd listened to Mother Heggy's advice. He should never have gone up to Mooncliffe for the Hunter's Moon. It hadn't helped Sylvie at all and because he'd acted so rashly, he was once again at Magus' mercy. There was nobody to help him escape, despite Tom's promise after his last imprisonment here. It was too much to expect the man to risk his own safety. Yul was alone and he was scared.

He knew that down in the Village, everyone would be gathered in the Playing Fields with Magus to light the Samhain Bonfire. They'd dance in great circles around the bonfire, several people deep, to symbolise the wheel of the year turning and never ending. There'd be singing and fireworks, which he'd always enjoyed. Food would be cooking on the fires around the field and people would eat to their heart's content, hungry after a day of fasting; Yul's mouth watered at the thought. After games and fun, the dancing and drinking would continue in the Great Barn well into the small hours of the New Year. Yul knew too of the other rites that took place tonight. He'd never witnessed them, as only a few chosen acolytes took part in the ceremony with Magus, but everyone in the community was aware of what happened in the Stone Circle at Samhain. It was the festival of the dead after all.

Then Yul heard footsteps approaching and quaked with fear. Jackdaw filled him with terror in a way that Alwyn had never done. His father had been a bully who relied on brute force; Jackdaw was more subtle and he shared Magus' enjoyment of a slower paced cruelty. The light snapped on and the door was flung open. Jackdaw beckoned, huge in the dark doorway. Slowly Yul tried to stand, his legs giving way beneath him at first. But he managed to stand upright and then attempted to walk across the byre. Everything tilted and spun around crazily. He put out a hand to steady himself but the wall wasn't where it should've been and he fell heavily to the floor. Jackdaw stood watching and laughed at his clumsiness.

'Hurry up, boy! I ain't got all bloody day.'

Yul tried again but just couldn't walk across the room. He'd thought his head was clear now but the poison must still be in his body, and he was very weak from lack of food.

'You're pissing me off now, Yul. If you can't walk then crawl, but do get a move on.'

Shakily Yul started to cross the stone floor on all fours but Jackdaw swore at his slowness and hauled the boy back to his feet. Yul felt himself sway and hoped that Jackdaw wouldn't let him drop to the ground again. He felt so fragile, as if his bones would shatter if he hit the stone floor too hard. But the giant of a man picked him up, tossing him over his shoulder as if he weighed nothing. They left the stable area and headed round the back of the Hall to the Hospital Wing.

Jackdaw strode inside, nodding to the nurse on duty, and made his way to a room near the end where he dumped Yul onto his feet. It was very quiet in here. There were four patients: three old people and Alwyn. Standing confused and unsteady, Yul was shocked at the sight of his father. He'd always been a large man and in his later days an obese one, but now he was shrivelled and withered, the skin hanging off him in folds. His piggy eyes were lifeless and droopy. Most of his hair had fallen out and he sat in a wheelchair like a dummy. Two of the other people lay on trolley beds, ashen faced and clearly very ill. The third was in a wheelchair but shaking severely and breathing with difficulty. All of them wore white tunics tied with white cords, their withered arms, legs and feet bare.

Yul stared at them and it slowly dawned on him that these were the Death Dancers who'd be going to the Stone Labyrinth tonight for the special ritual. But why was he here? Then it hit him like a stone between the eyes and he felt a terrible panic rise in his throat. As if in confirmation, Jackdaw pointed to a white tunic and told Yul to put it on and sit in the remaining wheelchair. Then Jackdaw left him amongst the dying people.

The other four were unaware of him – indeed, unaware of anything. Yul's heart thumped with absolute dread. Magus couldn't intend for him to die with them tonight up in the Stone Labyrinth; it must be a horrible joke, just another of Magus' cruelties. Carefully, he shuffled to the door but it was locked. He stumbled back to his wheelchair, head reeling, and sat there for what seemed like hours, though without a window he had no idea of time. The ragged breathing of the dying four was awful and Yul wanted to scream with horror. He shook uncontrollably even though it was warm in the room. Too warm in fact. He began to sweat, a clammy wave of dizziness washing over him.

When the door finally opened he almost choked with relief. Jackdaw wore a long black cloak and his face was grim. Yul tried to stand up but Jackdaw cuffed him round the head, making the room spin once more.

'Stay there and don't bloody move,' he growled. 'And I told you to put that tunic on! Do it now, boy, and be quick.'

He wheeled the four others out, one by one, and eventually came back to push Yul's chair down the corridor and out into the night. A large cart waited outside with two black plumed horses in the shafts. Jackdaw scooped Yul out of the wheelchair and laid him along the width of the cart next to the dying people, so all five of them lay head to toe like sardines in a tin. Jackdaw threw a blanket over the lot of them, pulled up the tailgate and went round to sit beside the driver. Slowly the cart rolled forward, jolting on the track.

The old people's shrivelled skin rubbed against his and Yul felt a wave of revulsion. He was young and healthy and he didn't belong with the old and the dying. He tried to move, tried to sit up, but he was so weak. His body, already exhausted by the effort of standing and walking even a little, wouldn't respond. He'd never manage to escape even if he could somehow get out of the cart, so he lay jostling against the dying person next to him as they trundled onwards. The track forked off just before the Village and as they approached it, Yul smelt wood-smoke and roasting meat and heard wild shouts and laughter as the community celebrated the festival.

He started to cry, sobs choking his throat, tears running hot down the sides of his head and soaking into his hair. He'd never again take part in the ceremonies, the dancing and feasting. Never again be with his family and the folk he'd known all his life. Never see his cottage, the Village, the woods, the hills – none of the places he loved. Everything was coming to an end this night. He loved life, loved Stonewylde and he didn't want to die.

The sounds and smells of the Village receded and the cart rumbled up the track of the Long Walk. In the lantern light Yul saw the skeletal branches of the trees above, interlacing into a tunnel. He remembered all the times in his life he'd walked along here, to and from ceremonies at the Stone Circle. The feelings of excitement and magic he'd experienced there, of being part of something beautiful and powerful and in tune with the Earth Goddess and her forces. He'd never imagined this horror – the Dance of Death before he'd even reached adulthood.

The cart stopped and Jackdaw hauled him out roughly. He was dumped onto a hard wooden sled with his arms laid across his chest. The air was cold on his bare skin, for the white tunic was skimpy and thin. He lay silently as the other four were laid out onto similar sleds. They were just outside the great stones of the Circle, and Yul turned his head and saw flickering light inside. The cart rolled away and the sleds were lined up side by side. Yul heard voices approaching, people getting closer, and then Jackdaw loomed into view again, black cloak flung back to reveal an enormous glistening torso covered with dark swirling tattoos. He crouched down, knees crushing Yul's chest as he leaned forward to leer into the boy's face. His breathing was heavy, his eyes gleamed with excitement. He produced a tiny bottle and forced Yul's mouth open with a grimy finger.

'Swallow!' he growled, pouring the liquid down Yul's throat. Yul gagged and choked on the bitterness and Jackdaw smiled, his gold tooth glinting. His face started to swim and melt away and Yul's fears were confirmed; he'd been drugged once more. Jackdaw laughed as he saw the change in Yul's eyes.

'That's a good boy, Yul. Taking your medicine nicely now, ain't you? We don't want you getting up halfway through and trying to leg it. This'll stop you wriggling but it won't knock you out. Magus wants you conscious for the ceremony.'

Jackdaw stood up as people approached, and positioned

himself by the sleds. Yul could see and hear although everything was strangely distorted and elongated, but found he couldn't move a muscle. The group wore hooded black robes and skull masks and for Yul, reality spiralled out of reach.

'How many folk wish to enter the Stone Labyrinth tonight?' asked Magus, his voice formal and ceremonial.

'Five,' answered Jackdaw, now wearing a bird mask. He looked like a real jackdaw.

'The five who enter the Stone Labyrinth must perform the Dance of Death. Are they prepared for this?'

'They are.'

'Have their closest relatives agreed that they should perform the Dance of Death?'

'They have.'

'And are these Death Dancers prepared for the Dark Angel, who may tonight come in their midst and take their souls to the Otherworld?'

'They are.'

Magus paused, looking in turn at each of the bodies on the sleds. He was quite terrifying in the skull mask.

'Bearers, step forward.'

Five robed people stood before him and he addressed them solemnly.

'Tonight you bearers may look Death itself in the face and you must turn away, for you belong in the Realm of the Living. Before you enter the Stone Labyrinth, you must be fortified. This wine is the fruit of the elder, the sacred tree of the dead, and represents the blood of the earth, the blood of death, and the blood of birth. Drink deeply of the wine in preparation for the part you must play in the Dance of Death.'

A squat female figure with a small cauldron and ladle came forward. One by one the bearers knelt before Magus, who held a ladle of the dark liquid to their mouths for them to drink. He then moved to the white figures, supine on the sleds, and poured a tiny amount of wine over their unresponsive lips. But when Magus came to Yul, the bearer stood aside. Jackdaw crouched and lifted the boy's head, tipping it back and opening his mouth. He winked as Yul's terrified eyes met his, only centimetres away. Magus slowly poured a whole ladle full of the wine down his throat, giving him time to swallow without choking. Yul felt the thick, warm wine slide down into his empty stomach. Jackdaw looked up and nodded, and Magus gave him another ladleful.

Yul, already drugged from the little bottle of liquid, felt his body melt into paralysis as if his bones were dissolving. Before him he saw Magus flex his claws and purr with pleasure. The Jackdaw strutted forward and bowed to the Cat. Then the black-robed bearers took up the ropes and began to drag the Death Dancers' sleds towards the entrance of the Stone Labyrinth.

3

Within the Stone Circle the transformation was complete. The circus of joy and celebration had become a carousel of darkness and death. Painted emblems of the dead danced and flickered on each great stone, lit from beneath by flaming torches. On the beaten earth floor the lines of the labyrinth were defined with black stones and candles in red glass jars, glimmering like tiny pools of blood to mark the sacred path. In the centre of this Stone Labyrinth rose a flat-topped pyre, a raft of death large enough to consume several corpses.

The first bearer dragged his sled under the elder arch, brushing beneath the hanging feathers and bones. The black-robed figure and his white-tuniced burden stepped onto the path of the labyrinth and the Dance of Death began. Yul knew that the pattern itself marked the dance, and led the dancer by twists and turns into the Realm of the Otherworld. Tonight at Samhain, with the veil between the worlds so thin, the dead would be visible. Echoing around the arena, the drums were like heartbeats thudding out their final rhythm and a lone voice chanted eerily in a song for the dead. The birds of the Otherworld were now here, having left the Village once the Samhain Bonfire was lit. Crows, jackdaws, rooks, blackbirds and starlings perched on every stone forming a ring of black feathers and bright eyes.

Finally it was Yul's turn to enter the labyrinth; he was the last. His bearer tugged and the sled moved forward, sliding across the soft earth. It was a strange sensation for Yul, lying inert on his back – lurching but gliding, and very slow. Reality had vanished and his world had imploded into this circle, this pattern; the red flickering lights below his vision, the torches and capering skulls and crows above. The drumming and chanting were deep and unearthly, and in the slight mist inside the Circle the temperature was dropping steadily. Yul's skin was cold; his feet and hands were numb already. He tried to close his eyes, wanting only to block out this vision of horror, but couldn't. The Dance of Death was inexorable.

The Great Barn was alive with merriment and laughter, the community having feasted well and all now freely drinking cider and elderberry wine. With the young children tucked up in bed, the older children and adults were having a riotous time. The Barn looked fantastical with all the candles inside the pumpkins and skulls lit and flickering. Flocks of black papier-mâché birds moved in the hot air or perched realistically on the rafters. The dancing was wild, the musicians tireless and Miranda sat on one of the benches at the edge fanning herself. She was hot and uncomfortable, too pregnant to join in the galloping dances. Sylvie sat listless and exhausted next to her, the earlier resolve to fight Magus now seeped away. It had been a long day and all she wanted was get back to her bed, but Magus wasn't here so she couldn't ask to leave. Would he be angry if she went back to the Hall now, having made such a fuss this morning about her joining in the celebrations?

She thought wearily about what he'd said to her earlier but her tired head was a jumble of confusion. If Magus intended to talk to her again in the morning she must sleep soon, as she'd need all her strength to stand up to him and his silver tongue. Perhaps she could use her gift of moon magic as a bargaining tool to help Yul? Sylvie closed her eyes, trying to block out the noise and heat of the celebration. The only thing that would make it bearable here tonight was if Yul were around. She wanted so much to see him, to make sure that he really was alright as Magus had said. She wondered what he was doing up at the Stone Circle tonight.

What sort of ceremony was taking place up there?

She concentrated hard and suddenly an image flashed into her mind: hundreds of black birds perched on the tall stones looking down; drumming and chanting, slow and sinister; red lights flickering in the mist; black-hooded figures with skulls for faces dragging heavy burdens after them. Sylvie felt terror, a suffocating sensation of being trapped and unable to move, a certain knowledge that something terrible was going to happen. She opened her eyes with a jolt, her heart thudding.

She noticed Rosie getting a drink from the bar and stood up, swaying slightly.

'I'm just going to speak to someone, Mum.'

Miranda nodded.

'Alright, and then we'll go home. I've had enough and I'm sure Magus won't mind us leaving, seeing as he appears to have already left himself.'

Rosie was pleased to see Sylvie but concerned that she looked so ill.

'It's okay, Rosie, I'm off to bed in a minute. But I wanted to ask you what Yul's doing up at the Stone Circle tonight. Is he alright? I've been having some really strange thoughts ...'

Rosie frowned.

'The Stone Circle? I don't know, miss. I haven't seen him since the last Moon Fullness 'cause he's been at the Hall ever since. We've all been very worried. So you ain't seen him neither?'

Sylvie shook her head, dread growing inside her.

'Magus told me this afternoon that Yul was fine, although Tom from the stables told me earlier that Yul was in a bad way. And Magus definitely said that Yul was going to the Stone Circle tonight.'

'Well, our father's up there. He's a Death Dancer and he'll meet the Dark Angel tonight. 'Tis time for him to let go of life and pass on into the Otherworld, but not Yul ... I'm really scared, miss. Something's not right here.'

The two girls stared at each other, their eyes wide with fear, united in their concern for Yul.

'I think he's in danger,' said Sylvie. 'I felt it a moment ago. He's trapped somehow and can't escape.'

Rosie nodded.

'I think you're right and I'll find Mother now and tell her. Are you alright, miss? Take my arm a minute – you look so faint.'

The girls held on to each other whilst all about them, the community whirled around in a mad carousel of music and laughter. Sylvie was pale as death, Rosie flushed and agitated. She patted the older girl's arm reassuringly, alarmed at her unsteadiness.

'You go on to the Hall now – there're horses and carts for Hallfolk outside so don't try to walk, will you? I'll let you know what happens somehow, and don't worry, miss, I promise we'll find Yul.'

The first sled had reached the centre of the labyrinth. The elderberry wine and potion had effectively paralysed Yul. He showed no more signs of life than the other four bodies, except for his eyes. As his sled lurched along its tortuous path, his beautiful grey eyes were once again wild and dilated, darting around to watch terrors both real and imagined. At last his sled entered the area in the centre and he was pulled around to face the pyre.

Seated on the top was a gruesome figure; a crone dressed in shreds of grey rag that hung from her sagging body. Her wiry hair sprang madly from her skull in long grey skeins. She wore no mask, but white unguent of some sort had been rubbed into her skin which gave her a cadaverous look and accentuated the wrinkles and seams that furrowed her face. Her toothless mouth was a cavernous hole, her eye-sockets pools of shadow. She held a lantern on her lap which shone up into her hideous face, creating macabre shadows. She cackled as Yul was turned to face her, and even in his hallucinatory state he recognised the evil laughter of Old Violet.

Magus, Jackdaw, another hag and a crow-masked figure stepped forward, and Jackdaw, who now wore a death mask, climbed the wooden steps to the flat summit of the pyre. He stood behind the crone, enormous and dark, his arms raised, whilst Magus, the hag and the crow man began to slowly circle the centre around the sleds and pyre, chanting to the drum beat. It was very dark, for there was no extra light and the torches on the stones only lit their immediate area. The cold was intensifying as the night grew later and mist curled in wisps just above the ground, glowing red above the tiny lights.

'You've completed the Dance of Death,' intoned Magus, 'and reached the Gateway to the Otherworld. The dead await, peering through the veil to see who approaches. They are beckoning, inviting you to join them. Death is merely a rebirth into another world and now is the time to let go your hold on this life and move on to the next.'

He paused, looking up at the sinister figures of Jackdaw and the old woman on the pyre.

'It is almost the hour of midnight. The old year is dying, the new one beginning, and the Dark Angel draws near. He alone will decide who accompanies him to the Otherworld. The Dark Angel alone will choose. Now is the time for the living to leave this circle and return to their realm. Bearers, depart!'

The bearers left the centre in single file and wended their way back around the path of the labyrinth. Finally they arrived at the edge of the Stone Circle, joining up with the others there – the drummers, singers and a few relatives of the dying people. Someone in robes started to organise a procession back down along the Long Walk as it was the custom to leave Magus and a couple of acolytes up in the Circle, alone with the dying. Nobody wanted to be in the Stone Labyrinth at midnight for the summoning. There were whispered tales of things that had happened over the years, and nobody wished to encounter the Dark Angel and look him in the eye.

Magus and the attendants who'd remained in the centre all now stood on the pyre platform. Yul could see the five of them clearly from where he lay helpless, hallucinating and in a state of terror. They seemed huge and grotesque so high up above him.

'By the power of the sacred Stone Circle and the wisdom of the dark birds, I summon the Dark Angel to the portals of this world!' called the crow-masked man, and Yul recognised Martin's voice.

'As the Crone of Samhain, I call on the Dark Angel as the veil stretches thin!' cried Violet, her withered arms upraised and face hideous with excitement. 'We summon you now to this Stone Labyrinth. We ask you to take these souls with you tonight to the Otherworld.'

'These five are ready and they await your presence this Samhain,' said Martin, his robe flapping like wings as he moved his arms. His beak nodded upwards repeatedly in exactly the movement of a crow.

'We summon you to the Circle tonight to take these five souls!' croaked the hag hoarsely. 'Take them tonight, Dark Angel!'

Vetchling, Violet and her son Martin bowed to Magus and made their way down the steps to the ground. They joined the others at the arch of elder leading out into the Long Walk, and only Magus and Jackdaw now remained with the five bodies. Yul glanced around as far as his eyes could move, for his head wouldn't turn at all. He knew that Magus and Jackdaw would soon leave too, and then the Dark Angel would come. And then he'd die.

Just as the procession was about to leave, there was a commotion under the Long Walk trees. Magus looked up sharply and in the flickering torchlight made out the figure of a woman. She was pulling at the bearers and drummers, pushing at the crone and her sister who blocked the entrance. The woman was held fast by the crow man but still tried to get into the labyrinth. She shouted and cried, and even in his drugged state, Yul recognised his mother's voice. He struggled to move, to show her where he was, but despite his very best efforts he couldn't move a muscle. He heard her calling him, her voice frantic.

'Bloody woman!' hissed Magus. 'What the hell's she doing here?'

'Shall I go and deal with her?' asked Jackdaw quietly.

Magus hesitated.

'No, Martin seems to have hold of her and I don't think she'd actually dare come in here anyway. It's a sacred space and she knows that.'

Yul's slow heartbeat had quickened slightly. Maybe he had a chance after all? Could she rescue him? But he thought of Jackdaw's brutality and knew the man would have no qualms about hurting a woman if Magus gave him the opportunity. The images swirled around in his brain but the effects of the elderberry wine seemed to be diminishing slightly, for he was thinking a little more clearly now.

'Magus, have you got my boy in there?' Maizie called desperately. She was surrounded by the bearers who barred her way, and Martin still restrained her. The two old women capered about, plucking at her shawl and poking her. Magus straightened to his full height on the pyre, facing her across the great radius of the Circle, the paths of the labyrinth flickering with the tiny red lights. The centre was dark and Maizie couldn't see clearly what was there. Who exactly lay on the sleds.

'It's not the custom to come here and question the magus at Samhain, at this crucial moment in the ritual!' he called sternly. 'You're disrupting our ceremony and you'll answer for it tomorrow.'

'Have you got my son in there?' she called again, ignoring the threat as if he hadn't spoken.

'I have your husband Alwyn here,' said Magus, 'and you're disturbing his journey to the Otherworld. Do you have any idea how serious this is? Have you forgotten how—'

'I don't care! Have you got my son in there? That's all I want to know and I won't go until you've told me the truth!'

Her voice was shrill with fear and anger. Magus swore softly.

'Just lie to her,' said Jackdaw quietly.

'She knows I've got him,' replied Magus. 'Somebody's told her.'

'Let me go and deal with her,' repeated Jackdaw. 'It'll only take a minute to shut her up and then she won't bother you again.'

'No,' said Magus. 'That wouldn't go down too well in the Village. It's alright, I can put her off.'

Yul lay as if made of stone, praying that his mother wouldn't be put off.

'Maizie, listen to me,' called Magus, in his most reasonable and conciliatory voice. 'I have got Yul here. He's eaten something bad, a poisonous mushroom or something, and he's very ill. He can't move and he's dying, I'm afraid.'

There was a loud shriek of anguish and Yul heard her sobbing.

'Why didn't you tell me?' she cried. 'Why didn't you come and get me? Has the doctor seen him? How could you bring him to the Stone Labyrinth without letting me know?'

'I'm sorry, Maizie, it all happened so quickly. The doctor said he can't possibly survive so I thought it best for him to leave us tonight at Samhain, with proper ceremony, and meet the Dark Angel.'

Yul could hear his mother sobbing and crying, screeching her grief and desolation. His heart felt as if it would break at the sound of her suffering. Then suddenly her sobs quietened.

'No!' she cried. 'No – that's not right. You told Sylvie that he were fine this afternoon, but you said that Yul would be up here tonight. How did you know that? You lied to her and you're lying to me! I don't believe you, Magus – my boy's not ill at all!'

She started to struggle again. Martin and the bearers did their best to hold her as she flailed her arms and tried to wrench away from their grip, and Magus swore viciously.

'Maizie,' he called sadly, 'I promise you I'm not lying. Ask Martin – he's only just left the labyrinth and he's seen Yul. The boy's completely paralysed. You know how fast poisonous mushrooms can act. He's only barely alive and his breathing's very slow. I'm afraid to say he really is dying and it won't be long now.'

'NO!' she shrieked. 'I never gave my permission for him to enter the Stone Labyrinth! 'Tis forbidden to take anyone in there without their closest relative's say so and I never agreed! I want him out now! *Now*, Magus! If my Yul's dying I want him to die in my arms, not in there with those old bodies. You bring him out!'

'I can't do that, Maizie.'

'Yes you can! I want to hold my boy one last time.'

'I can't bring him out, Maizie. It's just too late and—'

'NO IT'S NOT! You need my permission to have him in there and I don't give it! I don't give it, Magus! I'm going back to the Village now and I'll bring all the folk up here and let them see what you've done! You took my son in there without my agreement and everyone will know!'

She was almost screaming with hysteria, a heady mixture of panic and fury. Magus swore strongly again and Jackdaw fidgeted, begging permission to silence her once and for all. Magus stayed him with one hand and took a deep breath. He looked down at Yul. The boy lay like a corpse but his dilated eyes were wide open and watching everything. Magus smiled at Yul. In the flickering light his face grinned with wicked glee, like the Jack o' Lanterns painted on the stones.

'Maizie, listen to me,' he called. 'Stop shrieking and listen. I didn't ask for your agreement because I didn't need to. I decided to bring Yul in here tonight and I gave the permission myself.'

'You can't do that!' she screamed. 'You can't do that, Magus!'

'Oh yes I can!' he shouted back, triumphantly, still staring down at Yul. 'I can because I'm his closest relative too. I'm his father!'

Yul thought his heart had stopped in his chest. *Magus his father?* Could he be? He heard Maizie howl in anguish, a cry of pure pain as if someone had stabbed her.

'NO! You can't do this, Magus! How dare you do this now, at such a time? How can you be so *cruel*?'

She sobbed uncontrollably, unable to speak any further. With his eyes swivelled as far as they could go, Yul saw her sink to her knees, head in her hands. He knew then, with awful certainty, that it was true. Magus, this sadistic tyrant who'd so relentlessly singled him for punishment and humiliation, was his father. Magus laughed, the sound ringing out around the great stones.

'But I thought that's what you wanted? You said so earlier

today, and now I've acknowledged Yul as mine at least he'll die knowing who his father was.'

Maizie sobbed even louder at this.

'Go back to the Village, Maizie! You're not permitted to stay up here as the moment of midnight approaches. Come back in the hour before dawn with the other relatives, and then we'll know whether or not the Dark Angel has chosen to take our son to the Otherworld.'

Yul saw the group leave, surrounding his distraught mother and bundling her away. She was crying pitifully, overwhelmed with anguish. His hopes plummeted even further into utter despair. Maizie's arrival and her pluckiness in challenging Magus had been his only hope, but Magus had managed to fool her. He felt a surge of pure hatred for the man he now understood had fathered him – his vile cruelty was almost beyond belief. Yul was sure now that he'd die here tonight; he was so cold with no way of getting his circulation going. He realised then that the thin tunics would always ensure death for the old and sick.

'Do you want me to stay on here, sir?' asked Jackdaw, climbing down from the pyre.

'No,' said Magus. 'Go up to my office and I'll meet you there. I want a word with this boy first, just the two of us. I'll join you in a while and we'll have a drink and warm ourselves up. There's brandy in my office – Martin will show you. We don't need to return here until early in the morning, and I'd rather not spend any more time than I need to in the Circle at Samhain. Just so long as we're back here before all the relatives turn up, that's fine. Bring the cauldron over before you go, would you?'

Jackdaw passed him the cauldron and ladle and left.

Magus walked around the sleds feeling for a pulse in the neck of each Death Dancer. When he came to Yul, he crouched down. His fingers lingered, stroking the boy's throat almost tenderly.

'Well, son, here we are then, just you and me,' he said softly. 'Was it such a shock to learn that I'm your father? Did you never guess? I've spent all your life denying it but now you're about to die, perhaps it's time to finally acknowledge the truth.' His long fingers caressed Yul's windpipe. 'I hold your life in my hands. A tiny squeeze and it's snuffed out forever.'

His fingers paused, pressing slightly and then a little harder. Yul thought that this was it, but Magus released the pressure and continued to stroke Yul's neck.

'You began life in this Stone Circle and you'll be ending it here too very soon. The circle of life ... I remember the night you were born – what a night that was! And you've been the angel of my nightmares ever since, haunting me at every turn, never out of my thoughts or dreams. I've watched you grow up, Yul. I've looked on as Alwyn tried to knock the spirit out of you and break you. This year I've seen you turn from boy to man and challenge me as nobody else would ever dare, just as it was foretold. Old Heggy was right all along. It's strange – no member of the Hallfolk even begins to measure up to you and I almost feel proud of you. You're so very like me, flesh of my flesh.'

He sighed deeply, running his fingers over Yul's hollowed face, pushing the tangled curls back from his forehead. He reached across and took a ladle of the rich elderberry wine. He sipped it, savouring the heady taste, then knelt and lifted Yul's head, cradling it almost lovingly. Yul's eyes were locked in to his, staring in terror at this new facet of Magus. This apparently tender side scared him more than the cruelty.

'It should be easy to end your life now, Yul. I gave you life one magical night under a brilliant Blue Moon, when I took your mother's virginity. And I should be able to take your life away so easily – just a little pressure here would do it. You're very cold now, aren't you? Your body's shutting down and your pulse is so slow and weak. But I can't do it – not because I care and not because I don't want to. Believe me, your death is something I've dreamed about. But all these years you've been protected by that crone Heggy, bound by her spell, cast here in the Circle on the night of your birth.'

Yul looked up at him in amazement. Protected by Mother Heggy? Magus must have read something of the boy's surprise in his eyes, for he chuckled.

'No, I don't suppose you knew about that, did you? Thanks to her I can't take your life, much as I long to, because if I were to kill you the Dark Angel would take me too. That's the binding spell Heggy cast and it's the only reason you're still alive today. But tonight – this is different. It's not my doing if you die this Samhain. It's the Angel himself who'll decide your fate.'

Still Yul stared, unable to move or look away. He felt the man's power as he cradled him, the native force within him that was nothing to do with Sylvie's moon magic. Magus eyes, so dark and bright, gazed down into his and Yul sensed the iron will in his father's soul, the hard determination that drove him on, the absolute faith in his own strength and superiority.

'In a minute I'll leave you here on your own. You've defied me, challenged me, tried to put yourself above me, and now I want you to suffer. Tonight you'll know real fear as the Dark Angel walks the labyrinth. Being so cold and weak already, you'll probably die during the night, but should you survive the darkest hours, your death will be even worse.'

He paused and smiled grimly as he surveyed his helpless son.

'You know the customs of Samhain and the journey to the Otherworld. In the hour before dawn, if you can't move or show a sign that you choose life, then you'll be burnt on the pyre. A kindness for those poor souls who wish to bring an end to their suffering. And I know you won't be able to move, because Old Violet's little bottle of potion, which you drank so willingly from Jackdaw's hand, will prevent any movement for many hours yet. When I ask who chooses life you won't move or show any sign and it'll be your choice, Yul, not mine. Not my hand in any of this so I'll be safe from the binding spell. Jackdaw will put a torch to the pyre and you'll burn with the corpses.'

He chuckled again and drank more of the wine.

'This is very strong stuff. I must go easy – I don't want too many visions. I want to savour every single moment of this night, when I finally rid myself of you. I've looked forward to being free of you and that bloody prophecy for so long. But you can have more wine, Yul. Illusions and dreams will help you get through the night, while you lie here contemplating your death.'

Still cradling Yul's floppy head, he ladled more of the spiced wine down the boy's throat, slowly and carefully. Yul had to swallow or choke, but swallowing was so difficult Magus had to take his time. Then he tenderly wiped the boy's lips with the sleeve of his robe.

'There, that's more than enough to ensure some powerful visions. I can feel the effect and I've only had a few sips. And now I must leave you on your own with these four bodies. Did I tell you they're all already dead? No pulses, so it's just you, the corpses and the Dark Angel. You're surrounded by death. You're a brave boy but tonight even you will know genuine terror. Look out for the Angel, Yul, because he's here, that's for sure. Goodnight, my son.'

Magus bent and kissed Yul's forehead. He rose and stretched, looking down at the boy. His dark eyes glowed in the dim light and his mouth tightened momentarily. With a farewell salute, he turned and walked out of the Circle, leaving Yul alone with his hallucinations and dreams.

The small silvery creature sat up high on top of a great standing stone, a crow on her shoulder. She waved at him and smiled, then floated down to the misty ground inside the Stone Circle. She skipped along the labyrinth path, her ragged dress flimsy in the wisps of mist and hazy red lights. Her feet were bare, as were her thin white arms and legs. She was small and delicate and her face was beautiful. Her hair was a wild silver bird's nest of tangles and burrs around her.

'Blessings, Yul,' she said softly in a tiny angel voice. 'Well met again, my grandson.'

She threw her head back and laughed, revealing tiny sharp teeth. Her laughter tinkled in the air and wove a web of silver around the four dead bodies.

'You hold fast, my little Yul. 'Tis the place of your birth for sure, but not the place of your death. I'll help you through this

49

long and lonely night. Old Mother Heggy summoned me this Samhain, to protect you.'

Yul tried to smile at her, feeling better for knowing he wasn't all alone as the Angel drew near, but his face wouldn't move. He glanced upwards and saw the birds still perched above, watching him with bright beady eyes.

'Don't be scared of them. They're your friends, come to watch over you, and especially my crow. You'll see.'

The night wore on, growing colder and colder and Yul couldn't feel any part of his body now. Everything was numb with only a little kernel of his mind still functioning and that in a bizarre way, for the visions followed thick and fast. Many people joined him in the labyrinth, a host of ancestors all long gone, from centuries and centuries past. They poured through the veil and crowded in to gaze at him, appearing and then fading, but Raven let nobody come close. She sat by Yul's side and held his hand in hers, guarding him fiercely, waving them away and hissing at them to be gone. Or was this silver girl not Raven at all, but another moongazy girl, one who loved him and was here to protect him? In his delusional state, Yul had no idea.

Several times, in the corner of his vision, Yul saw a tall, black-robed figure processing around the Circle. At first he thought it was Magus come back, but then in a burst of lucidity Yul realised it was the Dark Angel himself stalking the labyrinth. The blackness around the figure was deeper than it should be, and Yul knew he mustn't look into the Angel's face, mustn't get a glimpse of those eyes or he'd be lost. He had a choice, and must at all costs avert his gaze should the Angel come close and peer down at him.

'Yul, Yul, don't go!' called the silvery voice later on, when the darkness grew thicker all around him. 'Don't leave me, Yul! You must stay and fight.'

She blew softly on his face, stirring his curls like a gentle whisper of breeze. He forced his heavy eyes open. He was so tired and wanted only to float into soft, grey sleep and never wake up. It was so tempting, so alluring, just sink into goose-down slumber and peace.

'YUL! Do you want your father to win? If you die tonight, what will happen? You must fight, Yul, for 'tis you alone at Stonewylde who can defeat him. Think of your moongazy maiden! He'll never have his fill of her. He'll drink her life away, gulp by greedy gulp until she dies at his hand, just as I died at his father's hand. You saw what he did to me, didn't you Yul? You saw that night on the cliff top how he devoured me, ripped me apart. 'Tis only you who can stop it happening all over again.'

Yul's eyes shot open – he had to protect Sylvie from Magus. He couldn't give in now, and with a huge effort he pushed the sleepy, enticing clouds away and tried to focus. He must stay and fight, never allow the monster who'd fathered him to destroy the girl he loved. Swivelling his eyes about, he located the thicker blackness standing right by the funeral pyre next to the other sleds. The souls had answered the summoning, and Alwyn was amongst them. But not Yul. He felt the shadow stirring, edging towards him, the only living being left in the Stone Circle. Even his silvery protector could do nothing to fight this spectre, should he gaze into his eyes. With a massive push of will, Yul closed himself off from the deadly summons, refusing to be lured. He sensed rather than heard a deep sigh, and then saw the Dark Angel drift silently out of the labyrinth and melt into the edges of the night.

And then, as if from very far away, he heard voices approaching, shockingly loud in the deathly silence of Samhain night.

'I reckon he'll have snuffed it.'

'I don't,' said Magus. 'That boy's strong and he'll have survived. But he won't be able to move, so he'll burn at dawn with the others. You have to take care of it, Jackdaw – I can't.'

'Aye, and I'll say the words, right enough,' came a cackly voice. 'I know 'em well. I'll speak the words for you, so 'tis not your doing and that binding spell's not crossed.'

'Yes, Violet, you take that role and leave me out of the whole thing this year.'

The five cloaked figures walked briskly around the labyrinth path and arrived in the centre. Raven shielded Yul from them, whispering comfort in his ear.

'You won't die here, Yul. 'Tis not your destiny. I'll help you and you'll choose life.'

'Well I'll be damned!' exclaimed Jackdaw, seeing Yul's eyes still open and watching. 'You were right, sir. Tough little bugger, ain't he?'

Magus laughed dryly and glanced down at his son.

'I told you he's a fighter,' he said, with a touch of something close to pride.

It was still dark in the hour before dawn, and the torches were burning low in their brackets around the stones, with many of the red lights on the path burned out and now extinguished. It was very cold and the new arrivals were snug in their thick cloaks, their breath clouding out in the still air. Magus' cheeks glowed and Yul knew he'd charged himself up with moon energy during the night; he could feel the hard quicksilver pulsing in the man. He was full of life and vitality and his eyes burned brightly. The five of them, Magus, Jackdaw, Martin, Violet and Vetchling, looked down at Yul lying on the wooden sled in his thin white tunic. He was pale and unmoving and, but for his dilated eyes, looked like a corpse. Every one of the five wished him dead.

'Soon 'twill be time, Yul,' cried the silvery voice. 'You must stir your cold blood. Move your toes and fingers, boy. Move them!'

He tried but nothing happened. He kept on trying, willing his body to move even a fraction, but nothing whatsoever happened. He was completely numb and paralysed. Magus crouched down and felt his pulse again, his fingertips hot on Yul's chilled throat. He gazed deep into Yul's frightened eyes and his black fire blazed in exultation. He smiled slowly and nodded, straightening up.

'He's still alive but only just,' said Magus, 'He's not going anywhere. We've about an hour until dawn and the relatives will be here soon. Have you got everything you need, Martin? The oil so they burn well? The wreaths for their heads and the special brand for lighting the fire? Good. As soon as Violet's said the words, you two men get the bodies up on the pyre as fast as possible. I want this over with quickly and I can't give you any assistance. Nothing must go wrong.'

Then Yul heard them coming, as did Magus and the others, and there were far too many voices. Unlike the Passing On ceremony, it was customary for none but the closest relatives to attend this burning. In the morning the ashes would be taken down to the Funerary Yew by the whole family and placed with due reverence and ritual under the great tree, together with a pebble. But this burning at Samhain, after the summoning of the Dark Angel, was only performed before a handful of relatives. However now, in the coldness of the hour before dawn on New Year's Day, a huge throng of people came up the Long Walk. From the corner of his eye, Yul could just see a massive crowd of Villagers led by his mother, all carrying burning torches. His heart leaped – he'd made it this far and there was still a chance!

Maizie stopped by the arched entrance and peered into the centre of the Stone Labyrinth. It was very dark inside the Circle and all she could make out were the five figures in their dark, hooded robes, and five still, white shapes on the wooden sleds.

'I don't believe it!' snarled Magus. 'She's brought bloody reinforcements!'

But he signalled to begin the ritual as if the size of the great crowd were entirely normal. The crone invited the Death Dancers to choose between life and death. They were commanded to show some sign if they wanted to stay in this world, or remain still and silent if they wished to be sped to the Otherworld and have their mortal remains burnt. The four corpses remained still and silent. Yul tried to move, tried to call out or move his hand. He struggled with every fibre of his being. But his numb, drugged body wouldn't respond.

He could hear his mother's voice calling to him from the entrance, begging him to make a sign. He could hear her choking on her sobs, pleading with him to choose life. She'd been convinced he'd be dead already. But now, although she couldn't see him clearly at all, somehow she felt he still held on to a thread of life. She kept on and on calling to him, but try as he might, he could make no movement at all. Then he heard another voice, the voice of his tiny, silvery grandmother.

'Come, Yul! 'Tis time and you *have* to move. If you don't show a sign now Magus will win and you'll be burned alive!'

He pushed and pushed, trying with every atom to move. How could his body fail him like this? Unless he made a sign right now, he'd die in the flames, burnt alive.

'Call on the Earth Magic, Yul! 'Tis your special place here and you're the chosen one of Stonewylde, so summon the power to you, Yul! Call the green magic now to give you strength!' she cried in desperation.

Yul was some way from the Altar Stone where the force was most powerful, but he knew she was right. The energy was here in the Circle, if only it would seek him out. His body was so weak, so cold, but he remembered that August night at the Corn Moon when he'd run round and round, calling up the storm. So in his mind he started to run now, his limbs free and strong. Round the Circle, round the stones, calling on the power of the Earth Magic, summoning the Goddess who lived below and beyond, raising the energy up, up into his soul ...

Raven rubbed hard on his frozen hands crossed on his chest. She chafed them with her small, rough hands, exhorting him to move. He could feel her and yet he couldn't – she was only a wraith and yet she had some substance. Her mass of tangled silver hair fell across his face and tickled him. He called and called, summoning the hidden power of the ancient Stone Circle, the power tapped by his ancestors, the green magic of old ... He called on the Earth Goddess who'd chosen him to lead Stonewylde.

'Sir!' whispered Martin urgently. 'I saw him move! He twitched.'

'What?' hissed Magus. 'Don't talk rubbish! He's paralysed – he can't move a muscle.'

'No, look! His fingers just moved. Look, sir!'

Magus saw it too.

'Give him some more of the potion quickly! Where is it? Quick!'

''Tis over yonder in the chest by the Altar Stone,' said Violet. 'But something's amiss. I feel another close by. A shade ... something, someone from the Otherworld who has no place here. She—'

'Never mind that! Go, Jackdaw! Get the bottle quickly!'

But as Jackdaw tried to cross the circle to fetch the paralysing draught, a great crow launched itself from a standing stone and flew straight into Jackdaw's face. It flapped and pecked in a wild flurry of black feathers, beak and claws. Jackdaw swore violently and tried to swipe it away. But the more his arms thrashed, the harder it attacked, coming from all angles, pecking and beating its wings, cawing crazily. He couldn't get out of the centre; couldn't move from the spot.

'What the hell is going on? Violet, say the last words! You two – get the bodies up onto the pyre! Quick!'

'I ask for the final time! If you choose to live, give us a sign. For now 'tis the hour of the burning. Do none o' you choose life?'

'Move, Yul, move! I feel the life force rising in you. 'Tis starting to work! Raise your hand!' cried his moongazy saviour.

There was a cry from someone in the crowd at the entrance.

'He moved! I saw him move!'

'YUL!' screamed Maizie. 'Are you alive, my boy?'

'Here, my sweet grandson, take my hands and let me help you.'

He gazed into her silvery moonstone eyes and felt such love and kindness flowing from her. His cold hands still lay crossed on his breast, and she took them in hers and tugged with all her strength. He felt the green energy snaking across the circle, seeking him out, finding its path to him and flowing beneath the labyrinth. With a sudden explosion of power, the Earth Magic poured from the ground up into his body. Yul sat up in one fluid motion, bolt upright on the sled, like someone rising from the dead.

The crowd of Villagers roared in delight, everyone cheering and laughing.

'He chooses life, Magus!' screamed Maizie, beside herself with joy. 'He's moved and now he can live. You're not burning our son! I'm coming to fetch him!'

Nobody knew the protocol when a Death Dancer chose life as it had never happened before in memory. Only the very sick or very old took part, and the cold night had always done its work by this point. But Maizie began to trot along the path of the labyrinth, hurrying around the twists and turns until she entered the centre. Magus glowered at her in silent fury, his face white. Jackdaw cracked his knuckles ominously and Martin, Violet and Vetchling muttered under their breath. They all stepped back from Maizie as she threw herself down beside Yul. She kissed his cold face, taking his icy hands in hers and rubbing them. She carefully laid him back down on the sled, for although he'd somehow sat up he couldn't move at all now. She pulled her warm shawl off her shoulders and tenderly covered her son with it, stroking his cheek as her tears fell on his chilled skin. His deep grey eyes gazed up at her, blazing out his love.

She glared up at Magus.

'You knew he were alive!' she choked. 'Yet you were prepared to burn him, your own son. I won't forget this, Magus. Nobody will forget this. The folk have seen what you tried to do here tonight and now they all know of your wickedness.'

'Maizie, you must—'

But she stood abruptly, ignoring him. She picked up the sled's rope and began to pull, dragging it slowly away from the centre and around the curved path. Several men in the crowd came forward to help and soon they were out of the Stone Labyrinth. The path back to life and rebirth had been trodden, and Yul emerged from his near death a different person – and one who now knew his true blood.

Tom had brought the cart and Yul was lifted up and laid carefully in the back, his head cradled in his mother's lap, covered warmly with people's shawls and cloaks. The crowd surrounded the cart as it moved away, the procession lit triumphantly by their blazing torches. The few grieving relatives who remained watched in silence as Magus and his assistants continued with the Samhain rite of burning the bodies.

Magus' face was as dark as the crows and rooks that perched on the stones. The pyre whooshed into crackling life and the birds rose as one. As the ashes floated high above the Stone Circle, the air was filled with the beating wings of hundreds of birds, speeding the four souls to the Realm of the Otherworld.

4

Magus stood looking out over the grey gardens. Dew and cobwebs laced the shrubs around the French windows in a delicate white shroud and the trees reached up to the overcast skies with bony black fingers. There was a desolate feel to the early morning that belied the excitement of the previous day's festival. Sylvie paused silently in the doorway of his office, loath to disturb the reverie of the man before her. He seemed dejected. There was something bleak in the set of his shoulders and his absolute stillness. He wore a dark business suit which gave him an Outside World air.

Sylvie had been summoned by a dour-faced Martin, who'd informed her coldly of Magus' request. He'd barely spoken a word as they made their way along the gallery of the wing and into the main body of the Hall. Martin's wintry grey eyes and air of disapproval had quashed her attempts at conversation and she struggled to keep up with his long strides, still feeling weak and shaky this morning. Sylvie still knew nothing of Yul, for as yet she'd seen nobody else this morning. Her mind raced with speculation as to why Magus should send for her so early, before everyone else was up and about for the New Year's Day breakfast.

Her tentative feelings of sympathy for him, standing so alone and pensive, were quickly dispelled when he turned and fixed her with an icy glare.

'Come in and close the door behind you,' he said tersely.

They sat on the sofas and his gaze scoured her face.

'I told you that we'd speak today, but this isn't the conversation I'd envisaged. Due to ... unforeseen events, I'm going away for a week or so. There're a couple of things I need to say before I leave. I've obviously reached you before you heard the gossip that will doubtless rage at the breakfast table today, once it's filtered up from the Village.'

Her heart jumped at this, dreading his next words.

'I wanted to tell you this myself, in case you get any ideas.'

He paused and saw the fear in her eyes. His face was impassive as he continued.

'Last night during the Samhain rituals up in the Stone Circle, I made an announcement. I let it be known to all that Yul is my son.'

He waited as Sylvie absorbed this astonishing news. She stared at him in mute incredulity and he watched the succession of emotions flit over her face, before finally reaching acceptance and understanding.

'You—'

He waved her to silence.

'I'm not discussing it other than to remind you that you're forbidden to have any contact with that boy. This changes nothing.'

'But—'

'No! He remains an ignorant, uncouth woodsman and nothing more, despite being sired by me. You're out of his league and you're to keep away from him. That is and remains my final word on the matter.'

Sylvie's eyes met his and she tried to mask her intentions, knowing only too well how perceptive he was.

'Is he alright? There was something wrong yesterday. I could feel it.'

'Yes, he is alright. And I heard of the part you played in this. Thanks to your meddling and scaremongering my plans for the future are now in jeopardy. You've a lot to answer for, and when I return I shall make sure you do. In the meantime, you're to attend all your classes every day and ensure that you work extremely hard. I've left a note for your tutor. When I get back I expect a full report from him on the progress you've made since coming here in March, and a complete record of your attendance. You're slothful and lacking in motivation. Your attitude is a mockery of all that we strive for at Stonewylde. This is your final year of secondary education and at this rate you'll fail your exams miserably. It's not acceptable. So whilst I'm away I expect you to make a concerted effort to cover the work you've missed. Now go back to your rooms and tell your mother that I wish to see her immediately. That's all, Sylvie.'

'But it's not—'

'I said *that's all*. I shall take this up with you when I return.'

His face was like stone. Sylvie stood up, smarting with the injustice. She knew exactly what she intended to do at the first opportunity.

Miranda returned a little later with an equally grim expression.

'Come on – breakfast time. Get a move on, Sylvie.'

As they made their way again down the long gallery she turned on her daughter.

'Things are going to change, Sylvie, starting from today. I've been far too soft with you. You're to sit with me at meal times so I can make sure you're eating properly. When you've finished breakfast this morning you're to see your tutor and find out what you need to do to catch up with your work. Then go and see Hazel in the hospital wing. Magus had told her to do a complete health check. And your weight's going to be monitored closely.'

'What? But Mum, why—'

'I don't want to hear it, Sylvie. Your attitude is just not good enough. You're going to spend every evening working in our rooms where I can keep an eye on you. You've so much ground to cover.'

'But it's not fair! I've only missed so much school because he made me ill! If you—'

'Don't be so ridiculous! It's *not* Magus' fault. You've been selfish and lazy, expecting us all to run around whilst you take to your bed and deliberately make yourself ill. I used to worry that you were anorexic, and now it's clear that you refuse food to weaken yourself intentionally and then get us all fussing over you. Well it's going to stop! I've the baby to think of now and I don't have the time or inclination to pander to you any more. Magus is very annoyed and it's up to me to sort you out.'

'Mum, I can promise you I've never deliberately made myself ill! I want to be fit and healthy and eat normally, believe me! You know how bad I was in London and why we came here – how can you even think I want to be sick again? It's Magus who's—'

'How *dare* you? We've discussed this before, Sylvie, and I'm appalled at you. It's thanks to Magus that you're alive today. He saved your life by bringing us here, and then healing you with his amazing gift. How you can blame him for your dreary hypochondria and self-harming behaviour is beyond belief. I'm ashamed of you, Sylvie!'

Sylvie's tutor was a rather grumpy middle-aged member of the Hallfolk, staying at Stonewylde for a couple of years whilst he completed his thesis. She'd never really taken to him but had found him to be generally amenable if not disturbed too much. Today he was curt and her heart sank. He glowered at her, furious to have his New Year's Day holiday taken up like this. He'd hastily compiled a list of coursework and areas of study where she must catch up, and presented it to her with a bad-tempered flourish.

'I've had to speak to all your subject teachers at extremely short notice when we thought we had the day off. Now that I've looked into it, I'm shocked at your attendance since the summer. You made a reasonable start in the spring but it very quickly deteriorated and you're now behind in every subject. You've a considerable amount of work to catch up with and I want to see you every morning with the fruits of the previous day's efforts. The last thing I need is Magus breathing down my neck. You've let us all down and there's serious work to be done, young lady, if you're going to even scrape through your exams.'

Even Hazel was cool with her. She gave Sylvie a comprehensive medical and drew up a chart to record her weight. The doctor frowned as she sealed the blood and urine samples in a box to be sent off for analysis.

'I'm really disappointed in you, Sylvie,' she said. 'I feel responsible for you being here, and I was so pleased that you'd made a full recovery from your illness in London. But this – this is something different. Magus says you're deliberately malingering to get attention, and that there's nothing physically wrong with you. I must say that apart from your obvious exhaustion after the full moon, and the fact that you lose so much weight by refusing food, I'm inclined to agree with him.'

'But it's his fault, Hazel! He makes me stand on the rock up at Mooncliffe and it drains my energy. He knows exactly what's wrong with me!'

'Oh come on!' said Hazel sceptically. 'Don't start fantasising as well as faking illness. Magus told me months ago about your so-called "moongaziness" and how you insist on going up to Mooncliffe each month. He's doing you a kindness, when he could simply lock you up in a room like your mother had to in the old days, to keep you safe. Don't pretend this is his fault when all he's doing is trying to help – that's a load of nonsense and I won't hear it!'

Sylvie stared at her helplessly.

'But Hazel . . .'

'No, Sylvie. Magus warned me you'd try to blame someone else for your apparent malaise but I can't believe you're blaming him of all people. You've got to face the facts – you love the attention that illness brings and that's all there is to it. It's a common enough syndrome but not something I'd have expected from you.'

'But I don't pretend to be ill!' cried Sylvie, her voice cracking. 'It's real!'

Hazel shook her head and stood up, ignoring Sylvie's tears and firmly ushering her from her office.

'I'm sorry, Sylvie. I just don't believe you so don't waste your time crying – it won't wash with me. Of course if these tests throw up anything, I'll reconsider. That's why Magus ordered them – to be absolutely sure we're not misjudging you. But you need to do some hard thinking about your life at Stonewylde. You didn't come here to mope about being pathetic, did you?'

'No, Hazel,' sobbed Sylvie, 'I only want to be happy here. Please, please believe me, I'm not putting—'

'Don't try to play on my sympathy, Sylvie. If you put me in a position where I must choose sides between you and Magus, I'm afraid you'd be the loser. He's been so kind to you and it's about time you woke up and started acting a little more appropriately to your situation. I'll see you tomorrow morning for your weigh-in.'

The turn of events had thoroughly depressed Sylvie. She recognised Magus' attempts to punish her for alerting Maizie to Yul's presence in the Stone Circle at Samhain. She was anxious for news of him, although judging by Magus' displeasure, Yul must be alright. A couple of evenings later, having endured dull days of endless school work and disapproval from all the adults responsible for her, Sylvie at last heard the good news she'd longed for. Harold caught her alone as she walked through the Tudor gallery. He emerged from the shadows of one of the doorways leading to guest rooms, and had clearly been waiting for her to pass by.

'Sorry, miss, to startle you. I got a message from Rosie for you and I been trying to find a way to get you on your own.'

'A message from Rosie? That's brilliant! Thank you, Harold.'

Sylvie was so relieved. She'd heard gossip and had gathered that Yul was now safely at home, but other than that there'd as yet been no details. She'd been wondering how to find out more and desperately wanted to see him, but didn't know where they could meet. She smiled encouragingly at Harold, who shyly scuffed his shoe along the deep wooden wainscot of the gallery. He was the same age as Yul, but much less sure of himself.

'Well? Can I have it then?' She held out her hand, but Harold shook his head.

''Tis spoken, miss – Rosie can't write. She said Yul's on the mend, but he's still very weak and their mother's keeping him indoors. She said Yul wants you to go to their cottage and see him, any time you like, he said. And he misses you. And . . . and he loves you.'

They both looked embarrassed at this but Sylvie grinned with bubbling happiness.

'Please tell him, or Rosie if that's easier, I'll come down to the Village just as soon as I get the chance. Everyone's on my back at the moment but I promise I'll visit. Tell him I love him too. Sorry, Harold. This is awkward I know. I wish he could read, then I'd write him a note.'

Harold looked up and nodded eagerly, his eyes alight.

'I told Yul I'd teach him.'

'You can read? How come?'

'I'm teaching myself though I'm not very good yet.'

'That's a great idea! Let me know if I can help? And do try to persuade Yul to learn too – Magus would hate it! Did you know Magus is his father?'

'Reckon the whole o' Stonewylde knows that now, miss,' chuckled Harold. 'What a thing! Who'd have thought it, the way Magus treats him? Mind you, I always thought Yul were a bit special.'

'So did I,' said Sylvie with a smile.

It took several days for the effects of the paralysing draught to wear off and for Yul's body temperature to normalise after the hypothermia. But he was young and fit and began to recover from the near fatal experience that Magus had subjected him to. Maizie kept him indoors and made up a bed in the parlour for him, because it seemed that most of the Village wanted to bring little gifts and wish him a speedy recovery. She couldn't have them all trooping up and down the rickety wooden stairs to the attic where he normally slept.

In the Village there was a backlash of anger against Magus. The main cause, apart from his brutal and inexcusable treatment of

Yul, was Jackdaw's return from banishment. Most people had been deliberately kept unaware of his presence at Quarrycleave earlier in the year, and he hadn't shown his face in the Village. But now the man had been brought back to Stonewylde without any explanation or apparent retribution, and many felt he hadn't been punished at all. People muttered and held whispered conversations, but such was Magus' power that nobody dared to criticise him openly. So solidarity was displayed in a show of support for Yul instead and he became the focal point for the Villagers. Maizie found her house crowded every evening with well-wishers.

Sylvie managed to get away one morning during a rare free hour. She'd been working as hard as she could in the evenings and was beginning to make a little headway in catching up with the work she'd missed. She was still struggling to cope with everyone's censure, but had persuaded Hazel that a daily walk was beneficial to her recovering good health. She slipped out of the Hall and went straight down to the Village to find Yul's cottage, having first checked with Harold exactly where to go. She was nervous about sneaking into the Village like this. She'd been at Stonewylde long enough now to know what was acceptable and what wasn't, and Hallfolk simply didn't visit Villagers in their homes.

Sylvie received puzzled looks from the Villagers out and about on their business. There was no festival and it wasn't the Dark Moon – why would Hallfolk be coming down here? The Village was bustling with women wrapped in warm shawls, leather boots on their feet and wicker baskets on their arms, gossiping to each other as they went about their errands. A group standing outside the baker's collecting their daily bread turned and stared at her, but she wished them a cheerful good morning and they smiled and greeted her in return. It was the same by the butcher's, the Village pump, and the laundry. Her presence in their territory was startling, and every time she passed a group she felt all eyes upon her and heard their barely concealed squawks of surprise. But Sylvie found that her friendliness was returned each time so,

65

reassured, she continued her walk past the pub and the Green, and along the track leading to Yul's cottage.

She began to feel anxious as she approached. She'd never seen Yul like this before as their friendship and developing relationship had been conducted in the fields, woods and hills of Stonewylde. She was also a little scared of meeting his mother face to face. But she found the cottage and walked up the path to the front door, her heart beating faster and her mouth dry.

Maizie recognised the beautiful ethereal girl at once, shimmering on her doorstep like a star. She smiled warmly, dried her hands on her apron, and opened the door wide. Yul, lying on his made up bed in the corner, looked up as the door opened and his wan face flooded with joy at the sight of her. Sylvie's shyness with his mother was forgotten as she flew across the room and knelt by his bedside, flinging her arms around him. She sensed Maizie's discreet withdrawal into the kitchen and held him in a fierce embrace, tears welling up and scalding her cheeks. She clung to him, her face buried in his dark hair, his arms holding her as tightly as she held him. At that moment she understood how much she loved him; he was more precious to her than anything or anyone and she knew with absolute certainty that they truly belonged together.

Sylvie cried as she held him, realising how close she'd come to losing him forever. He was so thin under the shirt; she could feel his ribs and shoulder blades. They finally pulled apart and when she looked into his deep, smoky eyes she saw that he still wasn't right. His pupils were a little dilated and his eyes seemed enormous in his pale and hollow face. His suffering was very apparent, even worse than the previous time in the summer, and something about him was different. It was as if he'd been to a place where no one should go; had seen things that nobody should see. Yul had looked death in the face and had only turned away at the very last minute.

'I've been so scared for you, Yul,' she sobbed, the tears streaming down her face. 'I don't ever want to be without you again. I love you so much.'

He tenderly wiped away her tears with his sleeve and kissed her mouth, gently but leaving her in no doubt that he felt exactly the same. Then he held her tight again, pulled her into his chest, kissing her hair and cradling her in his arms.

'We're almost there now, Sylvie. We just have to get through the next few weeks until the Winter Solstice and then we'll be free of him.'

There was a cough from the kitchen and Maizie appeared with rosehip tea and honey cakes. She smiled again at Sylvie and sat down with them, Leveret following her in from the kitchen. The little girl stared at their beautiful silver-haired visitor in fascination. She stood in her home-spun pinafore dress, the thick woollen socks slipping down her tiny legs into her little boots, and shook the mop of dark curls out of her eyes exactly as her oldest brother did. Then she too smiled and Sylvie was enchanted by her dancing green eyes and white pointed teeth, like a row of perfect seed pearls. Maizie gathered the child up onto her lap and surveyed Sylvie with equal intensity.

'Well, I can see right enough why my son's been so moon-struck these past few months,' she said, in the embarrassing way mothers have. 'And I must say 'tis good to be called on by Hallfolk for a friendly visit.'

'Oh please, don't think of me as Hallfolk,' replied Sylvie, unsure how she should address Yul's mother. 'I really hate all that stuff and I'd much rather live in the Village and be one of you. I'm not very popular up at the Hall – I don't belong there at all.'

Maizie nodded at this and handed her a heavy pottery mug of warm rosehip tea.

'Yul says that you're one of Magus' victims too. He's told me about your moongaziness and I'm sorry you've suffered so much, my dear.'

'Thank you, though it's nowhere near what poor Yul's been through at his hands – at least Magus wants me alive. That man has a lot to answer for.'

'Aye, he has!' agreed Maizie, her face grim. 'And he will answer for it too, I'm sure o' that.'

Sylvie managed to spend quite a bit of time with Yul over the next few days, snatching precious minutes alone with him in the cottage as his mother went about her daily routine. Sylvie dashed down to the Village every day when her lessons were finished, ostensibly on a healthy walk, and soon found she was warmly greeted by everyone she met. Word had spread that she was Yul's sweetheart even though she was Hallfolk, and this latest titbit fuelled gossip even further, as everyone was already reeling about the revelation that Yul was Magus' son.

Sylvie still found it hard to accept, although it was now so obvious. Their difference in colouring had masked the likeness between them but she wondered why nobody had realised before. She discussed it with Yul on one of her visits, not sure how he felt knowing that their enemy was in fact his father.

'In some ways it's a relief,' he said. 'It explains so much – I've spent my whole life wondering why Alwyn hated me.'

'So he knew all along?' asked Sylvie.

'Mother says it was impossible for my father to be anyone other than Magus. She and Alwyn didn't get together until after I was born, though she was forced to say they had. Apparently Alwyn had been keen on her for ages but she never liked or encouraged him. He was very jealous of Magus, but he was a Villager and couldn't compete with the master. Village men keep away from a woman if they know that Magus is interested.'

'How mediaeval – the droit du seigneur. But why did Alwyn pretend you were his when he knew you couldn't be?'

'Magus insisted. It was all part of the deal. After I was born he ordered Maizie and Alwyn to be handfasted straight away. Mother told me that she fought it of course, and at first refused to lie about whose son I was. But Magus turned really nasty. He publicly denounced her and denied fathering me, saying he'd been tricked by her. What could she do? She was only a young girl and everyone practically worshipped Magus for coming back and setting Stonewylde to rights.'

'Your poor mother – that must've been so humiliating and hurtful.'

'Yes, especially as apparently they'd been really close before, though I really can't see that myself. I just can't imagine Mother and Magus as a couple.'

'People change,' said Sylvie a little sadly, thinking of her own mother. 'They were probably very different in those days. But what about Alwyn? Surely he argued about having to pretend you were his baby?'

'Alwyn accepted it because you don't question Magus – and he was delighted to take Mother for his wife. He'd been after her for a long time but she'd always turned him down, so this was wonderful, having her handed to him on a plate. But he hated having to acknowledge me as his son and he took it out on me because he couldn't take it out on Magus. I suppose it's understandable.'

'No it's not!' said Sylvie fiercely, remembering the bruising and scarring she'd seen on Yul and realising that was just the tip of the iceberg; the emotional scars must go even deeper. 'It's child abuse and that's never understandable! It wasn't *your* fault.'

'True, but Mother said every time Alwyn looked at me he was reminded of Magus, as apparently I'm so like him. Alwyn started mistreating me when I was still very young and Mother was terrified he'd go too far one day and kill me. She begged Magus to take me in as a Hallchild but he refused – I suppose because it would've looked like perhaps I was his after all.'

'That's awful,' said Sylvie. 'To know that physical abuse was going on right under his nose but not put a stop to it – that's really terrible.'

'Mother says Magus never said anything to Alwyn – never told him to lay off me or control his violence. So it was clear Alwyn could do whatever he liked and Magus wouldn't interfere. It was as if Magus wanted me dead, and of course now we know he did.'

'And it's all because of this prophecy?'

'Yes. And Sylvie, you have to go and see Mother Heggy. I'm not allowed out of the house yet, and my mother's been through so much recently I don't want to upset her by disobeying her. You know Alwyn died at Samhain? It was no great loss and I won't pretend I'm sad, because I hated him. But it's not so easy for Mother – despite everything, they were handfasted for years and he fathered my brothers and sisters.'

'Are they alright?'

'Yes!' he chuckled. 'He might've been their father but they hated him too. They had to watch him beating me, remember, and they were terrified of him. Please go and see Mother Heggy, Sylvie, today if you can. The crow keeps visiting me and pecking at the window and it's driving Mother mad. She really doesn't like anything to do with Old Heggy. She even told Gregory to take a pot shot with his catapult!'

'I've seen the crow too so it must be a summons. I'll go right now and make up some excuse for being late back.'

'Could you take her some of the things people have brought me? We've got so much jam and wine and cake and she'd appreciate some treats, poor old thing.'

The crow was hopping around outside as Sylvie left with a laden basket for Mother Heggy. It flapped up onto her shoulder, cawing loudly in her ear.

'Yes, I understand,' she said with a smile as it scrabbled to hold on. 'I'm on my way.'

It stayed with her for some time as she walked through the Village, gripping clumsily onto her jacket. Several Villagers noticed and pointed it out to each other, remembering the crow on Yul's shoulder at the Summer Solstice ceremony. They knew it was Mother Heggy's creature and many made the sign of the pentangle in the air and touched their chests. The Villagers understood that Yul and Sylvie were under her protection.

'My little bright one!' crowed Mother Heggy at the sight of Sylvie on her doorstep. 'At last you've come. And only just in time, for 'tis the Dark Moon tomorrow.'

She pulled Sylvie inside the smelly cottage, shooed the cat off the chair and sat her down. The crow hopped about on the table

70

after a scrap of meat as Sylvie handed over the basket to the old woman.

'Very tasty too,' cackled Mother Heggy, smacking her shrivelled lips as she rummaged about inside it. 'And how is my boy? Does he heal well? I been sending reviving potions for him.'

'Yes, but ... he's changed. There's something different about him and I don't think that will heal.'

'No, 'twon't. He saw the Dark Angel at Samhain and he'll never be quite the same. There's a shadow on his soul now, but 'twill make him stronger and he'll need that strength. We're on the final path now, Sylvie. You know Sol must die, and 'twill not come about easy. Yul will need all his power and energy so tell him to get up to that Circle just as soon as he can.'

'You're not saying that Yul is actually going to kill Magus?' asked Sylvie, shaken at the thought. 'Surely that isn't right? I mean ... well, I don't know if Yul would do that, or even if he *could* do it.'

Mother Heggy shrugged, peering myopically at a jar of bramble jelly she'd unpacked from the basket.

'I don't know how 'twill happen,' she said finally. 'I only see so much. The old prophecy came to me like a thunderbolt when the boy were born, and 'twere clear enough. Yul is the fruit of his passion for sure, the child conceived under the blue moon and born under the red moon. In the brightness at the darkness – that's the full moon at the Winter Solstice, the darkest day. So 'twill be this Solstice, when Yul becomes a man.'

'How do you know it'll happen this Solstice?' asked Sylvie, still unsure quite how the lunar cycle and festivals fitted with each other. 'Is is always the full moon at the Winter Solstice?'

'No, 'tis rare for both to fall together at the same time, but this year 'tis the Moon Fullness on the eve of the Solstice. It don't happen very often like that and 'tis right it should be this year, when Yul reaches sixteen. Life is full o' these things happening all together in strange ways that don't seem possible.'

'Like a pattern you mean?'

'Aye, exactly like a pattern. Yul will rise up with the folk behind, and aren't they all gathering behind him now? At the place of bones and death – we know where that is, right enough. 'Tis six weeks to the Solstice. But Sylvie,' she gripped the girl's arm with her claws, peering almost sightlessly into her eyes, 'there may be a prophecy from long ago but ... Yul will rise up, without a doubt, but that don't mean he'll be sure to succeed, nor even survive. For I seen something else of late, but 'tis not clear.'

'Something else? What sort of thing?' asked Sylvie, wondering if it was to do with Magus' dreadful plans for her every month.

'There may be more than one death this Solstice,' muttered Heggy, her rheumy eyes gazing blankly. 'I see the number five, always five. But 'tis too many! Not five deaths, surely? I cannot see who must die, but I know one thing for sure. You and Yul are in great danger from Sol. Do you understand, girl? The magus is evil and Yul would've died at Samhain but for my Raven. I summoned her back through the veil to aid him and 'twas down to her that the boy survived. Has he told you my girl was there in the Circle with him that night?'

'No,' replied Sylvie with a shudder. 'He's hardly spoken about it, though he has terrible nightmares every night he says.'

'Aye, the Death Dance will haunt him for some time to come, poor boy, and maybe for the rest of his days. Well, you must listen to old Mother Heggy, my silver one, and do as I say. The prophecy may yet go unfulfilled and that's what Sol will hope for. He'll do everything in his power to stop it coming about as I foretold, and if he can get past the Winter Solstice, he'll be safe. The prophecy will lose its magic once the Solstice is passed and then Goddess help us all. We only have one chance and we must fight him, we who stand against him. Are you with us?'

Sylvie nodded, her eyes wide with apprehension.

'I love Yul. I'd do anything to stop Magus from hurting him.'

Mother Heggy pursed her lips at this and patted Sylvie's smooth hand with her withered one.

'Much will be asked of you, my bright one, almost too much. You must be brave and strong. 'Twill be a cage of sorrow for you, a cage that binds the silver nightingale with bars of gold. You'll see, you'll recall my words when you're captive. And the first task, the first thing you must do, is this: bring me something of Magus – hair or nail. I need something of his body for my spell.'

Sylvie looked sceptical but Mother Heggy was unperturbed.

'You don't believe but 'tis of no matter. Just bring me something and you must, without fail, bring it tomorrow. 'Tis the Dark Moon and the spell must be cast tomorrow night, when the banishing is at its most powerful.'

'I won't be part of murdering anyone,' said Sylvie a little shakily. 'I love Yul and I want to help, but—'

'You're as much a part o' this as Yul or me or Sol or anyone at Stonewylde,' snapped Mother Heggy tetchily. 'You were part of it from the moment you were conceived in the woodland under the red Harvest Moon, so don't go soft now you're needed! You ask your mother – she knows right enough 'twas no ordinary conception.'

'I'm sorry, Mother Heggy,' said Sylvie, her mouth trembling. She still felt fragile and so frightened. 'It's just the thought of causing someone's death . . .'

Mother Heggy regarded her with a toothless grimace.

'Nobody said 'twould be an easy path to follow, but if you love the boy you must do what has to be done. Now, we have two more weeks till the next Moon Fullness and we cannot let Magus feed on your moon magic again.'

Sylvie closed her eyes wearily, sick of the whole thing. Stonewylde had seemed like heaven on earth when they'd arrived here but now it was just a battleground.

'Aye, 'tis that,' said Mother Heggy, with her uncanny knack of reading thoughts. She pulled her filthy shawl closer around her bony shoulders and cocked her wizened head at Sylvie. 'And who do you want to win – Sol or Yul? Father or son? If you fail to get me what I need for my spell tomorrow, then the boy may well die at his father's hand this Solstice. The very spirit of Stonewylde will be broken, I can promise you that. And your life will be a misery o' pain.'

*

73

Sylvie stumbled back up the track to the Hall as the early November darkness closed in around her. The fallen leaves made a soggy carpet on the ground and several times she skidded and slipped, for she was always clumsy at this time of the month. Rooks cawed noisily around her, their voices raucous and abrasive. It was cold and damp and she was scared. How was she going to find Magus' hair or nail clippings? He was still away, but it might've been easier if he were around. She'd have to look in his rooms, and although she knew where they were of course, she'd never been anywhere near them before.

She was terrified at the thought of what she must do, and even more scared of Mother Heggy's talk of death. She still hoped that this terrible struggle between Yul and Magus could somehow be resolved peacefully. It was all very well believing in an old prophecy that spoke of rising up and overthrowing, but now that the reality of just how this was to be achieved was looming closer, Sylvie was very frightened. Magus had already proved that he had no qualms about resorting to violence, but she wanted none of it and was sure Yul didn't either. And as for Mother Heggy's remarks about five deaths ... Sylvie shuddered at the thought, and opening the garden door to their wing, climbed the dark stairs to her bedroom, grateful as ever to have a private entrance.

Miranda looked up from her knitting as her daughter entered their small sitting room, rosy-cheeked from her walk. Miranda sighed, rubbing her swollen belly. The baby was very active today and had had the hiccups this afternoon, which had been extremely uncomfortable. She was sure the baby was a boy and imagined him as a tiny Magus, complete with silvery-blond hair and brown eyes like dark chocolate. She was missing Magus and longed for his return; he'd be pleased with the way she was handling Sylvie. Her daughter was responding to the new, strict regime and had really knuckled down, eating properly and making progress with her schoolwork in the evenings.

'Why are you back so late?' Miranda asked sharply, anxious to keep Sylvie firmly in line. 'It's dark outside and you've been gone for ages.'

'I'm sorry, Mum – I lost track of the time.'

'Well don't do it again, Sylvie. You won't be allowed out at all if you can't manage your time and come home this late. Go and get on with some schoolwork before supper.'

Sylvie shrugged and went back into her bedroom, closing the door on Miranda and her huge bulge. She'd never thought they'd be like this, having always been so close. She'd lost her loving, friendly, funny mother and it made her so sad. Everyone was against her, not only her mother, but the teachers, her tutor, the doctor and all the other Hallfolk. Everyone was on her back, sniping and criticising, and now she had this request to worry about. Would Yul really die if she didn't help with Mother Heggy's spell? Sylvie couldn't quite believe it but didn't dare risk not doing her bidding just in case the old woman was right.

Sylvie sat with Miranda in the dining room, picking at her meal and far too nervous tonight to enjoy the food. Since her mother had started watching every mouthful she swallowed, eating had lost all pleasure anyway. They were surrounded by other Hallfolk, all talking and laughing together at the long tables whilst the servants scurried about, refilling plates and glasses and ensuring the Hallfolk had everything they needed. During the meal Sylvie felt Holly and her gang, a few tables down, staring at her and whispering. Holly had gathered quite a crowd over the past few months; Rainbow and the younger Hallfolk she'd teamed up with during the summer term were now joined by her original gang, including July, Wren, Fennel and some of the older boys. They were a large and noisy group and Sylvie felt uncomfortable knowing they were talking about her and glowering her way. Holly was very open about it. Her dark eyes held contempt and undisguised scorn as she glared insolently at Sylvie. Her pretty face twisted into an expression of malice whenever she caught Sylvie's eye, and she flicked back her thick, shoulder-length hair in a gesture of challenge. Sylvie sensed that Holly was building up to a major confrontation, and dreaded it. She knew how Holly had decided to make a play for Yul at the Autumn Equinox, and how he'd brushed her off. Sylvie now wondered if Holly had somehow found out about her and Yul's relationship, which would explain this increase in hostility.

Sylvie kept her eyes down and tried to avoid any kind of non-verbal contact with anyone on Holly's table. She had far more important things to worry about tonight. As the pudding was served, Sylvie sensed a good opportunity to visit Magus' rooms. All the Hallfolk were in the Dining Hall and would be for some time as coffee was also served in here, and the servants were busy with the meal and clearing away.

'Would you excuse me please, Mum? I don't want any pudding and I have to do some research for my coursework. I'll see you later.'

'Have some pudding first, Sylvie.'

'Honestly, Mum, I've had enough. You know I've put on weight and Hazel's happy with my progress. And you know I don't like lemon meringue pie very much.'

'Have cheese and biscuits and some fruit then,' said Miranda with a frown.

'Please, Mum, I'm really full and I've eaten loads. I need to do this research tonight and I don't want to be too late to bed as Hazel said I must get plenty of sleep.'

'Alright then, but where are you going – library or computer room?'

Sylvie thought quickly.

'I don't know yet, it depends which is quieter and what resources I need. Probably both.'

By giving two locations she'd buy herself a little more time should Miranda or anyone come looking for her.

'Okay, Sylvie, see you later. Make sure you work hard and don't be late for bed.'

Sylvie left the great Dining Hall and had no choice but to walk down alongside the table where Holly sat. She steeled herself to pass the large group, feeling her cheeks burn as everyone stopped talking and turned to stare at her in hostile silence. It was as intimidating as if they'd insulted her. She nearly bumped into

Martin in her headlong determination to get to the double doors without tripping over or embarrassing herself. He stood deferentially to one side to let her pass, holding a door open for her and watching as she hurried down the corridor out of this wing.

Sylvie sped across the stone-flagged entrance hall with its enormous antique ginger jars full of beautiful bronze-red chrysanthemums. She almost skidded into the great dinner gong and grabbed the carved newel post of the staircase. Swinging round it, Sylvie dashed up the first flight of stairs, wide enough for several people standing abreast. Huge paintings, banners and shields hung on the grand walls, so very high here, and at the half-landing, facing the gigantic stained glass window, Sylvie paused to catch her breath. She despised her lack of strength and tried to steady herself and calm her drumming heart, which she knew pounded as much from terror as lack of stamina.

Then she climbed the second half-flight of stairs and reached the first-floor landing. A wide oak-panelled corridor ran all along this main block of the Tudor mansion. This was where Magus had his apartments, in the centre of the south-facing front of the Hall, occupying the position of dominance over the vast stately home. Sylvie had looked up at these chambers many a time as she walked up the tree-lined drive, for the long series of windows were directly over the huge entrance porch.

She stood now at the top of the main staircase and looked up and down the corridor stretching darkly away to either side. There were many other rooms further on which she knew nothing about, but she did know the enormous oak door under the stone arch before her led into Magus' apartments. Despite all the Hallfolk downstairs finishing dinner in the Dining Hall and the many servants dashing about to serve them, it was very quiet up here. The carpet along the corridor was thick and the wood solid, and but for a distant hum from downstairs, Sylvie almost felt as if she were alone in the building.

Her heart was once again pounding and her hands trembled. She also had the dull nagging ache that told of her imminent period, and her head throbbed. She took a deep breath and approached the heavy door ahead. She was terrified but thought of Yul, telling herself this was to help save his precious life and she must be brave. She opened the door and stepped in quickly, shutting it silently behind her. Now she was safely inside, Sylvie knew she wouldn't be disturbed – nobody would come in here with Magus away.

5

The sliver of light disappeared as the heavy door fell shut behind her, and thick, soft darkness wrapped around Sylvie. In the silent blackness, she stood with her back to the safety of the door, heart knocking fast in her chest. Her instinct was to turn and run, escape this dark lair and find light and safety downstairs, to seek the security of familiar people around her. But Sylvie knew what had to be done tonight, which she alone could do, and she steeled herself, willing her hands to stop their violent trembling and her heartbeat to steady.

The air was strange inside the chambers; antique and woody, aromatic with incense and the exotic scent that Magus favoured. Sylvie breathed deeply to calm herself and felt his essence enter her lungs and infiltrate her body. She shook with nervousness, imagining his reaction if he were to suddenly appear and discover her purpose here. Although Sylvie's eyes were becoming adjusted to the blanket of darkness, she was still blind. It was totally black inside the room; no moon as it was almost Dark Moon, and a cloudy night anyway. There were no street lights at Stonewylde and the rooms downstairs were shuttered to the night. The darkness was absolute.

Realising that she needed to hurry up with her task, for time was of the essence, Sylvie forced herself to leave the safety of the door and felt all around the walls behind her for a light switch. She found nothing, so tentatively stepped out into the unchartered territory before her, feet shuffling in tiny steps, arms and hands flailing like a blind person's white stick. Her feet were silent on the thick carpet as she edged across the expanse. Without any warning she bumped suddenly into something hard, and groped at it frantically. It was a small table and with relief, Sylvie located a large electric lamp on it. Her patting, fumbling fingers found the switch and with a sharp click, the room sprang into vision around her. She gasped in utter amazement, looking around in wonder at the grandeur of the beautiful room. Its sheer size dwarfed Sylvie completely, frozen by the little table on the ocean of carpet. She felt like Alice stumbling into a world where she was tiny and everything around her far too large.

Set in the oak panelled inner wall was a vast stone fireplace, and a great mantelpiece ran above it. Over this hung a mirror of huge proportions, making the room seem even larger and deeper. An enormous leather sofa stood before the unlit fire, and over against another far wall was an antique desk, with a leather chair and computer. There were more sofas, chairs and occasional tables positioned around the room, a large television screen, a dining table and two chairs in a recessed alcove, and paintings and sculptures everywhere. Everything in the room was beautiful, a reflection of Magus' knowledgeable and refined tastes.

Along the outer wall in front of the diamond-paned mullioned windows was a long window seat covered with cushions, set behind a huge stone arch. This must jut out above the entrance porch below, Sylvie guessed, and made a slightly private area in the huge chamber. The massive wooden shutters hadn't been closed against the darkness, but Sylvie imagined that when Magus was in residence, with the great fire lit and the shutters drawn, it would be very comfortable and even intimate in this luxurious apartment.

Sylvie dragged herself out of her awed reverie, knowing she urgently had to find a piece of hair or nail. If they were to be anywhere it would be in his bedroom or bathroom, so she crept across the expanse of the room towards the door at the far end. She guessed that as with hers and Miranda's rooms, situated in one of the lesser Tudor wings, the grand chambers here would all connect with each other. The next room was a dressing room, bigger than the entire floor space of the flat she'd lived in all her life before moving to Stonewylde. Sylvie's jaw dropped at the magnitude of a room that existed solely to contain one person's clothes and shoes. The walls were lined with panelled wardrobes, tallboys, chests of drawers and glass-fronted cabinets. She had a quick look inside some of the cupboards and closets, noting how everything was immaculately stored and carefully organised, rows upon rows of ties, handkerchiefs, shoes, belts, riding clothes, shirts, cuff-links, suits ... the inventory was extensive. She couldn't begin to imagine how much his clothes and shoes must be worth, for he was a man of expensive tastes. She decided she'd look in here if she had no luck elsewhere, as there was a very slim chance there could be a hair on one of his jackets.

The next door led into his bathroom, almost Roman in its masculine opulence. She pulled the light cord, and soft, concealed lighting flooded the room, even larger than his dressing room. The huge bathroom suite was of rich black marble, with onyx and jade accessories and gold fittings, and a thick white carpet softened the hard lines. Luxurious white towels lay piled on every surface and bottles of priceless toiletries gleamed on shelves. Many large gold-framed mirrors twinkled the reflected lights and Sylvie could see herself everywhere in the bathroom, mirrored many times over like a mathematical multiplication puzzle. The walk-in shower was roomy enough for several people and the spa-bath huge and circular. Sylvie had a flash of a naked, tanned Magus emerging from his bath like a god from the pool of immortality, and quickly banished the thought.

She hurried over to the two adjacent wash basins and looked for his personal things: a razor, hairbrush, anything he may have left behind when he went away. There was a carved jade set – hairbrush, comb and clothes brush – on the black marble top, but all were immaculately clean. She couldn't imagine Magus tolerating any untidiness and pitied the servants responsible for looking after his rooms and clothes. She opened the cabinets one by one looking for nail clippers or a stray comb. Rows and rows of expensive products were arranged with spotless precision, everything a well-groomed man who took care with his appearance and personal hygiene could possible need. But not a hair or nail clipping in sight.

Feeling a rising sense of desperation, Sylvie closed the cabinet doors and moved into the next room – the bedroom. She found a switch on the wall and then this room also glowed with intimate lighting. She gasped again; how much luxury could one person command? Or even need? This room was also massive, a lair of crimson silk-lined walls and deep carpet smooth as velvet. The bed was antique, a great carved four poster large enough to sleep several people. The trimmings and covers were of exquisite Chinese silk, embroidered gold and scarlet on black, and the mound of pillows was sumptuous. The posts themselves were of a rich, dark wood carved with writhing vines of flowers and leaves. Sylvie had a Goldilocks-like urge to lie down on the great Daddy-Bear bed just to see what it felt like, for the extravagance and lavishness of such a grand piece of furniture was very inviting.

She looked carefully at the pillows, but of course the fine Stonewylde linen would've been changed since he left. Knowing Magus and his taste for luxury, he probably had the linen changed daily. She went over to the enormous carved dressing table and examined that minutely, but there was nothing. She slumped down on an embroidered stool in misery. This was impossible – she'd never find the hair or nails Mother Heggy needed, the spell wouldn't work and Yul may die. Sylvie's heart was heavy with disappointment and she felt close to tears at her failure. She gazed gloomily at her own dejected face in the ornate mirror before her, wondering what on earth to do now.

She sensed the movement rather than saw it. Reflected in the mirror, the door behind her, which had swung closed as she'd entered, was slowly and silently opening. Sylvie was already in a state of nervous fear; she now broke into a sweat, her heart drumming frantically in her ribcage. She looked around desperately for a place to hide and for a split-second considered dashing over to the bed and throwing herself underneath it. But there was no time as she was in direct view of the door, which was creeping open further and further by the second ...

The face that peered at her in the reflection, as pale and anxious as her own, wasn't that of the autocratic master of Stonewylde, but Cherry!

'Sacred Mother, you scared me to death, Miss Sylvie!' she squawked, coming into the room. 'What in Goddess' name are you doing in here?'

Sylvie swivelled around, waves of relief flooding through her, and suddenly felt very dizzy. She grabbed hold of the dressing table to steady herself.

'I ... I ...'

'Hold on, miss!' cried Cherry, bustling across the room. She put one arm around the girl to support her. 'Are you faint? You're white as a linen sheet. Put your head down between your knees, my dear. There, that's better.'

She stood holding Sylvie, clucking and fussing, and after a minute or so Sylvie sat upright. She felt a little better but had no idea what to say.

'Don't look so rabbit-scared, miss! You won't be the first maid to come in here unbidden,' said Cherry, shaking her plump jowls. 'I seen it all afore, and even known the more brazen ones creep in there,' she nodded towards the massive bed, 'and wait for him.'

'Oh no!' cried Sylvie in disgust. 'Oh no, Cherry! I'd never, ever do that!'

As soon as she spoke she realised what a good excuse that would've been to explain her presence here, but too late. Cherry smiled at her genuine horror.

'Aye, well ... I was wondering, seeing as how I heard that you and our Yul were sweethearts,' she said. 'I know you go up to Mooncliffe with Magus at the Moon Fullness, but I heard that he forces you to go and 'tisn't the usual thing he wants from you up there neither. He saves that for afterwards with someone else. He uses you up there for moon magic, I heard. Is that right?'

Sylvie nodded, her eyes round and nervous. Cherry patted her shoulder kindly.

'So you didn't come here to get into his bed, or rub your cheek against his clothes, or splash about in his bath, or any o' the other daft things I've seen girls do when he's got 'em in his thrall. So I wonder why you did come? You must hate the man if he's made you suffer up at Mooncliffe, and for what he done to Yul.'

Sylvie nodded again. She was useless at lying and racked her brains for a plausible reason why she'd sneaked in here. Cherry regarded her steadily, lips pursed as Sylvie sat on the embroidered stool in an obvious dilemma.

'Have you heard of Lily? About what happened to her?' asked Cherry eventually.

'No, I haven't.'

'She's the poor maid who were handfasted to that brute Jackdaw. You've come across him?'

'Oh yes, and Yul's told me about him too. He murdered his wife, didn't he?'

'Aye, that were our Lily, and Jackdaw was banished for it right and proper. But now he's back! And why? Magus is mocking us, treating us like fools, like we have no feelings, thinking he can do exactly what he likes and we'll just take it. Lily was my sister Marigold's girl, my little niece – apple of my sister's eye, Lily was. 'Twas bad enough at the time, but now that Jackdaw's back, 'tis like Lily's murder never mattered at all. So don't you worry about me knowing you hate Magus. Never thought I'd say this, but I find that I hate the man too, as does my sister.'

Sylvie looked up at her in relief.

'But you still haven't told me – why are you in Magus' bedroom, Sylvie?'

She noticed that the 'miss' had been dropped.

'I ... I came looking for something,' she said reluctantly.

'Aye?'

'Something that somebody sent me to find.'

''Twouldn't be a certain old woman who lives outside the Village up on the hill, would it?'

'Yes.'

'And would you be searching for something of Magus for a banishing spell, by any chance?'

'Yes.'

Cherry roared with laughter and clapped Sylvie on the back in a gesture that Villagers didn't normally use on Hallfolk. Together they searched carefully, looking everywhere in Magus' apartments, but despite the huge area it wasn't long before both realised the futility of their hunt.

'I'm in charge o' these rooms,' apologised Cherry, 'and 'tis more than my life's worth to allow any mess or dirt here. We'll never find anything and we'd better get out now afore someone realises we're in here. That Martin is always wandering and creeping about like a ghost. Come on, my girl.'

They turned off all the lights and left the chambers, but instead of going back down the main stairs they carried on further along the corridor, past several more closed doors. Eventually they reached the far end of the great block which formed the huge front face of the Hall, and went quietly down some narrow back stairs leading straight into the warren of corridors that were part of the servants' quarters.

'We'll talk to my sister Marigold. She may have an idea.'

Marigold, so like Cherry in looks, size and temperament, hugged Sylvie to her generous bosom once the details were explained. The three of them sat cosily in the cook's parlour, a small room next to the kitchens, and were quite private here. All notions of Hallfolk and Villager seemed forgotten in their united purpose of helping Mother Heggy with her banishing spell.

'Many of us feel the same,' said Marigold, 'but we have to be careful. 'Twouldn't do if some little weasel went and told Magus that people were gathering against him, would it?'

The three of them talked for a while, trying to think how they could get some of his hair or a piece of nail before the next night. Magus was due back any day but nobody knew exactly when. Sylvie was thinking along the lines of DNA, and wondered if Hazel would have any samples in her office, maybe some of his blood. But she quickly dismissed the idea, because even if the doctor did, it would probably be under lock and key. Then Marigold shrieked and slapped her great thigh so hard it quivered.

'I know, I know! Cherry, remember the album? The album old Rosemary used to keep of the boys?'

'Oh my stars – of course! Are you thinking o' the locks?'

'That I am, dear sister, that I am! I'm sure there's locks of hair in there.'

'What?' squeaked Sylvie in excitement. 'What album? Where?'

'Well, my dear, when the two little boys, Sol and Clip, were growing up they had their own nurse called Rosemary. Poor old thing, she were, doted on them boys but they treated her terrible, especially young Sol. See, their mother had nothing to do with 'em.'

'Raven?'

'That's right – Raven.'

The women exchanged glances.

'You're thinking I look just like her, aren't you?' said Sylvie.

'Well yes, my dear, you do. Peas in the pod.'

'Why did they have a nursemaid? Why didn't Raven care for her sons?' asked Sylvie.

'Oh no, she couldn't do that! They were kept away from her out of harm's reach,' said Marigold. 'Raven lived with Mother Heggy, and sometimes she lived wild in the woods, especially in the summer. I reckon she would've killed them boys if she could. She hated 'em as much as she hated their fathers. She were ill-used, the poor girl, first by old Basil, and then Elm. No reason to love the children she were forced to bear, especially not Sol.'

'No, she always despised Elm more than Basil. And Sol were ever his father's son in that respect.'

'In what way?'

'Sol were a thug as a boy, a real bully, and he used to fight the Village boys and beat 'em badly. Elm sent both boys away to school in the Outside World as soon as they was old enough. Mind you, that were after Raven had died.'

They poured some more tea, clearly ready for a good old gossip about the past, but much as she wanted to hear all this fascinating detail, Sylvie was very conscious of the time. Her mother could be looking for her and she had to get the hair to Mother Heggy tomorrow.

'So you think there may be some of Magus' hair in this album?' she asked.

'Aye, I do. Old Rosemary, she used to keep an album all about the two little boys as they grew. It were a big leather book full of photographs o' them that Hallfolk took, drawings they'd done and suchlike. And I'm sure she kept locks of their hair in that album from when they was very little. Now where would it be, Cherry? Can you remember?'

''Tis in that room where old Siskin works sometimes. You know, where all them papers and framed photographs are kept. We'll have to rummage.'

Sylvie started to get up. They both looked at her in surprise.

'Not now, maid!' said Marigold. ''Tis far too late. The Hallfolk are about and they'd see us if we started rifling and rummaging now.'

'We'll have a look tomorrow, dear,' said Cherry. 'Don't you worry – I can go in that room nice and early to get the cleaning done and nobody'd think twice. We have to be careful o' Martin, for he'd snitch as soon as look at us. But in the morning he won't question me going into any of the rooms with a feather duster. If that album's still about, and I don't see why it shouldn't be, I'll find it and get the lock of hair to you.'

'It's Dark Moon tomorrow and Mother Heggy said she must have it by the evening.'

'We know that, and don't you fear, we'll get it to you in time. And be happy to do it.'

'Aye, anything that'll help rid Stonewylde o' Magus, Dark Angel take his wicked soul!'

The two women didn't let her down. Sylvie returned to her bedroom after breakfast the following morning to find a twist of paper on her pillow. She opened it and stared at the small silver-blond lock of hair inside. She felt a sharp twinge of emotion looking at the tiny piece of Magus' childhood, so small and silky in her hand. It must've been difficult for him growing up without a mother, in the care of a harsh father who was interested in nothing but his own base pleasures. She pictured the little boy tearing around Stonewylde getting into mischief, fighting other boys and gaining a bad reputation, unloved by anyone except an old nursemaid and lashing out at the uncaring world, trying to control others with his strong will and angry fists. A little boy with nobody to nurture him and bring out his gentle side, and then sent away to a tough boarding school where he'd learnt to hide his darkness and present an amiable face to the world.

She stroked the silver lock, curled like a tiny crescent moon, and wondered if she held the means to Magus' downfall in her palm – maybe to his death. But she pushed the guilt and pity away and thought of Yul instead, still recovering from the terrible ordeal Magus had put him through. Whatever the reasons behind Magus' cruel nature, the fact remained that Yul was in danger from him, and indeed so was anyone else who crossed him, including herself. Sylvie hurried to Mother Heggy's cottage before her misgivings could get the better of her.

'I don't know if it's any good,' she said, breathless from climbing up the hill in the chilly November wind, 'because it was cut when he was a child. I'm sorry, Mother Heggy, but it's all I could get.'

''Twill do,' wheezed the old crone, fingering the lock of hair with gnarled fingers. 'Shouldn't matter how old it is so long as 'tis his own. Now I can get to work.'

'Will ... will the spell actually kill him?'

'No, not on its own. 'Tis not that powerful magic. I'm old and on the wane myself, not like I used to be. But 'twill weaken him just as I weakened Alwyn. 'Tis a symbol of intent, my spell-mongering. I do what I can to help the boy for he's the grandson of my Raven and the one with the Earth Magic. The Goddess chose him, as I knew she would.'

'But Mother Heggy, I don't understand why you hated Magus

so much when he was a child, before he'd done anything bad, and yet you don't hate Yul. Magus was Raven's own son, after all.'

''Tis true, but he were conceived from her suffering. She should never have borne children. If you could only have seen it ... My poor little Raven! Just a tiny, delicate little thing she was and he a great heavy brute of a man. 'Twas terrible how he forced her every single month, like his brother afore him, while she was moongazy and weak and couldn't defend herself. And he brimming full o' the power and energy he'd leeched from her through the stone, capering about like a wild torn cat and greedy with the moon-lust. No child of such a cruel union could ever be loved, not by me nor by her.'

Sylvie was silent, thinking of what little she knew of her own sordid conception. Did her mother resent her for it? Now that she'd conceived a baby in loving circumstances, had she realised the difference and decided that she didn't love Sylvie so much any more? It would explain why her mother had been so cold and uncaring recently. Sylvie swallowed hard, trying to push down the feelings of hurt and rejection. At least Yul loved her, even if nobody else did.

The crone had shuffled across to a dilapidated cupboard in the corner where she peered closely at the bottles and jars jostling on the shelves.

'But 'tis different with Yul,' Mother Heggy continued, decanting a green-tinged liquid into several smaller bottles she'd set out on the table, her hand remarkably steady for someone so old and blind. 'True he has his father's blood, but not his father's evil – the power and the strength without the cruelty. And Maizie were willing. She loved Sol, and in his own way he loved her, so Yul's conception was not cursed.'

Sylvie nodded bleakly at this, and taking the small bottles Mother Heggy pressed on her for Yul, hid them in a little bag she carried. Then after quickly hugging the old woman goodbye, Sylvie left for the Great Barn where she must join all the other women for the Dark Moon gathering.

It was an ordeal walking into the Barn, and Sylvie immediately located Holly and her gang over on one side of the enormous space. Once again they'd commandeered the pile of squashy cushions and were lying about on their backs, laughing and talking loudly. Another group of older Hallfolk women sat at a distance from them, examining a great heap of rushes. Sylvie fumbled at the pegs as she hung up her jacket, not sure where to sit. All she wanted was to hide herself away from everyone and not attract any attention from Holly's group. But it was difficult to avoid company here, so after some hesitation she decided to join the group of Hallfolk adults.

Hazel looked up at her arrival and the smile faltered on Sylvie's lips. The doctor was still cool with her, despite the daily visits in which Sylvie tried to get back to their previous friendliness. Magus had done a thorough job of turning Hazel against her.

'Can I join you?' she asked diffidently.

Hazel nodded, pulling a handful of dried rushes from the pile. This month they were making mats for the Villagers' cottages, one of the women explained to Sylvie. The rushes had been harvested in the autumn from the marshes where the river flowed into the sea, and these new circular mats would replace the worn-out ones on the stone kitchen floors. Sylvie sat down and watched how they selected the rushes and smoothed them out, before binding the ends with thin reed and beginning to plait. It was clearly more difficult than it looked, and timidly Sylvie began to pick out some of the long rustling leaves from the heap.

'I had the results back from your tests just after you left my office this morning,' said Hazel, plaiting efficiently as she talked. 'Magus is due home very soon and he'll be pleased to see them.'

'Are they alright? Is there anything wrong with me?'

'No, there isn't, so Magus was right all along.'

Sylvie's heart sank. Although she hadn't wanted there to be anything seriously wrong, this news would only strengthen Magus' case that she was faking the lethargy and exhaustion she suffered after moondancing for him.

'He'll be pleased that I've put on weight, won't he?'

'I expect so, although you haven't gained that much and your blood tests indicate there was some malnourishment. He won't like that at all.'

'But I am eating properly now, Hazel. I couldn't help eating nothing when I felt so ill, and you know I was asleep for most of that week after the last full moon.'

'Excessive sleeping is just another way of not facing up to life. Maybe it's time you woke up, Sylvie,' Hazel replied coldly.

A couple of the women in the group were Sylvie's teachers, and they looked across at her.

'I hope you've finished that history coursework,' said one of them sternly. 'Magus has requested a full report on his return and I've got my notes ready for him. There are still gaps in what you've submitted so far.'

'It's almost done,' said Sylvie. 'I should be able to finish it off tonight.'

'Too late for the report though.'

'How's the revision going?' asked another. 'You know the mock exams start soon. Have you caught up yet?'

'Nearly,' said Sylvie quietly. 'I've been working hard.'

'Pity you didn't try that earlier. The mocks will prove just how little effort you've put in over recent months. I always say they're a wake-up call.'

'Just what she needs,' said Hazel grimly. 'What a good job Magus realised how far you've slipped, Sylvie, and just in time, too. You're very lucky he's taken such an interest in your welfare.'

Sylvie swallowed her bitter retort, fighting down the tears of frustration and injustice that made her throat ache.

'And I hear your maths is quite dreadful,' continued the history teacher. 'I think you've left that too late to turn around and William's very annoyed you've let him down. Magus is always particularly proud of the high maths results achieved at Stonewylde. He'll be furious with you.'

'I'm doing my best,' said Sylvie, bent over the plaiting to hide her burning face.

'About time too. Oh for Goddess' sake, girl! What are you doing to those rushes? What a dreadful mess! Unplait all that and start again. Or go and do something a little simpler that you can manage.'

Sylvie gave up and stumbled miserably over to the group working on patchwork quilts, still avoiding the Hallfolk girls who were eyeing her malignantly across the stone floor. The group of Village women who were busy quilting welcomed her warmly and moved around their benches to make space for her. Maizie and Rosie were especially pleased that she'd joined them, Rosie even swapping places so she could sit next to her. Remembering Sylvie's clumsy attempts the month before, she offered to teach her how to sew properly. Sylvie tried hard to copy the girl's tiny neat stitches as she hemmed her hexagons, but glumly wondered if she'd ever find anything she was good at.

The conversation was mundane but comforting, revolving around simple things such as whose house pig was next due for slaughter, and when to shut the bees up for winter. Sylvie started to relax a little, managing to block out the strident laughter coming from the gang on the cushions. Then the women in her group turned to the favourite topic of the moment – the return of Jackdaw. He and Magus had been away for over a week now, but it was known that Magus was due home any day. The servants always fed any Hallfolk news back to their relatives in the Village, and there was much speculation as to whether or not Jackdaw would return with the master.

'I reckon he will. His things are still in the rooms over the stables where he were sleeping,' said Tom's daughter.

'He better not show his face in the Village,' said Edward's wife grimly. 'There'll be such trouble if he does!'

'Marigold said he comes into the kitchens like he owns the place, swaggering about and giving out orders. She said she's tempted to add a little Death Cap or Destroying Angel to one o' his pies.'

'She wouldn't do that!'

'Well, the poor woman has good cause to.'

'Aye, but then she'd be no better than those two old hags, Violet and Vetchling, and their nasty brews.'

'I'd poison him myself if I could,' muttered Rosie.

'Rosie! Don't say such things!' said Maizie sharply. 'He'll get his justice for what he's done to Yul without your hand in it.'

Sylvie glanced up at them and saw the naked hatred on Rosie's face.

'What did he do to Yul?' she asked. 'You mean at the quarry last summer?'

'No!' said Rosie, almost choking as she tried to explain. 'What he did at Samhain.'

'When he took Yul into the Stone Circle?'

'No, before that, when he had our Yul at his mercy in the byre. He burnt him.'

The group of women and girls stopped their sewing and looked sympathetically across at Rosie's flushed face. Maizie nodded, her eyes hard and bitter.

'Round burns the size o' your little fingernail,' she said. 'Jackdaw did it, Yul told us, when we noticed the marks all over his back, his arms and chest – he's covered in burns. Jackdaw did it just for fun, Yul said. My poor, poor boy ...'

Tom's daughter put an arm around her.

'Don't you fret, Maizie. That Jackdaw will be taken by the Angel, you'll see. There's justice in this world, and not only at Magus' bidding.'

'Aye, and I'd like to see him dead too.'

The women fell silent, bending their heads over their sewing once more as the ripples of this shocking comment reverberated amongst them. Now it had been said openly, and by a woman who'd always loved him. The dark clouds were gathering and Sylvie shuddered, thinking of the pitiful lock of silver hair in the Wise Woman's withered hands.

Knowing that his mother and sister would be in the Barn for most of the day, Yul slipped out of the cottage to visit Mother Heggy. He wasn't as strong as he'd thought and was pale and

93

exhausted by the time he arrived. She fussed over him, sitting him down and making a reviving brew in the old stone mug.

'You have but two weeks to get your strength back, boy,' she told him. 'He mustn't take her to Mooncliffe this next Moon Fullness for he must be as weak as possible when the Solstice comes in December. So no moon magic this month.'

'I know,' said Yul, worriedly. 'I need to organise it properly this time. Will I be well enough by then?'

'Aye, I reckon so if you get up to the Circle, my lad. That'll help, sunrise and sunset and this time o' year, 'tis easy enough with the days getting so short. Keep yourself warm, for you'll feel the cold in your bones for a while yet.'

Yul sat back, closing his eyes. He was so weary, and even when resting and sleeping he worried about Sylvie and the next full moon. He couldn't let her down again.

'I can't take her to Hare Stone, can I? That's the first place he'd look.'

'No, you must get her far away, somewhere he won't find her, but nowhere near Quarrycleave. That's a place of death and the big stone there at the head of the quarry, 'tis the same as the stone at Mooncliffe. 'Twill hold her moon magic just like the other one does and 'tis where he got the rock to make those stone eggs.'

Yul felt angry just thinking about the eggs. He'd love to smash the chest open and steal them away – that'd give Magus a nasty shock when he came for a fresh one to boost his dwindling energy.

Mother Heggy chuckled, and patted his arm.

'Now you're thinking a-right, my boy. It must be your plan, not mine, and you must use your wits. You may have the Earth Magic in you, but Magus is still bigger and stronger than you. So use your mind to outwit him, get things ready aforehand and think it clear. Use the man's own greed against him.'

'What about Jackdaw? He's very strong and he's as cruel as Magus. Much as I'd like to, I can't take both of them on at once.'

'Those who stand against you will fall, one by one.'

94

'You mean Jackdaw?'

She chuckled and shooed him out of the cottage.

'Go home, sleep, eat and get strong. Make your plans and let me get on with my banishing spell.'

After lunch in the Barn, Sylvie and Rosie along with many of the women went outside for a walk around the Green before resuming the afternoon's work.

'I'm pleased to speak alone,' said Rosie. 'Yul gave me a message for you this morning. He said to meet him under the tree afore you go back to the Hall tonight.'

Sylvie smiled and nodded, wishing again that he could read and write.

'I've got some medicine from Mother Heggy in my bag for Yul,' she said. 'I'll give it to you to take back for him in case I forget when I see him. He has that effect on me.'

Rosie grinned at this, but then looked serious.

'Be careful with Mother Heggy, Sylvie. And whatever happens, don't let on to Mother that you've seen her. Mother has a real wasp in her shawl about Old Heggy. She reckons all of this is her fault, 'cause if Heggy hadn't made that prophecy, Magus would've taken Yul as a Hallchild and wouldn't have turned against Mother. She'd never have been handfasted to Father and Yul would've grown up happy and loved. Mother blames Old Heggy for everything that's happened and she's told Yul he must never visit her again.'

Just then they heard a shriek of laughter and Sylvie groaned. Holly and her friends had come onto the Green and were heading their way.

'Hey, Sylvie! Wait for us! We'd so like the pleasure of your company!'

'You'd better go back to the Barn, Rosie, if they're going to join me.'

'Right enough, miss. 'Tis not my place to butt into your Hallfolk talk and—'

'No, no, it's not that, Rosie! I'd much rather be with you than any of that lot – you're far nicer company than them. I'd just rather you didn't get mixed up in all their nastiness. I'll see you back inside.'

Rosie squeezed her arm sympathetically and walked off back to the Barn, ignoring the girls' rude comments as she passed them. Sylvie quickened her pace, continuing the circuit of the Green. Holly came running up and overtook her, capering about in front of her and laughing. Holly was fit and athletic and Sylvie had a sudden memory of her leaping from the apple tree and landing on Yul, wrapping her muscular legs around his hips. She swallowed and kept her head down, forced to slow her fast strides.

The rest of them were coming up behind – July, Wren, Dawn and the group of younger girls.

'Why are you ignoring me, Sylvie?' asked Holly. 'Do you only mix with scummy Villagers now?'

'Villagers aren't scummy!' she said hotly.

'Ooh! Maybe you should move out of the Hall and live in the Village if you like them so much. You've been sitting with Villagers all day, haven't you?'

'No,' said Sylvie. 'I sat with Hallfolk making rush mats earlier on.'

'Not for very long. You've been with Yul's mother and sister most of the time, I noticed. You're very friendly with them, aren't you?'

'Not especially,' said Sylvie. 'I just preferred making patches for the quilts, that's all.'

'That's a lie – you're very friendly with them, Sylvie, and you were even walking round the Green with Yul's sister just now. I heard some interesting gossip this morning. I heard that you and Yul are sweethearts!'

Sylvie's heart sank. Holly fell into step beside her as the rest of the girls caught them up, and Sylvie felt Holly's dark eyes watching her, sizing her up.

'So you're not denying it then?' she asked, spoiling for a fight.

'I've got nothing to say to you!' retorted Sylvie.

'So *is* Yul your boyfriend? I want to know, Sylvie, and I'll find out if I have to go and ask him myself.'

'It's none of your business!'

'Ooh! I take it that's a yes.'

'Take it however you want, Holly.'

Sylvie strode as fast as she could, not looking at any of them, her long silver hair wafting around her as she marched doggedly on around the Green. She was now taller than Holly by quite a way and despite Holly's slim fitness, Sylvie's legs were much longer so Holly had to trot to keep up with her.

'We're sick of this, Sylvie,' said July. 'You know that Holly's keen on Yul. Why are you stealing another of her boyfriends?'

'Yeah, you're just a prize bitch really,' said Wren. 'First you take Buzz away from her – when you didn't even want him – and now you're taking Yul away too.'

Despite intending to ignore them, Sylvie found herself drawn into the argument.

'Have I missed something?' she asked. 'Is Yul actually your boyfriend then, Holly? How can I take him away from you if he's not?'

'Shut up, you cow!' snarled Holly.

'Why? Because what I'm saying is true? I heard Yul won't go anywhere near you and can't stand the sight of you. That's got nothing to do with me.'

'Yes it has! He was keen enough till you arrived! It's like Buzz, all over again!'

'You're so greedy, Sylvie,' said Rainbow. 'First Buzz, then Magus and now Yul!'

'Greedy for men! She can't get enough of it!'

'Stop it!' said Dawn, frowning at them all. 'There's no need for that.'

But they started to chant and dance around Sylvie, taunting and jeering, and she was reminded sharply of her school life in London.

'I wish you'd never come to Stonewylde!' cried Holly, skipping along. 'Nobody likes you! Why don't you go back to the Outside

World and whatever hole you crawled out from?'

'Why should I? This is my home now and I'm not going anywhere. Get used to it, Holly!'

'We don't want you here! Don't you realise how unpopular you are?'

'It's your fault Buzz was banished! And now you've got your hooks into Yul, just because Holly wants him. You better leave off him, Sylvie!' warned July.

'Yeah, and Magus too!' said Wren, still besotted after her stint as the Corn Mother at Lammas.

'You can't have them both!' cried Holly. 'It's not fair! Goddess knows what they see in you anyway, a skinny beanpole like you! Does Magus know about you and Yul? I bet he doesn't! I might just tell him. He'd be furious and it'd serve you right!'

Sylvie stopped. She was almost back at the Barn now and must deal with this situation, although she wasn't sure how.

'Look, Holly, if you're really interested in Yul you won't repeat any of this to Magus. I'm not the one he'd be furious with and he'll just take it out on Yul. You must've heard what happened at Samhain, so if you like him you won't say anything. Unless you want him to suffer?'

'Don't be stupid, of course I don't!'

'Then leave me alone and stop stirring it up!'

'You haven't heard the last of this!' Holly hissed as the crowd of girls swept in through the massive doors.

As the afternoon drew in and the light began to fade, the women in the Barn packed away their projects ready for the following morning. The Barn was used every night by different groups and everything had to be left tidy. The rushes and patchwork quilts were put to one side, along with the flax for spinning and the wool for felt-making. The women bid each other a good evening, and the Villagers hurried home to get the supper cooking. The Hallfolk were not so rushed as the servants had left earlier and would be busy on their behalf up at the Hall.

As they left the Barn the sky was pink and pearly to the southwest where the sun was setting. The birds still sang up in the great circle of trees that surrounded the Village Green, and Sylvie thought of the professor and all that he'd told her about the history of this part of Stonewylde. She remembered the great carved wooden face set into the wall of the pub, and the photo of Yul the professor had given her back in late summer. That photo was her most treasured possession, capturing something very magical that not many had seen, but Sylvie knew that Yul was the embodiment of the Green Man and all that he represented at Stonewylde.

She smiled to herself, remembering the funny little professor. They'd kept in touch since he'd left in August, e-mailing each other occasionally, and she must write again. He knew nothing yet about Samhain's terrible events and Magus' revelation, and she felt he should as he'd made it clear that he was on her and Yul's side. It was obvious that Stonewylde meant everything to him and she thought again how cruel Magus was, only allowing him back for a few weeks a year. The old man would've loved to spend his last years back in the place where he'd grown up and where he belonged. There were plenty of empty rooms at the Hall and he was no burden to anyone. Sylvie vowed that when Magus had gone, she'd make sure Professor Siskin was invited to return to Stonewylde for good.

The sky was now soft violet and grey; the sunset a vivid flamingo pink. The air was quite mild for November and Sylvie stood outside the Barn and breathed deeply. A stable hand had arrived with one of the large painted carts pulled by two horses, which were used to transport Hallfolk between the Hall and Village. Several Hallfolk women climbed in and settled themselves on the padded seats. Sylvie watched the cart roll away across the cobbles, soon overtaking the large group of women who'd chosen to walk the distance up the track to the Hall. She heard the gang of girls up ahead, still making too much noise in the quiet evening, and breathed a sigh of relief.

All was now calm and peaceful as Sylvie lingered in the shadows, waiting a little longer, her heart thumping with anticipation at the prospect of seeing Yul. She didn't notice Holly, who also loitered around the side of the Barn, hiding in the lee of a buttress. When Sylvie thought the coast was clear she hurried across the Green where plump woodpigeons pecked in harmony on the damp grass. She reached the yew tree and disappeared into the half-light. Holly was careful not to be seen as Sylvie melted into the shadows beneath the tree, and waited before moving forward herself.

Sylvie entered the yew's sphere and felt the atmosphere alter. The air was somehow different, time was a little changed and her skin felt strange. She thought of the scientific explanations possible; perhaps the oxygenation process caused by the transpiration of such a huge tree ionised the air all around it. But her heart told her it was the magic of the tree spirit causing the changes, however irrational that sounded. She smiled, knowing that in her old life she'd have laughed at such a theory but now knew it to be the truth.

Yul leant against the massive tree trunk, dark curls falling across his face, his grey eyes shadowed. She felt a starburst of excitement at the sight of him, tall and pale and waiting for her. She ran the last few steps and was enfolded in his arms, his lips bruising hers as he kissed her long and hard.

'I can't stay long,' she gasped, pulling away reluctantly. 'Mum will wonder why I didn't return with the others. They're all on my back at the moment and I must be careful. How are you feeling?'

'Much better thanks. I'm going up to the Circle tomorrow, which will help, and Old Greenbough's said I'm not to go back to work for a while. He's on our side, Sylvie! He said if we need help he'll do anything he can.'

'That's good news. We've got Marigold and Cherry up at the Hall too, and they said there are many others who feel the same way.'

'I think most of them do. The time is coming closer, Sylvie, and we need to make plans. The next Moon Fullness ...'

He felt her shudder as he spoke and held her close against his body, stroking her hair.

'Sylvie, I let you down last time and I swear it won't happen again. I'd die rather than let him to feed off your moon magic on that rock again.'

'No, Yul.'

She pulled back a little and looked up at him in the fading light. She could see the shadows in the hollows of his lean face.

'Dying wouldn't help. Awful as it is, I can survive moongazing on the rock. Don't sacrifice yourself for nothing.'

'No!' he said vehemently, shaking his head. 'He won't do it to you again. I've sworn an oath to myself. I need to get you away before moonrise next Moon Fullness – not so early that he has time to look for you, but not so late that there isn't time for us to get far away. You understand we won't be able to go to Hare Stone?'

She nodded. 'I don't think or act rationally at moonrise so I'll do whatever you say, and you know I trust you completely to take care of me.'

'I'll find somewhere we can hide, and once the moon's high the danger's mostly passed. I think Magus can only take your magic at the rising. But he must believe everything's fine and not get suspicious, or he'll lock you up or make Clip put another spell on you. I know it's awful, but you must go along with whatever he says over the next couple of weeks. Can you make him think you're coming round to his way of thinking? Because if he found out we're meeting like this . . .'

'I'll try my best. He's due back very soon, and I know he's going to give me a hard time, but I won't stand up to him—'

She stopped abruptly as he bent to kiss her again, his tongue skilful, his hands now more assured than the first time they'd kissed under this tree at the Summer Solstice. She'd wanted him then, but the feelings were now infinitely stronger. Everything was more intense and she felt herself dissolving into a wave of pure desire. Sylvie wondered if Yul felt the same, little appreciating just how tightly he controlled his longing for her.

'Stop, Yul,' she said shakily, pulling away from him. 'It'll show and Mum will know what I've been up to. I must go.'

She stumbled a few steps towards the grass.

'Will you be in the Great Barn tomorrow?' he called softly.

'Yes. I'll see you here again?'

'You will, but a little later, after sunset. Wait here for me if you can. I love you, Sylvie.'

She smiled and blew him a kiss as she turned away. Leaving the thrall of the ancient yew tree, she hurried home with wings on her heels.

6

Yul waited for a while beneath the boughs of the yew. He knew there was some special magic here; not the Earth Magic but something else, something primeval that called to him and fed a hunger in his soul. He belonged in this place and always had done. He leant back against the soft, flaking bark of the great bole and shut his eyes, his mouth still tingling from kissing Sylvie so hard. He took a deep, shaky breath. His body was highly aroused and his hands trembled from the torture of wanting her so badly but knowing he must rein himself in whenever he was close to her.

Darkness was almost complete as Yul pulled himself away from the massive trunk and ducked under the boughs and onto the Village Green. He looked up at the moonless sky now glittering with bright stars, feeling the magic of the Dark Moon deep inside. As he began to head for home and supper, his heart soared wildly from his encounter with Sylvie and the prospect of seeing her again tomorrow.

Nothing in the world compared to the feel of Sylvie in his arms; so willowy and pliant, so willing and passionate. Every moment they spent together was something magical, snatched and stolen time from their lives. One day Yul knew he'd wake to see her face next to his, feel the whisper of her breath on his cheek as they lay close together. He quivered with another rush of longing and then miraculously felt her hand slip into his as he walked across the Green. She'd come back! He turned, smiling, but his face froze into a mask of disappointment at the sight of Holly. Immediately he shook her hand out of his with a gesture of dismissal.

'What do you want?' he muttered angrily.

'That's not very nice, Yul!' she replied in a hurt voice. 'We've known each other all our lives and there's no need to be nasty.'

He continued to walk briskly, trying to throw her off.

'I need to talk to you,' she said. 'Please – just for a few minutes.'

'I've got to get home,' he said. 'My supper will be waiting.'

'It's important. Just a couple of minutes.'

'Alright then,' he sighed, 'but be quick.'

She slid her hand around his arm and guided him under the nearest tree, for they'd now crossed the Green and reached the other side. There was a very different atmosphere under the chestnut tree. It had shed most of its leaves, and the bare branches and twigs made an intricate pattern against the starry night sky. Holly stopped and Yul turned to face her, anxious to get this over with. He remembered how jealous Sylvie had been in the orchard during the apple harvest, and didn't want to do anything that might upset her again.

'What do you want then?' he asked brusquely, barely able to see Holly in the darkness.

'I want some of what Sylvie's been getting,' she replied and threw her body against his. She flung her arms round his neck in a limpet grip, trying to pull his head down to hers. Her lips brushed his as he jerked his head away and tried to shake her off. But she clung on tightly, deliberately pressing herself hard against him and despite himself Yul felt a jolt of desire, aroused as he was from his earlier passion with Sylvie.

'*Get off me!*' he snarled, grabbing hold of her arms and flinging her away from him. She stumbled backwards, shocked by his vehemence.

'Don't be like that!' she wailed. 'Why do you hate me? What have I done to you?'

'Nothing! Everything! I don't know!'

He was angry with himself for the momentary lapse, for wanting her even if only for a split second.

'Please, Yul, sit down and talk to me,' she said, her voice small and unhappy. 'Stop being so angry with me.'

She sat on the wooden seat built around the trunk of the tree and patted the spot next to her. Yul shook his head and remained standing.

'Okay, stay there if you like but I'll have to speak louder and anybody could hear us. It's about you and Sylvie – I know what's been going on.'

He sat down reluctantly.

'I don't know what you're talking about.'

'Oh yes you do!' The plaintive tone had been replaced with her customary supercilious drawl. 'I know what you've been up to under the tree with her. She gets about, doesn't she?'

'What do you mean by that?' he demanded.

'First Buzz, then Magus, now you. She can't get enough.'

Yul stood up abruptly, not trusting himself so close to her. He had an urge to slap her nasty little face.

'I'm not listening to this! You've got it all wrong. She's never been interested in Buzz or Magus.'

'But she's interested in you?'

'No, I ...'

He stopped, realising he'd made a blunder. She jumped in.

'I saw her going under the tree with you, Yul. I saw everything and we both know it's not allowed between a Villager and Hallfolk, not like that. I'm going straight to Magus.'

'No!'

He sat down next to her again and grabbed her wrist, peering at her in the darkness. He could only make out her shoulder-length blond hair but knew her face well enough to imagine her pretty feline features looking smug with malicious satisfaction. She didn't struggle in his grip but almost melted into him, reaching into his jacket to caress his chest.

'Yul, stop fighting me. What's she got that I haven't? You and I could have such fun together.'

'Stop it! Get off me! Look Holly, you really mustn't go to Magus. I—'

'Who'd suffer the most if I told him – you or her?'

'I don't know,' he said, not sure how best to play this. She was clever and manipulative and at the moment, at least one step ahead of him.

'Because I don't want you to be punished again, Yul, although it would be nice if *she* got into trouble. I could tell Magus—'

'NO! Don't, Holly, please, you mustn't say a word to him.'

'What's it worth?'

He shrugged, at a loss to understand what she wanted from him.

'You're very slow aren't you, Yul? I want you to kiss me like you kissed Sylvie.'

'No! I couldn't kiss anybody else like that!'

'Try, Yul. I'll be patient with you. Come on, it's not much to ask in return for keeping your secret. Not when Magus would be so very angry with both of you. My silence in exchange for a little kiss, just for old times' sake. You were keen enough once and I haven't changed. Come on, Yul.'

Reluctantly, knowing this was madness but unsure what else to do, he allowed her to link her hands behind his head and pull him down. Her lips fastened onto his and she kissed him. He remained passive, not responding in any way, and she pulled away from him.

'What's the matter with you? It's only a kiss, Yul, and Sylvie will never know. Kiss me properly or I'll go straight to Magus the minute he gets back and tell him everything.'

So he did, hating himself for it and hating Holly even more. It was mechanical and soulless and she felt horrible and tasted different. Finally, unable to endure it any longer, he wrenched himself from her clinging grasp. He stood up again, wiping his mouth hard with the back of his hand in the ultimate gesture of disgust.

'Alright, I've done it! Now let me go home, and leave Sylvie alone, Holly. If I hear you've been upsetting her ...'

'Yes? You'll do what, exactly? Don't threaten me, Yul! Or I might tell Sylvie what we've just been doing, and she wouldn't like that, would she?'

The light from the pub just illuminated her face as she looked up at him. Her eyes glinted and her smile was triumphant.

'That was very nice for starters, Yul,' she purred. 'Although a little more passion next time, I think. It's not long till our Rite of Adulthood, remember, and I'm looking forward to it.'

He turned on his heel and strode off, ignoring her laughter. He'd betrayed Sylvie and hated himself for it, realising he'd made a stupid mistake by giving in to Holly but also seeing it was too late to go back now. He must just make sure it never happened again. He crashed into the cottage, the door rattling on its hinges as he flung it open, and Maizie and Rosie exchanged worried glances. It was a while since they'd seen Yul in one of his terrible black moods.

Yul left his cottage the next morning whilst it was still dark, wrapped warmly against the chill November air. He started up the track that led to the Long Walk and the Stone Circle and was surprised to find Edward, the farm manager, waiting in the tunnel of bare trees.

'Blessings, sir!' said Yul, taken aback.

'Blessings to you, Yul.'

They fell into step together. Yul was pleased to see that he was now almost as tall as Edward, although he had a long way to go to match the man's huge physique.

'Why are you up here this morning, sir?' asked Yul. He kept an eye on the sky through the trees, not wanting to miss the sunrise.

'To look after you,' replied Edward with a smile, thinking the lad would resent this.

'But ... but I ...'

'Mother Heggy's orders. She says you need the Earth Magic and you must come here every day, sunrise and sunset. If Magus realises what you're up to he'll send Jackdaw to stop you. 'Tis why I'm here for there's nought I'd like more than a fight with

Jackdaw. So no arguing, young man – I'm coming whether you like it or not. We need you strong, Yul, as there's a lot of folk counting on you.'

Yul was silenced by this. He knew Edward to be one of Magus' staunchest supporters and wondered what had brought this change about.

'Thank you, sir, but I hope you don't mind. This must be a busy time of day for you.'

'I'm happy to do my bit. We need to hurry now, 'tis almost sunrise. And Yul – up here, you can drop the "sir".'

They entered the Stone Circle and, despite himself, Yul began to shake uncontrollably. This was his first visit since the night of Samhain, though he came here every night in his sleep. The Stone Labyrinth haunted him in his dreams, when he was most vulnerable and unable to fight back. The crows and skulls were still painted on the stones and would remain so until the preparations for the Winter Solstice. In the centre the ashes from the pyre marked a darker spot on the earth, although all remains of the fire had been cleared. The black stones and tiny red candles had gone and every trace of the labyrinth had vanished.

But still Yul felt sick with dread, remembering so vividly the stalking Dark Angel, the white corpses on the sleds and his own drugged paralysis. He knew that but for Raven's help he'd certainly have died in this place. The Stone Circle had always been a magical, beautiful place for him, somewhere that brought solace and harmony. Lately it had become the place where he received the Earth Magic from the Goddess, and the knowledge that he was destined to lead Stonewylde. But now, not only had Magus and his four acolytes poisoned his body here, they'd also poisoned this magical place for him, turning it into somewhere evil. He really didn't want to be here at all. He shuddered and Edward put a strong arm around his shoulders in an unexpected, almost fatherly, gesture.

'You were very brave that night, Yul, braver than any of us would've been. Accept what happened and put it behind you lad. Come on, up on the Altar Stone and forget about death.

Think o' life – the life force o' the Earth Goddess.'

Yul nodded gratefully, unable to speak as the emotions choked him. He clambered up onto the stone, not yet strong enough to leap as he usually did. Immediately he felt the throbbing, pulsing energy of the earth pushing up through the molecules of stone, channelling into his body. He felt it building as the sun came closer to the horizon. It was cloudy and grey but the sun was approaching whether or not the human eye could see it. The magnetic solar energy slid into alignment with this spot where the magnetic energy of the earth was strong and focused.

The sky remained a dull pewter grey, but Yul knew the precise moment when the sun appeared over the horizon for he felt an almost orgasmic jolt to his body. He stood with outstretched arms and the energy flooded through him, into every atom of his being, electrifying in its intensity and power. He felt filled, charged, fired up with the Earth Magic. He took a deep breath and relaxed, letting it saturate him. Gone were his fears and terrors. Suddenly he felt he could slay any foe who dared to challenge him.

About ten minutes later, when the sky was much brighter, he opened his eyes. He smiled across at Edward who stood some way off, leaning against one of the great stones. Edward was silent and strangely subdued as they walked back towards the Village, and after a while Yul broached a subject which was preying on his mind.

'You were angry with me in September, at the Apple Harvest, for speaking against Magus. Yet today you say everyone's counting on me. Why your change of heart?'

Edward looked at Yul, tall and filling out with hard muscle, but all said and done still a boy and not a man. The long dark curls and slanted grey eyes had masked his heritage, but now it was plain to see. He was so clearly his father's son, powerful, strong and a natural leader. The air around Yul crackled, although the boy didn't seem to be aware of it, nor of the tiny sparks arcing from his fingertips. There was absolutely no doubt that the Earth

Goddess blessed Yul with her green magic. Edward felt completely over-awed at what he'd just witnessed.

'I used to admire and respect Magus with all my heart,' Edward began. 'And in many ways I still do. He saved Stonewylde and made it a great place again, after all the years when the land had been abused and everything left to rot. But somehow Magus has missed the true path and gone wandering up one that's leading us all to a precipice.'

'What makes you think that?'

'I've heard about his plans for Stonewylde and I don't like 'em. I've young children and I don't want them growing up in a place that's gone bad, where us Villagers are nought but servants. More Hallfolk coming to live here, new houses to be built for them and us Villagers having to serve 'em all. That's how it used to be in the old days, my father says, and 'tis not what Magus always promised us. Seems to me he's abandoning all we hold sacred. He wants to increase the harvest from land and farm more aggressively too, and I can't hold with that. The Earth gives us what she can and she mustn't be forced.'

Yul nodded as this was one of the most fundamental principles of honouring the Goddess in the landscape. Take and enjoy her bounty, but never be greedy.

'And there's the matter o' Jackdaw,' Edward continued, an edge to his voice. 'Lily was my cousin. We all trusted Magus to punish Jackdaw fairly for killing her, and his banishment was just. But Magus has gone back on that and not even had the decency to explain why. I don't feel I can trust the man any longer, especially a man who tried to burn his own son alive.'

He glanced across at Yul, still bearing a haunted look of suffering, but also surrounded by an aura of energy that danced about him like a cloud of gnats.

'And then, Yul, there's you. You're the one who receives the Earth Magic now. Greenbough and Tom both told me so afore and I believed 'em, for they are good men and always speak true. Now I seen it with my own eyes I'll tell others too. 'Tis not us but Stonewylde herself that chooses the magus. You're chosen,

Yul, and after what I just seen this sunrise, 'tis my honour to support you. I'm behind you every step o' your path.'

They reached the Village and with a farewell salute, Edward mounted his great grey mare and rode back to the farm.

Before joining the fertile women of Stonewylde for the second day of menstruation, Sylvie went first to Hare Stone for the sunrise and then a walk along the ridgeway. She found she was increasingly able to sense the serpent lines of energy in the earth, just as Yul could feel her silver moon energy.

Walking along the Dragon's Back, up high in the hills, was exhilarating and set her spirit soaring. She could literally see the bigger picture when surrounded by the great sweeps and swathes of green hills and valleys, the recumbent form of the Goddess in the land. Sylvie walked along the green spine of the earth feeling the late autumn wind blow away the cobwebs, breathing deeply of the magical essence of Stonewylde and feeling herself restored by it. Arriving late at the Great Barn, all eyes turned to her as she made her entrance, windswept and rosy-cheeked, her eyes sparkling and hair whipped into silver tails. She resolved to spend a peaceful day in the Barn and try hard to avoid any trouble.

At the end of the day Sylvie watched the girls get into one of the carts to go back to the Hall. She savoured the peace once they'd left, standing amongst the trees and looking up at the bare branches feathery against the pale mauve sky. A blackbird sang sweetly, the liquid song pouring into the clear evening. Sylvie closed her eyes for a moment feeling a thrill of pleasure at the thought of seeing Yul. She walked across the grass and waited under the yew tree for him to return from the Circle. She was alive with excitement, longing for him to join her in their special place.

He arrived silently, appearing under the boughs in the shadowy enclosure formed by the yew. They gazed at each other, suddenly shy. Yul held back, crawling with guilt at the kiss with Holly. Sylvie was overwhelmed by his presence, feeling the difference in him straight away since his visits today to the Stone Circle at sunrise and sunset. He buzzed with energy, his eyes sparkling and long fingers plucking at the bark of the tree.

'It's because I haven't been up there for so long,' he explained, taking her hands in his. 'It's always stronger then. After a few days, it'll settle down.'

Sylvie was a little scared of him when he was like this, restless and vibrant with life and almost ready to explode with the magic. His eyes seemed to pierce her and he overflowed with power and energy; she felt it tingling in his fingertips. When he tried to take her in his arms she pulled away, apprehensive of the strength of the Earth Magic that hummed within him.

'I'm sorry,' she whispered, stroking his cheek. 'You're too much for me tonight, Yul. It's as if anything you touch will burst into flames. You set me on fire as it is; tonight you'd consume me completely.'

He smiled at this and contented himself with running his hands through her silky hair as they stood close, all the time watching her for signs that she'd heard about his kiss with Holly. It seemed the girl had kept it to herself and he prayed she continued to do so. He considered confessing to Sylvie now, to come clean and feel honest again, but when he thought of how angry and hurt she'd be he decided not to.

He was edgy and nervous, fiddling with her hair and shredding slips of yew, scuffing his boot on the ground. They talked of Magus' and Jackdaw's imminent return to Stonewylde and how careful they must be not to attract attention. But without warning, just as Sylvie started to explain about the banishing spell Mother Heggy had made on the night of the Dark Moon, Yul lost his temper. He was furious when he heard Sylvie had searched Magus' rooms. He swore vehemently and kicked hard at the soft earth beneath the tree with barely suppressed aggression.

'Mother Heggy had no right to put you in danger like that!' he snapped. 'Don't *ever* put yourself at risk like that again!'

'There wasn't any risk. Magus wasn't home so he couldn't have found me there.'

'He could've come back unexpectedly. And he still may find out what you've done. Sylvie, please don't do anything to make him angry with you. He's so cruel, so sadistic and I can't bear to think of him hurting you. Goddess, I can't believe Mother Heggy made you take a risk like that! How dare she?'

'Yul, she didn't make me do anything,' said Sylvie in a placatory voice, anxious to calm him down. 'She asked me to help and I agreed. I want to do my bit to defeat him. It's not just your battle; we're all in it.'

'Yes but you're more at risk from him than anyone else.'

'We're all at risk from him, Yul. Everyone at Stonewylde who crosses him is at risk.'

'So don't cross him!'

'I will if that's what it takes to stop him. I want him gone as much as you do and I have every right to help in the fight against him.'

'Sylvie, *I'm* the one who's going to overthrow him, not you! It's not your fight, it's mine. You keep well out of it and leave it to me!'

Furiously she turned and walked away from him, unable to believe what she was hearing. Besides which it was almost dark and she needed to get home.

'Don't turn your back on me!' he snapped, eyes flashing in the gloom. 'Come back here – I'm still talking to you!'

'Don't speak to me like that!' she retorted. 'You sound like your bloody father!'

He marched after Sylvie and tried to grab her.

'Sylvie, don't go! Look, I'm sorry, I ...'

She shook him off, running from the shelter of the yew tree onto the Green where she knew he wouldn't risk anyone spotting them together.

'Think about it, Yul! If you end up just like your father, what's the point in having a new magus?' she said, over her shoulder. 'I'll see you around, when you've got your arrogance under control.'

*

113

Yul was so angry after she'd gone that he didn't know what to do with himself or his rage. He didn't want to go home and upset his family again with his bad temper, so he decided to visit Mother Heggy and speak his mind, especially as this was her fault. He reached her cottage quickly and stormed in after a cursory knock.

'Blessings, Yul,' she wheezed from her rocking chair by the fire. 'Close the door. 'Tis cold out there.'

'Mother Heggy, I—'

'Come and sit awhile, boy. I hope Edward found you out today at the Circle?'

'Yes, thank you but that's not why I'm here. You had no right to send Sylvie snooping in Magus' rooms for stuff for your spells. NO RIGHT!' He slammed his fist on the table. 'She's *not* to be put in danger. I will fight Magus, not you or Sylvie or anyone else. It's between me and him, and I won't let you interfere or put Sylvie at risk. Do you understand?'

He quivered with anger, grey eyes flashing, and glared at the old crone who was not much more than a bag of wrinkles and whiskers. She peered up at him blindly and smacked her gums together.

'Spoken like a true magus.'

He glared even more fiercely, his breathing harsh.

'Do you understand, Mother Heggy?'

'I take orders from nobody,' she muttered. 'We're in this together and we must all do what's needed. You love Sylvie and want to protect her, I know, but she has a part to play in his downfall and you can't deny her that.'

'But I don't want her taking unnecessary risks and I don't want your spells either! I want to deal with him myself, one to one!'

'And you shall. But 'twill help weaken him, and it gathers the people behind you. Everyone knows I've cast a spell – Cherry and Marigold have seen to that. Never could hold their tongues, them two. The folk will all look at him with new eyes, watching for weakness or strangeness. 'Tis part of casting off an old magus and adopting a new one. Keep your temper under control, Yul,

114

and save it for them that deserve it, not we who're on your side.'

He hung his head, curls falling over his face, trying to calm his rage. He was so full of passion at the moment, and Mother Heggy continued rocking as he fought to contain himself. After a few minutes he looked up.

'I'm sorry,' he said, his eyes no longer sparking fury. 'I've no right to order you or anyone else around. But please, please, don't put her in danger. She's the most precious, most special, most . . .'

He stopped, choking on the words.

'Aye, but she's also brave,' said Mother Heggy, 'which is why she's a worthy partner for you. She might look like a delicate flower but she's not made o' petals and she certainly won't take no bullying from you.'

He grinned ruefully at this.

'I know, she's already put me in my place about it.'

'So listen to her, stop acting in passion and take her advice. She's clever and been in the Outside World most o' her life. She knows far more than you, who's nought but a simple, ignorant Village boy. Don't make her see you as a fool – you must be worthy of her too.'

'But how? I know I'm ignorant, but . . .'

'When this is over, all will change. You've much to learn, Yul and you're very young. But at the Solstice, when you become a man and take on the mantle of magus, you'll have a difficult lesson to learn. Being leader o' Stonewylde means sacrifice as well as power, and your sacrifice might start with facing your ignorance and swallowing your pride. You'll have to get proper learning to match hers, maybe in the Outside World. The struggle don't end at the Solstice, my dark boy. 'Tis when it begins.'

While Yul was running up the path to Mother Heggy, Sylvie walked angrily up the track towards the Hall. She was furious with Yul for being so high-handed and for his attitude towards the struggle with Magus. It hurt that he was shutting her out, not acknowledging either her role in the conflict nor her wish to help. She seethed with resentment at his arrogance. As night closed in around her she heard an owl calling in the distance, and then the sharp scream of a vixen in the woods nearby.

'Hello, Sylvie!'

Holly appeared before her on the track, just visible in the falling darkness. Sylvie groaned; Holly's cattiness was the last thing she needed right now. She kept walking, trying to avoid a confrontation.

'I thought you left on the cart.'

'I did but then I changed my mind. I wanted to speak to you in private and I didn't mind waiting. You weren't long tonight. Not as long as last night.'

'I'm not in the mood, Holly. Just leave me alone.'

Holly laughed her false, irritating laugh.

'I can guess what you're in the mood for! Just left lover-boy under the tree, have you?'

'What?'

Holly laughed again, skipping alongside Sylvie in a state of glee.

'I know where you meet Yul and what you get up to! Don't try to deny it!'

'Go away, Holly! You don't know anything.'

'You're so wrong – I know all about it! Didn't Yul tell you about last night?'

'What are you talking about?'

'No, I didn't think he'd tell you! Ha! Don't you want to know what he got up to with me?'

Sylvie turned and grabbed Holly's sleeve, shaking her with uncharacteristic fury.

'Just shut up! I don't want to listen to a word you say!'

Holly shoved Sylvie away, her face splitting into a grin of pure malice.

'Are you sure about that, Sylvie? You don't want to know what Yul and I did under the tree after you'd gone last night? You really shouldn't leave a boy all worked up like that – it's just asking for trouble. Poor Yul, but how lucky for him I came along.

116

Still, if you're absolutely sure you don't want to know . . .'

She took off with a laugh, running up the track leading to the drive, her laughter becoming fainter in the distance. Sylvie didn't try to catch her but her mind was racing. Surely Yul wouldn't have done anything with Holly? Or maybe he had, which was why he'd been so nasty to her tonight? And he'd liked Holly in the past, enough to get into a fight with Buzz over her. Sylvie gulped back her tears, misery squeezing at her heart. She could cope with anything if she had Yul by her side, but if he betrayed her, she'd never have the strength to stand up to Magus.

The long white tables gleamed in the soft candlelight as the Hallfolk ate dinner. Conversation bubbled, glasses and silver cutlery chinked and the servants hurried to clear the soup dishes away and bring the next course. Sylvie sat miserably next to Miranda, huddled in her seat trying to force down the meal. In contrast Miranda chattered non-stop, excited at the prospect of Magus' imminent return. There was a general buzz of anticipation in the air and Sylvie seemed alone in dreading his return. As Holly turned yet again to gloat at her, sniggering over some joke with her group of friends, Sylvie wished that she were anywhere but here. She noticed Hazel sitting up on the high table, near the head where Magus would dine should he arrive in time. Several of her teachers had given her meaningful looks already and she knew what they were thinking – Magus would be reading their reports very soon and he wouldn't be pleased.

Just as pudding was served the double doors were thrown open and Magus made his entrance. There was a moment of silence before he was greeted by cheers and a crescendo of noise as he strode down the long room to his seat. Sylvie felt her heart thudding faster but knew it was from fear rather than excitement. Miranda had flushed at the sight of him and was now giggling and talking too loudly, as were many of the women. He sat in his great carved chair, smiling at those around him and accepting a plate of food from Martin, who fussed over him deferentially. Sylvie noticed how the servants in the room had jumped to attention and become more nervous and jerky. She caught Harold's eye for a moment but he looked away immediately, denying their new friendship.

Sylvie gazed up the table at Magus, the returning hero. He glowed with health and vitality which she knew was thanks to her suffering on the rock. He wore a dark business suit with a snowy shirt and silk tie. His blond hair gleamed like burnished bronze, his dark eyes flashed with cleverness and energy. The candlelight gleamed on his skin, as smooth and rich as marble, hollowing his cheekbones, highlighting his strong nose and chin and emphasising the curve of his lips.

Sylvie was struck forcibly by his likeness to Yul. How had she never spotted it before? Seeing Magus, she could picture exactly how Yul would look at this age and knew she'd want him just as much then as she did now. Magus was so very attractive and every woman in the room watched him. Some were obvious about it, like her mother, Hazel, and Holly's gang, and others more discreet, but all were caught up in his magnetism and beauty. Would it be the same with Yul, Sylvie wondered? Would she have to share him with every woman at Stonewylde?

At that moment, Magus looked up and across the room straight into her eyes. She felt her cheeks flushing and her eyes widen but couldn't look away. His dark eyes bored into her and he inclined his head, his lips tightening into a half smile. It wasn't lost on Holly, whose head shot round to glare at Sylvie. She whispered to Rainbow and they both glowered at Sylvie for the rest of the meal. Sylvie felt awkward and embarrassed, her stomach churning so much she couldn't eat any more. She wondered what he'd do if he found out about the missing lock of hair from the old album. She also wondered when Mother Heggy's spell would start to work, because he looked as strong and powerful as ever right now. She shivered with fear, dreading the weeks ahead.

7

Sylvie sat in a maths lesson squirming with humiliation. William had just revealed her complete ignorance of quadratic equations to the whole class. Maths had always been a weakness and she'd missed the block of teaching on equations back in July. Sylvie stared at the textbook before her, cheeks burning as Holly swaggered up to the whiteboard and solved the complicated calculation easily. William smiled and nodded.

'Good – well done, Holly. You see, Sylvie? It's not difficult if you put your mind to it. I suggest you apply yourself to the relevant chapters, which you've clearly never even looked at. Work through the examples and complete all the exercises this evening and I'll take a look at them tomorrow.'

'But this evening I have to finish—'

Magus poked his head round the door.

'William, when the lesson's finished I'd like a word with Sylvie in my office.'

Sylvie tried to concentrate on the rest of the session, ignoring the whispers and daggered looks from the others. This would be the moment of truth now, for the medical test results were back and all the teachers' progress reports would be on his desk. She was terrified he was going to be angry.

Magus sat at his desk working at a computer but stood as she entered. He beckoned her over to the sofas and sat down opposite her. He regarded her steadily, his expression neutral. She quaked inside.

'I see you've made a complete recovery.'

'Yes.'

'And Hazel tells me there's absolutely nothing wrong with you other than deficiencies brought on by under-eating.'

'Yes.'

'She says you've put on some weight, and Miranda said you're eating sensibly now and applying yourself to your studies at last.'

'Yes, I am.'

'Good. I also have detailed school reports here from each of your teachers. The news there is not so good, as I'm sure you're aware. Everyone is disappointed with your progress and lack of diligence over the past months.'

'I'm working really hard now.'

'I'm sure you are. And you'll continue to do so. I want you up to speed in every single subject by the end of this term, which only gives you a few weeks. You're to have covered all the lessons and class-work you missed, and have all your course-work completely up to date. Is that clear?'

'I'll try, but I can't—'

'Yes you can! The mocks are looming too, so there's revision to be done for those as well. You'll be working every single waking minute of the day, Sylvie, to make up for all the time you've wasted making yourself ill.'

Sylvie hung her head, realising it was pointless to argue. She was keeping a lid on her bubbling resentment and sense of injustice and didn't want him to see it in her eyes.

'Miranda also tells me,' he continued smoothly, 'that you've been asking about new clothes for winter because you've grown so much taller.'

Sylvie frowned at this; she'd mentioned it to her mother but hadn't asked for the request to be passed on to Magus.

'Yes ... I wasn't sure what I'd do about clothes now I seem to have outgrown everything.'

'Mmn. I'll have to consider your request.'

'No, it wasn't—'

'Of course you can visit the Village stores and pick up some material to make clothes for yourself. Everyone's entitled to that.'

'I'm ... I don't know how to make clothes.'

'There're also the dressmakers. You may ask one of the Village women to run you up something to wear.'

'Yes, thank you.'

He fell silent and watched her. Then he smiled, his eyes amused.

'I expect you'd rather hoped to order some fashionable things on the Internet, the way all the other Hallfolk teenagers do.'

She looked at her hands, unable to keep eye contact with him.

'No, I hadn't actually. I'll go to the Village dressmakers,' she said quietly. 'I know I can't buy anything.'

'We'll see, but it does rather depend on you. You're in an awkward position, aren't you, Sylvie? All the others have wealthy and successful parents to provide for them, but you don't. Miranda may ostensibly work here as a teacher but over the months since you arrived at Stonewylde, she's missed a lot of work in order to care for you. Because of you taking to your bed, her attendance has been quite minimal and she's barely earned your keep.'

'I'm sorry.'

'I'm pleased to hear it. Maybe now you'll appreciate the con-sequences of your actions. And we're not just talking about your welfare either. There're your mother's needs too, for clothes, shoes and personal requirements. Yet you've prevented her from working to provide for herself as well, not to mention her baby.'

'I hadn't thought of it like that.' All Sylvie could really think of was Magus' dressing room and those rows and rows of shoes, clothes and accessories she'd seen.

'No, I don't expect you had. Let me remind you that nobody at Stonewylde gets a free ride. Everyone here works for their living in whatever capacity they can, be it ploughing the fields to grow our food, rearing children to provide future labour for Stonewylde or teaching the next generation of doctors and lawyers. Nobody takes and gives nothing back. All your contemporaries are at the Hall School because their parents pay me expensive fees, just like any other boarding school. You're the only one here who doesn't. And yet you expect me to provide you not only with education, accommodation, food and the necessities of life, but now a fashionable wardrobe too.'

'No, I'm sorry . . . I didn't think. It's alright, I can manage.'

'Good. Because I'm a generous man where it's deserved, but I won't be taken for a fool. When I became magus I banished all the spongers and leeches and I don't intend to start allowing them back in.'

Sylvie felt embarrassed. She'd expected a lecture about school work, but not this. She really wished her mother hadn't said anything about her needing new clothes, even though the situation was becoming a little desperate.

'However, there's one thing you can do for me that's worth more than every hour of labour given on the entire estate. I think you know what I'm talking about.'

She swallowed hard and nodded.

'Look at me, Sylvie, when I'm talking to you. You know what I need from you, what you alone can give me. Have you thought about it since our last talk, when I was so angry with you for interfering at Samhain?'

She nodded again, remembering Yul's words about not raising Magus' suspicions and going along with what he wanted.

'So will you freely give me the moon magic? Or will you persist in fighting me, threatening to leave, and starving yourself so you become weak and too ill to moondance properly and give me what I want?'

'I'll give it freely,' she whispered. 'I'm sorry I refused. I didn't realise how selfish I was being.'

He smiled and it was like the sun irradiating the land after a thunderstorm.

Life at the Hall became unbearable for Sylvie. The teachers continued to exert pressure on her in every lesson and she was loaded with extra work in all subjects. None of them had a good word for her despite the effort she was putting in, and they all made her feel stupid and worthless if she asked for clarification or assistance. The daily visits to Hazel continued and her weight rose slowly, now aided by Magus himself. He insisted that she sit by his side at every meal and monitored her eating carefully. He controlled everything she ate, always insisting she take more than she wanted or could comfortably manage. She felt like a turkey being fattened up for Christmas.

Worse, the fuss he made of her didn't go unnoticed. The other girls were beside themselves with jealousy at this attention and took delight in making nasty remarks. They also picked up on the fact that Magus wasn't being solicitous, but was actually coming down hard on Sylvie. With the other adults at the Hall being so disapproving and censorious of her too, the youngsters took the opportunity to victimise Sylvie with impunity. Holly was the ringleader and she had plenty of ammunition. Sylvie's unpopularity with the teachers was seized on, and Holly teased her constantly about her failure to keep up with the rest of the class. She picked on Sylvie's eating and weight gain, and her lack of winter clothes was a gift to her tormentors. Sylvie felt frumpy and plain in the out-grown summer things she still wore, topped with increasingly threadbare jumpers to keep warm. Holly swanked around in smart new outfits and took pleasure in humiliating her rival at every turn.

One morning Sylvie sat alone in the Dining Hall surrounded by breakfast debris. She'd been forced to eat a hearty cooked meal and, coming so soon after a huge dinner the night before, she now felt uncomfortably over-full. Magus had just left. He'd spent nearly an hour plying her with food, watching her swallow every mouthful. He'd stayed as everyone else gradually left the room just to make sure that she ate it all, with the added effect of making her late for school. Holly had given her a particularly venomous stare as she left to prepare for the first lesson of the day. Magus had finally gone and Sylvie was almost in tears, trying to decide whether to make a dash for the bathroom or wait a few more minutes and hope her stomach settled. She wasn't sure whether or not she'd make it there before she was sick.

'You're still here?' cried Holly, poking her head round one of the double doors. 'Not still eating, are you? Greedy pig – you're going to get so fat!'

She came into the great Dining Hall and started to make her way through the room to where Sylvie sat at the top table, pale and nauseous, holding a napkin to her lips.

'Brambling has sent me to fetch you as he's waiting to start the French lesson.'

'I don't feel very well,' said Sylvie weakly. 'Tell him to start without me and I'll come as soon as I can.'

'You can't skip lessons just because you stuffed yourself at breakfast!' said Holly, now standing in front of the table. 'You're thick enough as it is and Brambling's not at all impressed. He's furious you're not in there after all the fuss that's been made about your attendance. You should hear him – everyone's killing themselves laughing at his impersonation of you trying to buy a rail ticket in French.'

A young servant came in quietly through the door leading to the kitchens, and started clearing away some of the serving dishes from the long sideboard. Holly threw the girl a look, but otherwise ignored her.

'I'm so pleased it entertains you all,' muttered Sylvie. 'Tell Brambling I'll be along soon.'

Sylvie wished Holly would go; the nausea hit her in waves and the waistband of her old skirt dug in tightly. Holly glared at her disdainfully.

'Seen lover boy lately?'

Sylvie shook her head, not daring to open her mouth to speak.

'Well I have! I saw him yesterday when I was out riding and he was looking as gorgeous as ever, up at that stone on the top of the hill near the ridgeway. I told him about our little chat and he wasn't at all pleased that you know about us. He'd wanted us to keep it a secret so he could have us both, a bit like you keeping him secret from Magus. I suppose now Magus is back, you'll have to stay away from Yul, won't you? So I can have him all to myself, just like the good old days before you came! Yul and I always did have an understanding. Did you know we're going to be partners at our Rite of Adulthood?'

'Go away, Holly!' whispered Sylvie, feeling more nauseous than ever.

The Village girl came back in to get more dishes and glanced over at the two Hallfolk girls who shouldn't still be here.

'Get out!' yelled Holly. 'We're having a private conversation!'

The girl scurried away and shut the door behind her.

'Stupid half-wit peasant! Yeah, now Magus is back, you'll have to give up your bit of rough, won't you? And haven't you just got Magus wrapped around your little finger again? Goddess, it makes me want to puke watching him with you. Fussing over you, spoiling you, and he was practically feeding you breakfast just now. Does he like you being his little girl? That's sick!'

Unable to hold it any longer, Sylvie threw up over the littered table. Holly leapt back with a shriek of disgust.

'You revolting bitch! You did that on purpose!'

Sylvie sat ashen-faced and perfectly still, staring at the awful table-cloth in horror. She covered her mouth with the linen napkin and felt so humiliated. Not only had she disgraced herself before the girl who hated her most, she must try to clean up this dreadful mess too. She couldn't possibly leave it for that poor Village girl, and she'd be even later for French now. Sylvie felt tears well in her eyes yet again and wished that she were any-where but here.

Holly had already retreated for the doors but stopped there, hand on the brass doorknob. She turned and looked speculatively at Sylvie, sitting motionless and tearful at the table waiting for the tide of nausea to recede.

'Or maybe you didn't throw up on purpose? Maybe it's morning sickness! Now there's a thought – Mother and daughter pregnant at the same time! We know Magus is the father of your mother's baby, but I wonder if he's the father of yours too?'

A few nights later, Sylvie sat in bed trying to finish her geography revision for a test the next morning. The words swam before her eyes as it was growing late and she'd been looking at text practically since she woke up that morning. Outside, the wind was rising and dark clouds scudded rapidly across the large silver moon. She didn't want to see it. It was a constant reminder of the curse of her moongaziness, and although she hated drawing the curtains maybe she should. The wind rattled the diamond window panes and Sylvie shivered slightly, feeling warm and snug in her bed, but not free of the fear that haunted her. Every night the moon waxed fuller and she still had no idea what would happen at the next Moon Fullness.

She hadn't seen Yul since their argument under the yew tree the night after the Dark Moon. It was probably just as well, it had given her time to calm down and reflect on their fight. Sylvie realised they'd both been overwrought and was increasingly prepared to forget the whole thing. The business with Holly wasn't so easy to dismiss, however. She was desperate to know what had really happened between the two of them, but with Magus watching her so closely there'd been no chance to escape the Hall and find Yul.

Magus was still being strict and disapproving with her. He made her sit with him at every meal-time, he looked in on every lesson and checked up on her in the library in all her free periods. He took her to the formal garden if she said she needed fresh air and her lovely walks down to the Village to see Yul had become a thing of the past. Magus even visited at night to make sure she'd gone to bed and wasn't staying up late, coming into her bedroom to say goodnight and turn out her light like a stern father. She hated every second of it and felt suffocated by his constant attention. But she endured it because Yul had said she must keep Magus happy, although after the row with him she wasn't quite so sure that Yul knew best. She endured it because she had no choice.

She put the dull textbook aside and opened the drawer next to

126

her bed, pulling out her battered copy of *Wuthering Heights*. It fell open immediately to reveal its secret – Professor Siskin's photo of Yul. He'd printed it on heavy photographic paper and, despite Sylvie's constant handling, the photo was still clear and smooth.

She gazed at Yul's beautiful face, golden in the sunlight and smeared with green lichen and brown earth, his glossy curls long and full of twigs and leaves. His slanted, long-lashed grey eyes gazed out sleepily, a half-smile playing on his lips, and bright green foliage formed a glowing halo of leaves. Whenever Sylvie felt unhappy – unable to cope with Magus' attention, the nastiness of Holly and the girls, her mother's indifference, the criticism of her teachers and the doctor, or the loneliness of not seeing Yul for so long – she'd look at the photo and feel comforted by the sight of her own Green Man, so beautiful and magical. She missed him so much, despite Holly's spiteful attempts to ruin things between them.

Suddenly there was a pattering at her window too harsh for rain. Sylvie rose from her warm bed and looked out into the darkness, just making out a figure with pale upturned face standing on the grass below. It waved and disappeared, and a minute later there was a knock at the wooden door to the staircase in the corner of her room.

'Yul!'

She was overjoyed to see him standing in the arched doorway, his head almost brushing the top of it. The wind had whipped his face into a rosy glow and his hair into wild ringlets. His eyes sparkled brightly and he stood there slightly out of breath, obviously having run all the way from the Village. He wore an old leather jacket against the November cold, and dark trousers and boots. He was tall, lean and devastatingly good looking, and Sylvie had a sudden vision of him in the Outside World, maybe at college or university, surrounded by adoring girls all unable to keep their hands off him. She closed her eyes to block out the image and opened them to find him standing directly in front of her.

'Are you alright, Sylvie?' he asked, holding her at arm's length and looking into her eyes.

'I'm fine, just fatter than I was. I've been trying to come and find you but it's impossible to get away with Magus watching me like a hawk. How are you feeling now? You look really well.'

'I'm almost back to normal thanks. Sylvie, I need to apologise. I'm really sorry about what happened at the Dark Moon. I shouldn't have spoken to you like that.'

'It's okay. It was nothing really but I don't like being bossed about and you sounded so like Magus. It's bad enough with him trying to dominate me.'

'I know. I was wrong and it won't happen again.'

She laughed.

'Don't make promises you can't keep, Yul! I'm sure you'll do it again loads of times. So long as you know I won't take it and you'll never get away with it.'

He grinned at her and relaxed a little.

'I've brought you a present to say sorry,' he said, reaching inside his heavy leather jacket and producing an exquisite carving of a leaping hare. Sylvie gasped and gently took the tiny piece of polished golden wood from his outstretched hand.

'It's a moondancing hare. I made it from a little piece of our tree, the yew on the Village Green.'

She flung her arms around him in a fierce hug, kissing his cold cheeks and smelling the November night in his hair.

'You made it yourself? You're so clever! It's so tiny and perfect – thank you, Yul!' she exclaimed. 'It's the most beautiful thing I've ever seen, apart from you.'

He laughed but then his face grew serious.

'There's something else we must talk about.'

'Come and sit down,' she said, but looking around realised the only place was the bed as her chair was covered with a pile of school books. She wore her long nightdress made of fine white Stonewylde linen, given to her by Cherry when she first arrived, and although it covered everything except her hands, feet and face, she suddenly felt shy. Yul seemed not to notice and sat on the bed, frowning and preoccupied. She sat down next to him.

'I'm not sure how to start, really. I don't know quite how it happened, and I—'

'Yul, if it's about Holly, I already know.'

'I was worried you might,' he groaned, his face downcast. 'I saw her again the other day when I was up at Hare Stone looking for you. She started bragging about telling you and I was so angry with her I don't know how I controlled myself. I despise that girl! Sylvie, I—'

'Look, Yul, I don't know the details and I don't think I really want to. It'll only make me jealous and I hate feeling like that. But I understand how manipulative she is and I guess she tricked you?'

'Yes! I was a fool and I knew it straight away. She'd followed you and seen us together and she threatened to tell Magus if I didn't kiss her like I'd kissed you.'

'And did you?' whispered Sylvie, her throat tight and aching.

He nodded in shame, looking beseechingly into her clear grey eyes, now full of pain that he knew he'd inflicted.

'I'm so sorry, Sylvie! If it's any consolation, I hated it.'

'Oh Yul, how could you? I'd hoped Holly was all talk and I didn't believe you'd actually *kiss* her.'

His face twisted with guilt. He shook his head and half turned from her, unable to face her distress. She sat silently, fighting the emotions that slashed like a knife inside her.

'Do you want me to leave?' he mumbled.

She glanced down at the little golden hare still in her hand. It was perfect, completely capturing the essence of hare in its long ears and lithe body. He must have spent such time and care on it, and he'd even made it from their special tree. As with the corn favour he'd made her, Sylvie was touched by his thoughtfulness and romanticism. So she shook her head and laid her head against the hard leather covering his shoulder.

'No, Yul, I'm upset and angry, but I never want you to leave.'

At this he wrapped his arms around her and pulled her down on top of him onto the bed. He held her face just off his, her silver hair hanging like a veil around them, and gazed deep into her eyes. She saw his love for her, dark and a little dangerous, and felt herself dragged down into his soul where she knew there was a place for her alone and nobody else. Thoughts of Holly withered into insignificance.

'Kiss me, Sylvie,' he whispered softly. 'Kiss me and forgive me. You know you're the one I love.'

She began to kiss him, slowly and gently at first. She teased him with her softness and lightness, enjoying the control she had over him, the way he strained towards her so desperately. But soon her teasing gave way to the urgent need she felt blossoming inside, and their kisses became deep and hard. She felt his hands on her back through the soft linen of her nightdress, his leather jacket stiff between them as he clasped her hard against him, his mouth ravenous for hers. The walls of her bedroom disappeared as she entered the dark labyrinth of desire and took her first tentative steps along the path. Nothing mattered but this journey, and the two of them being together.

After a while and without warning, Yul stood up in a sudden and fluid motion, taking them both upright. But still she clung to him, her arms locked around his neck, unwilling to release him.

'Sylvie,' he murmured, and gently but firmly held her away from him. His eyes were almost black with passion and he laughed unsteadily, shaking the hair from his eyes. 'Sylvie ...'

She closed her eyes for a couple of heartbeats, then opened them to stare at him, her cheekbones flushed with longing, her breathing fast.

'I don't ... Yul, I've never felt like this before.'

He grimaced, brushing her messed-up hair away from her face with a trembling hand.

'You're lucky then. I feel like this all the time, every time I see you or even think of you ...'

He took a deep breath, his steely control slipping back into place, and gazed into her eyes once more.

'You don't know how much you fill my days and my nights,'

he said softly. 'Thinking about you, wanting you, dreaming about the day we can make love and be together. You're my whole universe, Sylvie, and Holly is just an irritating grain of sand. I can't begin to tell you just how much I love you and how much I need you. Don't ever, ever doubt it.'

He smoothed her hair again tenderly, his eyes searching her face.

'I must go,' he said quietly. 'It's dangerous to be here, this is so risky for both of us. But the Owl Moon draws closer and I have to tell you the plan. I'll come and get you in the middle of the afternoon as it gets dark early, now the Solstice is near. Have lunch as normal and, after a while, say you're feeling sleepy and need to rest before the evening. He'll approve of that. Tell your mother that you don't want to be disturbed, then come up here and put on your warmest clothes – lots of layers, because it'll be cold. Make up your bed so it looks like you're in it and pull the curtains shut so it's as dark as possible in here. Then wait for me. I'll come and fetch you and we'll get away as fast as we can.'

'Okay, it sounds a good plan to me except for one thing – what if the outside door's locked? You wouldn't be able to get in and I'd be trapped in here. Nearer the time, Magus may lock the door and take the key away. He's become a real gaoler lately and I'm almost surprised he doesn't keep me in chains.'

He grinned at her.

'I have my own key! Harold borrowed it and Tom got it copied by the blacksmith. I've tested it and it works perfectly, so I can rescue you even if the door is locked.'

'Brilliant! I feel so much better knowing there's a plan. I've been really frightened about it, worrying and having nightmares. And Yul, I – oh!'

She suddenly noticed the time on her small clock and her eyes widened in panic.

'I hadn't realised it was that late! Oh Yul, you must go now, quickly! Magus comes in here most nights and he could be here any time now. He's insisting on early nights because he wants me strong and healthy so I can stay on the rock for longer and give him all my moon magic. He goes on about it all the time.'

He kissed her quickly but longingly.

'Well he'll be disappointed, won't he? I'll see you in a few nights. Send a message with Harold or Cherry if anything happens and I'll come straight away. I won't let you down this time, Sylvie, I swear to you.'

The wooden door had shut with a cold waft of air and Sylvie had leaped into bed and yanked up the covers. The photo and her golden hare were now safely tucked away in her drawer and her love locked tight in her heart. She'd just picked up the book and was taking slow, deep breaths in an attempt to calm her pounding heart and trembling fingers, when with a peremptory knock, Magus strode into her bedroom.

'Time for lights out, young lady,' he said briskly. He sniffed the air and glanced around the room with a puzzled expression, but relaxed when his eyes fell on her.

'Are you alright? You're a little flushed and ... bright-eyed.'

She nodded, gripping her book and trying to shield herself with it. He came across to her bed and took it from her.

'What are you reading? Oh, *Wuthering Heights*. Are you enjoying it?'

'Very much,' she replied, quickly lying down in bed and pulling the covers up high to her chin. 'It's one of my favourite books.'

He stood looking down as she lay there, blond hair spread out on the pillow in a silky mass. He stared and stared until she started to feel uncomfortable. Then he sat down on the side of the bed, his weight pulling the covers tight over her, trapping her. He began to stroke the hair back from her forehead and she shivered with fear, remembering him doing the same when she was weak and he was angry with her. His eyes were deep and unfathomable, dark as a moonless night. He gazed at her as she lay trembling at his touch.

'Are you cold?' he asked softly. 'You're flushed and yet you're shivering.'

'No.'

132

'Then what's the matter?'

'Nothing.'

She was terrified, her mouth too dry to speak. His fingers, so like Yul's, began to trace her eyebrows and then down to her hot cheekbones. She remembered Yul doing the same but she'd welcomed his touch, whereas Magus' filled her with dread. Her silvery-grey eyes were enormous, the pupils dilated with fear as she gazed up at him helplessly.

'You're growing up, Sylvie, slowly but surely,' he said, his voice like rich velvet. 'Almost a woman now.'

His fingertips continued their slow journey down the line of her jaw. His thumb ran gently along the contours of her lips, still slightly swollen from kissing Yul so passionately, and she didn't know how to stop him without offending him. His eyes were compelling and so close, as mesmerising as a snake's. She saw a muscle in his cheek twitch and his nostrils flare very slightly. He seemed to be hesitating about something and she could hardly breathe, she was so scared. But she needn't have worried. He bent and brushed her cheek with his lips, his exquisite scent entering her lungs.

'Sweet dreams, my moongazy girl. I'll see you in the morning at breakfast.'

He got up, switched off her light and left the room, shutting the door firmly behind him. Only then did she breathe freely again, although his presence seemed to linger in the darkness long after he'd left.

The next day Magus escorted Sylvie from the Dining Hall and she felt every pair of eyes following them as he led her out, hand under her elbow. She knew the rumours Holly had spread after she'd seen Sylvie's sickness the other morning, and now walked glumly by Magus's side, trying to hold her head up and feeling queasy from the heavy food she'd just eaten. She hoped that whatever he had to say would be dealt with quickly.

He ushered her into the office and she saw Clip sitting on one of the sofas. He had a cake tin by him and hastily brushed some crumbs off his jacket. He looked pale and faraway, his face strained and eyes dull. Sylvie was reminded of some wolves she'd once seen in a zoo, their beauty and spirit marred by enforced captivity.

'Good morning, Sylvie,' he said listlessly. 'You're looking well.'

'She's very well now that she's taking care of herself properly at last,' said Magus smoothly, guiding Sylvie to the sofa opposite Clip and sitting down next to her. He took one of her hands in his and rubbed it encouragingly.

'She's seen sense at last, haven't you Sylvie? I'm so pleased with her, Clip. She's willing to make that little sacrifice every month for me and for Stonewylde. She knows what she has to do.'

Sylvie stared at her knees, wondering how she could pull her hand away without making him cross. She hated him touching her. He gripped her more tightly and she looked up suddenly. Clip was gazing at her intently, his pale eyes huge in his thin face and dominated by their enlarged pupils.

'She's seen sense then,' he said softly. 'No more fighting you.'

His voice that was like Magus' but not as deep or resonant, and Sylvie stared at him, remembering something, something she mustn't forget . . .

'No!' she cried. 'No, Magus, you promised! You said I didn't have to be hypnotised again if I co-operated. Please, *no*!'

She struggled, trying to escape, but Magus gripped her arm harder so she couldn't stand up.

'Just keep still, Sylvie, and then it'll all be over. This is for your own good and it'll make the whole thing so much easier for you. Come on, be a good girl and stop struggling. You know I don't want to hurt you.'

'Please, Magus, I *beg* you! I'll go to Mooncliffe, I'll do whatever you say, I promise! I won't fight you and I'll charge up all your moon eggs, as many as you want. Just don't hypnotise me, please – let me do this for you with my own free will!'

But Magus only chuckled, his grip as tight as ever as he slid a hand behind her to grasp her other arm too and hold her down firmly on the sofa. Clip knelt in front of her, taking her head between his hands so she couldn't look away. She closed her eyes, desperately trying to shake her head out of his grasp, whimpering for him to stop.

'Stop fighting, Sylvie, and just give in,' said Clip wearily. 'It's so much easier, believe me. Now look at me, look at me, look closely, Sylvie, deep into my eyes. That's right, good girl. When I count to three, you'll wake up and you won't remember this, just like before. Now, remember what I told you last time about Mooncliffe?'

When he'd finished he let go of her head and turned to Magus, his eyes resigned.

'Alright? Anything else or is that it?'

Magus smiled, releasing his hold on Sylvie's arms. She remained sitting exactly as she'd been before, staring ahead like a life-size doll, and he chuckled again.

'It's so easy, isn't it? No, I think that'll do for now, thank you Clip. There may be something else but that can wait for a bit.'

'I told you, Sol, this is the last time. I refuse to abuse my gift like this again and I'm not coming up to bloody Mooncliffe with you either, so don't even ask.'

'I don't need you, brother dear. Jackdaw's coming with me and I think he'll be far more effective than you were, especially if our friend Yul turns up on another rescue mission.'

'Sol, don't overdo it this month, will you? I know what Jackdaw's like, and what you're like too. Be careful, please – Sylvie's only a girl; remember what happened to our mother up there.'

'That was an eclipse,' said Magus tersely. 'Ordinary moongazing won't kill her.'

'Don't force her to carry on for hours on end, and do make sure she's warm enough.'

'You sound like a bloody nursemaid. What's with the sudden concern for her welfare? What's she to you anyway?'

Clip shrugged, and reached wearily for another cake.

'She's very vulnerable, and you're a cruel bastard. You take such pleasure in making others suffer for your own gratification.

I don't like to see you hurting and exploiting anyone, especially not someone as young and helpless as Sylvie.'

Magus laughed.

'Very touching. Bad memories, eh?'

'You could say that.'

'That was just an adolescent thing, Clip. I'm not like that any more.'

'Yes you are, Sol. You're just as bad and in fact I think you might be worse. All that's changed is now you're so much better at hiding it.'

8

$\mathcal{Y}$ul called on Sylvie again the night before the Owl Moon, anxious to ensure that nothing would go wrong at this late stage. He raced silently up the back stairs as soon as she returned from dinner having watched her room from the garden, and tapped on the arched door leading into her bedroom. He knew he had a little time before Magus came to say goodnight as this was earlier than his previous visit. Sylvie opened the door immediately, her face lighting up at the sight of him. She put her arms around him but then groaned, pulling away.

'What's wrong?'

'I'm so full. I feel sick.'

'Are you ill?' he asked anxiously, taking her hands.

She sat down on the bed weakly.

'I'm not ill but I've always had trouble eating large meals. I used to have so many allergies and sensitivities and I hate being forced to eat. Magus makes me eat so much and I just can't keep it all down. I'm being sick after meals now and that's why they were all cross with me in the first place, thinking I was deliberately starving myself. I just can't win.'

'Does he know it's making you sick?' asked Yul, unaware of eating disorders and food allergies.

'No he won't believe me, but every day he looks at my weight chart and he's angry again because I'm not gaining enough. In fact now I'm being sick so often I've started losing weight, which means every day he makes me eat even more.'

He sat next to her, holding her hand sympathetically.

'I just came to check that you're alright for tomorrow. You remember the plan?'

'Yes, I know what to do. It'll be easy: he said I have to stay in my room and rest all day tomorrow anyway. He even said I mustn't do any school work in case it makes me tired! He's such a hypocrite – one minute nagging me about not working hard enough and then actually stopping me from doing any at all. As long as he gets his moon magic he's happy, and my school work doesn't really matter.'

Then she turned to him, her eyes shining.

'Oh Yul, I'm really looking forward to spending the afternoon with you! I've missed you so much. It'll be great to have some time alone together.'

'I know – I'm looking forward to it as well, though I'm a bit nervous I must admit. Do wrap up very warm, Sylvie, as it's getting cold in the evenings. I'd better go now before Magus comes.'

'Yes, you only just left in time on your last visit! But Yul, there's one thing I'm concerned about. You said it's getting cold in the evenings but you understand, don't you, that I must get back here before then?'

'What do you mean?'

'I need to be home well before moonrise.'

'What?'

'Because I'm going up to Mooncliffe with Magus.'

He laughed and stood up, looking down at her with a smile.

'No, Yul, it's not funny – I mean it! I *have* to dance on the stone at Mooncliffe tomorrow. I want to give Magus my moon magic. You do understand, don't you?'

She looked up at him earnestly, her eyes great pools of moon-stone grey. His face fell in horror.

'Oh, no ... Oh, Sylvie, they've got you again! The *bastards*!'

'What do you mean, got me? I don't understand.'

'Never mind,' he said shakily, still staring at her in shock. He couldn't believe it – there was no chance to get her to Mother

Heggy before the moonrise tomorrow night, not when she was watched so closely. He wanted to scream with frustration but took a deep breath and kissed her quickly.

'Just make sure you're ready tomorrow afternoon, alright?'

'They've put a spell on her again!' shouted Yul, pacing the tiny room. The crow squawked indignantly, flapping its wings.

''Twas to be expected, however much she agreed to do what he wants,' mused Mother Heggy. 'He's taking no chances, an' it just shows how desperate he is for the moon magic. Did you get to steal some of the eggs, boy?'

'Yes, the key worked after a bit of twisting and Edward helped. There were a few fresh eggs left inside the chest. The ones lying on the grass outside were the used ones and there were so many of them! He's been gorging on her moon magic. We took the charged ones from the chest and hid them in the woods, and replaced them with used ones. They're so powerful, those eggs, and I hated having to touch them knowing what they'd taken out of her. Edward couldn't believe it either.'

'He'll be spitting angry when he finds they're missing,' cackled Mother Heggy. 'Especially when there's no new ones this month neither. Heh heh!'

'But he *will* get new ones this month and that's why I'm so worried! She's under the spell again and she wants to go to Mooncliffe!'

'For Goddess' sake, Yul! You're a man now; she's nought but a slip of a girl. Who's the strongest?'

'I can't force her to stay with me.'

'Course you can, silly boy. You must bind her tight till the moon is good and high and 'tis safe to release her.'

He looked at her in horror.

'I couldn't treat Sylvie like that!'

He stood gazing dejectedly into the fire. The crone pursed her lips and tutted, shaking her head at his misplaced sensibilities. She fondled the crow, now nestling in her lap, and rocked her chair steadily.

'Well, there is another way, Yul,' she said after a while, 'now I think on it. Up along Ash Wood, beyond Dragon's Back, there's a grove of old sycamore trees. D'you know the wood I mean, boy?'

'Yes ... behind Ash Wood, I think I know the sycamores there, though we hardly ever use those woods. Greenbough doesn't rate them highly, and there's more than enough for our work nearer home.'

'Aye, well, a whole group o' them sycamores up there have split trunks. They were coppiced long ago and then forgotten and left to grow strangely, like tree-cages. When I were a girl, the woodsmen put naughty lads in there to punish 'em. They'd bind around the trunks with rope and make cages so the boys couldn't get out.'

Yul nodded slowly, seeing her plan.

'You could put the maiden in one o' them. She'd be imprisoned, right enough, and you must be careful she don't make any noise just in case someone's out a-searching, but 'tis not as bad as trussing her up. Sounds cruel I know, but 'tis only for her own good and yours too, that Sol don't get her magic at Owl Moon.'

Jackdaw tapped at the French windows and was beckoned inside, but immediately Magus regretted the invitation, wrinkling his nose at the stench of stale tobacco. Jackdaw was particularly unsavoury today; greasy and unshaven, his protruding blue eyes bloodshot and bleary. He smelt unwashed too, and Magus decided not to bring him inside the Hall – and certainly not into his office – again. They'd have to meet elsewhere in future. He opened the French windows a little wider on the misty morning.

'You understand what's involved tonight?' he began. 'You'll help with the eggs and ensure that damn boy comes nowhere near the cliff-top.'

'Aye, sir, looking forward to a bit of action at last. But why don't I deal with the little bugger now? I could take him away, up to Quarrycleave maybe, have some fun first and then snuff him.'

Magus shook his head.

'It sounds easy but it wouldn't work. We tried at Mooncliffe last Moon Fullness and again in the Stone Labyrinth at Samhain. He should by rights have died on both those occasions, not to mention at Quarrycleave last summer, but clearly the Dark Angel doesn't want him. His time isn't up yet.'

He scowled at the look on Jackdaw's face.

'You've been away too long in the Outside World, Jack, and you've forgotten the reality of Stonewylde. The Dark Angel might sound like some fairy-tale fantasy to you nowadays, but I know only too well how real that spectre is. Yul's living a charmed life until the Winter Solstice and even after it, only *I* will be able to destroy him. It's his destiny and it's mine – they're linked together.'

'Right enough, Guv,' said Jackdaw, looking around the beautiful room with interest. 'You got some lovely stuff in here. Didn't notice it so much the other night at Samhain.'

'Never mind that,' said Magus curtly. 'You must keep Yul at bay if he tries to rescue Sylvie at Mooncliffe, though after last month, I can't see that he'd be that stupid again. I can't stress how vital it is that I take her moon energy tonight, so it mustn't fail. There are only a few charged eggs left and I want her to do the full load tonight, and more if she can take it. I've had some extras made up and I've ensured she's much stronger this month.'

Magus stood up, anxious to get Jackdaw out of his office and clear the air.

'Keep well away from the Village today,' he continued, ushering the brutish man towards the French windows. 'Martin tells me there's a lot of ill feeling about your return. The Villagers are complaining.'

'Load o' bloody peasants,' growled Jackdaw, forgetting his own origins. 'There's a few of 'em I'd like to put in their place starting with that old sow Marigold.'

'Once this Moon Fullness is done, we'll smooth things over. It's not long till the Winter Solstice and I'll certainly need your services then, so we'll make sure that everyone understands you're back to stay. Now, I want you up there by mid-afternoon, stacking the empty eggs around the rock in preparation. I'll bring the girl up myself just before sunset. You've charged up the two-way radios and got yours?'

'Aye sir, and don't worry, I'll make sure the boy don't trouble you,' said Jackdaw, rubbing his bristly jowls. He grinned, his gold incisor glinting amongst dark teeth. 'I know Yul's yours to finish, but there's a whole month till the Solstice, ain't there? Time enough for a bit of fun with him, if you don't mind. I'd enjoy that. He's a tough little nut to crack and they're always the sweetest.'

'We'll see,' said Magus, eyeing the thug with distaste. 'It depends on what you have in mind. But it could be useful to have him out of the way in the lead up to the Solstice, especially if you can weaken him for me. I'll think about it. We'll get through tonight first and discuss it tomorrow. Remember your brief for tonight, Jackdaw – keep your eyes open and your wits about you.'

Yul had the tree-cage ready by mid-day. He'd found the sycamore grove several miles from the Hall, hidden away in the Ash Woods, and had chosen an enormous tree to be Sylvie's prison. Its huge trunk grew almost a metre high and then split into seven separate trunks, each one as thick as his waist and growing straight upwards. The gap between each trunk was small, not big enough for someone even as slim as Sylvie to squeeze through. Only one gap was wide enough, which he could just slip through himself.

It was surprisingly roomy inside the cage. The bole of the tree was carpeted with a thick floor of soft moss covered by this year's fallen leaves. There was space enough for a person to sit or lie curled up inside the tree cage and to stand comfortably. Yul had ropes ready to tie across the larger gap once she was inside, and water and a lantern to hand.

Edward had lent Yul his beautiful grey mare, which had saved him a great deal of time in preparing the cage. He would've liked to ride all the way up here with Sylvie, but if she started to fight or thrash about it could scare the horse and he didn't want to risk her bolting and perhaps throwing Sylvie. He eventually compromised and decided to tether the horse halfway.

Finally, after checking everything was ready and that he had fine rope and a piece of cloth in his bag in case the spell made Sylvie resist, he mounted the mare and trotted off along the path towards the Hall. The mare was quiet and gentle, very different from the exhilaration of Nightwing, but Yul enjoyed riding her all the same. He had an affinity with horses and had always wanted one of his own. He thought often of Nightwing and had vowed that one day the dark stallion would be his.

He urged Edward's horse into a canter and together they flew down the woodland path, making a wonderful sight. The dark-haired boy on a milk-white steed, riding through the bare-branched trees to the palace ahead to rescue the imprisoned princess was like a beautiful picture from a book of fairy tales. Yul managed to stay in woodland until he was just outside the Hall, not wanting to be spotted by any Hallfolk. He carefully hitched the mare to a branch and continued the last part of the journey on foot. It was about an hour after lunch and Sylvie should be ready and waiting. His heart pounded as he tried the handle of the outside door leading to the staircase to her bedroom. It was locked, exactly as he'd feared.

Yul peered through the keyhole and saw that not only had Magus locked the door, he'd also removed the key, obviously determined to keep Sylvie captive. Yul felt in his pocket and found the key that Tom had had made for him. The door opened easily and he crept up the stairs, as quiet and terrified as a field mouse. His fear wasn't that Magus would catch him and hurt him, but that it would all go wrong and he'd fail Sylvie again. At the top of the stairs he tapped on the arched door and opened it silently, dreading what he might see. He pictured Magus standing there with Jackdaw, both grinning.

Sylvie stood by the window, dazzling in a vivid scarlet cloak made of thick velvet, with a great hood. She turned to face him and smiled. She wore a black outfit underneath – trousers, warm jumper, gloves, suede boots – which accentuated her tall, slim body. Her silver hair spilled out between the scarlet and the black, and her face was alive with excitement.

'Yul!' she whispered. 'I was so worried you wouldn't come! I'm all ready. Is that alright?'

She gestured to the bed where she'd stuffed an extra blanket and pillow. It was realistic, especially in the half light with the curtains drawn.

'It's perfect. Come on, let's go right now.'

They slipped out of the wing and into the woods, Sylvie's cloak billowing around her. Yul wished she were wearing something a little less brightly coloured and tried to hurry her along as fast as possible, out of anyone's sight.

'Do you like my new cloak?' she asked happily. 'It's a present from Magus to keep me warm while I moondance for him tonight. Isn't it lovely? And these amazing new clothes and boots – they were all a surprise. He said I must be very good for him tonight and give him all my moon magic and I mustn't make any fuss about feeling ill afterwards. I can stay in bed for two days if I'm tired but then I must get completely back to normal. He said if I can manage that he'll buy me some more winter clothes, really beautiful ones. I'm so excited! I'm fed up with Holly laughing at me for looking dowdy.'

Yul closed his eyes and groaned; he couldn't bear it when she talked like this. The sooner he could take her to Mother Heggy and have the spell lifted, the better. But he had to agree, the cloak was lovely and he'd never seen Sylvie dressed like this, all in black and looking so stylish; she was stunning. They reached the tree where he'd tethered the mare and Sylvie jumped with pleasure.

'Are we both going to ride her? We won't be too heavy for her?'

'She's very strong. She belongs Edward, and he probably weighs as much as the two of us put together. Can you ride?'

She shook her head.

'But I want to learn and I'm not scared.'

'Well now's your chance, Sylvie. We'll use this fallen trunk here to help us mount. I'll get up first and you sit behind and hold on tight to me.'

Soon they were up, Sylvie with her arms round his waist. Feeling her thighs gripping around him and her breasts against his back made Yul weak with wanting her. But he put a firm lid on his feelings and concentrated on guiding the mare back along the path towards the glade. Sylvie was chatty and animated, almost too much so, and he remembered how she was at Moon Fullness before the moonrise. Her hyper-activity could only get worse until the moon had risen.

The woods were misty and damp in the grey afternoon. Most of the leaves had fallen to make a soggy mulch on the woodland floor. Prickly sweet-chestnut cases were mixed up with the leaves, along with spiky beech mast shells and the split rinds of conker cases. Some yellow sycamore leaves still clung on to their branches, as did the serrated kipper-like leaves of the sweet chestnut, now a deep golden brown. But the sky was visible through the bare branches elsewhere, and although he was pleased it was so mild, Yul hoped the rain would hold off while he and Sylvie were outside.

Eventually they reached the little glade, a clearing deep in the woods where emerald green grass grew thickly. They dismounted and Sylvie darted about exclaiming over the dozens of fairy rings in the dell. The little toadstools sprouted in the wet grass in large near-perfect circles. Yul tethered the mare to a tree so she could crop the grass and take shelter if it did start to rain.

'Why have you tied her up?' asked Sylvie. 'Are we staying here? You remember I need to be back before it gets dark? You know it's the Moon Fullness tonight, and I must dance at—'

'Yes, I know,' said Yul wearily, thinking that maybe a gag wouldn't be such a bad thing after all. He really wasn't so keen on Sylvie when she was caught in Clip's spell – this wasn't the real her at all. 'Come on, we're going for a little walk up here. There's plenty of time.'

She skipped on ahead of him up the path. It wasn't cold and

she'd thrown back her hood and put her gloves in his bag. Yul tried to keep her mind off the moonrise by showing her some of the fungi growing on the woodland floor, remembering she'd shown an interest in it before.

'See this one, Sylvie? It's the Earth Star. See how it's split into segments like the points of a star.'

'It's lovely,' she said, bending down and looking carefully at the white star on the dark ground. 'Oh, those purple ones – they're Amethyst Deceivers, aren't they?'

'That's right,' he said, surveying the great troop of purple-lilac caps. 'They're edible. We'll come out mushroom harvesting one day and Mother can cook them for you to try. I love mushrooms on toast – it's my favourite breakfast. And look, there's Velvet Shank. See how smooth and velvety its stalks are, like the texture of your cloak. Oh, Sylvie, see those through there? Don't ever touch those – that's the Destroying Angel.'

'They're poisonous then?'

'Deadly poisonous; fatal.'

'They look quite innocent, just a white mushroom. I'd never know they were dangerous.'

'That's the trouble; some of the most deadly are the most innocent looking.'

'I love their names. They sound so beautiful, don't they? Amethyst Deceiver, Velvet Shank, Destroying Angel. You know so much, Yul.'

He shrugged, remembering what Mother Heggy had said about his ignorance.

'I know very little compared to you and the other Hallfolk. But I know a lot about Stonewylde and that's what matters to me.'

They covered some distance and he managed to keep her distracted for quite a time before she stopped on the path and began to fret.

'I really think we should go back now, Yul. It's getting late and I don't want to make Magus angry. Please let's go back now.'

'Just a little further, Sylvie,' he coaxed. 'There's a really lovely tree I especially wanted to show you. We'll get back in good time and I can make the horse gallop if you like, so our journey will be really fast.'

'Oh yes, I'd like that!' she cried and ran on ahead.

'Look, Sylvie, you must know these!' he said, pointing to a crop of bright red toadstools covered with white sugar crystal spots. They were too brilliant – poisonously scarlet, like something from a fairy tale. Sylvie, in her scarlet cloak, gazed down at the sinister toadstools growing under quiet silver birches and sighed. Yul remembered then a story Clip had told all the children once, long ago. It was a horrific tale about a wicked witch living deep in the woods, who lured children with exotic cakes, actually the caps of these red and white toadstools. She had a wooden cage hidden away where she'd fatten up her captured victims before feasting on their tender flesh and spinning their hair into thread for a magical cloak. Yul shuddered. The tale had terrified him as a boy and it still upset him now.

'Yes,' said Sylvie thoughtfully, remembering her encounter with the crones. 'I've seen these before – they're Fly Agaric! I always thought they were fatal but Mother Heggy told me she uses them in some of her potions as they have magical properties. And those two old women, Violet and Vetchling, they collect them too.'

'Let's see what else we can find,' he said, taking her hand in his and leading her deeper into the overgrown woods.

But he could only keep fooling her for so long, and eventually she stopped and refused to go any further. She was getting panicky, looking at the darkening sky between the branches.

'Please, please, Yul. I have to get back. You don't understand. Magus'll be so angry and I'm scared when he's angry. He frightens me, the way he looks at me sometimes. Please can we go back now? You promised you'd get me home in time and he needs my magic tonight.'

Yul knew it wasn't too far now to the tree cages, but he couldn't force her there without either tricking her again, or tying her up to prevent her making a break for it. He wondered how he could actually achieve this; it was all very well Mother Heggy saying he was much stronger than she was, but he wouldn't use brute force to subjugate her. He decided to try to trick her first, and guided her off at a tangent, explaining that this was a different way back, a short cut. But after a little while she became agitated again and convinced they were lost. He managed to reassure her and started to point out things he swore they'd already passed on their way, to prove they were retracing their steps.

'I know, Sylvie,' he said, sounding false to his own ears but getting desperate as he realised this ploy wouldn't last much longer. 'We're well on our way back now, so why don't we play a game as we go along? It's a sort of blind man's buff game from our celebrations at Beltane in the woods and it's really fun. You must wear this little piece of rope around your wrists. Let me show you.'

'Okay,' she said, 'as long as it won't slow us down at all.'

She held out her slim white wrists, smiling at him trustingly. He gazed into her exquisitely pretty face, her cheeks pink from the fresh air and her eyes bright, and felt a stab of guilt at the deception. Hands shaking in haste, he bound her wrists firmly together. He used much of the rope, going right up her forearms, and left a length as a halter with which to lead her. Then he took the gag out of his pocket and tied it firmly round her mouth. Her eyes were round with surprise but it was too late now. She was tied up, he had a lead with which to guide her, or pull her along if it became necessary, and she couldn't talk him out of it or cry for help. He saw the bewilderment on her face and took her by the shoulders, looking her into her clear grey eyes.

'I'm really sorry, Sylvie, and if there were any other way . . . But there isn't. There wasn't time to make a better plan than this. I'll look after you until the moon has risen and then I'll take you back to the Hall. Magus won't steal your moon magic tonight. But I'm so sorry to trick you like this.'

She started to make muffled noises of protest and pulled away. He tugged the rope bringing her back towards him. She pulled really hard, trying to run in the opposite direction and as he

148

yanked her back she fell, silver hair spilling everywhere as she hit the ground. He crouched over her trying to avoid the accusation in her eyes.

'I'm sorry, Sylvie, I really don't want to hurt you. Are you alright?'

She shook her head violently.

'Where does it hurt?'

She shook her head again. Sighing, he helped her to stand and led her further along the path. It was still about half a mile to the tree cage and he wanted to get her there as soon as possible. The light was beginning to fade, although it was difficult to judge the time on such a gloomy afternoon. Long skeins of mist appeared on the woodland floor wending around the tree trunks, and the cobwebs that laced the bare branches and dead bracken were jewelled with falling dew. It was becoming steadily darker and colder.

Sylvie followed him docilely for a while, only tugging on the halter in defiance now and again. But then she stopped dead without warning. When Yul turned to check she was alright, she swung her bound arms sideways at his head. The heavy clump of rope around her wrists hit him hard on the temple and he saw stars for a few seconds, the world turning black with shooting red and yellow flashes.

She took her chance. Yanking the rope from his limp hands, she ran back the way they'd come. He stumbled, trying to grab the rope, slowed by his dizziness and the pain in head. She was very quick but it wasn't easy to run with her hands tied so awkwardly in front of her and it didn't take him long to catch up. He leapt at her, knocking her down and landing on top of her. She felt lithe and wriggly underneath him, squirming onto her back to fight him. She thrashed about, trying to push him off and hit him in the face again with her bound wrists, fighting and growling like a captured wildcat.

Yul struggled upright and straddled her thrashing body, finally using his weight to subdue her. He remembered how effective it'd been when Buzz had sat astride him like this. Her eyes

149

screamed fury at him and he was sure that if she'd been free and had a weapon, she'd have tried to kill him. The moongaziness combined with the hypnosis had made her lose all reason and his head throbbed painfully where she'd hit him, proof of just how changed she was.

He gazed down at her lying stretched out under him. Her bound wrists were pulled above her head, his knees pinning her upper arms hard to the ground, and he felt her rib cage digging into him. He tried to figure out what to do next; they were almost there but he knew if he took any weight off her for a second she'd squirm and try to escape. But he couldn't spend long sitting on her like this; she was gasping for breath through the gag and he was crushing her badly.

Eventually, seeing no other option, he told her that she'd have to behave or else he'd hit her as she'd hit him. The words stuck in his throat but he had to get her to the tree cage quickly. Darkness was falling and soon the moon would rise and then she'd really be uncontrollable.

He pulled himself off and hauled her to her feet quite roughly to show her he meant business. He wound most of the rope halter around her, pinning her bound arms down across her stomach so she couldn't hit him again. Then, holding her from behind, he pushed her along. She resisted all the way, jerking and fighting him, until his patience wore thin and he became annoyed with her. He was only trying to protect her but she was making it so difficult. He shoved her along when she resisted, making her stumble, and prodded her hard when she wouldn't move. She was so stubborn and as his irritation increased he became rougher with her. At last he could see the tree cage up ahead in the twilight. Relief flooded him – now he just had to get her in there and seal the entrance.

Yul felt the moment when she understood his intent. She thrashed and squealed, digging the heels of her pretty suede boots into the earth. The scarlet cloak was driving him mad for he kept getting tangled in it. With a snarl of anger he wrenched open the fastening at the neck and ripped it off her. It was suddenly much easier to grab her bodily and lift her off the ground, especially with her arms bound to her. Despite her height, she was very light. He shoved her forcefully through the gap between the trunks of the tree cage, bundling her in and trying to avoid her kicking feet. He no longer worried about hurting her.

He knew she bashed her head on the trunk and scraped her leg as he thrust her through the gap, but he was beyond caring. He pushed her in hard and she fell down in a heap inside the small cage, giving him time to frantically bind the thick rope around the two trunks and seal the opening. His hands shook as he wrapped the rope around and around, leaving no gap she could escape through.

'Try getting out of that!' he snapped triumphantly, breathless with anger and exertion. His head was really painful and he gingerly explored the lump growing there. She hadn't tried to get up from the crumpled heap where she lay, but he knew she was conscious because she was watching him, glaring at him in the murky dusk. Yul turned his back on her and went to sit some distance away, drinking from the water bottle he'd brought up earlier. He was shaking and made a conscious effort to calm himself. He was so angry he felt like leaving her bound and gagged in that cage all night, just to teach her a lesson.

Eventually his breathing returned to normal and the anger evaporated. All he felt now was a dull throb on the temple where she'd hit him, and a weariness in his heart. Miserably he got up and went over to the tree cage. Sylvie was hunched over uncomfortably, her hands still tied to her stomach, a huddled black figure with the gag tight around her mouth. Her hair was all tangled up around the gag, spilling into her eyes in a silver mass and covering her face where she couldn't brush it away. She looked like a small wild animal, caught in a trap and waiting to be killed.

In the gloom, he saw that her eyes were desperate. She was pitiful and his desire to hurt and punish her vanished in an instant. She trembled almost convulsively and he realised her cloak was still lying outside the cage where he'd flung it in anger. Yul tried to push it through the gaps to cover her but it just fell in beside her. He put his hands through and pulled it over her, but she wriggled away from him and it fell off again. He wondered if the moon was rising yet, for her eyes were unfocused now, enormous and shining, gazing at nothing. She must be incredibly uncomfortable but she didn't seem to notice anything. Sighing, he sat down with his back to the cage and hung his head guiltily, not wanting to watch her captive misery.

9

Back at the Hall, all hell had broken loose. Earlier in the afternoon Magus had called in to their rooms and Miranda had assured him that Sylvie was fast asleep in her bedroom. He was pleased to hear it and stopped to chat for a few minutes.

'How are you? Everything alright?'

'I'm fine thank you, Magus. I missed you while you were away. I never seem to spend any time with you nowadays.'

'I know,' he replied, perching on the arm of the sofa where she sat knitting baby-clothes. He stroked her long red hair absent-mindedly. 'There's so much on at the moment. I've got a lot of business deals going through, which will mean greater revenue for Stonewylde. I'm also trying to set up the new building projects that I want to start after the Solstice and there aren't enough hours in the day right now.'

'Poor you,' she said softly, rubbing his leg where it lay, long and muscular, next to her along the arm of the sofa. She was desperate for his company. 'Is there anything I can do to help? I can write letters and reports, things like that.'

He laughed at this and shook his head.

'No, it's not the sort of thing anyone can help with. It's all up here.' He tapped his forehead. 'How you can help is by looking after that daughter of yours and making sure she dances up at Mooncliffe every Moon Fullness. You have no idea how vital it is to me, Miranda. You must make sure she's fit and healthy for it every month so you need to keep her weight up and not let her roam about wasting energy. I want her healthy and strong and I'm counting on you to make sure she is.'

'Of course,' she smiled. 'I know you have her best interests at heart. She's sleeping now, as you wanted, and she'll be fine for her dancing tonight. She certainly seems to love it.'

'Good – I'm really pleased she's taken to her new regime of healthy eating and more sleep so readily, and well done for your part in it, Miranda. I'll try and spend some time with you in December if I can fit it in.'

'Oh yes!' she said breathlessly. 'That'd be wonderful. I miss you so much.'

She laid her head against his thigh and sighed. He chuckled and reached down to caress her, feeling her melt against him.

'Not that long until the baby's due, is it? Less than three months? Then I shall have to make you pregnant all over again.'

She tipped her head back and gazed up at him adoringly, wanting nothing more than to bear his children.

'Anyway, I'll be back at about four o'clock to collect Sylvie. Make sure she's ready for me and wrapped up warmly in that new cloak, won't you?'

He patted her swollen belly and stood up, stretching. He paused to smile at her, then left purposefully.

But when he returned later he found Miranda white and trembling with fear.

'What's happened?' he asked, gripping her shoulders to make her look at him.

'She's not in her room.'

'Where is she then? In the bathroom?'

'No. Magus, she's ... she's gone.'

'GONE? What do you mean, gone?'

'She's not in her room.'

'You've already said that! Where is she?'

'I don't know!'

She burst into tears, screwing her eyes up like a child and crying pitifully. With a rough shake Magus released her shoulders, making her stumble, and strode past her into Sylvie's bedroom. He let out a roar of rage just as Clip came into the sitting room, wanting to check Sylvie would be warm enough up at Mooncliffe.

'What's going on?' he asked, glancing nervously towards the open door of Sylvie's room. 'What's happened?'

Miranda stood in the sitting room sobbing into her hands, her red hair falling over her face. Clip stared at her, his face suddenly white as if he'd seen something from the grave. Magus marched furiously back into the room, his face dark as thunder.

'I'll tell you what's happened! This stupid bloody woman has let Sylvie escape! WHERE IS SHE?'

'I don't know, Magus!' she sobbed. 'I'd tell you if I knew. I thought she was asleep but she was playing a trick. I'm so sorry.'

'You will be! The *one* thing I ask you to do – the *only* thing I want from you – is to look after that girl. And you're too bloody stupid to even manage that!'

His deep voice was frighteningly loud and his face almost purple as the blood pumped to his head. Miranda was terrified.

'Come on, Sol . . .' said Clip in a conciliatory tone, but Magus turned on him angrily, lips quivering with rage.

'Keep out of it, you drugged-up, useless bastard! This is your fault too – I thought you'd got Sylvie back under control again!'

He turned back to Miranda and advanced on her, his head lowered belligerently.

'When *exactly* did you last see her?'

As Magus stepped forward menacingly she stepped away from him, backing towards the sofa.

'I . . . I don't know for sure. I think . . . maybe about half past two? But . . .'

'What do you mean you don't know for sure?' he roared. 'Think! THINK! I need to know exactly! I need to work out how much time she's had to get away and where she could be now. THINK!'

'I don't know!' she sobbed. 'I thought she was in there but . . .'

'You stupid bitch! Stop bloody snivelling and answer me properly!'

Miranda had backed away until her legs were against the sofa and she could go no further. He towered over her aggressively, his breathing heavy, hands clenching with fury. Staring at her blotchy, distraught face he suddenly snapped completely. With a snarl he took another step forward, his hand raised as if he'd strike her, and she fell back onto the sofa in an ungainly heap, curling up to protect the baby. Magus glared down as if he'd like to throttle her, his chest heaving and his face utterly remorseless.

'Have you any idea what you've done this afternoon?' he raged. 'Of the consequences of your stupidity and ineptitude? No, I don't suppose so. You're too busy fawning all over me and gushing on about your bloody pregnancy. I told you how vital it was that I took Sylvie to Mooncliffe tonight – I've stressed it again and again. And you've failed to do the one simple thing I want from you ...'

He turned away from her, his hands shaking with fury, his mouth a thin white line.

'I can't bear the sight of you!' he hissed. 'I tell you, Miranda, if you weren't pregnant ...'

'But you love me!' she cried. 'You said I was special to you. You said only this afternoon that you wanted more children with me.'

He turned back to her and laughed harshly at this.

'*Love you? Special?*' His voice dropped to venomous calm. 'There's only one reason for making you pregnant and keeping you at Stonewylde. Think about it, Miranda – work it out. Goddess, how someone as dreary as you ever gave birth to a girl as magical as Sylvie is beyond me.'

She shrivelled into herself at his cruelty, shrinking from the vitriol of his vicious tongue.

'Please, Magus!' she sobbed, her voice high and strangled with tears. 'Please don't do this to me. I love you!'

His face twisted into a sneer of contempt and he laughed again. His eyes were black diamonds, glittering hard and cold.

'You love me? Of course you do! You and every other woman I take. But you're the only one fool enough to imagine I love

156

them in return. Why on earth would I love *you*?'

She stared up at him and finally understood. In that beat of a second, something inside Miranda quietly died and she bowed her head.

'You've gone too far this time, Sol!' cried Clip. He'd stood aghast as his brother destroyed the poor woman's dreams, but now he stepped forward, his thin face pinched with shock. 'Get out of here and leave her alone!'

'With pleasure!' spat Magus. 'I want nothing more to do with her. You're welcome to her, not that an impotent fool like you is of any use to a woman!'

He lashed them both with a look of scornful disgust and turned on his heel, storming out of the room and almost smashing the door from its hinges. Clip shut the door properly behind him and went to comfort Miranda. She was so distressed that she even allowed Clip to bathe her swollen eyes and hold her gently while she cried as if her world had ended.

Magus raced to the stables and bellowed at Tom to saddle Nightwing. While he stood impatiently, kicking at the cobbles in the stable yard, Magus yanked the radio from his pocket. Tom and the other stable lads heard him yelling at Jackdaw.

'She's bloody gone missing! She's not with you at Mooncliffe? No, I thought not. It's that little shit Yul – he must've taken her somewhere! If you see him, kill him! I mean it, Jack, forget what I said yesterday, just kill him! What? The reception's bloody useless on this damn thing! No, I'm riding up to the stone on the hill to look for them. You hurry down and look round the Village, and try his cottage. See if his bloody mother knows where they are and keep me informed.'

He thrust the gadget back in his pocket and yelled at Tom.

'Come on, man! Get a bloody move on!'

He snatched the reins from the ostler and leapt up into the saddle. Nightwing rolled his eyes and reared at the rough handling, and Magus pulled viciously on the reins, shouting abuse until he got the stallion under control. He grabbed the whip from Tom's outstretched hand and slashing at his horse's flank, clattered out of the yard.

Tom quickly saddled another horse and called to the stable boys to hurry down to the Village behind him.

'Where are you going, sir?' called one of the boys, scared by the frightening turn of events. None of them had ever seen Magus like this before.

'To Maizie's cottage – I don't want that brute Jackdaw turning up and terrorizing the poor woman. One of you lads take a horse quick and go and find Edward. Bring him to the Village too – there's going to be trouble tonight.'

He rode out of the stables and the boys ran after him.

The light was almost gone as Magus reached Hare Stone. Sylvie wasn't there and he roared his pure white-hot fury to the cloudy sky. Nightwing reared again, maddened by his ill treatment. His delicate mouth had been cut by Magus' aggressive handling and his flank slashed again and again by the whip. But Magus was a superb horseman and managed to keep his seat, curbing Nightwing with brutal skill. Wheeling him around, he kicked the stallion down towards the Village, cursing everything that lived and breathed as he went.

The scene in Yul's cottage was ugly. Jackdaw stood in the parlour with Maizie before him, her chin raised and defiance in her eye, whilst Tom stood beside her protectively. All six children were crowded into the kitchen where she'd pushed them, frightened for their safety. The scene was reminiscent of something from Alwyn's reign of terror.

'I tell you again, I have no idea where my son is and I'd never tell you if I did!' Maizie said, voice trembling and cheeks burning scarlet. 'How *dare* you come into my home like this?'

'Magus' orders,' replied Jackdaw, cracking his knuckles. 'Look, woman, I need to know where the boy is and I'll find out, one way or another. You'd do well to tell me now and save yourself a lot of grief.'

'Get out and leave her alone!' said Tom angrily. 'You were banished from Stonewylde for murder and you can't come back and order folk about! Who do you think you are?'

Jackdaw laughed at this, a harsh and mirthless bark. His blue eyes were alight with excitement; this was what he enjoyed most.

'Shut up, you old git! One more word out of you and I'll rupture your kidneys. What are you doing here anyway? You should be up at the stables knee-deep in horse shit, not chatting up lonely widows, you dirty old bugger. Now listen, darlin', I'll ask you for the last time—'

'I know where they might be!' cried Rosie from the kitchen, pushing herself forward.

'No, Rosie!'

'I think they've gone down to the beach!'

Jackdaw pulled her out of the kitchen and looked down into her pretty face, as flushed as her mother's.

'A little sister! Yeah, you're very like him. So what makes you think they've gone down there? You better not be lying, girl!'

She shrugged, shaking her dark curls from her eyes exactly as Yul did.

'I heard our Yul tell another Village boy he were going to the beach later on with his sweetheart. I don't want to say the wrong thing and I'm not sure, but 'tis where courting couples go at the Moon Fullness sometimes to the caves down there, to be private like.'

She simpered and Jackdaw stared at her, his ugly face furrowed with concentration. Perspiration beaded his bald head and trickled down his pierced face. The room was rank with the stench of his excited sweat.

'Yeah, I remember them caves. But why are you helping me when your mother ain't?'

'Oh, I'm not helping you,' said Rosie guilelessly, flicking her curls back and wriggling her shoulders. 'I want to help Magus.'

Jackdaw barked with laughter at this and chucked her under the chin with a dirty finger, leering into her face.

'And I'm sure he'll be grateful, you little peach,' he said.

At that moment Magus burst into the cottage. He took in the scene quickly and shouted at Jackdaw to get down to the beach and check the caves.

'Right, you! Up to Mooncliffe!' he yelled, grabbing Rosie by the arm and pulling her towards the door.

'WHY?' screamed Maizie. 'What are you doing? Leave my daughter alone!'

'I'm testing the whole lot of you stupid bloody Villagers! There must be a girl who gets moongazy at the Moon Fullness and I'll find out who it is tonight. That rock is going to be charged up by somebody, whatever happens. You, Tom, knock on every door and get all the girls in the Village to go up there immediately. Every single one! There's no time to waste – the moon's rising right now! Punishment tomorrow for any family who refuses to obey me. MOVE!'

Yul was trying to ignore the muffled cries coming from behind him. The Owl Moon must be rising for Sylvie was frantic, squirming around on the nest of leaves, unable to stand, unable to cry out. It was pitiful to hear and he put his hands over his ears to block out the noise. It was quite dark but he was scared to light the lantern in case Magus or Jackdaw were out looking for them. He wished he could silence her completely, but the gag was as tight as it could be tied and there was nothing more he could do. The sounds of distress went on and on and in the end he stood up and walked away, unable to free her and unable to bear it any longer. All around the owls hooted and called amongst the trees, eerie in the deepening darkness.

Up at Mooncliffe Magus stood tall by the great moon rock, his arms folded and face grim as he surveyed the crowded cliff top. Girls of all ages were gathered together with their anxious families looking on. Everyone was scared, not used to being shouted at, herded like cattle and ordered about like dogs. Many of the girls were crying as Jackdaw lifted them one by one onto the moon rock and left them standing there, while Magus looked for any sign of the jerking and shuddering that affected Sylvie. It was dark, as clouds obscured the sky and the full moon, but Jackdaw had rigged up a powerful lantern using his car battery. The effect was a harsh spotlight on each poor child as she stood alone and scared on the rock.

'Alright, when you've been tested, go back home!' shouted Magus, getting more irate by the minute at the lack of results. 'Come on, get a move on. Next!'

There was a background of angry muttering, and one comment rose above the general unrest.

'What about the Hallfolk girls? Why is it only the Village girls?'

'Good point,' said Magus loudly. He took out the radio and got through to Martin at the Hall, ordering every girl there to be sent up straight away in whatever means of transport was available, time being of the essence. This silenced the Villagers' muttering for a while but made the sounds of children crying even more obvious.

Then a little girl of about five years old was wrenched from her mother's arms by Jackdaw and swung up onto the rock. She cried and cried, shaking with terror and cold. Magus watched intently as she stood sobbing her heart out, her shawl slipping from her shoulders. Her mother stepped forward, trying to reach her, but Jackdaw yanked at her arm to stop her.

'Let me take her down, please,' begged the woman, her heart breaking at the sound of her little girl crying so pitifully. 'She's terrified and I can't bear it!'

'Get back,' growled Jackdaw. 'Magus ain't finished with her yet.'

'I can't decide if she's just shaking from crying or really shaking properly. She's probably too young to be moongazy anyway,' muttered Magus. He glared around at the crowd in exasperation. 'Sacred Mother, I wish they'd all stop this bloody bawling!'

'Shall I shut her up?' asked Jackdaw.

'NO! Don't you touch her!' the mother screamed, trying to push past him. Casually, without even thinking what he was doing, Jackdaw grabbed the woman by the throat and held her at arm's length. She started to choke and there was a furious roar from the crowd.

A black crow came out of nowhere, flying into the bright spotlight in a flurry of feathers and flapping. The crow launched itself straight at Jackdaw's face. He released the woman, who scrambled up onto the rock and scooped her little girl to safety. Jackdaw hit out frantically at the crow just as he'd done at Samhain in the Stone Labyrinth, trying to thump it away from his face. The crow attacked again and again, pecking and clawing, stabbing with its vicious beak. Its raucous cries of attack mingled with the man's oaths and yells.

Then Jackdaw screamed, long and piercing, and doubled over clutching at his eye. Dark blood trickled between his fingers. The crowd shrank back in horror as the man stumbled about in the harsh spotlight, screaming in agony. Still the crow attacked, pecking and tearing at Jackdaw's hands. He fell to his knees and the crow landed on his head, its claws digging in to the shiny skin that covered his skull. The sharp beak stabbed down repeatedly, slashing at Jackdaw's wounded eye. Magus stepped forward, as horrified as the Villagers at the terrible sight. He grabbed one of the stone eggs and tried to bludgeon the crow with it. The crow cawed loudly and Jackdaw jerked round at the sound. In that split second the egg came down with a heavy thud, not on the crow but on the back of his bald skull.

Jackdaw cried out, a low howl of anguish. Completely disorientated, he clambered to his feet again. With the bird latched onto his head he staggered about, maddened and clumsy with pain. Thick blood oozed from the messy eye socket. He screamed and stumbled, thrashing about madly, and then all seemed to happen in slow motion. He tripped and started to fall and the crow spread its great wings and took off. Jackdaw slowly toppled over backwards, his arms flailing wildly. His bald head cracked down full force on the edge of the great white moon rock and split open as easily as eggshell.

*

Yul approached the tree cage with trepidation. Sylvie was silent, or so he'd thought, but as he got nearer he heard her little mewing sounds of misery. He could see nothing in the darkness.

'Sylvie!' he said softly. 'Sylvie, it's me. I'm going to light the lantern now. It'll seem very bright at first so close your eyes.'

In the soft light of the flame he saw she was still curled at an awkward angle and must be in pain with her hands bound tightly to her body and the gag tied hard around her mouth. She wasn't covered by the cloak and trembled violently, her eyes looking up at him in desperation and begging for release. Her distress was terrible to witness.

Fumbling with guilty haste Yul untied the thick rope that fastened the cage. He reached in to help her out but she couldn't move; she'd been lying awkwardly for so long that her legs were numb. He half climbed into the cage himself, squeezing through the gap, and untied the tight knot of the gag. Her mouth was white and unmoving and she could only stare up at him in mute misery. Yul was almost crying, wondering how he could've gone off and left her at her most desperate time. He had great trouble unbinding the rope round her torso but once it was free, with her wrists still bound together, he pulled her half upright and dragged her through the narrow gap and out of the cage. He carefully stood her upright but she crumpled at his feet, her legs unable to take her weight.

Yul felt worse than ever before. Last month at the moongazing he'd watched Magus put her through hours of suffering and this month he'd done exactly the same thing. He'd never forgive himself for this. He pulled the beautiful scarlet cloak out of the cage and tried to wrap it around her as she lay motionless on the earth. Then he knelt over her, fumbling at the bindings around her wrists, wondering why he'd tied her so very tightly. Eventually the hemp rope unravelled to reveal her wrists, swollen and bruised. Her arms were damaged right up to the elbows and her hands were very cold and white. He scooped her up and sat down with his back against the tree cage, gathering her into his lap. Wrapping the cloak around her as she curled into him, desperate

163

for warmth, he held her in his arms, rocking her gently, chafing her hands and kissing her head. His tears fell silently into her silver hair.

The Villagers had scattered, parents trying to cover their children's eyes to protect them from the hideous scene at the moon stone. The air was full of children's crying and the shocked, hushed voices of the adults. Nobody could believe what they'd just witnessed. Magus stood in silent disbelief, gazing down in the glaring spotlight at the blood-splattered rock and the body that lay sprawled on the grass. Shaken out of their obedience to Magus, the crowd started to head down to the Village, meeting the first group of Hallfolk girls on their way up the cliff path.

'Don't go up there,' they warned, shaking their heads, and the Hallfolk turned back when they heard what had happened.

By common consensus the Villagers trooped into the Great Barn, feeling the need to be together at such a time of crisis. Hot drinks were made and children wrapped in warm blankets. Gradually, as the shock of Jackdaw's death lessened and the full impact of what Magus had done began to sink in, they started to get angry.

'He's got no right to put our children through that.'

'Who does he think he is, dragging us up there in the middle o' winter?'

'Aye, and why was that Jackdaw back anyway? He's banished!'

'How dare he touch our girls, force 'em up on the rock!'

''Tis what he's been doing to that lovely girl Sylvie every month.'

'That crow was Mother Heggy's, you know.'

'Where's Yul? He should be here.'

'He must be off hiding the poor maid away so Magus can't get at her again.'

The complaints grew louder until eventually, in the absence of any clear leader, Tom climbed onto the dais where the musicians played at the celebrations. Everyone quietened down, wanting to hear what he had to say.

'Folk, I ain't one for speeches. But we need to think on what's to be done after this terrible night. Something's happened to Magus. He's been good to us in the past, right enough, but he's changed. The man's turned bad, evil, just like his father afore him.'

He paused to let the growls of agreement die down.

'At the stables tonight I heard him on that there radio thing speaking to Jackdaw. And I must tell you this – Magus told Jackdaw to kill Yul!'

There was a roar of disapproval at this and Tom raised his hands to quieten them.

'I know, I know! 'Tisn't the first time it's happened neither. Twice now that boy's been locked up in the stone byre by the stables for days on end, and been beaten, starved and tortured. First time Magus had Alwyn to help him, second time it were Jackdaw, and that poor boy has suffered, I can tell you. You all seen the state of him when he came back to us. We know what Magus tried to do to him at Samhain.'

The Great Barn echoed with people's angry voices.

'To my mind, Magus must be scared o' Yul to treat him like that – he must see the lad as a threat. Yul's no ordinary Village boy but neither is he Hallfolk. Pardon my impertinence, Maizie, for being personal here but now 'tis finally acknowledged that Yul is Magus' son, not Alwyn's. We know 'twas Mother Heggy's crow that killed Jackdaw tonight. And we all remember what happened at the last Summer Solstice, when the crow sat on Yul's shoulder and Magus dropped the sacred fire. Some of us know there was a prophecy, many years ago, about Yul.'

The Villagers buzzed excitedly about this and again Tom quietened them. Then Edward arrived from the clifftop and joined him up on the dais, taking over. He knew the people would do as he said and was well used to managing and leading.

'Listen well, folk. We must bide our time and wait patiently, go about our business as normal. We must keep Yul safe until the time is right, and most of all, we must not make Magus angry. He's not right any more and who knows what he may do next?'

The Villagers muttered loudly again, recognizing the truth of these words.

'Tis nearly the Winter Solstice when Yul will turn sixteen,' continued Edward, 'and I reckon things'll fall into place then. But until then, we must keep our heads down. When the time is right, Goddess willing, we'll have a worthy new magus to be the guardian of Stonewylde, to lead us in our festivals and our celebrations.'

The crowd roared at this and Edward had to raise his voice.

'A magus to bring up Mother Earth's magic and share it amongst the community. I seen for myself the boy being blessed with the Earth Magic, and 'tis a sight to behold! We will stand together and wait for Yul, for the good of Stonewylde! For the folk of Stonewylde!'

There was cheering and clapping at this as the people felt themselves bound together with a new sense of solidarity and purpose.

Yul felt Sylvie slowly respond to his body heat and the gentle chafing of her hands and wrists. He knew he must get her back home soon as it was getting colder and she should be tucked up safely in bed. She no longer trembled but lay docilely in his lap, her head against his chest, curled up like a kitten. She rarely spoke much after moongazing, and he realised that she wasn't going to come round any more than this, so he stood carefully and found that with a bit of help she could now stand. He picked up the lantern, leaving everything else to collect another time. With his arm around Sylvie's waist to support her, he led her back through the woods to the glade where Edward's grey mare waited patiently.

They rode back slowly, Sylvie sitting in front this time so Yul could hold her. He let the mare choose her way in the darkness until the Hall lights became visible ahead. Yul extinguished the lantern and lifted Sylvie down, light as a goose down quilt, and carried her towards the back door of the Tudor wing. He saw lights in her room and was scared what he might find, but knew he had to take her up there, as she was as vague as ever and couldn't possibly manage it herself. He opened the door and climbed the narrow stairs, almost tripping over her cloak, then pushed the arched door. It swung open to reveal Miranda sitting silently by the window.

She was perfectly still in the soft lamplight, her long red hair hanging down over her shoulders. Her eyes were so puffy they'd almost disappeared. What had happened here tonight? She rose as he entered the room.

'Yul!' she said softly, her voice raw. She gestured for him to put Sylvie on her bed. He did so and stood back, unsure of what to do next.

'Sylvie, darling,' Miranda whispered. 'You're back now.'

Sylvie's eyes were closed and she seemed to be sleeping. Her mother tugged off the black suede boots and unfastened the cloak, pulling it out from underneath her. She tucked Sylvie under the bed covers fully clothed and turned to Yul, her head slightly bowed to conceal her swollen eyes.

'Thank you,' she said.

He shifted uncomfortably.

'I'm afraid I hurt Sylvie tonight. I was trying to protect her but I ended up harming her, and I'm very sorry, ma'am.'

She shook her head and looked down at the floor, hiding behind the curtain of hair.

'Thank you, Yul, and sorry I misjudged you. I'm grateful to you.'

He nodded, feeling that if he spoke he might embarrass himself by crying. It had been a terrible night and all he wanted was to get home. With a final glance at Sylvie lying peacefully in her bed, he left down the back stairs and rode the patient grey mare back through the foggy November night to the Village.

On the cobbles outside the Great Barn, the Villagers milled around as they continued to discuss Edward's and Tom's words. The men headed for the Jack in the Green to speak further over a pot of cider, whilst the women gathered their children together

to take them home. The Village buzzed with eagerness and speculation. Only Maizie seemed unaffected by the excitement stirred
up by Tom's and Edward's speeches.

As she led her children back to the cottage, Leveret fast asleep
in her arms, Maizie felt her heart heavy in her chest. She alone
recognised the enormity of what the men had said tonight in
the Barn. As she'd done so many times since Yul's birth, Maizie
cursed Mother Heggy and her dangerous prophecy. She knew
how iron-willed and utterly ruthless Magus could be and it was
too much to ask a young lad to take him on, support of his
people or no. Maizie alone seemed to understand that the fight
ahead was unfairly matched and the outcome far from assured.
She ignored the excited chatter of all those around her, filled
with fear for the life of her eldest son.

10

Just before dawn the next morning an ill-assorted group gathered on the cliff top a little way from the disc of white stone. A chill wind whipped their hair and cloaks as seagulls screamed and drifted around them. Magus stood granite-faced before the mound of wood, hastily assembled overnight by Martin and a couple of young servants. Jackdaw's body lay within the pile, hidden beneath a piece of hemp cloth. No embroidered pentangle for him, nor the community's comfort for the bereaved. Vetchling huddled against her sister Violet, her dirty face grimed with tears for her son. Her daughter, Jackdaw's sister Starling, supported her on the other side, as squat and bellicose as her mother. Martin stood beside them with his young wife, and three small boys looked fearfully on.

The wood smelt strongly of the resin Martin had splashed over the funeral pyre to ensure a thorough blaze. Magus glanced at the group mourning the passing on of the most hated man at Stonewylde. Not the normal send-off, and it must be done quickly, for the sooner it was over the sooner the Villagers could put the incident behind them.

He produced a lighter from beneath his cloak and bent over the pyre. The wind extinguished the tiny flame instantly, and Magus cursed as he tried again and again to set light to the body and its cradle of branches. Martin stepped forward to shield him, and at last there was a sharp crackle as the wood ignited. The flames flared wildly to one side as the salty wind gusted, but the pyre burnt well, the heat and smoke causing the group to step back. The little boys stared at it in fascination.

Standing tall on the desolate cliff top, his black cloak flaring out behind him, Magus looked up into the leaden grey sky. His face was as bleak as the cruel sea far below.

'Dark Angel, take the soul of Jackdaw now, before the sun rises, to the Otherworld. He was killed before his time and we ask that you accompany his soul as he passes through the veil. He will be missed by his family. He served me well.'

Vetchling let out a wail as the fire consumed her son's body. Starling patted her mother's arm and clasped Jay, Jackdaw's young son, to her great thigh. She ignored her own little boy who stood next to Martin's child, sucking a filthy thumb and gazing at the blaze with vacant eyes.

''Twas Heggy's crow that killed my boy!' Vetchling cried. 'She sent it to do her bidding. May the Dark Angel take her and all!'

'Aye, sister, but on whose account was the crow sent? 'Tis that dark-haired brat who's to blame for this. Maizie's bastard – he's the one!'

'You speak true, Violet. Angel take his soul too.'

Magus' dark eyes rested on her wrinkled face and he nodded.

'Four weeks,' he said softly, his words stolen by the wind. 'Four weeks until the Solstice and then at last I shall be free of him.'

The white gulls screamed around their heads as the fire burnt away to nothing, leaving no trace of Jackdaw's presence at Stonewylde.

'Mum, aren't you coming down to breakfast?'

Sylvie stood uncertainly outside her mother's bedroom.

'No,' came the muffled reply. 'Go on down without me. I'm not hungry.'

Sylvie frowned. She felt disorientated this morning. She'd been horrified to wake up and find herself badly bruised and aching all over. Her wrists and lower arms were agony; the skin was swollen, chafed red and covered with bruising and her upper arms hurt too. Her leg and the right side of her body was scraped and sore, there was a large blue lump on her forehead and her ribs hurt if she breathed too deeply. She had vague memories of Yul pulling and pushing her, of being bound and gagged and then shoved into a cage. She remembered his anger and her desperation to escape; to go to Mooncliffe and dance for Magus. She knew Yul had treated her badly but was at a loss to explain why. She'd hoped that her mother would shed some light on what had happened. Magus must be furious with her as she'd promised to give him all her moon magic and she'd broken that promise.

'Can I come in, Mum? I want to talk about last night.'

'No! Go away, Sylvie, *please*. Just leave me alone.'

'Are you alright?'

'Go to breakfast and your lessons, Sylvie, and leave me in peace.'

All day Sylvie waited in terror for Magus' summons. He'd be furious, she knew, but it wasn't her fault. She hid her injuries as best she could, pulling her tatty jumper sleeves down as far as they'd go to conceal her wrists and shielding her forehead behind her hair. But Magus was nowhere to be seen. The summons never came, and eventually her lessons finished and she returned to the Tudor wing to start the pile of homework that awaited her. In her bedroom she discovered a large and shiny bolt attached to the arched staircase door, a brass padlock securing it shut. Miranda was still in her room and Sylvie began to worry about her mother.

When it became too much, she ignored her mother's wishes to be left alone and went into the darkened bedroom anyway. Miranda lay curled up on her bed, and Sylvie was shocked to see her looking so dishevelled. Miranda's face was puffy and her eyes dead. She didn't want to talk; all she would say was that it was over between her and Magus. She refused to say anything about the night before, other than the fact that Yul had brought Sylvie back quite late and had apologised for hurting her. Miranda didn't even ask where she was hurt, she simply closed her eyes and told Sylvie to shut the door behind her.

The atmosphere in the Village was strange. People went about their business as usual but it was as if everyone held their breath. The events of the previous night were discussed in shocked voices, and in the cold light of day nobody could quite believe what had happened up on the cliff top. Everyone was worried that Magus would turn up, clattering over the cobbles on Nightwing, harrying them and maybe even punishing them for daring to speak out against him. The planned Story Web had been cancelled and there was a feeling of anti-climax after the excitement and anger of the Moon Fullness.

As Yul walked through the Village he sensed a change in attitude towards him. Many people nodded, almost in deference, whilst others glanced at him fearfully as if he spelt danger. He'd heard of what had happened at Mooncliffe and was shocked; Magus' cruel treatment of the girls strengthened Yul's determination to rid Stonewylde of such a tyrant. Of Jackdaw's gruesome death he said nothing, but Mother Heggy's words rang in his head over and over:

Those who stand against you will fall, one by one.

Yul made his way up the path to Mother Heggy's hovel, anxious to unload his guilt about poor Sylvie.

'Couldn't be helped,' she said firmly, a blackened clay pipe clamped between her gums. ''Twas that or the rock. At least she's not weak and drained today, and he has none o' her quicksilver flowing in his veins.'

Yul nodded, knowing she was right, but unable to forget the damage to Sylvie's wrists when he'd finally unbound the ropes, and the way she'd been bashed and scraped against the tree as he'd thrust her so roughly into the cage. He also remembered his anger with her. He couldn't justify it, nor banish the terrible thought that he was becoming like his father. Heggy surveyed him and chuckled.

'Aye, boy, you are your father's son, right enough, and you must watch yourself in the future. You like things your own way just a mite too much and you brook no argument with them that don't agree with you. But you're not cruel, Yul, and you love the bright one with your soul and your heart. Learn from it, and then put it behind you and think on what's to be done. Four weeks till the Solstice. Four weeks to prepare. Build up your strength, my boy, and make your plans. Take yourself up into the land and open your heart to the song of Stonewylde. The Goddess herself will help you prepare.'

The next day Hazel collared Sylvie at breakfast. Her normally attractive face was grim and frowning.

'Why didn't you come for your weigh-in yesterday?' she demanded. 'I'll see you this morning before lessons start.'

As Sylvie faced the doctor in her office in the hospital wing, she thought sadly of how Hazel had once been her friend. She remembered the kindness of the young intern in that awful London hospital; the only friendly face amongst the wolf-pack. Hazel had been so warm and caring then – what had Magus done to make her so cold? Sylvie stepped down off the scales and Hazel tapped the figures into her computer, barely looking at her.

'You're not gaining anything. Eat properly and don't start messing around again, or I'll be forced to keep you in the hospital under constant supervision.'

Sylvie nodded glumly, keeping her head down to hide the nasty bruise on her forehead.

'I saw Magus before breakfast,' Hazel continued, 'and all I can say, Sylvie, is I hope you feel guilty.'

Her head shot up. Was Mother Heggy's spell working? She tried not to think of the tiny crescent of silver hair.

'That poor man! After all he's done for you, I don't know how you can repay him like this. I don't understand how it works, but you know that your moongaziness is essential to him and without it he seems to become weak. He's been in a terrible state since the full moon and I'm really quite concerned.'

173

'I'm really sorry, Hazel, but it wasn't my fault. I—'

'Nothing's ever your fault, is it Sylvie? There's always someone else to blame. Save your breath; I'm not interested in your pathetic excuses. Magus had a message for me to convey to you. He said that nothing's changed, even though you've let him down so badly after promising to help him. You must continue to catch up with your school work and on no account are you to leave the Hall. He was adamant about that. He hasn't mentioned it, but I'm assuming he still wants your eating monitored, so you're to sit near me in the Dining Hall whilst he's unable to join us. Do you understand?'

'Yes, but . . . doesn't he want to see me?'

She still couldn't believe she'd get off without a lecture from Magus as well.

'No he does not!' Hazel's eyes were stone cold as she stood up from her desk and glared at Sylvie. 'He doesn't want to see anyone and certainly not attention-seekers like you. He's shut himself up in his rooms and just wants to be left alone. I've never known him like this before, and it's all thanks to you.'

During the next few days the pressure on Sylvie became so relentless she wanted to scream. The teachers continued to hound her in every lesson; Magus had done a good job on them too, she decided. She was constantly humiliated in front of her peers, who seized their chance to join in making Sylvie the scapegoat of every class and butt of every joke.

Holly had a field day. She also used Sylvie's lack of smart winter clothes as a weapon against her. The new clothes Magus had promised her after the Owl Moon never materialised because she hadn't moondanced for him. She was forced to continue wearing her thin summer skirts and dresses with layers of old jumpers to keep warm, and she'd borrowed a stretched and shapeless cardigan of Miranda's, which had longer sleeves than any of her own shrunken woollens, to cover the purple bruises on her wrists. None of last year's winter clothes fitted now she was so much taller, and as she was restricted to the Hall she couldn't even ask the Village dressmakers for help. Hazel continued to watch her at meal times, although it was nowhere near as bad as the force-feeding Magus had subjected her to. Sylvie finally stopped being sick after every meal, but still found the constant monitoring hard to bear.

She dreaded the evenings up in the Tudor wing, trapped with Miranda moping in her bedroom. Her mother wouldn't go downstairs and face anyone. She wasn't teaching any of her classes and had trays of food sent up at meal-times, which she picked at half-heartedly. Sylvie offered to eat with her, thinking that at least she'd avoid Hazel and the Dining Hall, but Miranda refused this, wanting only to be alone. She'd grown wan and dull-eyed, crying constantly and carping at Sylvie when she wasn't lying listlessly on her bed. Clip had called in briefly and reversed the hypnosis he'd subjected them both to, apologising for his weakness at giving in to his half-brother's demands. He promised to call in again, but first he had to spend a few days out in the open. He said he had much thinking to do.

Sylvie's greatest distress, however, was caused by Yul. She hadn't seen him since the Owl Moon and still didn't understand why she was so injured, or what had actually happened that night. She didn't know Yul had tried to visit, but the downstairs door was bolted from the inside, rendering his new key useless. Nor did she know that on Magus' orders, Martin had instructed the servants to inform him if Yul was seen anywhere near the grounds, and to keep watch on Sylvie to ensure she didn't leave the Hall.

As the days passed and the swollen skin on her wrists and forearms turned to deep black bruising, she became increasingly upset. Hiding the bruises was difficult, for all her sleeves were far too short, and constantly wearing Miranda's baggy old cardigan with its worn, stretched sleeves made her feel frumpier than ever. Her upper arms were marked too and her ribs were painful when she breathed deeply. The scraped skin down her side and on her thigh scabbed over and the lump on her forehead turned purple. She felt a wreck, her body damaged and her clothes thin and too small. She dreaded her lessons and hated spending time anywhere near Miranda. Life seemed unbearable.

Several days later she returned to the Tudor wing, after an awful day enduring Holly's vindictive teasing, to find Clip and her mother discussing the future. Since Clip's kindness towards her at the last full moon when her world had been blown apart by Magus' cruelty, Miranda had warmed slightly to the wispy, gentle man. They both looked up as Sylvie entered the room despondently, clutching the heavy pile of books and folders.

'Come and sit down,' said Miranda. 'We're talking about options for the future.'

Clip smiled at Sylvie, sensing the girl's utter dejection. His eyes were sad and she thought he looked old and tired.

'Cheer up,' he said. 'It's not as bad as that, Sylvie.'

'It is,' she replied. 'It's worse. I'm working really hard at school but I still haven't caught up with everything I've missed. It's not my fault but nobody seems to care about that. I'm stuck at the bottom of the class, none of the teachers like me at all and I'm sick of feeling stupid.'

'Well it may not be for much longer,' said Miranda. She sat hunched on the sofa, her beautiful red hair lank and dull, her eyes lifeless. 'I think it's time we considered going back to the Outside World.'

Sylvie's heart almost burst in her chest at this.

'NO! Mum, no! We can't! I don't ever want to leave Stonewylde!'

'Well I do. There's nothing for me here. Magus ... Magus has been very clear about his feelings for me, and how he felt about me all along. I feel a complete and utter fool. I don't know if I can continue to live under his roof – it's too humiliating.'

'Mum we can't leave! We can't afford to, you've said that yourself. Where would we go? It's impossible!'

'I've promised your mother that if you really wanted to leave,' said Clip softly, 'then I'd help you. Remember, Sylvie, Stonewylde legally belongs to me, and although I don't use money as such,

I do have access to a large account. I don't want you to leave and I really hope you'll stay, but if you insisted then of course I'd help. I'd find you somewhere to live and support you until your mother's able to work again. Miranda's had no salary since she came here, and anyway, I feel responsible for your plight. I'm very ashamed of the part I played in bringing you both to this awful situation. You've no idea how terribly guilty I feel about everything.'

'But I don't want to leave!' cried Sylvie desperately. 'Please, Clip, don't do this.'

'I think the decision is mine to make,' said Miranda, 'and I need to consider it very carefully. But I really can't see a future here, not now I know the truth about Magus. It's just too painful for me.'

'But what about me?' wailed Sylvie. 'Don't I have any say in the matter? It's my life too! I won't go, Mum. Leave if you must, but I won't.'

'No, Sylvie, that's not one of our options. If we do go, then we leave together. I need to think about it. But if things are as bad here as you make out, surely you'd be better off in the Outside World? We could put Stonewylde behind us and make a fresh start – you, me and the baby.'

As Sylvie lay in bed that night listening to the wind pick up outside, she thought about her mother's words. Maybe she was right; maybe it was time to start again. Miranda wasn't the only one whose idyll had been shattered and Stonewylde wasn't the paradise Sylvie had thought. She had no friends but many enemies and she couldn't keep up with the relentless school work. She'd missed so much both since coming here and before that in London and doubted she'd ever fill in all the gaps in time for the exams. She'd fail every subject miserably and everyone would be deeply disappointed with her for letting them all down.

Magus was determined to leech her energy every month on the moon rock and, worst of all, even Yul seemed to have turned against her. If only he'd explain why he'd hurt her so badly, what had happened that night, she might've been able to forgive him. But as it was, she felt let down and bewildered.

And there was worse to come. The Solstice was fast approaching and the thought of the looming conflict between Yul and Magus filled her with horror. She'd said that it was her battle too and that she wanted to help, but that was before Mother Heggy had started talking about five deaths. She'd imagined Yul somehow overcoming Magus, forcing him to leave Stonewylde, but realistically how could that ever happen? Magus' actions at Samhain had proved he was prepared to kill his own son. Sylvie didn't think Yul was intending to kill his own father, but how else was Magus ever going to leave? He certainly wouldn't go voluntarily and hand Stonewylde over. Would there be some sort of accident, maybe brought on by Mother Heggy's spell? And if so, Sylvie wondered if she could live with the guilt of knowing she'd contributed to a man's death by stealing a lock of his childhood hair.

Sylvie wanted to help Yul, but she wanted no part of anyone's murder. And these things happened at Stonewylde – first Alwyn and now Jackdaw. She'd heard the gossip about what'd happened that terrible night at Mooncliffe and felt partly responsible for the man's death; if she'd been up there with Magus, none of it would've happened. Mother Heggy – she was the key. The cake for Alwyn, which Sylvie herself had delivered, and Magus' lock of hair – was Mother Heggy using her to help bring about these awful deaths? Sylvie shuddered at the thought, but knew too that what the old woman had said about Magus' plans for Yul was true. And if Magus succeeded, could she live under his dominion knowing the boy she loved had died partly because of his involvement with her? The thought of any more deaths – surely not five? – was awful. Maybe, Sylvie thought despondently in the darkness, it would be easier to leave now and let the events at Stonewylde unfold without her.

Yul stood with his back to Hare Stone and surveyed the sweep of land that filled his vision and his soul – the flanks of the

Earth Goddess. The breeze ruffled his hair, the curls long and unkempt from his lengthy trek through the hills and valleys of Stonewylde. He was dirty and hungry after roaming the land for a couple of days, but had needed to get away from everyone and set his mind free. He was living in limbo, aware of time passing. Every rotation of the Earth brought him closer to his destiny at the Solstice in three weeks' time. He knew that his entire life had been leading to the event ahead, although he understood that the outcome was far from assured. Mother Heggy had stressed that what she'd seen at his birth was just one possibility. Nothing was fixed. In his heart he knew he was the true magus. Stonewylde called him to lead the folk and guard the land. But he also acknowledged Magus' power and intelligence. He didn't make the mistake of under-estimating the man he now accepted was his father.

With a final gaze around the panorama of green hills and grey skies, Yul touched the great stone reverently and made to leave the magical spot where the moon spirals were so strong. He paused, suddenly remembering lying on the grass with Sylvie in the warm summer sun, gazing at the tiny pulse beating in her throat. Unbidden, another image flooded his mind. Sylvie lying curled in the belly of the Goddess, pale and still, the tiny hare of yew wood clasped in a lifeless hand. He shook his head to clear such macabre thoughts, and sent his love across the boulders and through the woodland to the Hall. He hoped she'd feel it and understand.

Yul made his way to the dolmen further along the Dragon's Back ridgeway where he'd slept for the past couple of nights. It was dry and sheltered, if cold, in the Neolithic stone building. He'd trapped and skinned a rabbit earlier, and would now roast it over a fire. One more night out in the open, he decided, and then he'd go back to the Village. He wanted to be around during the Dark Moon next week as he hoped Sylvie would be permitted to join the other women in the Great Barn. He'd been told she was forbidden to leave the Hall, but surely Magus wouldn't break with tradition so fundamentally. He might get the chance to see her again on the Village Green and explain what had happened during the Owl Moon; he really hoped that she'd forgiven him for his rough treatment. He'd no idea how ugly her injuries were and would've been mortified if he'd known.

The smoke trickling from the open mouth of the dolmen alarmed him as he'd collected wood earlier but hadn't lit the fire. As he approached, Yul saw Clip's tall angular frame standing in the entrance and he almost turned around and disappeared back into the hills. But he knew he must face up to whatever waited for him, so he pressed on up the incline and joined his half-uncle by the great stones.

'Blessings, Yul,' said Clip. 'I hope you don't mind, but I've lit your firewood and brewed some tea. Come and join me.'

Clip was a regular visitor to the dolmen and kept a few basic necessities in the back of the cave-like structure. They sat on opposite sides of the fire in the entrance, gazing out at the view below them and sipping from chipped pottery mugs.

'The magic is strong for me here,' said Clip softly. 'I always feel that the Stone Circle is the mind of Stonewylde, but this place is the heart.'

'And the Village Green is the soul,' said Yul, ill at ease with this enigmatic man. There were times when he felt drawn to Clip and his shamanic gift, but he knew the man's weaknesses too well to trust him.

'Yes, I can see that. The Green Man – he's your spirit guide, you know. You'd feel his presence powerfully on the Green.'

'Under the yew.'

Clip nodded, watching Yul through the smoke that curled like a veil between them. He saw echoes of his brother in the strong face that gazed out across the land. Yul's cheekbones, nose and jaw were as chiselled as Magus' and spoke of the same strength of character and determination.

'You'd make a worthy magus,' said Clip. 'The Earth Magic is in you and the Goddess has chosen you – I can feel it. My brother has had his day and his cruelty has become excessive. I'd thought he had that side of his nature under control, but lately ... You're a brave young man, and should you defeat him at the Solstice, I'll support you.'

Yul glanced at him in surprise and Clip was struck by the beauty of the boy's deep grey eyes. Yul nodded and fed more wood to the fire. He began to prepare the rabbit on the spit and Clip watched him carefully, admiring the practicality and economy of his actions.

If only his brother had accepted this boy as his son, how different things could've been. Yul might've tempered his father's hard heart and brought out the kindness and fullness of spirit that Clip was sure were locked away inside Magus' steely personality. Apart from that brief few months with Maizie, Magus had never loved anybody but he could've loved this boy, and through that love become a better person. But it was too late for that, and Clip knew that now there was room for only one of them at Stonewylde.

Magus lay in his black spa-bath, the deep and fragrant water bubbling gently around him. His eyes were closed and he dreamed of steak, bloody and tender. His mouth watered. Not long now and he'd be able to eat a decent meal. It was almost a week since the cliff-top funeral following the Mooncliffe fiasco. His iron will had stood him in good stead as he'd starved himself since then, eating just enough to remain functioning whilst he spent every waking hour working in his rooms. He'd worked diligently, closing many deals and setting up new ones. Throughout his self-enforced exile from everyday life, he'd let it be known that he was languishing on his sick bed unable to throw off a mystery illness.

Magus smiled to himself at the thought of the three weeks ahead. He'd been informed that Sylvie was buckling under the strain; struggling with the mountain of school work piled on her over the past weeks. He knew she'd had no contact with Yul. Martin had ensured that she was watched every minute of the day and the bolted and padlocked doors had prevented any visits from the bastard upstart. He could imagine the atmosphere in

181

her rooms at present, with Miranda moping around like a kicked dog. Today he'd launch the plan that would bring his moongazy girl to heel once and for all. He stood up and stepped out of the circular bath, wrapping himself in a thick robe. His gaunt face stared out a hundred times all around the black marble bathroom. Magus' mouth split in a grim smile of satisfaction – he looked really dreadful.

The students sat around in the music room sipping drinks and eating snacks during break time. Sylvie was half hidden in the window seat, gazing out over the lawns with unfocused eyes. She felt fragile this morning after another big argument yesterday evening about leaving Stonewylde. Miranda hadn't decided yet and Sylvie thought privately her mother was still clinging to a shred of hope that Magus would relent and say it had all been a misunderstanding. Although Miranda hadn't gone into details, Sylvie had worked out what had happened that night. Magus must've lost his temper and finally shattered her illusions, though Sylvie still found it hard to believe that Miranda had laboured under her misconceptions for so long. Hadn't she noticed how Magus was with the women who surrounded him? Had she really deluded herself into thinking he cared only for her, and didn't enjoy any of the other women who fell at his feet?

Last night Sylvie had once again argued the case for staying put. Having considered carefully, she'd decided in the end that despite her fears about the conflict to come, she just couldn't leave Stonewylde. The alternative was too terrible to contemplate. Back in the Outside World, with schools, shops, traffic, pollution, grimy people scurrying about their business – how would she ever fit into that sort of society after reconnecting with nature at Stonewylde? She remembered all her old medical problems, those awful allergies and sensitivities to the modern, toxic world which she knew would return if she went back to the grey prison of the Outside World. She couldn't face hospitalisation again, nor the prospect of a life without the magical forces of Stonewylde. Sylvie knew she was unhappy at the moment due to the pressure of school work and her peer group's unkindness, but after the Solstice things would be different. And of course there was Yul ... As if she'd picked up on Sylvie's thoughts, Holly approached and sat beside her on the window seat.

'Wakey wakey, Sylvie – no time for napping now! It's your favourite lesson next, maths with William. He's such a good teacher, isn't he? Did you know he's my mother's cousin?'

'That figures,' muttered Sylvie. How could she ever overcome her unpopularity amongst the teachers when the whole lot of them were so inter-related and clannish?

'I do hope you've done that stats homework or he'll go mad,' smirked Holly.

Sylvie looked away and shrugged.

'Oh dear, are we a little down in the dumps today? I wonder why? Is it because Magus has abandoned you? Just when you thought you were well in there, too. That's what he does, Sylvie – takes up with someone for a while and then drops them. You're not so special after all, are you? And nothing from Yul either. Are you fretting under your house arrest? It'd drive me mad, not being able to go out.'

'Go away, Holly.'

'Still upset about Yul kissing me?' she taunted. 'It's not long till our Rite of Adulthood and I'm *so* excited about that.'

'You really haven't got a clue, have you Holly? You've no idea what's going to happen at the Winter Solstice.'

'Why? What is going to happen, Miss Know-it-all?'

'Never mind,' said Sylvie wearily, gathering her books and files and standing up. She looked down at Holly, pretty and immaculately turned out as ever. The girl smiled nastily up at her, spitefulness animating her features.

'The only thing that's going to happen is I shall celebrate my coming of age with Yul. I'll think of you, Miss Frumpy, as we drink the special mead and eat the ceremony cakes. I'll toast you as we lie together on the rabbit-fur rugs next to the Solstice bonfire to keep ourselves warm while we make love.'

She rose too, barely reaching Sylvie's chin. Her brown eyes raked Sylvie from head to toe.

'How can you bear to be seen looking like that, Sylvie? I'd lock myself in my room if I looked such a tatty mess. It's no wonder Magus has lost interest – he's a man of style and expensive tastes and you look even worse than the Village girls. At least their clothes fit.'

'Alright, let's move on to revising standard index notation,' said William, scribbling a jumble of numbers on the board. 'Sylvie, come up and convert this number to standard index form please. This is an easy example to start us off, so I'm sure even you'll have no trouble.'

Sylvie stood before the white board, the marker pen in her hand and her back to the group of students who sat around the couple of large tables. She felt their gleeful anticipation and knew that William was going to have fun with her today. He'd never be allowed to get away with this victimisation at any school in the Outside World but could behave how he liked here. She gazed blankly at the squiggles on the board's shiny surface; they meant absolutely nothing to her at all. She'd missed this teaching too and the whole topic was a complete mystery to her.

'Convert the number to standard index form,' repeated William. 'For crying out loud, girl, just have a try! We learn through our mistakes, so take a risk! If you're wrong I'll show you where to put it right.'

But it wasn't as simple as that. If she was wrong he'd spend the rest of the lesson referring back to her mistake until she wanted to die with humiliation. Besides, even having a try was beyond her now; standing up here in front of everyone, her mind had gone completely blank with panic. She stood with her face close to the board, horribly conscious of her awful floral cotton skirt and woolly socks, and closed her eyes in despair. William must've made some kind of gesture behind her back, for the others students burst out laughing simultaneously.

'I don't know how to do it,' said Sylvie woodenly. 'I don't have the faintest idea. I missed this work when you covered it.'

'Of course! How silly of me to have forgotten that. Every single time we turn to a new topic for revision – and I stress the word *revision* – you trot out the same lame excuse.'

'I've tried to study it by myself,' she said, still with her back to the class.

'Clearly without success.'

'I asked for some help last week!' she burst out, turning to him with flaming cheeks. 'And you said you didn't have time!'

'I've already taught this topic and I'm not teaching it again!' he retorted. 'Why should *you* be entitled to special one-to-one teaching? You should've been capable of picking it up from the textbook anyway. But everything we do seems beyond you, doesn't it, Sylvie? Is there anything in the mathematics syllabus you do know?'

'Probably not,' she said bitterly, turning to go back to her seat.

'Not so fast! Stay where you are, young lady, and let's have a little try, shall we? Let's see if there's any aspect of mathematics where you feel you might have just the slightest inkling of understanding.'

Sylvie stood with her head bowed, feeling the sharp stabs of many pairs of bright eyes watching avidly, feeding on her distress. This was pack hunting at its most effective, and her heart thumped with anger. She was tempted to hurl the whiteboard marker pen at William's sneering face.

'Telling the time?' called out Holly, flicking back her hair. 'Adding up? Counting?'

There was another burst of laughter.

'Now, now, Holly, let's not be unkind,' said William. 'I do hope you're not implying that poor Sylvie would be better off down in the Village School with the dullards! How about some simple, basic—'

The door opened and Hazel looked in.

'Excuse me,' she said. 'Magus wants to see Sylvie straight away.'

Sylvie had never imagined the summons could bring such relief. Tight-lipped, she gathered her things and stumbled from the room, chased out by whispered barbs from Holly and her friends. William simply glared, robbed of his victim, and instructed the class to start the revision exercise.

'Why does he want to see me now?' asked Sylvie as they crossed the entrance hall and headed for the great staircase. Hazel shrugged.

'I've no idea. He hasn't seen anyone for over a week now, not even me. I'm seriously concerned for his health. He called me in just now and asked for some anti-depressants. Then he asked me to fetch you.'

They climbed the stairs and Hazel paused, looking hard at Sylvie.

'I'm counting on you to do something to help him, and make sure you don't upset him. I've never seen Magus like this before and I'm worried. Try to get him to eat if you can – he's lost a lot of weight by the look of him.'

They stood before the stone arch leading into Magus' apartments and Hazel knocked quietly on the oak door, then left Sylvie to face the man alone.

Magus' aromatic fragrance filled the huge room, enveloping Sylvie as she stepped across the thick carpet. A fire crackled in the arched stone hearth and pale sunlight filtered through the diamond-paned windows. He lay on the leather sofa before the fire, a silk cushion beneath his head and cashmere rug draped over him. He looked vulnerable and exhausted. Gone were the arrogance and power. His face was hollowed, the cheekbones sharp, and he looked more like Yul than ever. There were dark shadows under his eyes and the lines around his mouth were etched deeper. Magus looked like a man who'd been suffering, a man in torment. He smiled slightly, his deep brown eyes soft as she approached. He raised his arms weakly to pull her down for a light kiss on the cheek. Then he indicated an armchair nearby where the late November sunlight fell onto her face.

He gazed at her until she became uncomfortable.

'I'm sorry to hear you've been ill,' she said finally to break the silence. He grimaced.

'Now I know how you feel after the moondancing,' he said. 'I'm so weak I haven't even been able to eat.'

'But why? What's wrong with you?'

He shrugged and his dark eyes locked into hers.

'I need your moon magic, Sylvie. You promised to come with me but you let me down. And now I'm like this.'

'I'm sorry,' she whispered. 'I didn't mean to.'

She wondered if he saw through her. All she could think about was the lock of hair and the Dark Moon spell. She hadn't fully believed in it before, but seeing this fragile-looking man lying so pathetically on the sofa in his pyjamas, she realised that Mother Heggy had done it again. This was the outcome of her previous visit to these chambers and nothing to do with her lack of moondancing for him. He was just using it as an excuse to make her feel guilty and had no idea of the truth behind his frailty.

'You look beautiful this morning, Sylvie.'

She shook her head, wanting none of his compliments.

'I was just told I look a tatty mess.'

He raised an eyebrow at this.

'Your hair shines in the sunlight like spun silver and I've never seen anyone more exquisite. I can feel my spirits lifting. Why didn't I send for you before?'

He rose shakily from the sofa and bent to throw a couple of logs on the fire. In his dark silk pyjamas he looked lean and starved, the open neckline revealing collarbones and hollows not normally visible. He crouched by the hearth and looked up into her eyes. The arrogance may have gone but the charisma remained, deepened by pathos.

'I need some company, Sylvie. Will you stay for a little while and talk with me? Cheer me up?'

'Of course, especially given the alternative.'

He lay back down on the sofa again, shutting his eyes momentarily as if in pain.

'Which is?'

187

'Maths with William. I try hard but I'm not doing so well at the moment.'

He nodded sympathetically.

'Forget maths then and stay here with me.'

He closed his eyes again weakly and Sylvie glanced around the enormous room in fascination, not having fully appreciated the luxury of it on her last furtive visit. The Tudor setting was superb, infinitely grander than her own smaller rooms, and Magus had surrounded himself with beautiful things. She was over-awed by the splendour and opulence, such a contrast to Clip's mediaeval tower with its shabby furnishings and strange collection of ethnic objects.

'How did you get that nasty bruise on your forehead?'

He was watching her as she gazed around.

'Oh ... it was ... it was an accident.'

'I see – it looks nasty. And how's your poor mother?'

'Very depressed.'

He put a hand to his temple and groaned.

'I don't think she'll ever forgive me for losing my temper like that. I really did shout at her, but I was so angry with her for letting you go wandering off into the night when you were moongazy. You know how dangerous it is and I was furious at her negligence. She only thinks of the baby and nothing of you. But I've been too ill since to go back and try to make amends with her.'

'She looks as awful as you do.'

'Poor Miranda. She always did have unrealistic expectations about our relationship, even though I never pretended anything otherwise.'

Sylvie nodded at this, for it was perfectly true.

'I was angry with her but I never wanted to hurt her. I'd like to make it up, but if her heart's set against me I doubt she'd listen to me now. My temper's always been my downfall.'

He shook his head ruefully and, despite herself, Sylvie felt some sympathy for him. He'd lost so much weight and he looked depressed and rather tragic.

'Can I get you anything?' she asked. 'Would you like a drink?'

'Yes, that'd be nice. There's a fridge over there, behind the panelling. A glass of water please, and do have something yourself if you like.'

She busied herself at the fridge and brought him over a glass of iced water. He took it from her outstretched hand, but then grasped her fingers.

'Sylvie! What on earth is this?'

He stared at her wrist. The baggy cardigan sleeve had fallen back and the shrunken jumper beneath failed to cover her wrist. He took hold of the other one and examined that too, peeling her sleeves back. He gently traced the deep black bruising around her slim wrists, all the way from the base of her palms up her arms to the elbows.

'This is terrible! What happened?'

She squirmed, not knowing what to say and feeling suddenly tearful at this unexpected sympathy.

'Who's done this to you? Who was it?'

'I ... I don't know.'

'Come on, Sylvie, you don't get injuries like this without knowing how. It must've been terribly painful. When did it happen?'

'On the night of the Moon Fullness.'

'Just as I said! You go wandering off and you get hurt. But this was no accident, was it? These are rope marks – someone tied you up, didn't they?'

She nodded, not wanting to get Yul into trouble but knowing there was no other rational explanation for the pattern of bruising.

'And it was Yul! Wasn't it?'

She nodded again. Magus shook his head, his face turning even paler. She looked into his eyes fearfully. They glittered with fury.

'How dare he treat you like this? What an awful thing to do to someone!'

'Oh no,' she said quickly, 'it wasn't like that. I think he was trying to protect me.'

'Protect you? From what?'

'From ... from you. From going up to Mooncliffe with you.'

The words sounded hollow even though she longed to believe them. Magus' face was a mask of anger and concern, and Sylvie realised then just how little sympathy or real care she'd been shown for so long. And especially not from her own mother, who couldn't seem to care less any more, being so wrapped up in herself. Magus' dark eyes softened as he saw her lips trembling, fighting to hold back the tears.

'But why? You wanted to come up there with me, didn't you? I remember you saying you'd give me your magic willingly. Didn't you?'

'Yes, but then you made Clip hypnotise me!' she said. 'And you promised you wouldn't.'

'Not really hypnotise, Sylvie, just suggestions to help ease the discomfort for you. And anyway, that's not the point. How dare that boy tie you up to prevent you coming to me! I can't bear to think of it – you poor little soul.'

He shook his head in disbelief and again, Sylvie felt the urge to sob her heart out at this unexpected sympathy.

'And I suppose the bruise on your head was caused by him too? Sacred Mother, but he's brutal! Any other injuries I should know about?'

He saw her glance down involuntarily at her leg.

'Go on, show me.'

Feeling embarrassed, she pulled up the cotton skirt slightly and rolled down her long woolly sock to show him the scabbed scraping all the way down from thigh to ankle. Magus gave a low whistle and looked at her in distress.

'I won't have Village boys – or anyone, for that matter – doing this and getting away with it. I shall punish him as soon as I'm up and about again, rest assured.'

'No, Magus, please don't! He didn't mean to, I know he didn't!'

'So how did he inflict that horrible injury all down your leg?'

'He put me in ... a sort of cage, I think.'

'WHAT? He imprisoned you *as well* as tying you up? Is there anything else the boy did to you that I ought to be aware of?'

'No, and it's not how you're making it out to be. He wouldn't hurt me deliberately.'

As she said it, Sylvie had a flash of memory: Yul shoving her hard along the path and bundling her roughly into the tree cage. Her words rang false in her ears. He may've been acting to protect her, but Yul had hurt her in anger and it had been intentional. Magus shook his head and frowned, picking up on her confusion.

'I know you feel weak after moondancing for me, Sylvie, but I'd never hurt you like this, you know that. Now can you see why I warned you away from him? I always said he was too rough for you.'

'But I—'

'There's something I should show you, Sylvie, something that'll help you understand why I've forbidden you to have anything to do with him. Maybe then you'll believe me when I tell you that boy is brutal and dangerous. But I'm too ill to deal with it now and we'll talk about it later.'

'Of course. I'm sorry if I've tired you.'

He looked very pale and she stood, ready to leave. Feebly he reached up and touched the hem of her skirt.

'It's just so distressing for me to see someone as special and delicate as you knocked about by a Village lout like him. I'm exhausted, Sylvie ... could you leave me to rest?'

'I do hope you feel better soon,' she said, turning to go. He still had hold of her hem and his dark eyes were pleading.

'Would you come back this evening to have supper with me? I can't face eating downstairs in the Dining Hall and I've been off my food for days now. But if you were here, Sylvie, I may discover my appetite again. Would you mind?'

Sylvie nodded. How could she possibly refuse such a request?

11

When she returned that evening to have supper with Magus, Sylvie found him dressed casually in one of the loose white linen Village shirts and dark trousers, looking as strained and pale as he'd done earlier. Supper arrived via the dumb waiter, concealed in the wooden panelling of the interior wall.

'I'm sorry, Sylvie, I feel too weak to serve you and I really can't do with the bother of summoning someone. Would you do the honours?'

She found an ornate wooden trolley by the small service-lift in the wall, and loaded the hot dishes and plates onto it. Then she wheeled the antique trolley over to the dining table in its intimate alcove, already laid with linen, silver and candles, and served them both. The light meal was delicious but Magus only toyed with his food. Sylvie found it ironic that their roles had been reversed in this way; she was now the one urging him to eat more. She sympathised with him, talking of how she'd suffered from his force-feeding, and he apologised.

'I'll never do that again,' he promised. 'I had no idea how awful it is to eat when you're feeling so delicate. I only wanted to build you up so the moondancing wasn't so debilitating for you. I'm sorry, Sylvie, truly sorry for anything I've done to make you suffer. You should be treated like a princess.'

Afterwards Sylvie cleared the dishes back into the dumb waiter and pressed the switch for the lift to descend to the floor below, whilst Magus switched on the huge television screen.

'Come and sit next to me,' he said, patting the soft leather sofa. 'I mentioned that I wanted to show you something. This is distressing and I'm sorry to break the pleasant mood but I think you should see it. Your injuries have upset me a great deal.'

'Really, Magus, I'm absolutely fine,' she protested, sitting down next to him at a safe distance. She felt very strange being alone like this with him, although he was as weak as a kitten and not threatening or overbearing at all.

'I'm sorry, but nobody at Stonewylde can behave the way Yul did with impunity. You may remember I banished Buzz because of what he did to you? That Village boy and the way he's abused you have been preying on my mind all afternoon. You need to understand why I've been so adamant, ever since you arrived, about your having no contact with him. I know you always thought I was being high-handed, Sylvie, when I forbade you to fraternise with him. But you really don't know the full picture. That's my fault – I should've told you more, but I'm just not used to having to explain myself. I'm so sorry, Sylvie, that you've been assaulted twice and on both occasions by my sons. I'm ashamed to have fathered such monsters.'

Sylvie glanced at him, noticing his serious expression and the way his hands shook slightly. She felt a sudden rush of pity for him – this was a different man to the golden god-like figure who demanded obedience so forcefully. This Magus was quiet and almost humble, clearly suffering in his weakened state.

'These are photos of Buzz,' he continued, 'taken after his fight with Yul in August. I'm sure you remember the incident well, as it wasn't long after this that Buzz assaulted you. Buzz was admitted to the hospital wing and Hazel photographed his injuries, recording these images almost daily as he began to heal. I wanted a record of Yul's brutality because it was so very shocking.'

'I heard that Yul was defending his sister.'

'Just so – and one can understand that of course.'

'So why take photos? I don't understand.'

'Because at that point I wasn't intending to punish Buzz further – Yul had already done that very thoroughly, as you'll see. Buzz had only kissed the Village girl and fumbled about with her blouse – nothing more had taken place, by the girl's own admission. Yet the Villagers were up in arms about it and wanted Buzz whipped or even banished. I'd hoped that by showing them these photos of Buzz's injuries, they'd see that he'd had punishment enough for his misdemeanour. It wasn't until he also attacked you that I realised he'd intended to take it further with the Village girl too. That young man had no idea about self-control or how he should conduct himself.'

Magus paused, the control in his hand and regarded Sylvie steadily.

'Anyway, now perhaps it's lucky I have this record to show you. I want you to look carefully, Sylvie, however upsetting it is. I want you to see what sort of a beast lies beneath Yul's boyish charm. Remember that Buzz was much larger and heavier than him. Try to imagine the sheer viciousness and violence of this attack, to cause such uncalled-for damage. Yul isn't normal, that's for sure. He has the brutality of someone with a severe personality disorder and he fought like someone mentally unhinged. Buzz never had a chance to fight back, that's how sudden and ferocious Yul's attack was. Yul was totally unharmed in the fight, other than his hands, and you'll see only too clearly why they were damaged.'

On the enormous screen that showed everything in great detail, Sylvie watched a progression of the most terrible series of injuries she'd ever seen. Hazel had catalogued Buzz's suffering meticulously and Sylvie looked at each photo in horrified fascination. She saw how the passage of time had created an animation of vivid discoloration and grotesque swelling, before finally beginning to heal the damage. She'd had no idea of the extent of Buzz's disfigurement, only seeing him a month later when many of the visible injuries had all but healed.

She was sickened at the sight of his face: the eyes puffed-up like dark plums, his nose bent and swollen, his mouth looking like a piece of raw meat. His body was mottled with a camouflage pattern of deep bruising that passed through every shade before eventually fading to a dull, dirty yellow. The bruising was all over his torso, revealing injuries to his ribs and on his back, especially around his kidneys. Finally Sylvie could stand no more and turned away in distress. Magus switched off the slide show before it moved on to another injury and looked into her eyes.

'Do you understand a little better now, and appreciate why your injuries have upset me so much? They're nothing compared to Buzz's, but nevertheless they indicate that Yul has no qualms about hurting you too, if he thinks it warranted. Has he done anything else to you, Sylvie?'

She swallowed, wanting to defend Yul but feeling unable to, given the appalling photos she'd just seen. She couldn't believe he'd deliberately inflicted such dreadful damage on another person.

'My upper arms and ribcage are quite painful too. He pinned me to the ground and crushed me, I think. I don't remember it too well; the moon was close to rising and I was frantic. I'm scraped all down the side of my body, not just my leg. And he gagged me. My mouth was sore for a while, although there weren't any marks. That's all, I think.'

Magus nodded slowly.

'And what about ... how can I put this ... in passion? Has he done anything to violate you? Anything of a sexual nature.'

Sylvie blushed scarlet. She thought of their kisses, of the increasing desire she felt for him, and recalled the tentative caresses they'd shared. She remembered the night when he'd come to her bedroom and pulled her down on top of him on her bed and she'd wanted him so badly it hurt. But she shook her head, avoiding Magus' eye. Yul had never done anything she hadn't wanted; he'd always been the one to hold back when her emotions overwhelmed her natural reticence.

'I can see that something has gone on between you,' said Magus quietly, shaking his head sadly. 'I do hope it hasn't gone too far, Sylvie – that would be terrible, for more reasons than I can say at this point.'

'No,' she whispered, horribly embarrassed. 'Nothing much has happened. And ... Yul has never made me do anything I didn't want to.'

'Yes, I imagine you believe it was all mutual and Yul wasn't forcing himself on you. Maybe it was, but just remember the power of the Earth Magic. I know only too well the effect it has, not only on the recipient but on all who come into contact with it. It's extremely powerful stuff, the very essence of Stonewylde and nature's wild, procreative forces. Yul will use the Earth Magic to overcome any shyness or reluctance you may feel. I speak from experience here, Sylvie. I've never been turned down by a woman, ever. In fact I often turn them away. You've seen how your mother behaved with me. Was she ever like that before, with anyone else?'

Sylvie shook her head, knowing that what he said was true. The change in Miranda had been profound and had happened almost overnight.

'I'm not fool enough to imagine it's just my charm and good looks that excite women,' Magus continued. 'I know it's the Earth Magic and it can almost be a curse at times, attracting too much adoration and attention. So just remember that with Yul. Since he's stolen my Earth Magic, he has access to all that sexual energy and if he made any advances you'd find him impossible to resist.'

Sylvie swallowed hard at this, again knowing it was true. She'd felt the compelling force in Yul after the ceremonies and his rituals at sunrise and sunset. But surely there was more to it than that? He loved her and wanted her so much, and that was nothing to do with any green magic of Stonewylde. She felt the same about him and had done since before he started to receive the Earth Magic. She shook her head and turned away from Magus, staring into the blazing fire. He got up slowly and turned off the screen. Pouring them both a small glass of mead, he sat quietly next to her on the sofa whilst they sipped at it.

'I'm sorry, Sylvie. I've upset you. But you need to be in possession of the facts. Go and think about it tonight. Will you visit me again tomorrow if I ask for you? I feel so much better for seeing you today, and at last I've managed to eat something. I'm feeling stronger already and I'm grateful to you. Thank you for helping me like this.'

Back in her room, Sylvie found it impossible to concentrate on her pile of homework, and the angry notes from teachers about the afternoon's missed lessons upset her. The mead and heat of the fire had made her body relax, but her mind was reeling with the horrific images she'd seen on the screen and Magus' words of warning about Yul's passion. Eventually she pushed the books away, unable to concentrate, and went to bed. She moved about restlessly for hours as sleep eluded her. She was worried that Magus was manipulating her, and more worried that he spoke the truth. If only she could see Yul and talk to him.

Magus was as gentle and charming again the next day, sending for her mid-morning during a history lesson. Holly hissed with spite as Sylvie bundled up her things and left the school room. She followed Martin up the stairs, not dreading the encounter as she'd done the previous day, but still wary of Magus and any further revelations he might make today. She needn't have worried. He seemed a little brighter and they ate lunch together at the dining table looking out over the grounds. He reminisced about his early days of leadership at Stonewylde and some of the difficulties he'd faced trying to set right the years of neglect. She felt a grudging respect for him as she understood more fully what he'd achieved as magus.

'Stonewylde is my life,' he said softly, sipping at his glass of water as the meal lay largely untouched on his plate. 'I'd never voluntarily give up my guardianship of the place.'

'Can't you manage a little more of your food?' Sylvie asked, not wanting to discuss anything to do with the forthcoming conflict. Magus was still pale and drawn and his eyes were weary. His hands trembled as he pushed the plate away and she felt a pang of pity for him. The sun glinted suddenly on his blond hair and she almost choked as an image of the tiny lock of child's hair rose unbidden into her mind. She wondered if there was any way to reverse Mother Heggy's awful spell. It was one thing going along with all the talk of ousting Magus, but quite another to see the weakness and suffering of the man himself as he sat quietly in the sunlight, talking of his hopes and dreams for Stonewylde.

'No, I can't,' he said. 'I can't face it.'

He lay on the sofa after lunch and closed his eyes. Sylvie sat in an armchair fidgeting, worried about her lessons. It was maths again this afternoon and she didn't want to arrive halfway through. Not after leaving early yesterday before William had finished his daily bout of mortification. He'd be angry enough without her being late today, and she hadn't managed to finish the homework last night either. She wondered if she should creep off to the lesson now, whilst Magus slept.

'Do you want to go, Sylvie?' he asked, opening his eyes.

'Oh, I didn't mean to disturb you. I'm just worried about my classes this afternoon. If I don't go now I'm going to be late and I'm in enough trouble as it is.'

'What have you got next?'

'Maths.'

'Would you rather go to maths or stay here with me?'

She laughed harshly at this.

'I'd rather walk across hot coals than go to maths!'

'It's that bad? Stay with me, then. I feel much better when you're here. I'm so weak since that terrible last Moon Fullness when Yul prevented you from helping me like you'd promised. Perhaps I'm picking up some of your energy now?'

'I don't think it works like that,' she said doubtfully. 'It's not like the Earth Magic.'

'Then maybe it's just your presence. Whatever the cause, I don't feel so terribly depressed when you're here. Would you mind staying?'

She needed little persuasion to miss another session on standard index form, or whatever new horror William might humiliate her with. She spent a peaceful afternoon sitting on the long sofa working on an essay for the history lesson she'd missed that morning, whilst Magus rested beside her. He lay with his head on a cushion against her leg, saying that being close to her helped his recovery. He was so weak and listless that he no longer seemed a threat, and she found some comfort in knowing she was helping him; anything to lessen her guilt over the spell.

As the afternoon grew dark she fed the fire and lit the lamps, pulling the huge oak shutters across the long expanse of windows. It was cosy in the great room and Magus watched her moving quietly about.

'I like you being here with me, Sylvie,' he said. 'I'm feeling much better. Would you mind missing school for a few days?'

She came over and sat down on the floor, hugging her knees and gazing into the fire.

'Would I mind missing school?' She laughed bitterly at this. 'I hate school! Of course I wouldn't mind – you're the one who was so cross about my absences and my lack of progress.'

He chuckled.

'Yes, I was, because I thought you were malingering. But now I know better. Now I'd be a hypocrite to chastise you for taking to your bed for a week and not eating – it's exactly what I've done. Have you caught up with the schoolwork yet? I heard you'd been putting in a lot of effort recently and I saw how diligently you worked this afternoon.'

She shook her head, feeling a welling up of the despair that any thought of school inspired.

'I've tried so hard. I've worked and worked, but there are so many gaps. It's not just since I started moondancing for you – I missed almost two years of school in London because of the bullying, my illness and all the time in hospital. I've tried to study by myself and fill in the gaps but there are so many, and none of the teachers have been very supportive or offered any extra help, even when I've asked. I guess they can't be bothered with someone who's just not worth the effort.' Her voice started to crack and she swallowed hard. 'I hadn't realised how little I knew until all this revision started. I'm so stupid and slow and I'd always thought I was alright.'

'Don't be silly, Sylvie – you're not stupid at all.'

'Well that's how the teachers have made me feel – completely useless. And the others, Holly and her gang, they tease me about it and laugh every time I can't answer a question or get a poor mark in a test. I can't . . .'

To her dismay she burst into tears, bowing her head over her knees and sobbing. Magus leant over to stroke her hair.

'Don't cry, Sylvie,' he said gently. 'It's really not the end of the world. It's only school work.'

'But I'm *useless*!' she sobbed. 'I can't do anything. They all laugh at me, William picks on me and I can't bear it any longer!'

The frustration and misery of the last few weeks and the pressure of all the work came flooding out and she couldn't stop crying. Magus slid down onto the thick, velvety rug next to her, sitting with his back against the sofa. He put an arm around her shaking shoulders and pulled her in close to him, enfolding her in soft linen and heavy scent. Gradually she relaxed into his embrace and felt the unique comfort of being held by someone big and strong. He gave her a clean handkerchief and stroked her hair gently, a small smile on his lips.

'Sylvie, calm down a minute and listen to me. Maybe I can help – listen.'

She managed to stop crying and sat quietly, shaken by the occasional gasping sob.

'If you like, I can make a call to your tutor who I imagine will be in his room changing for dinner. I can tell him that we've decided to defer your final year of secondary education. You could take some time off lessons now and catch up with everything you've missed, and then start this year again next September. You'd still have a lot of work to do, but it would give you a chance to really get to grips with everything you've missed and I'm sure you'd achieve much better results, even if they are a year late. You've been very ill and it's entirely acceptable to defer your exams and course-work. Would you like me to do that?'

She stared at him incredulously, hope flaring inside her.

'Won't the teachers mind? Are you allowed to do that?' she gasped, her throat constricted with disbelief.

'Sylvie, I can do anything I want. I'm in charge here, not the teachers – they work for me. Shall I make that call?'

She nodded, unable to believe that at a single stroke he could remove the relentless and crushing stress that had blighted her life since Samhain.

'But Sylvie, there's one condition.'

'Yes?'

'You'll keep me company until I'm better again. You'll look after me and come here every day to cheer me up and help me get well. Is that a deal?'

She smiled, sniffing and gulping back the tears, her heart soaring with relief. She nodded again happily and he bent to kiss her forehead.

'Silly thing,' he said fondly. 'If you'd only told me how much you were suffering I could've done this long ago. I want you to be happy, Sylvie, and I'll do whatever I can to make it happen. You've been so good to me the past couple of days and I won't forget it.'

Martin stoked up the fire and turned to his master, who sat at his desk tapping away at a keyboard.

'Are you ready for that steak now, sir?'

'Is she back in her room?'

'Yes, sir, all tucked up for the night, I'd imagine.'

'Fine, send the food up then. Goddess, but it's been a long haul! A decent bottle of wine too. And Martin . . .'

'Yes sir?'

'When I've finished eating, bring me a woman.'

'Anyone in particular, sir? The young doctor perhaps?'

'No,' he frowned. 'She'll talk and fuss too much. She thinks I'm seriously ill. No Hallfolk – it could get back to Sylvie. Get me a Village girl, someone fresh.'

'Very good, sir. Anything else? Shall I wait up and take the girl back later?'

'No . . . no, I'll keep her till the morning. Be ready to escort her down the back stairs and away first thing though, as Sylvie will be joining me for breakfast tomorrow.'

Martin smiled and plumped up the cushions along the sofa.

'Enjoy your evening, sir.'

'I'm sure I will, Martin. I've earned it. This past week of abstinence has been hell.'

'You can't just miss a year of school like that!' said Miranda angrily.

'Not miss it, Mum – defer it, he said. I'll go back and do this year again next September.'

'But I don't want you to do that! Magus should've asked me first.'

'I don't think he wants to speak to you,' said Sylvie, feeling a prickle of guilt at the lie. Surely it was kinder to let her mother recover from her infatuation and broken heart – seeing Magus at this point would only stir it all up again. Sylvie was sure Magus would never love her, not in the way Miranda wanted. Miranda's face fell and she looked down at her knitting.

'How dare he make this decision and not consult me? I—'

'Please, Mum, don't get funny about it. I can't catch up, and this way I'll get better results when I do take my exams.'

'And what if we leave?'

'Come on, Mum, you know we can't leave. Anyway, my schooling would be even worse then. How could I start at a new school now, halfway through my final year? Please, don't make a fuss. I feel so relieved. It's like a great weight has been lifted suddenly and I can suddenly stand up straight again.'

'It just annoys me that he thinks he can do this without even asking me. I'm your mother after all! What were you doing in his room anyway? Did he send for you?'

Sylvie looked away guiltily.

'I've been spending a bit of time there over the past couple of days. Magus has been ill and he asked me to keep him company.'

Miranda swallowed, keeping her head down and trying to hide the sudden violent resentment she felt towards her daughter. When she looked up again, Sylvie was sorting out her school books and folders and putting them tidily into the book shelf in their sitting room, her eyes shining with happiness.

'I don't know what he's playing at,' Miranda said slowly, 'but be very careful, Sylvie. Whatever you do, don't be fooled by him the way I was.'

'Mum, I've always known what he's like. You were blind to it, not me. Remember the arguments we used to have about him? When I told you there was another side to him and you wouldn't believe me? I don't trust him at all, but he's been very sweet the last few days and it won't do any harm to spend time with him.'

Miranda eyed her sourly and went back to her knitting with renewed vigour.

Sylvie was relieved when there was a knock on their door the next morning and she found a maid standing outside with a pile of clean laundry. It was Rowan, the girl who'd been the May Queen at Beltane all those months ago. Like Miranda she was now quite heavily pregnant, but unlike the dreary and embittered older woman, Rowan glowed with vitality and ripeness. Sylvie smiled tentatively but Rowan refused to meet her eye.

'Thank you,' said Sylvie. 'I'd been hoping these would come back soon. I've got nothing else to wear. '

The new black trousers and jumper were the only things that fitted her properly and she'd wanted to wear them for days. Magus noticed the difference too, when she joined him for breakfast, his eyes following her about the room. The slim black outfit set her figure off perfectly and her hair shone in a silver cloud almost down to her waist. Sylvie sensed a change in him today. His eyes sparkled and glowed with some of the old lazy charm. As she brought the plates of croissants and fruit to the table, he caught hold of her hand and examined her wrists again.

'Still there, I see.'

'Bruises always take ages to fade on me,' she said, looking into his dark eyes. 'But they don't hurt as much anymore and my ribs are fine now.'

'Good,' he said. 'I don't like to see his marks on you. Come and sit down so we can eat – I feel ravenous today.'

She watched in bemusement as he consumed a couple of croissants and a bowl of fruit salad in quick succession.

'Your appetite's come back!' she said. 'You look so much better today.'

'It's because you're here with me,' he said, smiling across the table at her. 'I feel infinitely better. What power you have, Sylvie, to cure someone just with your presence.'

She frowned at this, not convinced.

'You seem different today,' she said. 'There's something else . . . Did you get a good night's sleep?'

His face split into a grin and he looked so like Yul.

'I had a wonderful night, Sylvie, absolutely wonderful.'

After breakfast he took her over to his desk and sat down with her.

'We're going to order you a new winter wardrobe,' he said. She stared at him in wonder and he laughed. 'Don't look so shocked! I said I'd buy you new clothes after the Owl Moon.'

'Yes but . . . we had a deal and I didn't moondance for you.'

'That wasn't your fault, Sylvie. I can see the pain and suffering you went through trying to escape that damn boy's clutches. You'd have danced for me if you could've, so I'll keep my side of the deal. There are several websites for department stores that offer a courier service so we can get some clothes quickly for you. And I'd like to get some decent designer things too – some really special outfits to do justice to your beauty. They may take a little longer to arrive. You'll need shoes and boots as well, and maybe some jewellery? Perfume and cosmetics? Let's go on a virtual shopping trip and see what lovely things we can find for you.'

Two hours later Sylvie sat in the window seat gazing out at the wintry sky. She couldn't believe what had happened. They'd visited several sites and Magus had urged her to choose whatever caught her fancy. At first she'd been shy, not sure if he'd approve of her taste, or what sizes and designs she should try, and not certain how much she was allowed to spend. He'd sensed her awkwardness and hugged her briefly.

'I love your lack of greed,' he'd said. 'You're not avaricious in the slightest. I've seen some of the girls here with rich parents indulging in spending frenzies that shocked even me, and I'm not renowned for my restraint when it comes to money. But you, Sylvie ... you're delightful. You make me want to buy you the earth.'

'But is it alright to order so much? This will cost a fortune.'

'Sylvie, I'm worth a fortune. I have considerable personal wealth. You remember my company in London? It's extremely successful and there's money pouring in from all sorts of ventures. I'm a rich man and I can't think of a better way of spending it than buying things for you. You're so appreciative.'

She smiled shyly at him. She'd never had money in her life, and certainly never been able to splash out on fashionable clothes. She'd always had to make do with second-hand things and any new stuff had been cheap and shoddy. This was a different world.

Magus had taken over as they shopped, realising her lack of experience when it came to serious spending. He'd picked out item after item, urging her to choose whichever colour she preferred and accessories to match. She had no idea how much money he'd spent on her, for after a while the figures meant nothing and she lost count, and Magus didn't even seem to look at the prices anyway. She felt a thrill deep in her stomach at the exhilaration of such extravagance. When they'd finally finished, they stood up and he'd taken her hands in his, gazing down into her moonstone eyes.

'You've given me a lot of pleasure this morning,' he said softly.

'No ... no, you've been the kind one. Thank you!' she smiled. 'Thank you, thank you!'

He chuckled and held her close in a brief hug, kissing the top of her head in a fatherly way.

'This is just the beginning,' he said. 'Your life is going to change so much, my moongazy girl. I want to spoil you, pamper you, indulge your every whim!'

She giggled at this.

'No, Sylvie, I mean it. You know how desperately I need your moon magic, how you alone can give me what I crave. And in return, you'll never want for anything. Every month you'll dance for me on the rock and you'll see what a generous and grateful man I can be. You'll be my princess and everyone will know how special you are. They'll see exactly just how much you mean to me.'

Now she sat on the window seat as they waited for lunch and her heart began to sink. She'd been caught up in the excitement of buying beautiful new clothes, things that would make Holly and her gang green with envy, but the meaning of Magus' words now trickled through her self-delusion. He'd spoken as if she'd be with him for ever, as if they'd be living here at the Hall with their whole future spread before them. A future patterned by the thirteen full moons when she'd go up to Mooncliffe willingly and stand on that rock, pain shooting through her body as the stones drank her magic.

Maybe Magus was imagining she'd get used to it. And maybe over time he'd only keep her there long enough to feed him what he needed, with no extra stones to fill. It was a dream ... but a dream that couldn't exist after the Solstice. That knowledge sliced through the fantasy he'd created. He had no idea what Yul had planned for him in less than three weeks' time.

Sylvie still didn't trust Magus but realised she was warming to him. He'd treated her very kindly over the past few days, just as he'd treated her when she first came to Stonewylde. He could be a gentle and congenial person when he wanted to, and she remembered how he'd healed her in the woods, restoring her health and probably saving her life. How could she repay him now by playing a part in this conflict? Even by keeping quiet she was helping to bring about his downfall.

She thought of Yul, and realised it was the first time she'd done so today. If she warned Magus what was to come, what would happen to Yul? Would Magus really kill him, as Yul believed? It was impossible to imagine this generous man setting out to murder his own son in cold blood – surely Yul must be mistaken. It was true, she knew, that Magus hated him and wouldn't tolerate Yul's challenge to his supremacy. But maybe she could negotiate between them, help them come to some arrangement? She'd give Magus her moon magic every month and he'd leave Yul alone and allow them to see each other. She needed to speak to Yul and try to sort this out.

Magus sensed her dejection, surprising after the excitement of the shopping spree, and after lunch decided they needed some fresh air. He told her to fetch her cloak and helped fasten the clasp around her neck, releasing her great swathe of hair from beneath it. He let it slip through his fingers in silky strands. His eyes were bright as he gazed down at her.

'You are lovely,' he murmured, his eyes roaming her face.

She felt a pang as she wore the scarlet cloak remembering the last time when she and Yul were together; she wondered what he was doing now. Magus took her arm in his and they went downstairs side by side. Several people in the entrance hall looked up at the striking pair descending the great stairs and Sylvie was gratified to see that one of them was Rainbow; this would now get back to Holly. Hazel was there too and she greeted them at the foot of the stairs.

'You're better!' she exclaimed, looking up at Magus with a twisted half smile. Sylvie felt sympathy for the doctor; her eyes held the same expression that her mother's had, and it could only lead to heartache.

'I am indeed,' he smiled, putting an arm round Sylvie's shoulders. 'All thanks to this little moon goddess.'

Hazel's eyes followed them as they swept past her, and Sylvie felt the young doctor's pain.

They went into the formal garden with its gravel paths, clipped yews and stone statues. The December sky was like lead and a chilly wind flicked at them, stinging their cheeks and eyes. Magus had walked with her here before, when he was being so hard on her, but the atmosphere between them today was very different.

'I should've brought my gloves!' said Sylvie, and Magus took

207

one of her hands in his. He began to tell her the history of this garden and formal gardens in general. He talked of the Renaissance ideology, of the concept of imposing order and symmetry on the chaos of nature, and was eloquent and knowledgeable. She listened to his lively conversation and found herself wondering if it would pall after a while, living with someone so clever, or whether it would always be entertaining and stimulating.

'Of course, you'd have to visit Italy and France to see the best examples of those Renaissance gardens. When the weather's a bit warmer, maybe March or April, we could go and visit if you like. We could spend a month or so in Europe, travelling and touring. What do you think?'

'Oh yes!' she exclaimed, completely forgetting that if Yul were successful, that would be an impossibility. 'I've never been abroad before.'

'What? Oh Sylvie, in that case, we must start soon! We'll go wherever you want, wherever takes your fancy. We'll look at the globe in my office when we get back. We can visit such wonderful places . . .'

And then, at that precise moment, surrounded by the order and symmetry of the formal Italianate garden with its raked gravel and perfect hedges, Sylvie started to think seriously about what a life with Magus would actually be like; life with a very wealthy man who could go anywhere and do anything, and wanted to share it all with her. Life with a man who could have any woman he wanted, but who believed she was unique.

Sylvie knew she had something Magus wanted more than anything else in the world. It was something he couldn't take away from her, but would have to accept in small portions every month, something he was prepared to coax from her. She knew that it was painful and debilitating to channel the moon magic for him, but would it be worth enduring that pain in order to keep a man like him in her thrall? Would it be worth the sacrifice in order to live like a princess?

12

Sylvie awoke the next morning and stretched in her bed, luxuriating in the knowledge that there were no more lessons to face for a while. The pressure was off. After weeks of being ostracised and ridiculed by her peers, nagged and censured by the adults, ignored by her mother, it was heaven to be spending time with someone who actually appreciated her company and found her delightful. She hopped out of bed eager to start the new day and wore her black outfit again, unable to bear the thought of her scruffy old clothes. Holly had been right – how had she stood looking so awful? What must Magus have thought of her floral skirts, bobbly old jumpers and woolly socks? Hopefully today the courier service would deliver some of the new things they'd ordered. Her heart jumped with excitement at the prospect and she decided to go straight to his rooms now for breakfast. After all, she must keep her side of the deal.

But as Sylvie left the bathroom and made for the door, her mother emerged from her bedroom in a dressing gown. The pregnancy, now in the last months, had suddenly become hugely apparent. The bump was enormous and Miranda had gained weight everywhere, her arms and legs puffy with extra flesh and fluid. Even her face seemed bloated, and her beautiful chestnut-red hair had become quite lank and lifeless. Gone was the sparkle and vivacity of her early pregnancy, to be replaced by a heavy dullness. Sylvie felt sorry for her. It must be awful carrying that great bulge around and feeling so ungainly.

'Are you going down to breakfast?' asked Miranda, shuffling across the sitting room in her slippers to draw the curtains. Sylvie nodded, pausing by the door, eager to be gone.

'Hold on a minute and I'll come down with you. I feel a little more able to face the world now.'

'That's good, Mum,' said Sylvie, her heart sinking. 'That's really great news. But I can't ... I'm sorry; I'm not going down to the Dining Hall. I'm having breakfast in Magus' rooms.'

Miranda frowned at her.

'Has he sent for you? I didn't hear a knock.'

'No, but ... he said he wanted me to keep him company until he's better. He's ordered me some winter clothes and that was the deal.'

'I see. So he's arranged for you to miss a whole year of school just so you can prance about in new clothes and keep him amused, has he?'

'No Mum, it's not like that. He says I've helped to make him better. I must go – I promised.'

'And what about me, Sylvie? I'd really like to have you with me as I go downstairs and face all those people again. I'm dreading their looks and comments. They must've all guessed what's happened and I feel so humiliated. I need some support – I thought you'd be happy to help me.'

Sylvie looked away guiltily. She wanted to sip fresh orange juice from crystal glass and talk with Magus; bask in his warmth and appreciation. She certainly didn't want to walk into the Dining Hall next to her heavily pregnant mother with everyone staring and sniggering. Miranda was right, gossip was rife, and Sylvie really didn't need any more aggravation. Not now that everything was so rosy.

'I'm really sorry, Mum. I've promised Magus I'll spend the next few days with him and I can't go back on that.'

'I think you've spent quite enough time with him lately – he doesn't own you. We'll send a message to say you're busy today.'

'No!'

210

'But you don't enjoy going there, surely? Not after what he's done to all of us. You, and me, and Yul.'

'Well . . . no of course not, But he isn't that bad. I mean, I know he hurt you and Yul, but he hasn't actually done anything to me.'

'What about Mooncliffe? Have you forgotten what he put you through? Clip's told me about it and it's appalling that Magus used you like that. And what about your awful weakness and illness afterwards? If that's not harming you, I don't know what is!'

'But that's not his fault really – it's what the moongaziness does to me. He tried to make it less painful for me, but—'

'Listen to yourself, Sylvie! He's got you exactly where he wants you, eating from the palm of his hand. You are so shallow! What about poor Yul? I thought you were "in love" with him. Where's your sense of loyalty?'

Sylvie felt herself flushing angrily.

'*My* sense of loyalty? Where have *you* been these last few months when I needed you? You've neglected me and ignored me, not even noticed when I was upset or frightened or badly hurt, but now you expect me to come running just because you've finally realised what a fool you were! You haven't been here for me since Beltane, Mum, so don't you *dare* pull that one on me now!

Miranda stood by the window, the morning light unflattering on her puffy face, her mouth bitter. Sylvie was torn between pity and outrage.

'Well if that's how you feel, Sylvie . . .'

'Alright then! You win – I'll go and tell Magus you said I must have breakfast with you instead.'

'No, Sylvie, only if you want to! I'm not forcing you. I thought you'd want to help me and you'd be pleased I'm ready to start picking up the pieces of my life again. I thought you hated Magus as much as we all do, but it seems I was wrong.'

'No! Well . . . yes. I mean: I've got to know him better over the last few days and he's not as horrible as I thought. He really likes me and he's actually very good company.'

'Of course he is! Why do you think I fell in love with him? I'm not a complete fool, Sylvie. You know how strong and independent I used to be and I'd never have fallen for him if he'd treated me badly from the start. Magus is charming and flattering and funny while he's still hunting, but you wait till he's got his claws into you! Then the charm and flattery evaporate and you realise just how cold and cruel he is inside. You saw it happen to me, Sylvie.'

'I know, Mum, but—'

'But you're arrogant enough to think it'll be different with you! You think you're special – that *you're* the one he'll change his ways for.'

'No, Mum, you've got it all wrong! I don't think of him in that way, not like you and all the others do. It's different, my relationship with him.'

'Oh don't make me laugh, Sylvie – of course it isn't different! You've got a crush on him and you're naïve enough to think he feels something for you. You're playing with fire, Sylvie – I've heard all about Magus now and how he operates. You're much, much too young for him and he'll chew you up and spit you out just as he has all the rest.'

'No he won't! It's not like that between us and honestly, Mum, he's different with me. He can't do enough for me and he watches me all the time, can't take his eyes off me. Not that I want anything like that, of course, but he really thinks I'm unique. He said so.'

'For God's sake, girl, you're only fifteen! What on earth do *you* have to interest a sophisticated man like him? And don't say it's your pretty face and long blond hair, please! Nubile girls are ten a penny to him and he can – and does – have any girl or woman he wants, here or anywhere else. You're not that special!'

'Oh but I am,' said Sylvie softly, stung by her mother's diatribe. 'I'm the only one who can give him what he really needs because I'm the only one who's moongazy. He'll do anything for my gift of moon magic. To Magus I'm more special than anyone else in the world.'

Miranda stared at her daughter, wanting very much to slap the smugness off her lovely face but knowing how bad a move it would be. Sylvie gave her a little smile, and slipped on her black suede boots. She flounced out of the sitting room, shutting the door just a fraction too hard.

But when Sylvie tapped on the great oak door there was no reply and she didn't like to go in without permission. Where was he? She stood by the stone arch uncertainly, unsure what to do now. She couldn't go back to her room, not after the row with her mother, nor could she go down to the Dining Hall for breakfast. She looked down over the staircase balustrade to see if he was in the entrance hall below. She saw the gleam of blond hair and thought for a moment it was him, but it was Martin who looked up. He climbed the staircase slowly, watching Sylvie.

'Were you looking for the master, miss?' he asked deferentially, his grey eyes cold.

'Yes ... I thought ... I was going to join him for breakfast.'

'Really? Did he invite you?'

'No, not exactly, but I thought ... oh well, I must have misunderstood.'

'Yes, miss, you must have. Magus breakfasted some time ago and then went riding.'

'Oh. I see.'

'I expect he'll send for you when he wants you. He's a busy man and he'll let you know when he has time for you.'

Sylvie flushed and looked down at her feet. She felt a fool. Martin gave a small smile.

'Will that be all, miss?'

His meaning was clear and she nodded, moving away from the oak door. She decided to do some work in the library, having nowhere else to go now and unsure if she was still forbidden to leave the Hall. She sat alone in the window seat in the silent room surrounded by thousands of books, bored and unmotivated now that the intense pressure to complete her coursework was off. She waited all morning for Magus to return and come looking for her. At lunch time she thought about going to the Dining Hall but again didn't want to walk in and face the huge crowd.

So Sylvie stayed where she was, her stomach rumbling, becoming ever more impatient and frustrated as time wore on. Why hadn't he sent for her? After all the time they'd spent together recently and the great fuss he'd made of her, his absence felt as if he'd stood her up. Eventually she had enough of hanging around waiting for him and decided to go upstairs and see if one of the luxurious bathrooms was free. She closed the books she'd been reading and stood up, just as the door opened and Holly walked in.

'Well, well, it's Queen Sylvie herself,' she sneered, shutting the door behind her.

'Leave me alone, Holly,' said Sylvie. The girl came over and faced her across the antique writing table, head cocked to one side. Her eyes danced with malice.

'How do you do it, Sylvie?' she asked. 'We're all dying to know. While Magus is away, you've got Yul running round after you and secret assignations under the trees in the Village Green. Then Magus comes back and suddenly you're shut up alone in his rooms all day, and he doesn't even come out for meals. And now we hear you're excused from school. What's your secret? We'd love to know.'

'I'm sure you would, but knowing wouldn't help you much, Holly. You've either got it or you haven't.'

Holly's face twisted dangerously, her cat's eyes narrowing.

'You're a smug little bitch and I hate you! We all hate you!'

'It's mutual.'

'Now that you're tied up with Magus, I think I'll pay Yul a visit. Take up where we left off under the chestnut tree.'

Sylvie shrugged, tossing her long silver hair behind her shoulders. She felt good in her svelte black outfit. Better, she could see the jealousy fizzing in Holly's eyes and smiled.

'You'll be wasting your time, Holly, because Yul doesn't want

214

to know. He only kissed you because you tried to blackmail him but it won't work again because he really can't stand you. I'm afraid he only wants me, Holly, so bad luck.'

'You wait, you cow!' hissed Holly. 'Once Magus gets bored of you I promise I'll make your life a misery.'

Sylvie laughed, heading for the door.

'Well don't hold your breath, Holly. Magus is far from bored with me. Quite the opposite in fact! It's a pity he likes to keep me all to himself up in his rooms, else you'd be able to see just how special I am to him!'

When Sylvie returned to her room Miranda was nowhere to be seen and she breathed a sigh of relief. Then she noticed a note from Magus on the table asking her to join him for dinner in his apartments at eight o'clock. She was pleased at this, but cross that she'd wasted the whole day moping about and waiting for him. She trooped off down the wing to see if the white bathroom was free.

She lay in the marble bath a little later, her head emerging from a sea of fragrant foam and her thoughts drifted as she relaxed in the hot, silky water. She remembered how she'd brought Yul here on the eve of the Summer Solstice having rescued him from the quarry. He'd been overwhelmed by the grandeur and extravagance, poor Yul. He had no idea of the luxury of the Hall or the lifestyle here and was out of place anywhere other than the Village and his woods. It wasn't his fault, of course, simply the way things were. Sylvie remembered how she'd once longed to live a simple life in the Village, wearing a home-spun shawl and carrying a wicker basket. She smiled at the notion and felt the hot steam bring beads of perspiration to her pink face as she luxuriated in the white marble tub.

When Sylvie walked back into the room in her bath robe, glowing and smelling lovely, Miranda wordlessly handed her another note from Magus, just delivered by Harold. Sylvie's heart sank thinking he was cancelling the dinner; she certainly didn't relish the prospect of an evening with her crabby mother. But instead he asked if she'd wear the evening dress that had arrived that day. It was only then that Sylvie spotted the boxes lying on the table and hurried to rip them open, crying out with delight as she removed the tissue paper.

Miranda sat down and picked up her knitting, pointedly ignoring Sylvie's rapture as she examined her beautiful new things. The dress was sleeveless, a deep shimmering green made of watered silk, cut on the bias. There was a black pashmina of the finest texture imaginable, elegant high-heeled shoes and lovely underwear. Sylvie felt like Cinderella as she took the things into her room to get changed.

Magus greeted her with a glass of amber mead. He wore a dark suit over a black shirt and looked strikingly attractive, his illness now passed but his face still hollowed and interesting. His blond hair gleamed in the candlelight, for the room was lit by many tiny flames. He smiled, kissing her cheek lightly, his black eyes glittering. Sylvie felt nervous standing in the figure-hugging dress, her neck, shoulders and arms exposed. He'd removed the pashmina as she entered the room and she felt embarrassed, unused to such a sophisticated and adult style of dress. Without the wrap she was also very conscious of the disfiguring purple bruises on her wrists and arms. Her hair fell like a curtain of silk to her waist and she felt Magus' eyes on her, taking in every detail of her appearance. He toasted her and drank his mead in one go whilst she sipped at hers. She loved the taste of it but knew it made her dreamy and drowsy.

A log fire blazed in the great fireplace and they went to stand by it, for Sylvie was shivering a little.

'Have you had a good day?' he asked, pouring them another glass of mead from a crystal decanter.

'Yes, thank you. I worked in the library and did some research for my history coursework, for next year.'

'Good. I missed you today, Sylvie. I've been out riding for most of the day – I needed the air and the exercise after being cooped up in here for so long. And Nightwing needed a good hard ride too. That horse forgets his manners if I neglect him for too long. But I've blown my cobwebs away now and reminded Nightwing of who's the master.'

'I rode a horse with Yul recently.'

It was a silly thing to say, but she had a ridiculous urge to make him jealous. She was still annoyed that he'd abandoned her all day without letting her know.

'Really?' He seemed unperturbed. 'I didn't think the boy had a horse.'

'He borrowed it, an enormous white one.'

'You mean a grey. That would probably be Edward's. Interesting to know he's been helping Yul. Drink up, Sylvie – the mead will warm you. Let me pour you another one. So you shared the same horse, did you?'

She nodded, sipping her third glass of mead and knowing she must slow down. She'd eaten nothing all day and could feel her body becoming warm and tingly already. Everything seemed a little unreal as he smiled at her, eyes bright and fathomless.

'How very intimate. Was this before the moon-rise?'

'Yes, we went through the woods and I felt as if we were part of a fairy tale. It was misty, and there were amazing red toadstools everywhere.'

'And tell me, did you ride to the cage he kept you in? I'm intrigued by this cage and I really can't imagine how he came by such a thing.'

'We rode quite a way and then he tied the horse up in a clearing in the wood, and the cage was just a bit further on.'

'A metal cage?'

'No, it was made out of tree.'

'A wooden cage?'

'No, a tree cage.'

'Of course – I know the tree cages! I used to go there as a boy and had great fun up there!' He laughed. 'What a clever idea ... but he had to tie you up first to get you in there, I'd imagine. Is that how you were injured?'

'Yes, I guess so.'

Sylvie put the empty glass down on a small table and stood looking into the fire. She suddenly felt very weary and wondered why she was here at all. Magus again sensed the change in her mood and pulled a bell rope by the fire. Almost immediately there was a discreet buzz from the dumb waiter.

'Go and sit down,' he said, nodding towards the beautifully laid table. A great silver candelabra glowed on the snowy linen, making the cutlery and glass twinkle. He opened the panel and began to bring dishes of food over. Sylvie watched in a detached way as he looked after her every need, serving her tiny portions, fussing over the napkin on her lap, pouring her some iced water.

'I don't want you getting intoxicated,' he said, smiling. 'You can have some more mead later, but I think you've had enough for now, don't you? And see, Sylvie, I'm not over-feeding you any more. This isn't too much, is it? Now we've ordered all those new clothes you mustn't put on any weight or nothing will fit!'

She enjoyed the meal and felt her spirits revive as she ate. After a while she began to sparkle and laugh, teasing and joking with him. By the end of the meal she'd cast aside all her earlier misgivings but still felt slightly removed from the moment, as if somebody else were in her body. The sensation was quite pleasant. Then Magus stood and took a jewellery box from the mantelpiece.

'I almost forgot – these arrived today and I thought they'd complement your dress.'

He opened the box to reveal a necklace and bracelet of opals and diamonds. They were exquisite, gleaming and glittering in the candlelight. Sylvie gasped, unable to speak. She'd never even dreamed of owning such valuable jewels and gazed at him incredulously, round-eyed and open-mouthed.

'Lift your hair up and I'll fasten the necklace,' he said gently, smiling at the disbelief on her face. He stood behind her as she raised the mass of hair with both hands. Very carefully he circled her neck with the jewels and closed the clasp, bending to brush the soft skin of her nape with his lips. She shuddered involuntarily and his eyes gleamed enigmatically.

'Now give me your wrist, Sylvie,' he whispered, and started to fasten the beautiful bracelet on her.

'These bruises are so ugly,' she said, looking at the livid marks on her slim white arms. 'They spoil the effect of the dress and the jewels.'

'Oh I wouldn't agree at all,' he murmured, kissing the inside of her wrist. He looked into her eyes, his nostrils flaring slightly as he breathed in her scent. 'There's something quite intriguing about such juxtaposition.'

'What do you mean? You're not saying that you like the bruises?'

'I merely meant they remind me why you should be here with me, not hiding in the woods with some Village boy. Wouldn't you agree?'

'Oh Magus, don't make me say—'

'Would you really rather be outside in the cold now? Can you hear the wind? It's horrible out there and it's so warm and cosy in here, so intimate. Come on, if you've had enough to eat, we'll sit on the sofa by the fire and keep you warm.'

'I've got the pashmina.'

'No, don't put that on,' he said softly. 'I like to see your skin.'

They sat together on the leather sofa sipping at another glass of mead as music played softly in the background. Sylvie felt relaxed and happy, mellowed by the mead and fine meal, and very grown up. Magus knew her interests and how to impress her and he chatted easily, engaging her in the conversation and making her laugh. She felt warm and safe in the comfort of his luxurious chambers, with the great log fire burning and the soft leather of the sofa cradling her body. Gradually she curled into him as the effects of the mead and the heat overcame any last vestiges of shyness. He slid an arm around her and held her gently, careful to keep his touch very light. He looked down at the silver head on his chest and smiled to himself in satisfaction.

'I enjoy your company so much, Sylvie. You've such an enquiring mind and you're very well informed for someone so young.'

She smiled, her head nestled into him. This was music to her ears after the weeks of being told how little she knew. He stroked her hair softly, enjoying the pure silkiness of it, the way it slipped and entwined itself around his fingers. Then he picked up one of her hands and ran his long fingers from the palm slowly up to the inside of her elbow and back down again, tracing the bruised skin with a touch like swansdown.

'There's one thing that puzzles me, Sylvie.'

'What's that?' she murmured, feeling quite sleepy.

'You're such an intelligent girl. You clearly enjoy intellectual conversation and you've said you find me interesting.'

'Mmn?'

She was very relaxed; the touch on her arm was so subtle.

'What do you find to talk about with Yul? What's he done, or seen, or read? What does he know? He's never left this estate – he's barely left the Village. Never read a book, never seen a film. He must be very dull and uninformed and I'd have thought, intellectually at least, you were a million miles beyond him.'

Sylvie swallowed and the caressing of her arm stopped. She realised she'd hardly thought about Yul all day and feeling guilty, pulled herself from the comfortable cradle of Magus' arms. Her mass of hair tumbled everywhere as she sat upright, face flushed.

'We always find things to talk about and often we don't need to talk at all – it's just good being together.'

He held up her wrist and examined the bruises. His dark eyes met hers in a mocking gaze.

'I see. And yet despite such deep spiritual compatibility this strong, silent one manages to inflict these terrible injuries on you. He imprisons you in a cage, cracks you over the head, takes the skin off one side of your body, and almost breaks your ribs as you lie crushed beneath him. Not to mention tying you up and gagging you. Do you enjoy being kept in bondage and treated roughly?'

'No, of course not! And it's never happened before – it was only because of the moongaziness and he never meant to hurt me. I'm sure he didn't.'

'I understand. Well, I just hope he has the intellect and

intelligence to satisfy you in the future, for there's nothing worse than being saddled with some ignoramus who bores you witless. You'll find the Neanderthal brutishness will begin to pall after a while.'

She stood up, stung by his tone, and felt the room sway.

'I think I'll go now,' she said tightly.

'Alright, Sylvie,' he said smoothly. 'You do that, if you've had enough of my company. But you should visit my bathroom first and do something about your hair and your face. Your mother might get the wrong idea if she sees you looking like that.'

Angrily she went through to the black marble bathroom and gasped when she saw herself reflected many times over in the gilt mirrors all around her. Her cheeks were very flushed, her eyes unnaturally bright and her hair was messed up all around her head. She looked exactly as if she'd been doing something she shouldn't.

When she returned several minutes later, smoothed and cooled down with cold water, he'd poured them both another drink.

'Have this before you go,' he said, smiling. 'I'm sorry, Sylvie, I didn't mean to upset you. I was only teasing and you shouldn't rise to the bait, but I really don't think he's worthy of you. A simple Village lout and a princess like you – it's all wrong. You deserve the very best.'

'Please don't be nasty about him,' she said, accepting the glass from him and sitting down again. 'I enjoy coming here while you're getting better, but you know I like him and I don't want to hear you say horrible things about him.'

He shrugged.

'I don't like the horrible things he's done to you. Drink your mead.'

She swallowed obediently.

'Anyway, how can you call him a simple Village lout? I thought he was your son.'

'He is, but he's still a lout. Relax, Sylvie, and stop being cross with me. Come here and snuggle up again – it makes me feel better having you close.'

221

She put her empty glass on the side table, her head spinning as she'd had far too much to drink. The mead was powerful and she wasn't used to drinking alcohol. She rested her head against Magus and he held her lightly; she felt so warm and drowsy in the heat from the fire.

'Yul's very like you, you know,' she murmured, her eyelids heavy.

'I'm sure he is,' said Magus softly. 'But why make do with a copy when you can have the original?'

Sylvie awoke late the next morning on Magus' sofa, a silk cushion under her head and the pashmina draped over her. Her head throbbed and her eyes wouldn't focus at first. She sat up feeling confused and then, as the reality of the situation hit her, horribly embarrassed. The clock said it was almost mid-day and there was no sign of Magus. The fire had burnt out but had not yet been re-laid. Her hair hung in her face, and when she looked in the mirror over the mantelpiece, she saw her eyes were smudged dark with mascara. She felt a complete mess.

Sylvie crept back to the Tudor wing hoping she wouldn't meet anyone on the way. She still wore the evening dress and jewels, and it was obvious she'd spent the night with Magus. She was lucky for the only person she saw was Martin, who composed his face into a respectful smile as he passed her in the corridor.

'Good afternoon, miss. I hope you slept well.'

'Er . . . yes, thank you, Martin.'

'Are the master's rooms available to be cleaned?'

'Yes, of course. I'm sorry if I was in the way.'

Miranda was waiting in their rooms in fine fettle, accusations ready to hurl.

'I promise it's not what you're thinking, Mum! We ate dinner and drank some mead, and we were sitting on the sofa by the fire chatting and then the next thing I knew it was morning. I'm so embarrassed. I must've dropped off to sleep and I've only just woken up. I don't know where Magus is. Don't give me a hard time, please.'

Miranda could see Sylvie was telling the truth, but glared at her daughter as she unwrapped the soft pashmina.

'What on earth are those? Are they real?'

She touched the milky opals and brilliant diamonds around Sylvie's throat, her face twisted as if she'd swallowed something sour.

'They were a present and I'm sure they're real. Can you imagine Magus buying fakes?'

Miranda turned away, her throat tight.

'Go and get changed and wash that make-up off your face,' she spat. 'You look like a slut, Sylvie, coming back in such a mess, dressed like that and dripping with jewels. What on earth would people think if they saw you like this? I hope nobody did see you?'

'Only Martin.'

'Well that's a relief. Now hurry up and we'll go down to lunch.'

'Oh no, Mum, I really couldn't face lunch. My head hurts and I need to lie down – the room's spinning.'

So Miranda went alone to lunch, and then down to the Village for the afternoon to join the women in the Nursery. Sylvie was delighted that she'd started going out again; it was just what her mother needed and would distract her from carping on about Magus all the time. Sylvie thought she might go for a walk herself but she still felt sleepy so she had a rest on her bed and before she knew it, Harold was knocking on the door. He carried a couple of boxes and seemed a little awkward with her, clearly not wanting to engage in conversation. There was also another note from Magus, inviting her to join him as soon as possible and stay for dinner. It was getting dark, almost four o'clock, and Sylvie realised she'd slept for most of the day. She felt satiated with sleep, lazy and languorous.

Dressed in another set of new clothes, Sylvie went back to Magus' rooms. He was on the phone but smiled and waved her to the sofa. She kicked off her boots and lay down, picking up a book to read. She realised she should've brought some school work with her as she'd done nothing today, but she really couldn't be bothered to go back and get it. She relaxed, listening to Magus' voice in the background rattling away in a language she didn't recognise.

'Sorry,' he said eventually, coming over to her and kissing her briefly on the lips. She recoiled slightly. He usually kissed her cheek. She looked up at him wide-eyed and he smiled down at her.

'You look very well rested. Good night's sleep on my sofa?'

She flushed at this.

'I'm sorry – I don't even remember falling asleep.'

'I don't mind at all, and I thought it best to let you sleep rather than wake you up and send you back to your cold bed. You looked so cosy curled up here by the fire and it was lovely to see you while I ate breakfast. I hope Miranda didn't mind.'

'Well, yes, she did but we sorted it out.'

'Good – and how is she? Will she speak to me yet?'

Sylvie realised that she didn't really want Miranda speaking to him at the moment. She was enjoying coming here every day and Miranda would just complicate things.

'No, she never wants to speak to you again.'

He laughed.

'Well that's going to be difficult, seeing as how we live under the same roof. She'll come round, I'm sure, but I don't want her giving you a hard time. You've had a bad experience recently with all the teachers hounding you so if there're any problems with your mother, let me deal with her. I expect she's a little jealous of you at the moment.'

'Yes, I suppose she is. She says I'm shallow.'

He sat down next to her and put his arm round her, squeezing her affectionately.

'I've never met a girl less shallow than you, Sylvie, so don't listen to a word she says. Oh, by the way, we had a big delivery today. Look over there – all those parcels are for you.'

'Wow!'

She was overwhelmed by the number of things he'd bought

her. It hadn't seemed so much when they were sitting at the computer, but there were boxes and boxes with the clothes inside all beautifully wrapped in tissue paper.

'I don't think it'll all fit into my wardrobe,' she said, as they stood looking at the piles of unpacked clothes and shoes.

'I thought you might say that,' he smiled, passing her a glass of mead. 'So I've organised a room for you just down from here, beyond my bedroom. You can keep all your new things in there and it could be a bolt-hole for you too, if Miranda's on your back. Pregnant women can be quite irrational at times and besides, you're practically grown up now and need to be more independent of her.'

'Thank you, Magus,' she said. 'You're so kind to me.'

'Not at all. You've given me so much pleasure, Sylvie, over the past few days. Being rich for the sake of it is no fun, but being able to treat you to whatever you want gives me such a buzz.'

He poured her some more mead and sat working again at his desk for a while. Sylvie lay on the sofa by the fire, sipping her drink and reading. They ate a leisurely dinner and watched a film, and she felt herself becoming drowsy after a while. She knew she should get up and go back to her room, but it was so comfortable here. She curled up against Magus and he stroked her hair and played with the long silky strands. She felt her eyes closing, and he shifted so that she lay more heavily against him. His scent was heavenly and his hands very gentle as they soothed her to sleep. She drifted away.

When she woke the following afternoon, Magus had just come back from a ride. His cheeks and eyes glowed and he looked bright with well-being. Sylvie had been dreaming about Mother Heggy and the crow and now, looking at Magus bursting with health and vitality, she realised what a load of rubbish the idea of a banishing spell was. She couldn't believe she'd been ridiculous enough to take it all so seriously, let alone feel guilty about it. She smiled lazily up at him and stretched, her body arching like a cat's on the sofa. He gazed down, his eyes slowly travelling the length of her.

'Have you been asleep all this time?' he laughed. 'You look so content and there's no need to get up if you don't want to. Do you want any lunch?'

'No thanks, I'm not really hungry, just a bit woozy.'

'Oh dear – then you won't want this?'

He'd brought her over a glass of mead, glowing gold in the weak sunlight that streamed through the windows. Smiling, she took it from him and laid her head back languidly on the pile of silk cushions, sipping its fiery sweetness. She was getting quite a taste for it.

'Let me run you a bath, Sylvie,' he said, refilling her glass a little later. 'You lie there and I'll call you when it's ready.'

She sipped and sighed, wriggling her toes with pleasure, picturing the luxurious black marble bathroom. It'd be fun to try out that enormous circular spa-bath. She idly wondered what Miranda was doing today – probably down in the Village again talking babies. An image of Yul flitted through her mind and she felt a twinge of guilt as she'd hardly thought of him at all in the last couple of days. Her head was heavy from all the sleep and spoiling and she didn't want to think of him now; it was too much effort. She closed her eyes and basked in the warmth of the December afternoon sun and the heat of the log fire.

Sylvie must've drifted off for she was awoken by a knock on the door. Magus was still in the bathroom, so she called for the visitor to come in. Hazel entered, her eyes sweeping the room and missing nothing. Sylvie tried to sit up but she was a little dizzy from the mead, so remained spread out on the sofa in disarray. She smiled up at Hazel, hoping she'd be a little friendlier now. The doctor stared down at her stonily.

'Where's Magus?' she asked. She stared at Sylvie lying dreamily in her expensive new clothes, cheeks flushed and silver hair spilling everywhere, an empty glass on the floor beside her.

'In the bathroom I think,' said Sylvie, waving vaguely in the direction of the other rooms.

'Are you drunk?'

'No! Of course I'm not.'

'Sylvie! Your bath– oh, Hazel.'

Magus strode into the room and frowned at the young doctor.

'To what do we owe the pleasure of this visit? I thought I'd always been very clear that anyone who wishes to see me phones first, or checks with Martin that it's convenient. Never turn up here unannounced.'

Hazel gazed up at him, her eyes begging for kindness.

'I'm sorry, I just wanted to make sure that Sylvie was alright.'

'Well of course she's alright. Why wouldn't she be?'

'It's just that ... you were concerned about her health before and you wanted me to check her daily, but she hasn't turned up for her weigh-in for several days now.'

'Oh that!' Magus shook his head. 'No, I don't need you monitoring her any more. She's under my personal care now.'

'She looks a little thinner,' said Hazel, glancing down at where Sylvie lay stretched out.

'She's fine. I'm not worried about her weight any more and if she wants to be slim, that's fine by me. Isn't that right, Sylvie?'

She smiled up at him and nodded.

'And are you fully recovered, Magus? You called me in a week ago and asked for anti-depressants, but you're looking well now.'

He brushed Sylvie's hair with his fingertips and Hazel saw the way the girl gazed up at him, her soft grey eyes slightly unfocused. She was definitely thinner and Hazel understood only too well what was going on.

'As you say, I'm well now and fully recovered, thanks to Sylvie's attentions. So if that's all, Hazel?'

The doctor turned on her heel, smarting with humiliation. She felt like an intruder on an intimate scene, although it was clear that Sylvie wasn't being coerced into anything – not yet anyway. Magus was so clever. And the worst thing of all, thought Hazel bitterly, was that she'd have given anything to be in Sylvie's place.

'Sylvie, you're going to have to leave tomorrow.'

'No! Why? I don't want to.'

It was two days since Hazel's visit and Sylvie still hadn't left Magus' rooms, the hours passing in a pleasant haze. Sylvie gazed at him now with drowsy eyes, reluctant to make any effort to move at all.

'It's the Dark Moon tomorrow and you need to go to the Great Barn with the other women.'

'Oh no, I'd forgotten about that,' she groaned. 'What a pain. Do I have to go? I really can't be bothered – I'd rather stay here.'

'You'd better go or tongues will start wagging if you don't. You can come straight back to me in the evenings though, so it won't be too bad.'

She twisted on the sofa and looked up into his dark eyes, deep and heavy as they rested on her. He lifted her languid hand and examined her wrist.

'His marks are beginning to fade. I don't ever want to see anyone else's marks on you – we both know you belong here with me.'

Sylvie saw the muscle in his cheek twitching and remembered him looking like this before, sitting on her bed in the Tudor wing and stroking her hair as he came to say goodnight to her. She'd been terrified then, and now she wondered why. He was so easy to control if she kept him happy; she knew exactly what she was doing.

'Let me sleep,' she mumbled. 'I'm tired.'

'You can't be tired – you've done nothing but lie around all week. Wake up, Sylvie! I need to talk to you.'

'What?'

'I don't want you mixing with the Villagers tomorrow in the Great Barn. You're to sit with the Hallfolk where you belong. If you're going to be my princess, you must behave accordingly.'

'But the Hallfolk girls hate me.'

'Don't be silly, of course they don't. They may be a little jealous, but just ignore it.'

'No, it's really much worse than that. They've been ganging up on me all summer and autumn and they say the most awful things to me. Holly's the worst – she really loathes me.'

'Does she? Would you like me to send her away?'

She looked up at him startled, her head against his thigh as she lay full-length on the sofa, her hair cascading over his lap. He gazed down at her impassively, one hand lightly fingering her throat and the sharp line of her jawbone.

'What – banish her?'

'Not banish exactly. I could send her away from Stonewylde to live with her parents in the Outside World. Holly's father is my second cousin.'

'Would you really send her away just to please me?'

'Sylvie, my angel, when are you going to realise? I'd do anything to please you. You only have to say what you want and it's yours.'

She smiled, feeling a thrill of power, but shook her head.

'No, don't send her away. She's been awful to me but I can deal with her.'

'I'll speak to her, then – I'll speak to all of them. But you're not to sit with the Villagers tomorrow, do you understand?'

His fingers played on her throat, kneading the tender skin gently.

'But Magus, I usually—'

'No! It stops now. I'll give you the earth, Sylvie, but only if you obey me. That's the deal – you do as I tell you.' He looked down into her eyes. His face was lit by the flickering firelight, hollowing his cheeks and making his dark eyes glow.

'You might see Yul tomorrow.'

She looked away, feeling guilty. She'd barely thought about Yul lately; he'd just faded into the background now that her days and nights were filled with indolence and luxury.

'You understand, don't you Sylvie, that if you want to enjoy all this you'll have to give him up completely?'

She didn't respond and kept her eyelids lowered. His thumb traced the outline of her lips.

'Sylvie, you can't expect this level of privilege and still enjoy your bit of rough on the side.'

'He's not my bit of rough!'

'Oh, I think he is, and you have to end it. And there's another thing, while we're on the subject of Yul. I believe he has some silly notion about wanting to take over from me as magus – I've never heard anything more ridiculous! Can you imagine that illiterate boy running this estate? Tomorrow, when you tell him it's finished between you, you can also tell him this: if there's any nonsense at the Solstice, I'll banish him from Stonewylde.'

'You wouldn't do that to him!'

'Oh yes I would,' he said quietly. 'I'm the magus and I'll do whatever I think best. I've put up with a lot of aggravation from him, but no more – he's overstepped the mark this time.' He tapped her wrists. 'How dare he prevent you from being with me at the last Moon Fullness? I expect you to tell him all this tomorrow when you say goodbye to him. Any attempts at a coup and he's out for good. You'll do this for me, Sylvie, to please me and to prove that you'll obey me.'

She started to sit up but his hand on her throat restrained her.

'Don't go, Sylvie. You don't want to go back to that cold bedroom and suffer a long lecture from your mother, do you? She hasn't seen you for days and she'll be raring to go. Stay here with me.'

'But Magus, I can't obey you,' she said in a small voice. 'I can't give Yul up. I'm sorry but I can't.'

His mouth hardened and something in his eyes changed, glittering as brilliantly as diamond as he looked down at her.

'Oh come now! Did you really think you could live so intimately with me in my private apartments, with every single thing your heart desires, every need anticipated, and still carry on with that Village boy as well? You can't have believed that, Sylvie. You must've realised that if you belong to me, I don't share.'

'Oh Magus, why does it have to be like this? Why can't you and Yul get on together? You're alike in so many ways, and—'

'No!' said Magus sharply. 'Remarks like that show just how little you know me. You'll never see Yul again in that way, and tomorrow you'll say goodbye and end this ridiculous liaison once and for all. That's my final word on the matter.'

He poured Sylvie yet another glassful and let her sit up to drink it, then laid her back down on the sofa and turned down the lights. His face was tense and angry but there was no sign of it in his soothing touch. Eventually he felt her body relax into sleep. Almost there now – he'd played her so carefully and skilfully. He thought of how easy it usually was, getting what he wanted, but Sylvie was different and what he needed from her was different too. He remembered Jackdaw's words: the toughest nuts to crack are always the sweetest. And he remembered something else he'd heard his father once say, a long time ago, which now made perfect sense:

A moongazy girl is hard to find, but worth more than all the riches in the world for the unique gift that she brings.

13

Sylvie was grumpy the next morning, not used to waking up before mid-day anymore, and still wore yesterday's clothes having fallen asleep in them the night before. She refused breakfast and sat in the window seat with a cup of coffee, her head aching, and scowled at the floor. Magus had clearly been up and about for a while and was curt and business-like.

'I've spoken to Holly and the other girls and you won't have any more trouble. They've gone to the Barn already and you'd better get down there soon – it's almost ten o'clock.'

Sylvie ignored him and turned to stare out of the window. He frowned and stood over her, his hand heavy on her shoulder.

'Remember what I said last night. Don't mix with the Villagers but if Yul's hanging around outside waiting for you, speak to him for a few minutes and tell him that it's over between you. Then come back with the other Hallfolk girls – I'll be waiting and I've a special present for you tonight. Understood, Sylvie?'

She nodded sullenly, sipping her coffee noisily.

'Stop making that disgusting noise and answer me properly!'

She glared at him.

'Yes!'

He stared out of the window at the grey December morning.

'Are you sulking because of Yul?'

'No.'

'Then what's the matter?'

232

'My head hurts and my stomach aches. It is the Dark Moon, you know.'

'Of course. I'll get you something for that.'

He returned from his dressing room with a pill.

'Poor darling, this'll help you. Now come and give me a hug and show me you're not sulking.'

Reluctantly she stood before him, angry with him and angry with herself. She had no idea what to do about Yul and was ashamed that she'd hardly thought of him during the past week. The days and nights in Magus' rooms had passed in a blur. Sylvie hadn't been able to face the fact that this man, with whom she was now so comfortable, might be gone in two weeks' time. Gone ... or worse still, dead, if Mother Heggy's dire warnings were true. The whole thing was barbaric and it just couldn't happen. She'd have to try to stop it somehow.

And now she had such a special relationship with Magus, how did Yul fit into her life? How could she ever share herself between the two of them? Sylvie couldn't see how it could all possibly work. She dreaded seeing Yul today knowing that she'd betrayed him and allowed Magus to lure her into his world of indulgence. She didn't want to leave this comfort to trek down to the cold, wintry Village and face reality. She'd much rather go back to sleep by the fire.

'Come here, Sylvie.'

Magus held out his arms and pulled her in close, holding her against his broad chest. His cashmere jumper was soft under her cheek and he smelt gorgeous. Sylvie put her arms around him a little awkwardly and hugged him back. It was like embracing a great pillar of protection. She relaxed a little, feeling her irritability begin to lessen.

'That's better,' he murmured. 'Don't be grumpy, my sweet girl. It won't be as bad as you think.'

He stroked her hair gently and she found his touch reassuring.

'But I don't want to go down there!' she said petulantly. 'It's cold and grey and I'll have to sit and talk with Holly and her gang all day and do stupid sewing or something equally tedious.

233

It's boring and I don't want to go – I want to stay here.'

Even to her own ears she sounded like a spoiled child, but she really didn't care. Magus, however, was patient.

'You have to go, Sylvie. It's the Dark Moon and you know it's one of our customs. I take it you are menstruating?'

'I usually start around mid-day, but I can tell it's on its way,' she said. 'Please let me stay here with you instead, Magus. You said I could have whatever I wanted and that's what I want. Please?'

He laughed at this, still holding her close.

'You can have whatever you want, of course, but you also have to obey me. You need to show everyone you're fine. Can you imagine the gossip if you don't go? All the talk there'd be about why you're not menstruating? I think you know what I mean . . .'

Sylvie gulped. He smiled at her embarrassment.

'Would you like me to take you down in a car, so you won't get cold?'

She nodded, closing her eyes and clinging to him. If only she could curl up by the fire and forget everything.

'Go and have a quick shower and get yourself ready. Make sure you look elegant, and I'll drive you to the Village in twenty minutes.'

The room Magus had given her was a little further down the building but still within Magus' luxurious apartments. It could be reached via the corridor but also through the interconnecting doors of his chambers, and was grand and comfortable. It was full of the gifts he'd bought her; some of her new clothes hung in the wardrobes but many were still spilling out of their boxes and tissue paper, strewn all over the bed. The dressing table was littered with costly bottles of perfume, cosmetics, toiletries and the lovely jewellery he'd given her, whilst the floor was cluttered with shoes and boots. The four-poster bed remained unused as Sylvie spent every night on the large leather sofa by the fire. She looked around now at the mess and knew she should make the effort to put all these beautiful and expensive things away. She sighed – maybe one of the servants would do it as she certainly didn't have time today.

Sylvie returned to the sitting room showered and smartly dressed, wearing a little make-up to hide her pallor. Magus nodded approvingly, and handed her a glass of mead.

'I know it's a little early in the day, but it'll help you relax until that pill starts to work. Try it – this one's brewed with blackberries.'

Sylvie drank it, the warm sweet liquid like nectar in her mouth. Mead made her feel so calm.

'You look absolutely lovely, Sylvie – designer clothes really suit you. Hazel was right, you've lost a little weight this week and you're so tall now the clothes hang perfectly on you like those beautiful, willowy catwalk girls.'

Giving her a final hug, he wrapped the scarlet cloak round her shoulders and led her down the wide staircase to the hall below. Several people looked up curiously but quickly glanced away when Magus' dark eyes rested on them. Sylvie felt odd being amongst others again, having spent so much time closeted alone with Magus in his chambers.

He ushered her through the grand entrance hall and porch and out onto the gravel drive. The silver Rolls Royce was waiting, its engine running quietly. Magus opened the front passenger door for her and Sylvie sank into the fine leather seat, enveloped in the softness of it, savouring the expensive smell. The last time she'd been in this car, she realised, was the day of her arrival. She remembered sitting in the back and catching Magus' eye in the driver's mirror as they passed through the gates and entered the world of Stonewylde. She closed her eyes, feeling a little strange and disorientated.

'I love this car,' she said as they purred away down the drive.

He chuckled and patted her knee. She felt like a rich man's plaything basking in luxury, wearing her costly clothes and perfume.

'After the Yule celebrations I'll take you up to London for a few days. Not the London you know, of course – I'll show you my world. We can shop in Knightsbridge, go to concerts, the ballet and the theatre. We'll drive up in the Rolls if you like and stay at my house in Mayfair.'

She nodded, excited at the thought of such a treat and once again forgetting the reality of what life would be like after Yule. The drive took only minutes in the car and very soon they pulled up on the cobbles outside the Great Barn. Magus switched off the engine and turned to face her. The Village Green looked cold and muddy, the dull brown trees encircling it starkly bare except for the yew tree, which now had a dark and ominous appearance. The cottages seemed to be huddled together for comfort, smoke rising from every chimney and then snatched away by a bitter wind that swept the grey skies.

Sylvie's eyes filled suddenly with tears which spilled down her pale cheeks.

'Please don't make me go in there, Magus,' she whispered. 'I really don't want to. I just can't face everyone.'

He took her chin in his hand and gazed at her. He'd groomed her well during their days and nights together and today she would finally cut the ties with his son. It had to come from her, and once she'd broken that bond she'd be even more vulnerable to him. There'd be no question of duress; she'd have made the choice herself and would be all the more desperate for affection because of it. And all the more willing to give him what he needed.

'You have to do this, Sylvie,' he said softly. 'Show the women what you've become now – my beautiful princess. And if Yul is waiting later on, you must face him and get it over with. Simply tell him it's all finished between the pair of you and then leave. Promise me you won't linger or get drawn into arguments and swear to me, Sylvie, that you won't let him touch you. I absolutely forbid that.'

He held her gaze and she saw something new in his eyes; a nakedness that frightened her with its intensity. And Sylvie realised that maybe she didn't know what she was doing after all.

'Swear to me!'

'I won't let him touch me,' she whispered. 'I'll say what I have to and come straight home.'

'Just remember what I told you about the intoxicating and

irresistible effects of the Earth Magic – I don't want him tricking you with it again. Remember his brutality and what he did to Buzz. We know that Yul is a potential killer and I don't want him anywhere near you.'

She bowed her head and he smiled, exhaling sharply. He patted her leg again and stretched across to open her door. A cold blast of air entered the warm cocoon of the Rolls.

'Are you feeling better now?' he asked solicitously. 'Headache and stomach ache gone?'

Sylvie nodded; they'd vanished and she felt as if she were floating on a cloud. Her head was light and uncluttered and her body was hollow. She gave him a small smile and Magus leant over and brushed his lips against hers, his breath warm on her mouth.

'Don't let me down, my moongazy girl. You know this is what you really want.'

She slid from the car. With a little wave, and feeling as if her feet didn't belong to her, she pushed open one of the double doors to the Great Barn and went inside. The warmth and noise of many women hit her and she stopped dead, feeling confused. A sea of faces stared up at her, arriving late and looking startlingly beautiful in her scarlet cloak. She stood there, unsure of what to do, overwhelmed by a sense of unreality. But then a group of Hallfolk girls came rushing up to her, smiling brightly and all chattering at once. They took off her cloak, admiring it, and hung it on the pegs with the other coats. Then she was led over to the pile of cushions where they sat stitching the quilt they'd started last month. They still hadn't got very far with it.

'Are you feeling alright, Sylvie?' asked Dawn, noticing Sylvie's pale face and unfocussed eyes.

'Yes thanks, I'm fine,' said Sylvie.

She felt awkward with them, and when she caught Holly's eye the girl gave her a strained smile.

'It's good to see you again, Sylvie,' she said in a high, unnatural voice. 'We've been wondering where you were recently.'

Sylvie noticed Holly's eyes were red and swollen.

'I don't know why,' she replied. 'You saw me in the library last

237

week, remember? You said you'd make my life a misery when Magus grew bored of me.'

Several of the girls gasped and Holly stared at the floor.

'I'm sure she didn't mean it!' said July quickly. 'You know how silly Holly can be.'

'She meant it,' said Sylvie. 'Holly's never made any secret of hating me.'

'That's all in the past now,' said Dawn. 'Isn't it, Holly?'

Holly nodded, still unable to look up, and Sylvie realised she was crying. The scene was becoming increasingly dreamlike under the strange effects of the pill Magus had given her. There was a little silence and then the girls started talking about the ski trip planned for January.

'Are you coming, Sylvie? Most of the Hallfolk go every year.'

She shook her head, trying to stitch one of the patchwork pieces but finding her fingers weren't working properly.

'I don't think so. Magus has just said we'll be spending a few days in London after Yule, but he hasn't mentioned skiing.'

The girls exchanged careful glances at this.

'I love those boots, Sylvie,' said Rainbow. 'They're gorgeous.'

'And your trousers and that top – you look great.'

'Thanks.'

'Are they all new? Did you go away for some serious shopping?'

'No, Magus bought them for me on the Internet.'

'We saw all the boxes being carried up to his rooms and we wondered. Has he bought you lots of stuff?'

'Yes, loads. There's so much it's almost completely covered my new room.'

More glances were exchanged.

'You are lucky, Sylvie.'

She looked up at the group of blond girls watching her, their eyes bright with envy.

'We're really sorry we were horrible to you before,' said Wren.

'We were just upset about Buzz being banished,' said July.

'We thought it was your fault, but now we know it wasn't. Magus told us the truth and he's explained a lot of things. We're all sorry and we hope you'll forgive us and be friends.'

'Well, if you want but it really doesn't matter – I don't care.'

'It does matter!' said Holly. 'I want to be your friend, Sylvie. Can I get you a drink?'

She insisted, despite Sylvie's protestations, and when she'd gone Sylvie shook her head.

'Is something up with Holly? She looks like she's been crying all morning.'

'She has,' said Rainbow. 'Magus was cross with all of us but he really laid into Holly. It was so scary! He grabbed her shoulders and shouted right in her face. I thought he was going to hit her and so did she. And he said if she was ever mean to you again he'd banish her instantly, just like he did with Buzz. She's terrified!'

'Please don't tell him we told you that,' said Dawn, frowning at Rainbow. Sylvie merely smiled and accepted the drink that Holly brought her.

Later on, when she went to the lavatories attached to the Great Barn, Rosie followed her in.

'Blessings, Sylvie! I was hoping you'd sit with us again this Dark Moon. 'Twas fun last month.'

'I know, I wanted to but I'm under orders today to sit with the Hallfolk girls. I'm sorry, Rosie – I'd much rather be with you.'

'Oh well, can't be helped. Not much longer, eh? I've a message from Yul. He's been so worried about you and we've heard all sorts from the servants. 'Tis said you sleep in Magus' rooms every night and never come out o' there.'

'I sleep on his sofa.'

'That's what they said.'

'How do they know?'

'They go in every morning to clean and lay the fire and they find you fast asleep on the sofa. They're calling you Sleeping Beauty.'

Sylvie felt annoyed at this.

'It's not really any of their business, is it?' she said stiffly.

'Well, no. Anyway, Yul will be outside at the usual place, he said, just after sunset as he'll come straight down from the Circle. Is that alright?'

'Yes, but Rosie . . .'

'What's wrong?'

Sylvie shook her head. How could she tell this sweet girl that she was going to finish with her brother? She remembered Rosie's words, spoken in the summer in this very place, about not hurting Yul and she cringed with guilt at what she had to do. Her only comfort lay in knowing that this way she might avert the coming confrontation at the Solstice.

'Nothing. It doesn't matter.'

Many Village women started to leave just before the sun set, wanting to get home before dark to start cooking, and the Hall servants had already gone. Sylvie had given up trying to sew and was curled miserably on a large floor cushion by one of the fires. She knew Hazel was watching her from across the Barn and had been all day, but hadn't approached her. Sylvie's stomach ached with cramps. The effects of the pill and mead had long worn off and she felt a little sick, having barely eaten anything. Her headache had returned too and the last thing she wanted was to meet Yul under the yew tree in the cold, dark evening.

'Are you coming back to the Hall now, Sylvie?' asked Dawn, packing up the sewing for tomorrow. Sylvie lifted her head and shook it wretchedly.

'We'll wait for you till you're ready to go, like Magus wants.'

'Well you'll have to wait a while. I need to see Yul outside.'

'That's alright. We'll tell the cart to come back and wait too.'

Sylvie shrugged, not really caring if she inconvenienced them. Magus had said she must talk to Yul and she knew she had to get it over and done with. But how could she face him? What was she going to say? Shivering under her cloak, she left the Barn and crossed the Village Green to the yew tree. It was windy and very cold after the warmth of the Barn.

Yul leant against the massive trunk, looking taller than ever. Sylvie couldn't see his face clearly in the near-darkness, but as she approached he stood upright and wordlessly pulled her to

240

him. Magus' words about not letting him touch her were forgotten already as he held her in a tight embrace, cradling her as if she were the most precious thing in the world. She stood like a stone carving in his arms, her heart thudding with despair. She must tell him she no longer wanted him. She must deny everything she'd felt for him; the love between them that had been growing since the spring when she'd first watched him digging her back garden.

Sylvie suddenly recalled the moment when she'd found him sitting on the bridge down by the river, wrapped in a cloak of loneliness and misery. She remembered how her heart had cried out to him then, wanting to light the darkness that filled his spirit. The bond between them – that flash of telepathic understanding that had connected her soul to his – suddenly snapped back into place. With his powerful arms around her and his heart drumming in her ear, Sylvie could feel his brightness and life-force, the essence of him that called to her and joined them as one. The trappings of Magus' privileged lifestyle started to unravel under the blaze of love that raged inside Yul. Sylvie hugged him back fiercely – how could she have ever considered it could be over between them? He felt perfect in her arms.

Yul kissed her gently, murmuring her name, covering her face with small urgent kisses. She melted into him, loving the smell of him, the feel of his skin and hair against hers. His kisses became hungrier and all the old emotions came flooding back as she kissed him deeply, losing herself in his darkness. How'd she forgotten this magic? How'd she doubted the strength of their attachment? She clung to him tightly, glorying in his leanness and energy, realising that Magus had been wrong. This feeling was nothing to do with the Earth Magic and its effect – this was the magic of Yul himself, the darkness to her brightness. Magus would never understand the strength of this instinctive, over-ruling attraction between them. Eventually they pulled apart and he took her face in his hands and peered at her. She was trembling violently.

'I've missed you, Sylvie,' he said softly. 'I love you so much and I've missed you every single minute. You've been in my mind all the time, day and night.'

He bent and started to kiss her again, saving her from having to lie to him. Sylvie hadn't thought of him constantly, nor had she missed him. She'd denied him, betrayed him and agreed to give him up forever. Her mother had been right all along – she was shallow. Shallow and naive, easily swayed by Magus and his excessive generosity and persuasive flattery. She'd dropped Yul as if their love was nothing, in exchange for a few new outfits and compliments and a glass of mead. She hated herself. Remembering the girls waiting for her in the Barn, and Magus waiting at the Hall, she reluctantly pulled away. She had to say something now . . .

'Yul, I don't have long. He's expecting me back.'

'I bet he is,' muttered Yul. 'I heard he's keeping you a prisoner in his rooms. He hasn't hurt you, has he?'

'No, no, not at all – he's been very kind to me.'

'Bastard! Remember what he's done to us and don't be taken in by him, Sylvie.'

Too late for that, she thought. She took one of his hands in hers and held it to her cheek. She'd forgotten Yul's raw energy; the feeling that together they could set the world alight. She'd forgotten the sheer excitement and magnetism of him.

'Yul, I'm sorry but I've got to tell you something. I . . . you . . . things have changed and I . . . I realise now that you really can't try to overthrow Magus at the Solstice or force a confrontation with him. You must forget Mother Heggy's prophecy and all that horrible stuff about death and people falling one by one. Your mother was right – Mother Heggy has caused so much trouble and you must put all this aside. I know Magus has treated you badly but you—'

'What?' he said incredulously. 'Treated me *badly*? Sylvie, he tried to *kill* me! If you could've seen him in that labyrinth at Samhain – he was going to burn me alive! And before that, up at Mooncliffe, he stuffed so many cakes down my throat I nearly died of poisoning. And that's not to mention what he did to me in the byre back in the summer and what he hoped would happen at Quarrycleave. I hadn't realised that I've been protected all this time by a binding spell, but that comes to an end on the eve of the Solstice and Magus knows it.'

'Oh come on, it—'

'Sylvie, you must understand – if I don't deal with Magus this Solstice, he'll kill me. It's that simple. Is that what you want?'

'No, of course not. But I don't think he feels that way any more and I'm sure he just wants things to be peaceful and normal so he can get on with his plans for Stonewylde. As long as you don't challenge him, he won't do anything to you. I'll speak to him and make him promise – I know he wants to please me.'

He pulled away from her angrily, his eyes flashing in the gloom.

'Are you completely mad? He doesn't want to please anyone but himself and whatever he says to you will be a lie. You're back under Clip's spell, aren't you?'

'No! I haven't even seen Clip.'

'Then Magus has you under his own spell and he's been working on you – and by the sound of it he's done a good job. Has he talked to you about the next Moon Fullness, by any chance?'

'Well yes, but—'

'There you are then! That's all he's interested in – stealing your moon magic. He knows he has to get it this month or he's finished.'

'Stop being silly, Yul. He does want me to go to Mooncliffe with him, but it's not as dramatic as you make out. I thought perhaps if I went up with him this month to keep him happy, then maybe—'

'Sacred Mother!' he shouted, spinning around and stamping his boot into the ground. 'What has he *done* to you? Have you forgotten already how it feels when you're standing on that rock? Don't you remember how much it hurts you? He's tricked you, Sylvie, and you *mustn't* go up there with him! If he gets your moon magic this month then I'm dead. He'll be too powerful for me to fight and he'll kill me. Please, Sylvie, stop being so stupid and listen to me!'

He grabbed her shoulders and shook her but she shrugged him off angrily.

'Don't call me stupid and don't you *dare* touch me like that! I'm still recovering from the last time you had a go at me!'

He stepped back and stared at her, unable to read her expression in the darkness. All was silent save for his uneven breathing as he struggled to control himself.

'I'm sorry I hurt you last month, Sylvie, but you know why it happened and you accepted the risk.'

'I know you didn't want Magus to take me to Mooncliffe but you didn't have to be so brutal! You really hurt me and I was injured all over. I know what you're like now, Yul – I've seen pictures of your attack on Buzz and they were absolutely horrific. You obviously have a violent streak and I think maybe you're a greater danger to me than Magus is.'

Yul hung his head.

'I never meant to hurt you but I had to get you into the cage or you'd have run off into the woods. I feel really bad about it, Sylvie, believe me. And as for Buzz – yes, I know I gave him a bad beating, but he'd have done the same to me if he'd got in first. He was much heavier than me, remember, so I had to go in hard and bring him down before he got the upper hand. And he had it coming. If you'd seen the way he'd beaten me over the years, when we were younger ... He's always been so much bigger than me and he used to bring his gang along to hold me while he hit me, knowing I was always battered and bruised anyway and nobody would notice a few more bruises. Buzz deserved every punch I threw that day, believe me.'

'Maybe he did. But there's a vicious side to you I didn't know about and I won't go along with your violence. I won't be a part of this rising up against Magus. It's archaic, all Mother Heggy's talk of death and spells and people getting hurt. Magus is a civilised, educated man who knows how to run Stonewylde properly, and you're not. He's shown me a different world and I'm just not sure of anything any longer.'

Yul stood before her silently. He reached out to her but she brushed his hand away impatiently.

'Don't you love me any more, Sylvie?' he asked, his voice strangled with pain. 'What's happened?'

'I don't know! I thought I did ... I'm just not sure now. I'm sick of this conflict and being torn in half.'

'But you said ... I thought we loved each other? I thought we belonged together? Sylvie, please – without that there's nothing. You're the reason I must do this! You're my reason to live, my reason to fight, and—'

'*No I'm not!* I'm not a prize to be fought over! I'm not some silly, pathetic girl who has no say in anything. Don't make *me* the excuse to justify your violence towards the man who's your own father, your own flesh and blood! I won't be dragged into it like this!'

'But Sylvie, I never wanted to drag you into it! You're the one who argued with me right here, under this very tree, about how it was your battle too! I—'

'No! I don't want to hear any more!' she shouted. 'I was going to finish with you tonight, Yul – I'm sorry but that's the truth. Magus persuaded me that it was the right thing to do. Then when I saw you and we kissed ... I realised I still love you. But that's not a good enough reason for this stupid battle of yours with Magus. He's not a bad man like we thought, not deep down inside. There's another side to him I've got to know in the past week – he's kind and he's fun and I think he's also rather lonely, despite being adored by everyone. You're his son, Yul! Why can't we sort this out? I'm sure we could ...'

But he'd turned away, choking on his tears. He'd never expected this betrayal, despite Heggy's warnings. He stumbled a few steps away from her and sank to his knees on the earth, hunched over and crying into his hands. Sylvie looked at him helplessly, trying to ignore the merciless throbbing in her head. She still felt sick and hollow as if she weren't really here at all.

'I must get back, Yul – there'll be trouble if I'm out any longer.

I'm so sorry to upset you but maybe we can talk again tomorrow if I can slip away.'

She went over to him and put her hand on his shoulder. He shook with huge, silent sobs as if his heart were breaking.

'I never once doubted you!' he choked. 'I never thought you'd do this to me. You were the *one* person in my life I counted on—'

'Please, Yul, stop! I love you. It's just . . . I can't agree with this awful conflict and the idea of getting rid of Magus. Get rid of him how? No thought's gone into this other than Mother Heggy's mad prophecy and I can't bear the idea of people getting hurt. Magus has been good to me and he cares for me, and—'

He cried out at this and leapt to his feet, angrily wiping his face with the heels of both hands.

'You've been deceived, Sylvie! He's evil and he'll make you suffer for trusting him. How can you be so *blind*? If you—'

'I've got to go. He'll be cross if I don't get back soon.'

She started to walk away, her stomach aching and head pounding.

'Sylvie! Come back tomorrow! We can't leave it like this. Tomorrow at mid-day – I'll be waiting. Promise me you'll come.'

'I'll try,' she said over her shoulder. 'But I can't promise.'

'She's turned against me!' Yul cried, sinking onto the hard chair. 'She doesn't love me as she did. What can I do?'

He felt a wrenching pain in his chest that stifled his breath. Mother Heggy nodded in sympathy as she rocked in her chair, a thick hairy shawl clutched around her and the familiar shapeless hat pulled low on her head. She wore ancient hobnailed boots on her feet and her dress was little more than a thick grey sack reaching her ankles. Somebody kind had recently knitted her some fingerless mittens which covered her gnarled hands, leaving only the filthy nails poking out like horny talons. The skin on her face was furrowed like a field and just as dirty, and her features had fallen in on themselves so her nose curved into her puckered mouth and her whiskery chin rose up to meet it. She was very old indeed. The crow perched precariously on the back of her chair, beady black eyes blinking rapidly and sharp beak nodding in time with her rocking.

'She still loves you, my dark one,' Mother Heggy wheezed. 'She's deceived, but not for ever. He cannot mask the evil for ever and she'll shine clear in the end. Have faith in her, my boy.'

'But she's completely under his spell! I can't stand it knowing she's with him night and day. He's so powerful and clever and she's only a young girl. She's too open and trusting and she really has no idea just how cruel he is. I can't bear it!'

'Two weeks, Yul, only two more weeks. She still has much to endure, the poor child, trapped in his golden cage, and 'tis as well she's strong and clever herself.'

'But she brushed me off tonight, Mother Heggy. And she said she might go to Mooncliffe with Magus to keep him happy.'

'NO!' screeched Mother Heggy. 'Oh no, she mustn't do that! She's in great danger! I see five, five – always five.'

'Five what? What do you mean?'

'In the leaves, in the bones, in the ashes and in the runes and cards. Everywhere I seek the truth, I see five. Five deaths at Stonewylde this Solstice – not one, but five!'

Yul stared at her in horror. Her face was creased into a mask of fear and bewilderment as she rocked frantically in her chair.

'Five deaths? Are you sure, Mother Heggy? Do you know who?'

'No I don't, and maybe 'tis not even decided yet. But Sylvie must not go to Mooncliffe! 'Twould give him the power and strength to fight and maybe defeat you, and 'twill be the Moon Fullness in the Winter Solstice. The brightness in the darkness and the most dangerous time for him to drink her magic. The moon magic will be more powerful than ever and strange too, as 'tis during an eclipse. You know what happened to my poor Raven at the eclipse and the same may happen to Sylvie, if he gets her on that rock at the Solstice. Remember my words, Yul. Five deaths, and I know not whose!'

14

Magus had everything ready when Sylvie returned to his chambers, weary and depressed. She was ushered straight into his black marble bathroom where the circular bath brimmed and bubbled with hot, fragrant foam. She slipped into the water with a groan of relief, and lay there sipping mead. All she wanted was to block the horrible events of the day from her mind and forget everything. She emerged much later, glowing and relaxed, wearing a pair of black silk pyjamas he'd laid out for her. They were newly arrived that day; a brief camisole top with shoe-string straps and wide, loose trouser bottoms. She wrapped her hair in a white towel and carried her comb and the empty glass back into the sitting room. Magus was on the sofa reading some papers but rose as she padded in on bare feet.

'Sylvie, you are exquisitely beautiful,' he murmured, pouring her another drink. He sat on the sofa and pulled her down onto a cushion at his feet. He unwrapped the turban, and taking the comb, started to detangle her hair as the warmth of the blazing log fire dried it to pure silver silk. Sylvie became drowsy from the heat, the hot bath and two glasses of mead on an empty stomach.

'Are you hungry yet?' he asked, still playing with her hair, teasing it out so the strands slipped around his fingers.

'Not really,' she mumbled, eyes closed. 'Just sleepy.'

'Lie down here while I eat then,' he said. 'I'm starving. Come and join me if you change your mind, and when I've finished I'll give you that special present.'

She nodded and crawled onto the sofa, falling instantly asleep on the soft leather.

Later, when Magus had finished dinner, he took his glass over and looked down at her curled up fast asleep. The black camisole top showed off her pale arms and shoulders to perfection. Her hair tumbled around her delicate face, flushed slightly from the heat. He closed his eyes momentarily and took a deep breath. Then he sat beside her and smoothed the hair off her face, calling her name. Eventually she opened her eyes, drowsy and confused.

'Wake up, my darling girl. Are you sure you don't want to eat?'

She shook her head, still half asleep.

'I've got you some more mead here.'

She was so sleepy that her numb fingers almost dropped the glass.

'Steady,' he said, holding the mead to her lips.

She could barely sit up and leant against his shoulder, her hair spilling over his chest and into his lap. Magus held her close, stroking her slim arm. Her skin was as silky as her hair and he felt a jolt of pleasure at the beautiful perfection of her; at the possession of such a prize.

'Now tell me, Sylvie,' he murmured, 'everything that happened while you were away from me. I missed you today. I've grown used to keeping you by my side.'

He had to shake her to keep her awake and, in a muddle, she began to tell him about her day in the Barn.

'So the girls were friendly, were they?' he asked. 'Did they treat you well?'

'Yes,' she mumbled. 'They were nice to me.'

'And Holly? Was she suitably contrite? She bloody well better've been.'

'Yes, she was alright.'

'Only alright? In that case, I'll have another word with her in the morning.'

'She tried to be friendly.'

'And so she should.'

Then came the part she'd been dreading. Sylvie couldn't think straight but knew that she must. The room was spinning and she felt very confused, her mind a jumble of what had really happened and what she should say had happened. All she could remember clearly was Yul on his knees sobbing silently into his hands.

'And Yul? You were back late, so you must've spoken with him. What happened?'

'Nothing,' she said quickly, too quickly. 'Nothing at all. He just said he'd missed me.'

'Missed you? Did you tell him it was over between the two of you?'

'Yes, yes I did.'

'And was he upset?'

'He was very upset.'

'Did he get close to you? Did he touch you?'

'No,' she whispered, keeping her head down. She sat very still, hardly daring to breath.

'So he didn't even try to get close? I can't believe that. I don't think you're telling me the truth, Sylvie,' said Magus softly. 'Did he try to kiss you?'

Even in her confused state she sensed the edge to his voice and felt his body tense like a steel coil.

'No.'

'DON'T LIE TO ME!' he shouted, turning on her and grabbing her arms hard. He shook her and she flopped like a rag doll, her hair flying out about her. He released her suddenly and she shrank back into the corner of the sofa, huddling as small as she could, her eyes now wide open. He leaned over her until his face was only centimetres away from hers. His black eyes glittered dangerously, boring into her terrified gaze and she bowed her head, trying to retreat from the thrust of his anger.

'I'll ask you again, and you'd better tell me the truth this time. Did he kiss you?'

'Yes,' she whispered, unable to meet his eye.

Magus took a deep breath.

'Look at me, Sylvie. Look at me! That's better. Now tell me: when he kissed you, did you enjoy it?'

She stared at him like a rabbit caught in headlights, trembling and white-faced.

'Yes,' she whispered once more.

He seized her upper arms again very hard, deliberately squeezing and pinching her soft flesh in a vice-like grip. She cried out in pain but didn't dare try to pull away from him. Magus' merciless black gaze locked into her pleading grey eyes as his fingers dug viciously into her skin.

'You'll never kiss him again,' he said, very softly. 'You've let me down, Sylvie. You've disappointed me and I won't forget this. I do hope you told him you'd be spending the Moon Fullness with me.'

'Yes,' she gasped. Her upper arms were agony and she whimpered in distress. With a final sharp dig, he let her go.

'Good! Now, my moongazy girl, I shall give you your present, not that you deserve it. I should be punishing you for disobeying me, not giving you gifts. But this is the Dark Moon and I wanted you to have it tonight.'

Magus reached down and picked up a large square jewellery box, with an exclusive Bond Street jeweller's name and logo embossed onto the velvet in gold leaf. Sylvie sat hunched in fear, her arms on fire with pain, trying desperately not to cry. Smiling charmingly as if he'd not been angry with her just seconds before, as if he'd never hurt her at all, Magus carefully opened the box to reveal a necklet such as she'd never seen before. It sparkled in the firelight revealing a fire of its own that dazzled the eye. The high choker was studded with hundreds of diamonds, each one glittering with prismatic light. There were concealed hinges in the centre and it lay slightly open, with four long clasps that slid into holes on the other side to fasten it. A tiny gold key on a chain nestled in the velvet. Magus picked up the collar with delicate fingers and opened it fully.

'Sit up, girl,' he commanded. 'Lift your hair off your neck.'

He reached across and fitted it carefully round her throat, then snapped it shut. She heard the clasps sliding in and clicking into the holes, and he took the key and locked it. The thick collar was a snug fit around her slim neck, twinkling beautifully as it caught the light.

'Now let your hair go . . . oh yes, that is exquisite! Do you like it, Sylvie?'

'Yes, thank you very much,' she croaked, still fighting back the tears.

'That's good. Because now I've locked it you won't be able to take it off again unless I choose to unlock it, which I certainly don't intend to do.' He put the chain round his neck and slid the key under his shirt. 'I've commissioned two wrist bands for you as well, to match your collar. You'll sparkle like a princess and you'll never forget that you belong to me. What do you think of that, Sylvie?'

She shook her head in confusion, still unable to believe what he'd just done to her.

'I don't . . . I mean, thank you, Magus. Thank you.'

'Poor child, you sound so dry. You may have just one more drink and then you can lie down and go to sleep.'

He poured her another glass and watched as she drank it. Her head was really spinning now, the room going in and out of focus. Her stomach was hollow with hunger and the throbbing pain in her upper arms was excruciating. He gazed at her with heavy eyes that gleamed darkly.

'Are you feeling alright, Sylvie? There, lie down here and let me stroke your hair, just how you like it. Go to sleep now, there's a good girl.'

He ran his fingertips down the swelling bruises that had appeared in ugly blotches and lumps on her delicate white skin.

'You do bruise easily, don't you? I didn't mean to mark you but you must understand what happens if you disobey me. You were told you couldn't carry on with that boy and yet you deliberately defied me. You need to learn that I get angry, Sylvie, very angry, if people disobey me. Now go to sleep, my darling.'

*

She was awoken by a kiss on each eyelid and smiled, still dreaming of Yul who'd haunted her all night. But she found herself staring into black eyes that dragged her soul into a maelstrom of darkness and she recoiled in shock, pulling away from him abruptly.

'Good morning, my dearest girl. Feeling better today, I hope?'

Sylvie struggled to sit up, the black pashmina he covered her with every night falling off and her blond hair tumbling about her in a tangled mass. She felt terrible; her head pounded and stomach ached, and her throat was as dry as bark.

'Good morning,' she managed, blinking at him in the bright morning sunlight. It was far too early for her.

'Go and get dressed,' he said. 'I'll start breakfast without you – I've been up for ages and I'm hungry.'

She sat up fully, holding her head in her hands. The heavy diamond collar felt strange round her neck and had rubbed the tender skin sore.

'Hurry up, Sylvie! The girls have gone down to the Barn already and I'll give you a lift again if you get a move on. Make sure you cover up those horrible arms – I don't want everyone seeing how angry you made me.'

When she returned to the table feeling fresher and more awake, there was hardly anything left to eat. Sylvie was very hungry having eaten virtually nothing the day before.

'Can I ring for some more?' she asked, gulping down coffee and the one remaining croissant. Magus looked up from the newspaper he was reading, the harsh sunlight etching shadows and hollows on his handsome face.

'No there isn't time now. You should be down at the Barn already – it's your own fault for over-sleeping.'

She hung her head, feeling vulnerable and tearful at his complete change of personality and attitude towards her. How had she ever thought him so kind and amusing? So considerate and charming?

'Don't sulk! Look, there's plenty of coffee left and I've just

253

remembered – I've got some cakes here. If you're so hungry, have one of these.'

He passed her over a cake tin and she looked at the speckled cakes inside.

'But aren't these the special ceremony cakes?' she asked, remembering what had happened that night to Yul up at Mooncliffe.

'No, they're just some saffron cakes that Marigold makes for me. They're delicious, but if you don't want one . . .'

'Yes, I do, please. I'm starving.'

He put two on her plate and watched as she ate them quickly, washed down with coffee. He smiled, folding the newspaper, and got up from the table.

'Enough? Right then, let's get you down to the Barn. Your collar looks beautiful, Sylvie. It's catching the sunlight and sparkling everywhere.'

She touched the heavy band around her neck and found she couldn't look him in the eye. He was acting as though nothing had happened last night; as if he hadn't hurt her at all. If he'd only say sorry for losing his temper or show some remorse for his cruelty it'd be different. But the most frightening thing, Sylvie realised with a jolt, was that Magus hadn't actually lost his temper. His viciousness had been controlled – almost calculated. She wanted to confront him about it, to protest at the outrageous way he'd treated her, but she simply didn't dare.

'It was very generous of you, Magus. Thank you.'

'You know I like to buy you gifts – just make sure you deserve them. No more disobedience today or you really will be punished tonight. If the boy's out there at the end of the day, ignore him and come straight home to me. Don't even speak to him – do you understand?'

'Yes.'

Sylvie stood up, desperate to escape the luxurious room that was rapidly transforming into a cage. Magus came around the table and took hold of her shoulders, looking deep, deep into her frightened grey eyes. She was unable to look away. There was something different about him today, a dark fire that she hadn't noticed before.

'You haven't apologised for making me so angry with you last night, Sylvie.'

His hands slid deliberately from her shoulders to her slim upper arms. He held them lightly at first, exerting a subtle pressure on the swollen, bruised skin. Then slowly, deliberately, he squeezed. Sylvie flinched and her eyes widened as the pressure increased. She saw his black eyes, fixed on hers, register her pain. Something flared inside him as she flinched – she saw it clearly. Something deep within his soul surged at her suffering, and in that split second he lost her for ever. She could never forgive that terrible flicker of pleasure. She gasped sharply and then whimpered, and Magus smiled calmly at her.

'Well?'

She wanted to cry.

'I'm very sorry,' she gabbled in a strangled voice, wanting only for the pain to end. 'I'm sorry I made you angry . . . *please stop!*'

'That's better,' he said smoothly, releasing her arms. 'Make sure you behave more appropriately today – I won't be so lenient if you disobey me again.'

The morning was a complete blur of sounds and images. Everything was strangely surreal and many of the women appeared weird and distorted, their voices coming from far away, but when she looked twice they returned to normal. The Hallfolk girls were all over her again and very excited by her diamond collar, which attracted a great deal of admiration. Holly was even more upset than the day before; today she had a red mark across her face with four points bright against her cheek. Every time Sylvie looked, the mark pulsated like a blood-red jelly fish and Sylvie knew something was wrong. It must be the cake Magus had given her – why else would she be floating like a ghost above the ground?

'What happened to your face, Holly?' she asked in a voice that wasn't hers. Holly stared silently at the floor.

'It was Magus,' piped Rainbow. 'He told her off again this morning, and when she tried to say something back he slapped her hard. He was really horrible! We don't envy you, Sylvie, being alone with him up in his rooms day and night. We used to think you were so lucky but not any more. Magus is a monster, isn't he?'

'Ssh!' hissed Dawn, looking worried. 'Shut up, Rainbow – Holly's fine.'

'Yes, I am,' said Holly quickly, putting her hand to her cheek. 'Absolutely fine.'

As mid-day approached, Sylvie wondered how she could get outside to see Yul without anyone noticing. The effects of the cake were beginning to wear off but everything still appeared slightly bizarre and dreamlike. Hazel came over to Sylvie, as she lay on the cushions gazing up at the rafters in a daze, while the girls chattered around her. The doctor loomed overhead and Sylvie stared up into her face. Time slipped and she imagined she was back in her London hospital bed with the intern doing her rounds.

'Good morning, doctor. How are you today?'

Hazel crouched down and scanned Sylvie's face, her expression concerned. She put her hand on Sylvie's forehead, then took one of her wrists and felt the pulse.

'What's happened to you, Sylvie? What's been going on?'

'I've been very silly,' she muttered. 'I got it all wrong and I've made a big, big mistake.'

'Are you eating? What's he given you? Your pupils are so dilated! Sylvie? Sylvie can you understand me?'

She nodded weakly, her tongue feeling heavy in her mouth.

'I'm alright. I'm sorry Magus doesn't want you any more, Hazel. I saw your eyes the other day – you're hurting badly.'

Hazel looked away.

'We've all made a big mistake, I think,' she said quietly, 'and learnt our lesson. But I'm worried about you, Sylvie. Tell me what he's been doing to you.'

'It's alright, the Solstice will be here soon.'

'What? Sylvie? You're hallucinating, aren't you?'

The doctor stood up, uncertain what to do for the best. She knew the girl had been drugged, and she'd seen her drunk the other day. But what could she do? Magus wouldn't permit a challenge from anyone, not even the doctor.

'It's okay, Hazel, really. Don't worry about me.'

Shaking her head, Hazel glanced down in consternation at the prone girl.

'I'll go and see your mother tonight and we'll sort something out. You can't carry on like this, Sylvie, and I'm not sure if Miranda understands what's going on. You shouldn't be alone with him in his apartments – we've got to stop this going any further.'

The time came for lunch to be served and Sylvie saw an opportunity to get out while everyone queued for food. She was frustrated at missing lunch when she was so hungry but it couldn't be helped – she had to see Yul. While the girls went over to the food tables she went to the lavatories and then slipped out through a side door.

It was a cold December day but she hadn't put on her cloak, knowing she was less obvious without it. The cold air revived her a little although she still felt oddly disassociated from reality. She walked around the Green quickly on unsteady legs, keeping close to the trees so as to be unobtrusive, until she reached the yew. The branches hung down so low and thickly it was impossible to see underneath to the trunk. But as she ducked under a bough she saw Yul's boots and her heart jumped with relief.

It was wonderful to see his face again as she hadn't seen him clearly at all last night. His hair was longer, hanging down in curls almost to his shoulders, and he looked older somehow. His eyes were clear and bright as they found hers. She read the anguish in his look, the fear of being hurt all over again, and she stumbled towards him as he tentatively held out his arms. She fell into them, feeling his heart beating wildly against her as she clung to him.

'Yul, I only have a few minutes,' she mumbled against his chest. 'I've got to be back before anyone notices I've gone. I can't risk him finding out I saw you today. Yul, *please*!'

The desperation in her voice made him pull away and look carefully at her.

'Are you alright, Sylvie? Your eyes look funny – what's happened? And what's this round your neck?'

'Another of his horrible presents. He gave me cakes for breakfast and I think they were the same as he forced you to eat – I feel really strange.'

Yul's face darkened with anger. He took her by the arms and she jumped, yelping with pain.

'What?' he cried in alarm. 'Did I hurt you?'

She moaned in distress as darts of pain throbbed in her upper arms, trying to hold back her tears. Carefully Yul rolled up one of the sleeves of her jumper, blanching as he saw the faded bruising on her wrists and forearms.

'Is that what I did to you?' he whispered.

She nodded. He pulled the sleeve up higher and she winced, even at his gentle touch. Then he saw the fresh, livid marks on her upper arm, swollen into welts and turning black now as the deep bruises started to develop fully. Sylvie felt him shaking and his voice came out in a strangled hiss.

'And this was him? That's it – I'm going to get him right now! I ...'

'No, Yul, wait! Wait till the Solstice, until the time's right. He did this because I kissed you yesterday but as long as I obey him he won't hurt me again. It's better to hold on as we planned. But I have to go now – if he finds out I've seen you he really will do something awful to me, I know it.'

'Sylvie, yesterday—'

'I'm so sorry about yesterday! I was wrong and I've been stupid. He deceived me, made me think he was kind and caring but I was an idiot to fall for it. He's almost impossible to resist when he's being nice and I was taken in by him, but today I saw something in his eyes, something I won't forget.'

'I can't let you go back to him, Sylvie!' said Yul desperately, holding her close. 'You're not safe there.'

'I am, really, and it's only for what ... twelve days now? I can manage that.' She gently extricated herself from his arms.

'Goddess, I hate him!' muttered Yul. 'I can't bear to think of you trapped in the same room alone with him.'

'It's alright, I'll be fine and at least he's off your back for the moment. But be careful and Yul, whatever happens ... however you have to do it, make sure he doesn't get me at the Moon Fullness, please. You were right – he's counting on taking my moon magic to power himself up and I don't *ever* want to give it to him again.'

Nobody seemed to realise she'd been missing but her rumbling stomach was a nuisance all afternoon. Holly spent a great deal of time trying to be friendly, falling over herself to be nice to Sylvie.

'Holly, you're trying too hard. Leave me alone.'

'I'm sorry but please don't push me away, Sylvie. I want to be your friend and I'm so very sorry for all the things I said to you. Please don't hate me.'

'I don't hate you,' said Sylvie wearily.

Holly looked at her with frightened eyes and Sylvie didn't have the heart to enjoy her victory over the bully; Holly was now too pathetic to gloat over. When it was time to leave, Sylvie got ready with the other Hallfolk girls and they left together, choosing to walk today. Nobody noticed the tall, blond man waiting silently in the shadows by the side of the Great Barn. He smiled as Sylvie headed straight up the track towards the Hall, and urged the black stallion onto the Green for a circuit of the trees. It was as well for Sylvie that she hadn't thought to slip away and disobey him, because he'd have caught her red-handed.

The next few days passed slowly for Sylvie, still a prisoner in Magus' apartments. He decided she needn't go to the Great Barn for the full four days as not everyone did, and her appearance had been noted by all. Now Sylvie had seen through Magus' false charm she became aware of the extent and methods of his manipulation. He kept her underfed and hungry, drunk and drugged, and constantly sleepy from the roaring fire and hot baths. She knew it was all part of his plan to control her and keep her weak; he didn't want her thinking lucidly or standing up to him, and needed her compliant and docile as the full moon and Solstice approached.

Sylvie thought that if she went along with it, he wouldn't hurt her again. She was frightened of the pain he may inflict on her, having recognised his repellent sadism, and tried really hard not to anger him again. She was in a very vulnerable position, trapped like this at his mercy, but knew she just had to hold on for a while longer and then they'd all be free of him for ever. Any qualms she'd had about ousting him had vanished.

One afternoon Clip came knocking on the door. Sylvie hadn't been awake long and was curled up trying to concentrate on a book. She'd already been given two glasses of mead and there'd be no food for her until dinner that evening, unless she asked for one of the special cakes. Her stomach hurt badly with hunger pangs and her hands shook; she couldn't focus on the page at all. Magus sat working at his desk in the corner of the room, well away from the blazing fire. He'd barely spoken to her today. Some days he was all over her, unable to resist stroking her and playing with her hair, other days he was curt and cold and almost seemed to hate her. Sylvie didn't know which frightened her most.

Magus looked up sharply when the knock came, annoyed to be disturbed. He was even angrier to see Clip, who breezed into the room and sat down on the sofa without waiting to be invited.

'I'm busy, Clip,' he said tersely. 'I'll have to see you some other time – you know you should check first to see if it's convenient.'

'Don't worry, Sol, it's just a social call. I'll talk to Sylvie.'

He smiled but his eyes registered his shock at the sight of her lying on the sofa so pale and thin. She blinked up at him, confused and unsure if he were really there. Although she tried

260

to avoid the cakes if she could, she believed her meal last night had been spiced and she was still seeing strange things today.

'Are you alright, Sylvie? Your mother hasn't seen you for ages and she's been worried about you.'

'I'm fine thank you,' mumbled Sylvie.

'You've lost a lot of weight since I last saw you. Are you eating enough?'

Magus strode over from his desk and perched on the arm of the sofa. He rested his hand proprietorially on her shoulder and glared at his half-brother.

'Of course she's eating enough! She's in my care and she's fine, and you can tell Miranda that. Was there anything else?'

'Yes, I wonder if Sylvie'd like to go for a little walk with me to stretch her legs? It's very hot and stuffy in here and she looks so droopy. Do you fancy that, Sylvie?'

'No she doesn't!' said Magus sharply. 'She's perfectly happy here.'

'I would like some fresh air,' she whispered, and Clip noticed how Magus's hand tightened into a white-knuckled grip on her thin shoulder. She closed her eyes and winced.

'Then we'll go for a walk later,' Magus said smoothly. 'I'm expecting a very important call any minute from Japan, which is going to take some time. I really can't leave the room right now.'

'I wasn't asking you to come, Sol,' laughed Clip, and held his hand out to Sylvie. 'Come on, young lady – put on your shoes and get your cloak. It's quite mild out today.'

Magus started to protest angrily, but then the phone rang and there was nothing he could do. Clip hustled Sylvie out quickly, supporting her discreetly as she stumbled and swayed against him, barely able to stand.

15

'For Goddess' sake, what's he done to you?' Clip muttered furiously as they hurried towards the stairs. 'We'll go to your mother's rooms. Cherry!'

He'd seen Cherry below, in the hall, and half carried Sylvie down the stairs.

'Cherry, I'm taking Sylvie over to Miranda in the Tudor wing. We don't have a lot of time. Get her something to eat quickly – anything – and bring it there, would you?'

'Yes, sir, yes!' said Cherry. 'Poor little mite.'

Miranda hugged Sylvie as if she'd snap her in half. Then she held her daughter at arm's length and surveyed her carefully.

'I've been so worried about you, darling. Oh, look at the state of you! It's even worse than Hazel told us. Is she drunk, Clip?'

He nodded, guiding the swaying girl to an armchair in the little sitting room. She sank gratefully into its depths, a pathetic huddle with white face and vague eyes.

'He's obviously dosing her up with mead to keep her quiet and obedient – Hazel was right. And Yul told us about the cakes. I know only too well just what they can do to you. Is that right, Sylvie? Has he been feeding you too much mead and those special cakes? '

Sylvie nodded but then closed her eyes wearily as the sitting room revolved around her in a sickening carousel.

'And I'm so hungry,' she whispered. 'I've barely had anything to eat in the past few days. He's starving me.'

'He always goes too far!' Clip barked angrily. 'There's no need for this cruelty. Can't he see how he's damaging your health?'

Miranda took one of Sylvie's limp hands in hers.

'I can't bear to see you like this. What's he been doing? Has he hurt you?'

'No, not really. He calls me his princess and he's given me so many presents. But apart from once, he hasn't hurt me so don't worry, Mum.'

'But I do! I hate you being in there alone with him and it's not right. I'm worried that—'

There was a knock and Cherry bustled in with a tray.

''Tisn't much – I hope it'll do,' she said, and stood back to watch as Sylvie devoured the sandwiches and glass of milk. Her plump face was filled with concern and she shook her head in disapproval.

'Miss Sylvie, I were thinking . . . I could leave food in that room he's given you,' she said. 'I can get into it through the door from the corridor. I've got a key on my master key-ring and I could leave the food hidden somewhere for you.'

Sylvie looked up at Cherry with unfocused eyes and nodded slowly.

'Would that work, Sylvie?' asked Clip gently. 'Can you go to your room for a little while to eat, without Magus noticing?'

'I don't know . . . I sleep on his sofa and I use his bathroom. I spend all day and evening in the sitting room with him. I'm only allowed to go into my own room to get dressed when I wake up, but Magus goes in there every day too. He always chooses and lays out clothes for me to wear.'

'I'll be careful,' Cherry promised. 'I'll leave a tray under the bed and he'd never look there. 'Twon't be much, but still more than you're getting now.'

'Thank you, Cherry,' said Clip. 'That'll really help.'

Miranda leant over to kiss her wan daughter, tears in her eyes.

'Sylvie darling, I'm so very sorry about everything. I've failed you and I've let you down and now . . .'

'Don't, Mum – I'm sorry too. I was horrible to you and I must've hurt you so much.'

'We've both been manipulated and used, but he'll never come between us again.' She turned to Clip. 'I'm sorry, Clip, but we've got to get her out now – I can't just stand by and let him do this.'

'But Miranda, you know what we've all agreed. Whilst Sylvie's staying in his chambers, he's staying in there too. You know we said that if—'

'I don't care! I've changed my mind – I can't bear this. She's my daughter and she's not safe with him.'

'I honestly believe she is,' he said, concern creasing his craggy face. 'It's not in his interest to harm her, not with the Moon Fullness so close. He's keeping her quiet and weak but he won't actually damage her. I'll remind him that she needs to be strong enough to moondance for him – that's all he cares about. But we really mustn't rock the boat at this stage as we need him complacent and convinced that all's well. If we took Sylvie out now he'd be furious, and then he'd start snooping about and we can't have him discovering what's going on, not with the Solstice so close. There's just too much at stake to alter our plans now.'

'But what if he—'

'Mum, I'm alright, really,' interrupted Sylvie, a bit brighter now she'd eaten something. 'Please, I want to do my bit to help. What's been going on? Have you got everything organised for the Solstice? What's going to happen?'

'Oh Miss Sylvie, 'tis so exciting!' said Cherry, clasping her chubby hands together. 'There's all sorts o'—'

'Ssh, Cherry,' said Clip. 'I'm sorry but it's best Sylvie doesn't know what's planned. We don't want her blurting something out by mistake, do we? And Sylvie, we must go out to the garden now because as soon as Sol's off the phone he'll come looking for you.'

Sylvie and her mother kissed goodbye, Miranda clinging tearfully to her thin daughter. Clip led her quickly to the formal garden, Sylvie now much steadier on her feet, and the cool winter air revived her too. They strolled around the gravel paths between the clipped bushes and Sylvie breathed deeply of the fresh air, making the most of this unexpected freedom from her prison. She smiled gratefully at Clip.

'Thank you for rescuing me,' she said. 'I was so pleased to see you today.'

'It's about time I did something to help,' he replied. 'You have no idea how guilty I feel, Sylvie, for all the wrongs I've done to you and your mother. And I should never have hypnotised you or taken any of your moon magic. I feel dreadful about it.'

Sylvie squeezed his hand, feeling a return of the old warmth that she'd always felt towards him.

'Don't worry, Clip,' she said. 'I understand how hard it is to go against his wishes. I know you've never meant to harm me.'

'But I shouldn't have been so weak,' he said ruefully. 'I've always been scared of my half-brother. All my life I've been unable to stand up to him. I know exactly what Sol's like and I admire you, Sylvie my dear, for what you're enduring, being with him day and night. He's absolutely obsessive and it must be dreadful for you.'

'It was alright until he found out I'd kissed Yul at the Dark Moon. That's when he turned so nasty and started playing cat and mouse, sometimes kind, sometimes cruel. I never know how he's going to treat me from one hour to the next and it's terrifying sometimes, the way his mood changes so dramatically. Worst of all, I think he enjoys watching me suffer.'

Clip nodded.

'He's always been like that, ever since he was a boy. It's bordering on a personality disorder I think. You're a very brave girl, Sylvie, but I mean it – I really don't think he'll harm you and I wouldn't dream of leaving you with him if I thought you were in any danger. Just try to keep him happy, and whatever you do don't stand up to him or cross him in any way. Don't give him any reason to hurt you. It's only for five more days. The Solstice is almost here! And after that—'

'SYLVIE!'

Magus was furious. He strode up to them and took hold of

265

Sylvie, putting his arm round her. She leant against him and looked up at him guilelessly.

'I'm so pleased you came, Magus,' she mumbled. 'Please take me back. I feel so weak.'

'Of course, my darling.'

He scooped her up into his arms and started to walk back to the Hall with Clip trailing along beside him.

'You're a fool, Clip! I told you she shouldn't go out – it's much too cold for her and she's very delicate.'

'You've changed your tune! When I think back to that last Moon Fullness at Mooncliffe . . . You won't be saying she's too delicate next week on Solstice eve, will you?'

'That's different. And she'll be better wrapped up then.'

'I think she'll struggle to give you any moon magic, being so thin and feeble. You should be feeding her up for the event like you did before, if you want to maximise her moongaziness. She's so weak and—'

'I don't need your advice!' snapped Magus. 'I know exactly what I'm doing. Now go away, and don't come barging into my chambers like that again. I'll see you tomorrow morning, about eleven o'clock, in my office. We need to discuss the Solstice ceremony and make arrangements for the Story Web at Yule.'

'Fine – I've got some good ideas for that. See you tomorrow then. Goodbye, Sylvie. I'm sorry if the walk was too much for you.'

Back in the grand sitting room, with the fire roaring, Magus laid Sylvie gently on the sofa and removed her cloak. She closed her eyes, trying to hide the excitement she felt bubbling inside her. He poured her a goblet of mead and sat by her, holding the crystal glass to her lips.

'There, you'll feel better with this inside you. You should never've gone outside with him. Don't ever do that again – you mustn't go anywhere without my permission.'

'I'm sorry,' she said. 'I just wanted some fresh air. I was silly to go without you.'

He smiled and smoothed her hair, then fingered her neck and the choker.

'Remember what this collar symbolises, Sylvie. You belong to me and you must stay by my side at all times and never stray.'

The next morning Sylvie was awoken once more by kisses and pretended to be asleep, desperately hoping he'd go away and leave her alone. When the kisses touched her lips she opened her eyes wide in horror and saw not hard black eyes, but deep smoky-grey ones.

'Yul!'

She tried to sit up but he pushed her back down and kissed her again, holding her face in his strong hands. It felt so good and she wrapped her arms around him, pulling him in closer, kissing him back. She wondered if she was dreaming because he shouldn't be here, they were in Magus' chambers and ... Sylvie jolted fully awake and pushed him away in panic, struggling upright.

'Why are you here, Yul? What's happening? Is it the Moon Fullness already?'

He smiled, smoothing the mass of silky hair back from her face.

'Not yet. Magus is in his office discussing the Solstice with Clip and we've got half an hour at most. All the doors to the corridor are locked – you really are a prisoner here. But I came in through your room with Cherry's key, right down the corridor, and then up through all these connecting rooms. I'll leave the same way and down the servants' back stairs at the end of the corridor. Harold's waiting there to guide me out in case I get lost. I just can't believe this place! The size of all these rooms, Magus' bed and that bathroom ... Here, Cherry's given me some breakfast for you – better eat it quickly while you can.'

Sylvie wolfed down the thick bacon sandwiches and gulped at the glass of milk whilst he watched, horrified at the sight of her. She wore another pair of the black silk pyjamas which Magus liked to dress her in, not allowing her to fall sleep in the expensive designer clothes. At his insistence, she now wore the pyjamas at all times other than when he made her change for dinner.

Although the loose bottoms covered her legs, the skimpy top showed just how thin she'd become; jutting collar bones, pointed shoulders and stick arms. Her jaw and cheekbones were unnaturally prominent making her eyes seem even larger in her hollow face. The huge diamond collar, so thick around her neck, sparkled in the sunlight that poured in through the windows, and her silver hair cascaded around her shoulders and down to her waist in a wild tangle. Yul felt a jolt of desire at the sight of her, and couldn't bear the thought of Magus seeing her like this every morning and night, so exposed and defenceless, yet more desirable than ever in her vulnerability.

She looked up at him, chewing frantically on the sandwich.

'Stop staring at me,' she said with her mouth full.

'I can't help it – you're too beautiful.'

She smiled, swigging down the milk.

'You can bring me breakfast in bed any time you like,' she said, finishing the last crumb of the sandwich and licking her fingers. 'Oh that was lovely!'

'I'll have to go, Sylvie. It's all so close now and I can't risk anything going wrong. But you wait – you shall be fed bacon sandwiches to your heart's content once the Solstice is over, I promise.'

Yul took her in his arms again and held her gently, not squeezing her too hard as she felt so frail and delicate. He tried not to look at the livid bruising all around her upper arms knowing he'd go mad with anger and spoil their brief time together. Nor could he bear to look at the other, faded marks on her lower arms.

'I've got something for you, Sylvie.' He fished inside a pocket and brought out a small woven pouch, old and grimy with a dark leather drawstring. 'It's from Mother Heggy and it's for protection. She said to tell you it belonged to Raven, and you're to wear it round your neck when you moondance at the Solstice.'

'Okay,' said Sylvie, taking the tiny bag a little doubtfully. 'I'll need to hide this away from him. And where will I be moon-dancing? I won't have to go with Magus to Mooncliffe, will I?'

'Oh no! Don't worry, we've got everything organised – just be prepared to leave on the afternoon of the Moon Fullness.'

'Who's "we"?'

'It's best you don't know, then you can't give anything away. I'm sorry ... there are so many people who ... well, never mind that now. You have to remember that whatever happens you won't be going to Mooncliffe. I'd die before I let you down again.'

Sylvie nodded, clinging to him, burying her face in his curls. She loved him – how could she have almost given him up for that man? She felt so ashamed of her betrayal and started to cry.

'Don't! Please don't, Sylvie,' he begged. 'It breaks my heart to see you trapped here in his lair. It's been decided that this is the best way, but I hate it. You're being sacrificed to keep him content, so he stays in here with you thinking he's got what he wants and has already won. He mustn't find out what's going on behind his back down in the Village. Dry your eyes, Sylvie, please. I feel so guilty about this.'

'I just wish it were all over,' she whispered. 'I'm terrified about what's going to happen and I don't want there to be any violence.'

'Neither do I, believe me. I've had more than my share of violence.'

'So what will happen to Magus? How are you going to get him out and become the new magus yourself? '

'Sylvie, I have absolutely no idea how this will work. Mother Heggy's prophecy only said I'd rise up and overthrow him. Unfortunately it didn't explain how. I'm trusting to destiny and instinct.'

'Please, Yul ... promise me you won't kill him. I couldn't bear that.'

He hesitated at this and gazed deep into her eyes. She felt his spirit blazing out, strong and true.

'I don't want to kill anyone, Sylvie, but I can't promise you that. I'll do what I have to when the time comes. Just believe that I'll try my very best to do what's right, and soon this nightmare will be over and everything will change.'

'I want to be with you, Yul, and feel safe.'

'We'll be together very soon. Just imagine – seeing each other whenever we like, no more secret meetings – we'll be just like any other sweethearts. I can't wait!'

He kissed her tears, tasting their saltiness.

'Lie down as if you're asleep and try to look hungry.'

'I am hungry! It'll take more than a bacon sandwich to fill me up.'

Yul gazed down as she lay back on the sofa with her hair spread out in a fan of silver. Sylvie smiled up at him, her pale grey eyes so pretty, and he tingled with weakness and longing, wanting only to throw himself on top of her. There was something magical about her that drove him wild; how could Magus resist her? That was what really worried him – surely he wasn't alone in feeling this craving for her?

That night Sylvie had a terrible nightmare. Maybe because she'd eaten proper food that day, the mead hadn't sent her to sleep quite as soundly as usual. Magus was chasing her through the maze in the formal garden wielding a double-headed axe made of white stone. He was mad, his eyes manic, his mouth snarling open in a rictus of rage – he'd become the Minotaur. Snakes writhed around the maze, silver and black, hissing at her with forked tongues and needle-like fangs, trying to stab and envenom her as she ran around desperately seeking the exit. Sylvie sat up screaming, kicking the pashmina to the floor and flailing wildly.

Magus came rushing in through the dressing room and bathroom from his bedroom, for her screams had reached him even there. Pulling on a heavy black silk robe, he raced over to the sofa and scooped her into his arms, holding her tight.

'It's alright, Sylvie,' he said soothingly. 'It's alright, my darling, I'm here.'

'Who are you?' she whimpered, still thrashing about trying to escape the monster. In the near darkness lit only by the glowing embers of the dying fire, she saw the gleam of his blond hair. *'No! Not you!* Where's Yul?'

'Stop it, Sylvie, and wake up! You're safe now.'

But she fought, trying to escape, punching at him. He tried to calm her but she wriggled wildly, shouting that she hated him and wanted only Yul. Then Magus grasped her by the arms exactly where he knew it would hurt most and shook her till her head snapped back and forth.

'Be quiet, you stupid bloody girl! Be quiet!'

She screamed with the pain as he squeezed her damaged arms, then he let go to slap her hard round the face. That quietened her and she fell back gasping for air, finally fully awake, trying to catch her breath after the hysteria.

Magus got up and turned on the lamps, flooding the room with soft light. He found her goblet and filled it with mead.

'Drink this,' he commanded. 'All of it. Then we're going to have a talk, you and I, and put things straight once and for all.'

Sylvie forced the drink down her throat, feeling the familiar warm sensation as it hit her stomach. She shivered with fear and cold, unable to remember what she'd said while she was dreaming. She closed her eyes. Awake or asleep, this was all one long and terrible nightmare. Magus poured himself a brandy and sat next to Sylvie on the sofa staring into the amber pool in his glass.

'I'm sick of this attachment you have to Yul,' he said finally, in a cold, clipped voice. 'It's been going on for a long time and you've persistently disobeyed and defied me over him. I thought, the other night when you made me so angry, that we'd cleared it up once and for all. I explained that to deserve this level of privilege, to earn the right to have your every desire and whim taken care of, the one thing I require from you is obedience. And I made it abundantly clear that any feelings you once had for that boy were to be erased for ever. Did I make that clear or not?'

'Yes, Magus, you did,' she whispered, her voice quavering.

He turned his gaze on her and stared, his eyes narrowed and merciless. Sylvie trembled. She had no idea what he might do to her next – it could be anything. She recalled the flare of pleasure in his eyes as he'd witnessed her pain and knew he was capable of any kind of cruelty. She thought of Yul, at Magus' mercy twice in the stone byre for days on end. She understood how Yul must've felt, and why he'd never be dissuaded from getting rid of this man. To have someone taking pleasure in your pain and enjoying your suffering was the worst experience, and Sylvie was petrified as to how he might hurt her next.

Magus poured her another crystal goblet of mead. She didn't want it but maybe she'd need to be dead to the world. She began to force it down, feeling slightly sick. Her face both stung and felt numb where he'd slapped her so hard, and her arms were agonising where he'd dug into the livid bruises.

'Right then, Sylvie, shall I enlighten you and explain fully why I'm so adamant that this relationship with Yul finishes? I'd hoped that everything I'd told you already about Yul – his killer instinct and his use of Earth Magic to trick you – would be enough to put you off, but clearly it wasn't. I know he's kissed you, and presumably it's happened on several occasions?'

'Yes,' she whispered, remembering Yul's presence only that morning.

'Has it gone any further than that?'

'No!'

'But judging from the way you're so obsessed with the damned boy, doubtless it would sooner or later. He'll be sixteen soon, and so will you next summer. And you and he must never, ever have a sexual relationship.'

He turned on the sofa so he faced her, staring straight at her. She tried to look away but he reached across and grasped her chin in his hand. He examined the bright red slap mark on her cheek and shook his head sadly.

'Why do you make me do it?' he asked. 'I really don't want to hurt you. When will you learn not to anger me?'

'I'm sorry,' she said, her eyes lowered. Her breathing was quick and shallow and her lips trembled; she was terrified of him.

'Listen to me, Sylvie. And look at me – I want to see your eyes.

It's a sad and sorry tale and one that I'd hoped to spare you, but it seems I shall have to tell you the truth after all.'

His hand gripped her chin tightly as he spoke, telling her of a romantic encounter he'd enjoyed in some woods one autumn, many years ago. He was at a big charity ball but soon became bored networking and talking business, and wished he were back at Stonewylde watching the Harvest Moon rise at Mooncliffe. He danced with a young, pretty red-haired girl in a fairy costume who'd caught his eye, and before he knew it they were heading for the woods together. She was a little tipsy and all over him, eager and giggly. One thing led to another and they made love in the woods on a carpet of fallen leaves under the red September moon. It was a bit of naughty fun for both of them but especially for her, whose old-fashioned parents were at the party and had no idea what their wayward daughter was getting up to outside. Afterwards they went back into the party and joined in the dancing again, little guessing the consequences of their union.

Magus watched Sylvie's soft grey eyes closely. He knew that the alcohol he'd given her had made her slow. He also knew she was cold and frightened and not really thinking straight. But he was delighted to witness the exact moment when Sylvie fully understood the implications of what he was saying.

He was her father; that was shock enough. He saw that fact registering and being accepted with horror and surprise. But the next realisation – that was the one he enjoyed the most. It hit her, more powerful and devastating than any physical punishment he could inflict on her. He watched the intense pain and sorrow blossom into a bloom of utter despair, and savoured every moment of her grief.

If Magus was her father, then Yul must be her half-brother.

Sylvie woke very late the next day, having been awake for much of the night. The afternoon passed in a haze of misery. She was numb inside, unable to cry any more although she'd shed enough tears during the night. At dinner that evening she found it hard to swallow even the meagre portion of food Magus served her.

He was so solicitous, constantly enquiring if she were alright, patting her gently and smiling sadly. He revelled in every second of her suffering and she felt a sharp desire to stab him with her dinner knife. The mead and her unhappiness made her much bolder than she'd been of late. She really didn't care if he chose to hurt her – nothing could hurt more than this, and nothing mattered any more.

'If you knew you were my father, why didn't you say so from the beginning?'

'I only knew when Miranda finally told me the circumstances of your conception. You know how she always refused to talk about it at all. But recently I persuaded her to tell me and that's when I realised. It was a huge shock to me of course – I had no idea.'

'But you must've recognised her!'

'No, not at all. It took place many years ago, remember, and she was only a girl herself, just sixteen. And it was a brief encounter, very dark in the woods, and of course she was in fancy dress wearing a mask. Why on earth would I recognise her now?'

'Does Mum know it was you?'

'No, not yet, but she'll have to be told.'

'What about Yul?' Her voice caught in her throat. 'He must be told too.'

Sylvie knew what this news would do to him. Yul loved her as fiercely and deeply as she loved him, maybe even more so. He couldn't be her brother; it was too cruel. And yet it made sense – why she had the silver Stonewylde hair, why she looked so much like Raven and why she was moongazy. Everyone had said her father must be Hallfolk. Who'd have thought it was the magus himself?

She found that she hated him. Discovering her father's identity after all these years brought no rush of love or happiness, and the revelation strengthened her determination that the plan to overthrow Magus would go ahead regardless. If she and Yul had no future together, they must still rid Stonewylde of this evil man and send him off to the Outside World. Yul would still be the new magus and the only difference was now he'd have to stand alone, without her as his partner.

'I want to be the one to tell Yul, not you,' she said, imagining how Magus would relish Yul's distress at the devastating news.

'That's a good idea,' he said gently and she frowned at his easy capitulation. 'I'll arrange it for tomorrow and he can come here to see you. And now, my lovely daughter, I have another beautiful present for you, arrived today.'

Sylvie shut her eyes and groaned; she'd come to loathe his presents. A whole mountain of boxes had been delivered earlier containing the latest clothes he'd ordered. Magus had insisted she try some of them on and was pleased that they fitted her. She was now stick thin and he'd forced her to parade around the room for him, saying she was his gorgeous catwalk girl. He'd obviously settle for her as a trophy daughter if he could have nothing else.

He brought out another Bond Street jeweller's box and opened it to reveal two heavy bracelets to match the choker, very wide and studded with diamonds. He clipped them round her slender wrists and they snapped shut exactly as the collar had. Once again he locked them using his gold key. They felt like handcuffs, which she supposed was the idea. A collar and cuffs; his property and his prisoner.

'Do you like them, Sylvie?' he said, stroking her arm.

'No I hate them!' she cried, jerking her arm away from him. 'And don't touch me! You make my skin crawl – if you're my father you shouldn't be touching me like that!'

He laughed and the sound made her shudder.

'Touching you like what, exactly? I've never behaved inappropriately towards you, Sylvie, not once. Think about it. If you've misinterpreted my actions, maybe the fault lies with you; maybe it's you who thought of me in that way? If you did, you must quell those feelings, however difficult that may be, and never think of me like that again.'

He laughed at her look of disgust and slid his arm around her, pulling her close to him and ignoring her tight-lipped resistance.

'I'm so proud to have such a beautiful daughter,' he murmured. 'My sparkling princess.'

Sylvie drank mead until she could no longer sit upright, but sleep still eluded her. The room was spinning and she felt nauseous. Magus was a blur, a noise in the corner of her consciousness, and nothing was real any more. She realised suddenly she was going to be sick and lurched to his bathroom, stumbling into furniture on the way. She just made it and retched violently into the toilet bowl. Magus was there, holding her hair back, his arm around her waist as she heaved and heaved. Because the contents of her stomach were almost totally liquid the experience was fairly brief, but all the more painful for it. Eventually she swayed upright, clammy and deathly white.

'Please let me go back to my mother,' she begged.

'Absolutely not – you stay with me.'

'Then can I sleep in my room down the corridor?' she groaned. 'I just want to lie down on a proper bed.'

'No, my darling,' he said. 'I like you on the sofa where I can sit with you. Come on, back we go.'

He picked her up and carried her to the sofa where the fire still blazed. He laid her down and sat next to her, his hand on her hair. Sylvie looked up at him, her face ashen and her eyes dull with grief.

'Why do you treat me like this?' she said softly. 'Why are you so cruel to me?'

He chuckled, his fingers still playing with her hair. His eyes were hard as he gazed at her, burning with that darkness she'd grown to dread.

'Cruel? You're the one who's cruel. Look how you've treated me since I rescued you from your hardships. Twice now I've changed your life at a stroke, taken away all the bad things that caused you suffering, wanting only to make things perfect for you. I've bought you gifts, given you every single thing I could think of that might please you. At the Dark Moon I asked you specifically not to let my son – your brother – touch you, yet you

276

ignored me and upset me terribly. When you had that nightmare last night and I came running in to comfort you, you rejected me so cruelly. You said you hated me, and you punched me and pushed me away. Can you imagine how that felt?'

He paused, gazing into the crackling flames in the hearth. He took a deep breath, and when he spoke again, his voice was almost wistful.

'I could've loved you, Sylvie. It's been a long time since I loved a woman, and that was only a brief, impossible interlude which came to a bitter end. Apart from that I've never loved anyone, not one single person – parent, child, sibling or lover. But I thought I loved you and I wanted to make your life so special.'

'Why can't—'

'No! You've thrown it back in my face, all of it. You're ungrateful and heartless and you'll pay dearly for that, believe me. I could've given you the earth, you know.'

'No, Magus,' she whispered. 'You couldn't have. The earth isn't yours to give.'

16

Magus woke her up at midmorning the following day – not with kisses but a rough shake of her shoulder. Sylvie felt even worse than usual, her throat scratchy as sandpaper and head pounding relentlessly like a pneumatic drill. Her stomach hurt badly and she'd pulled muscles with that awful retching the night before. She sat up and rubbed her eyes, the diamond collar and bracelets heavy and uncomfortable against her skin, but glinting brightly in the sunlight that streamed in. Magus sat at the other end of the large sofa watching her struggle to regain consciousness.

'Yul has been sent for,' he informed her. 'He'll be arriving at the Hall in a little while so I want you up, showered and dressed straight away. You must look your most beautiful when you tell him that you're his sister. I've put out the clothes you're to wear and you'll love the dress. It's one from that mediaeval collection we admired from Milan, and very appropriate, given the setting.'

'Can I have some breakfast please? After last night I feel—'

'No,' he said curtly. 'Too late for that, and anyway, if you're going to deliberately make yourself sick then you don't deserve any food. Now go and get ready – Yul will be here soon.'

Sylvie did as she was told and after showering, went to her room. The servants had cleared all the mess a while ago and the room was now immaculate, the wardrobes and chests full of expensive outfits, her perfume and cosmetics arranged neatly on the large dressing table. The dress she must wear lay spread on the four-poster bed and despite her resentment, she was over-awed at its beauty.

It was of heavy brocade silk, a deep rich purple with a sweet-heart neckline and long pointed sleeves. Tiny seed pearls and amethyst beads were embroidered into the full, flowing skirts. The boned bodice was smooth and silky, with a long line of hooks that must be laced up with thick satin ribbons from the back. Sylvie slipped on the gossamer-fine shift first, then stepped into the heavy dress, pulling it up around her. She froze as Magus opened the door, his expression inscrutable.

'Go away! I'm getting dressed and I want some privacy.'

'Mediaeval clothes weren't designed to be put on unaided,' he replied with a smile, his earlier coldness now replaced by friendliness. 'And neither are the modern replicas. It'll be my pleasure to assist you, my lady.'

Sylvie slid her arms into the long tight sleeves, her heavy bracelets catching in the material. The points came down over the tops of her hands, but the slashes in the sides of the sleeves revealed the diamonds as she moved her arms. The dress was the ideal foil for the diamond choker around her throat. The neckline sat low on her milky white chest, revealing her delicate collar bones and the heavy, priceless collar.

'Turn around and I'll lace you up,' said Magus softly. He began to tug hard on the laces, firmly and methodically pulling the material tighter and tighter as she breathed in. Gradually the dress was fastened to skin-tight, unyielding perfection. Sylvie could barely breathe and she certainly couldn't bend, but when she saw her reflection in the full-length mirror she knew the effect was stunning.

Magus picked up her hairbrush and brushed until her hair shone around her in a silver cloud. He helped her slide her feet into the embroidered slippers that matched the outfit, for she couldn't bend to do it herself, and then surveyed her critically.

'Make-up,' he said. 'You need to cover up the marks on your cheek and put on some eye shadow and mascara too. All that crying hasn't done you any favours.'

'Why are you making such a fuss about my appearance?' she asked sullenly. 'What's it to you? Surely you don't care how I look when I'm seeing Yul alone?'

'Who said you're seeing Yul alone?' he asked.

'Well I'm not telling him in front of you!' she said, smoothing foundation into her skin to cover the faint but tell-tale imprint of his hand on her cheek.

When she was made-up to his satisfaction, they left her room and returned through all the other chambers back to the sitting room. Sylvie stood by the windows ignoring him, looking out across the drive with its avenue of bare trees, to the lawns and then parkland off to the side, and the wintry hills beyond. She yearned to be freed from this prison. It was so long since she'd been outside, at liberty to roam where she wanted and enjoy the fresh air. She remembered walking around Stonewylde with Yul; in the woods, the ridgeway, the Stone Circle, the hill at Hare Stone.

As the memories flooded in, her heart turned to stone. They'd never be together like that again. She thought of Yul's curly dark hair, always falling in his face, full of bits of wood and leaves. His grey eyes, slanted and long-lashed, smouldering with tightly controlled passion as he watched her. His body, long-limbed and slim but strong too, and so very tough and resilient, bearing witness to the beatings and cruelty he'd been subjected to all his life. She remembered his beautiful golden brown back criss-crossed with ugly scars, and his hands, long-fingered and square nailed, often dirty but always so gentle.

A sob escaped her throat and then Sylvie dissolved into tears, finally understanding fully that these thoughts, these memories, were now forbidden. She had to deny them. She could still love him – nothing would ever stop that – but it must be a sister's love and she could never again experience that deep melting sensation as he kissed her or touched her. She must never hunger for him and long for him, as she'd done for so many months, always in the certain knowledge that one day her longing would be fulfilled. She sobbed silently as if her heart would break, the bones of the corset tightening cruelly around her ribcage as she cried.

Magus came and stood close behind her, grasping her arms gently. The bruises were hidden under the silk but he knew exactly where they were. He exerted the tiniest pressure and she caught her breath sharply.

'I really think you should pull yourself together, Sylvie,' he said softly, as her body convulsed with suppressed sobs. 'You'll still be able to see him, after all. In fact, you'll be seeing him in a few minutes and I want you calm and composed, so be a good girl and stop this silly blubbering. You'll smudge your make-up if you carry on like this.'

He gripped her arms a little harder, pinching on the damaged flesh under the tight silk sleeves until she could no longer keep silent but cried out in pain.

'Leave me alone!' she sobbed. 'I hate you! I wish you were dead!'

He laughed, letting her go and turning her to face him. He put a finger under her chin and tipped her face up so their eyes met, hers soft and grey and full of tears, his black and gleaming. He took a handkerchief from his pocket and carefully dried her cheeks.

'I do enjoy a girl with spirit – so much more fun. You'll learn to love me, Sylvie. When I decide to be kind to you again, you'll lap it up and come running back like a little kitten, desperate for my attention. Think how keen you were only a week or so ago, how much you enjoyed all the pampering and spoiling. But of course you didn't know you were my daughter back then. Anyway, it's almost time to go downstairs.'

'Why? What for?'

'So you can tell Yul you're his sister, as you wanted.'

At that moment there was a discreet knock and Martin came in. He ignored Sylvie, his face expressionless.

'All is ready, sir,' he said.

'Thank you, Martin. Come on then, my moongazy girl – time to make your entrance.'

'I want to see Yul alone!' she cried, shaking his hand from her elbow.

'Oh no, Sylvie, such an important announcement must be made to everyone – or everyone that matters, anyway. Come on!'

She began to struggle and Martin stepped forward, his grey eyes cold.

'Would you like some assistance, sir?' he asked quietly.

Magus shook his head and roughly spun Sylvie round to face him, thrusting his face into hers.

'Do you want us to carry you downstairs kicking and screaming, you stupid girl?' he demanded brusquely. 'Stop this behaviour at once or you'll suffer for it later. You know I mean it, Sylvie.'
He grasped her damaged arm again and she had no choice but to move; the pain was excruciating. She followed Martin down the stairs, with Magus behind her prodding her in the back.

'But I want to tell Yul alone! Not in front of you! Please, Magus!'
'You'll do as you're told, girl. Move yourself!'

She understood his intentions when they entered the mediaeval Galleried Hall. Magus regularly held his court of justice here and now the great room, with its stone-flagged floor, vaulted ceiling and oak-panelled walls, was filling up with Hallfolk. They milled around, pouring in through various arched doors that led into the vast area, and as Magus and Sylvie made their entrance into the packed hall, everyone fell silent. She faltered and stopped, horrified at the sight of such a large crowd to witness such an intimate, awful moment. But the vicious grip, so agonising on her upper arm, forced her forward to the dais at the far end of the hall. The great carved throne stood empty and waiting for Magus, an ornate stool at its foot. Magus guided her up onto the dais and indicated she should sit on the stool.

Sylvie felt as if she were on a film set; everything seemed staged and unreal. The bodice of her purple silk dress fitted like a tight glove, flowing into the heavy skirts that swirled in a mass of pearls and amethyst around her. She sat down carefully, straight backed as the rigid steel bones in the bodice bit sharply into her ribs and waist. It was so painful and she couldn't breathe properly, having to take small, shallow breaths which made her feel dizzy. Her hair fell about her face and shoulders, almost down to her waist, in a shining silver veil, and the thick diamond collar and wristlets glittered brightly, startling against her very white skin. The bones in her face were fine and sharp after her starvation, like delicately carved alabaster.

Sylvie sat perfectly still, her grey moonstone gaze fixed on the half-hidden carvings of Green Men and dancing hares up in the high vaulted roof. She'd become a fairy-tale princess, not flesh and blood at all. Every single eye in the great room was on her; she had the rare gift of true beauty and everyone feasted on it. Magus relaxed on the throne chair, enjoying the attention Sylvie was attracting. She was an exceptional trophy. He revelled in her charismatic beauty and the beguiling air of tragedy about her. Reluctantly he dragged his eyes away and looked around at the crowds of Hallfolk, all of them related to him in some way. Nearly everyone was blond and there was a definite genetic link, clearly visible when they gathered together like this.

And then Yul arrived, dark and different, but also clearly one of them. It was apparent in his cheekbones, the way he held his head, his long limbs, and in his nose and jaw. Magus had never before seen it as clearly as he did now, with the boy surrounded by his kin. But Yul shone brighter than any of them; something fine and honed glowed from deep within, something magical crackled in an aura about him. Magus hated him with a vengeance, but the dark hatred was shot through with a surprising glint of pride. His son was so much greater than any of these others in the room.

All eyes had turned to watch Yul's arrival through one of the arched doors. He wore his festival clothes, the flowing white shirt and black trousers and boots giving him a mediaeval air to match Sylvie. He strode in and stopped, unsure what was expected of him but not nervous or awkward in the slightest. He stood straight, chin raised proudly, shaking the curls from his eyes in his familiar mannerism.

283

Then he saw Sylvie on the dais. Magus noticed with satisfaction the effect she had on him. Yul's body stretched, seeming to yearn towards her. His eyes brightened and his lips parted, none of which was wasted on Magus, so perceptive and astute. It was plain that the boy was absolutely in love with her, which made the forthcoming revelation even more delightful. The buzz of noise that had greeted Yul's arrival died down and all eyes now turned to Magus, who'd summoned them there. He rose from the carved chair, tall and commanding, and anticipation throbbed in the air.

'Blessings to you, my Hallfolk,' he began, his deep voice filling the great room. 'Thank you for gathering here today at such short notice, and welcome to all the visitors who've arrived early for the festival. I wanted to speak to you before the Winter Solstice ceremony and the Yule celebrations and holiday. I know most of you are leaving for Switzerland after the twelve days of Yule for our annual skiing trip. Sylvie and I may join you some time later in January.'

There was a burst of excited chatter at this news and he raised a hand for silence.

'I've two important pieces of news to tell you all today. The first I believe most of you know already, but I'd like to make it official. The young man you see standing there, whom you've known as Yul, a Village boy training to be a woodsman, is in fact my son and therefore one of the Hallfolk.'

There was a great eruption of noise as people turned to each other. Behind one of the many arched doorways leading into the Galleried Hall, two women who didn't belong at the gathering met each other's eye.

'Has to tell the truth now, don't he? Got no choice any more, and after all those years of hiding it!'

Cherry pursed her lips and nodded, jowls quivering.

'Aye, sister. But our Yul ain't no Hallfolk! Look at him now, so handsome and full o' the magic. He's better than all o' that lot put together!'

'So what's this about then?' said Marigold. 'What's Magus

playing at now? I don't like this, not one bit. I reckon he knows there's something going on. He's heard something, and I bet 'tis from Martin, that miserable old sod.'

They both looked across the crowded hall at Martin, standing tall and sombre in another doorway and watching the proceedings intently. His eyes were on Yul and his expression was one of bitterness.

'He hates Yul, don't he? Look at his face! We must be careful, Cherry. If Martin gets any wind o' the plans afoot, he could spoil everything.'

'Aye, Marigold, he'd snitch straight off. Go running to Magus telling tales. And Goddess help us all if Magus finds out what the folk got planned. We must guard our tongues, right enough.'

''Tis not long now. Not long till our Yul takes his rightful place.'

'We won't be hiding away like this then, will we? Skulking in corners and not being allowed to show our faces. Us Villagers'll take our rightful places too.'

'Aye, we will if all goes well. But I don't know ... something's not right here. Magus is too clever and he looks so pleased with hisself. Oh, I feel for that poor maid. Look at her now – what's he done to her?'

Yul stared across at Sylvie, who sat bolt upright and as pale as death. Her eyes found his and he poured his love to her across the room, ignoring the noise and the people, sending a silent message of comfort and adoration. But he saw there were tears in her eyes. Sunlight shone down on her through one of the stained-glass windows up high above her, and in the shaft of bright blue light, her tears sparkled almost as brightly as her diamonds. She was bathed in a pool of mediaeval azure as if someone from the past had shone a blue-filtered spotlight on her. She shook her head sorrowfully at him, her message unclear.

'It's unusual for one of the Hallfolk to have been raised in the Village, for normally a Hallchild is brought up here at the age of eight,' Magus continued. 'Unless of course he's completely daft, which Yul certainly isn't. There's no doubt that Yul is my son and I want to formally acknowledge this and tell you all that after the celebration, he'll be coming to live with us at the Hall. He and Sylvie have formed a strong attachment and I know they like to spend as much time together as possible. So with Yul living here under the same roof, they can see each other as often as they wish.'

There was more chatter at this, for nobody could understand Magus' thinking. The Hallfolk had assumed Magus wanted Sylvie for himself; he'd kept her up in his rooms for two weeks now, barely allowing her out. They'd all seen the boxes and boxes of presents that had arrived for her and the diamond jewels she wore were clearly priceless. Why was he now handing her to his son?

Yul was utterly confused too. He frowned at Magus and looked at Sylvie for enlightenment. But she was staring down at her hands in her lap, and he realised from the slight shaking of her shoulders that she was still crying. Something terrible had happened, he was sure, and perhaps something terrible was still to come. Magus was playing with them, pretending to free them as he prepared to pounce. Yul could bear it no longer. He'd only answered the summons today because Clip had advised him to, thinking it best to keep Magus happy. But he wasn't taking orders from Magus, nor playing the victim in his cat and mouse games; he'd moved beyond that. Yul stepped forward and called out in a voice very like Magus', deep and clear.

'I am your son and there's no doubt of that, as you say. But as for being one of the Hallfolk – I tell you all now, I will never, *ever* be Hallfolk! I'm proud to be a Villager, the lifeblood of Stonewylde, not a Hallfolk parasite. I will *not* be coming to live at the Hall. I don't belong here and I don't want to belong here.'

His deep grey eyes flashed and Magus, lounging on the throne up on the dais, smiled lazily. Yul thought again of the silver cat of his nightmares, and shivered. Something bad was going to happen – Magus was too purring and complacent.

'Of course, this is all a shock to Yul so please excuse his rudeness,' he replied smoothly. 'He didn't know why I summoned him here this morning. He didn't know I was going to acknowledge him in public as my son, nor invite him to live here. Such grandeur must seem daunting to someone raised in the Village, and we'll make allowances for him. But Yul, there's a second piece of news today. Sylvie already knows and she insisted on being the one to tell you.'

He smiled again at Yul, his dark eyes hooded with veiled menace like a cobra about to strike. Yul straightened himself, preparing to take whatever Magus gave. He knew that look of excited cruelty only too well.

'Sylvie, stand up,' commanded Magus.

She obeyed, swaying slightly like a slim reed in the breeze. The amethysts and pearls in her skirts caught the light, the diamonds sparkled and her hair shimmered around her. She glittered like a star and people caught their breath at her perfection. Sylvie slowly raised her eyes to meet Yul's, and in them he read all her sorrow. What had she done? His heart began to hammer in his chest as the dread grew inside him. He had the most terrible, awful premonition of what was to come: she'd submitted to Magus, maybe given herself to him in a deal to stop the imminent conflict, or maybe Magus had taken her by force. This magical, moongazy girl, so pure and precious, was now the latest in Magus' long line of women. She was too young of course, but only by six months, and Magus made his own rules.

Yul took a deep breath, flexed his fingers and steeled himself ready to do what must now be done. There was a clear path from him, in the middle of the hall, to Sylvie on the dais. People had instinctively parted to make a way through and slowly he began to walk towards her, hesitant, dreading what she was about to say and worried that she might faint away altogether. She was as white as death and looked alarmingly fragile.

'Tell him, Sylvie,' said Magus, a small smile on his lips. 'Tell him the wonderful news.'

Yul stopped a few steps away from her, the dais balancing their heights so their eyes were level. She brushed the tears from her cheeks with the back of her hand and glanced towards Magus in supplication. He nodded at her encouragingly.

287

'Go on then, Sylvie. You wanted to tell him yourself and everyone's waiting to hear.'

She swallowed, and cleared her throat in the absolute silence.

'The night before last,' she said, in a small voice that filled the silent Galleried Hall, ' . . . I discovered . . . I can't . . .'

'Tell him!'

She tried again, her voice faltering.

'He told me . . . the truth is . . . it was him, Magus. It was Magus who . . . forced himself on my mother in the woods when she was a girl. It was him who made her pregnant. Which means that he's . . . he's *my* father too.'

She saw the awful shock flash in Yul's eyes, and then the light in them die as the truth hit him, just as it had hit her the night before. Magus had risen angrily to seize hold of her, and she cried out as he gripped her hard.

'No, please not my arm . . .'

'That's not what I told you!' he shouted. 'I don't force girls! You've twisted it!'

'Let go of her!' Yul roared and leapt forward to pull Sylvie from his grasp.

'My mother *was* forced!' cried Sylvie, flinching before Magus' fury. 'It wasn't all fun and lovely, the way you told it. She was only a young girl and she didn't want that! She wasn't willing. *You're* the one who's tried to twist it!'

'NO!'

'Yes,' came a clear voice from above, cutting through the stunned silence. 'Sylvie's speaking the truth – it was rape.'

There was a collective gasp and every head in the hall looked up. Miranda stood above in the gallery which ran around one wall. Her red hair gleamed as she held onto the balustrade and gazed down at them all.

'Thank you for inviting me, Magus,' she said quietly, but in a voice that carried right across the hall packed with shocked faces. 'And just as well you did, for as Sylvie says, you're twisting the facts a little.'

'We'll discuss this later, Miranda,' hissed Magus, his face like thunder. His moment to stick the knife into Yul was now completely ruined.

'I'm sorry, but as you've chosen to make Sylvie's parentage such a public affair, I don't think you should deny the truth at this point,' replied Miranda coolly, her chin tipped with defiance.

Sylvie had sunk down onto her stool, her legs unable to hold her, and stared up at her mother with admiration. This was the old Miranda, the woman who stood up for herself and fought the rough deal life had given her. Yul had stepped forward and taken one of Sylvie's hands in his. She felt him trembling and knew that she was doing exactly the same.

'Everyone may leave now!' called Magus. 'I—'

'Not so fast!' cried Miranda. 'We were talking about how I was raped in some woods at the age of sixteen and how, out of that dreadful act, I conceived my beautiful Sylvie.'

'I do *not* rape girls!' bellowed Magus in outrage. 'Everyone here will testify to that! I've never, *ever* had to force anyone.'

'That's true,' came another voice, similar to Magus'. Up in the Gallery, Clip stepped out from behind Miranda and surveyed the pool of upturned faces and his brother's murderous expression. 'You've never forced anyone in your life, Sol. As you say, you've never had to. But I'm ashamed to confess that I have. *I* took poor Miranda's virginity that night, not you. Sylvie is *my* daughter!'

There was another explosion of noise, and Yul stared at Sylvie, his eyes flaring with hope. Was it true? Cousins? And only half cousins at that! She looked at Yul with the same frantic hope in her eyes. Magus was beside himself. He paced the dais like a caged panther, desperate to go up into the gallery to silence them but not daring to leave the hall to do so.

'Don't be ridiculous, Clip! You're a shaman – you're celibate!' he raged. 'And you couldn't make love to anyone even if you wanted to. You know full well you've never been able to.'

'Never been able to here at Stonewylde, with you mocking and taunting me,' said Clip calmly. He leant over the balustrade and met his brother's eye unflinchingly. 'You always had to be the best at everything, didn't you, Sol? You even turned love-making into a competition and of course I couldn't compete with you. You're right – I could never manage it. But once, just once, I did. At that dreadful fancy dress party in the Outside World, I saw a lovely young lady dressed as a fairy queen, who knew nothing about me or you or Stonewylde. She knew nothing of all my failures, of the way you'd teased and taunted me for my lack of success with women. And I managed to make love to her, under the red Harvest Moon in the woods. At least, to me it was making love, a dream come true. But to her it was rape. And of course I *never* imagined a child would come of it.'

'Is this true, Mum?' cried Sylvie, staring up at them. 'Is Clip my father and not Magus?'

'Yes, Sylvie, it's true,' said Miranda, looking down at her sparkling daughter on the dais, all bathed in blue stained-glass light and her eyes shining with hope. 'Clip realised who I was on the night of the last full moon, after Magus humiliated me and showed his true colours. The memory slid into place and Clip put it all together.'

'It was when Miranda cried and her long red hair fell over her hands,' said Clip ruefully. 'I've never, ever forgotten that. It's an image that's haunted me all these years – that poor girl standing up afterwards, all covered in leaves and earth. She cried into her hands with her lovely hair hanging over her face ... I'm so sorry, Sylvie. This is a terrible way to find out I'm your father. I'm so very sorry that it had to be like this.'

The Hall erupted as the Hallfolk began to discuss these extraordinary revelations. Sylvie had risen again and flung her arms around Yul, who held her tightly as though he'd never let her go.

'I love you,' she whispered, in the mayhem and noise around them. 'I love you more than anything in the world, Yul. I thought I'd lost you for ever, but now ...'

'Shall I get you out?' he whispered back. 'I hate your being trapped here in this vipers' nest. I can take you away now, Sylvie.'

'No, it's only three more days. It's almost over. Best to wait for the right time, as the prophecy said.'

She looked up and her eye fell on the Green Man in one of the stained-glass windows above. She smiled, hugging Yul tighter, and kissed his cheek. Miranda and Clip had left the gallery and were on their way down. Excited noise from the startled Hallfolk rose like a cloud of bees ready to swarm. Magus stepped forward and roughly pulled Sylvie away from Yul.

'Don't touch her, boy! Upstairs, Sylvie!'

Yul looked Magus in the eye, his steely grey gaze steady.

'Three more days,' he said softly. 'Under blue and red, the fruit of your passion will rise up against you, with the folk behind, at the time of brightness in darkness, and overthrow you in the place of bones and death. You have three more days, Magus of Stonewylde. Three more days until I finish you.'

17

Magus leant against a tall standing stone watching the boy on the rock. It was still half-light, the sky a palette of lavender and mauve with a hint of pink. A cold breeze rippled across Magus' cheeks, numbing his lips, but the boy seemed oblivious to it. He sat cross-legged and straight-backed on the Altar Stone facing the lightest part of the sky, his eyes closed. Dressed in browns and muddy greens, his hair long and curly, he looked like some sort of woodland spirit. Like the Green Man.

As Magus watched, a curious spectrum of emotions flickered inside him. Strongest of all was hatred, and had he been able to, he'd have killed the boy right now with no hesitation. He stood in silence, remembering the moment when Yul had been born next to that stone almost exactly sixteen years ago. The sun had set and the full moon had risen; a red moon at the Solstice, a highly unusual conjunction indicating rare magic afoot. The eclipse was total, the face of the Moon Goddess finally becoming a deep blood red at the moment when the ceremony reached its mystical and powerful climax.

Magus remembered the scene so clearly; the dark Circle packed with silent people, all lit by the flickering light of the great Solstice Fire. The young dark-haired girl – his Maizie – had crouched down on the earth and moaned in a long drawn-out wail of agony, unable to stifle the sounds of her labour any longer. Then the unmistakable, primeval howl of a new-born baby echoed around the sacred circle. Magus' heart had leapt at the unexpectedly early birth of this child, not his first, but certainly the one he imagined would be special. This one had been conceived at Stonewylde during a Blue Moon with a Village girl who'd given him her virginity and then stolen his heart. How could this baby, born so magically during a total eclipse at the Winter Solstice, be destined for anything other than greatness?

But then ... with Maizie still down on the earth floor and the bloody afterbirth staining the sacred ground, Mother Heggy had exacted her revenge against the Hallfolk for the death of her beloved Raven. In just a few heartbeats, before the totality of the eclipse had slid past, the crone had blighted both his love for the simple Village girl and his hopes and dreams for their child. She'd cut the cord with her white-handled knife and triumphantly delivered the baby, still bloody, onto the Altar Stone. And then she'd screeched her wild and dreadful prophecy to the hushed crowd.

Magus recalled the cold whisper of destiny in his heart as he'd picked up the tiny child, hot and velvet-skinned from the womb, and had the terrible, unspeakable urge to smash its fragile skull on the Altar Stone. For Mother Heggy's words had triggered a nightmare vision in his soul, one which had haunted his dreams since childhood: he lay in agony, alone and cold in the silver darkness, with a terrible pulsing in his head as the life-blood spurted out of him and the creeping blackness closed in. This vision, premonition perhaps, had burst into his mind as he held his son over the Altar Stone thinking perhaps he could cheat destiny and destroy the key to his downfall.

For Magus never doubted Mother Heggy's words. The prophecy – or was it a curse? – held within it a truth and certainty that grabbed his heart and squeezed. The Wise Woman was powerful, terrifying, and had always hated him and his kin with a vengeance. So he'd raised the baby high but he'd hesitated, and then Mother Heggy had risen up like a ragged spectre and screamed her summoning spell. She'd called on the Dark Angel to bind the child with his shadowy protection, to keep him safe from the evil intent of his father. A thick mist had swirled into the Stone

Circle at her call, bringing spirits from the Otherworld and a deathly cold unlike any winter chill.

Magus still shuddered at the fearful memory; the awful paralysis that had stilled his hands as he clutched the screaming child. The crone had snatched the baby from him and completed the magical words that would ensure Magus' death if he ever tried to kill his child. Magus had felt the cold presence of the Dark Angel at his shoulder and had recognised the Wise Woman's power. But she'd paid for the potent magic invoked that night. Her abilities had waned, as if everything had been drained from her, used up in that terrible summoning of the Angel of Death.

Now, as Magus looked at the young man sitting on the Altar Stone, he felt the hatred flowing in his heart as strong and blood-red as ever, and the same desire to smash his skull. The binding spell that Mother Heggy had cast that night at the Winter Solstice red moon only enabled Yul to grow up in safety. The spell expired at sunset on the eve of the Winter Solstice when its purpose was fulfilled and the boy attained adulthood at last. Finally Yul would stand alone and unprotected and Magus smiled at the thought. Then, at last, he'd free himself of the horror that had haunted him since childhood – that cold, lonely haemorrhaging in the darkness.

The sky was palest apricot to the south-east horizon where the sun would soon rise. Shredded ribbons of cloud lay above the skyline, glittering pink and bright, mirroring the sun that had yet to clear the rim of the earth. Yul's body yearned towards the horizon, his hollow-cheeked face serene, his eyes shut. Suddenly great rays of golden light beamed up around the skyline and the boy's eyes flashed open as the light washed over him. Magus frowned in disbelief, blinking in the blinding light. It seemed that Yul himself glowed, giving out light and brightness. He stood in a fluid movement facing the glorious sun, his slim frame arched to accept the caress of light.

Then Magus felt something moving, a rumbling beneath his feet. The glowing boy quivered as the force thrust up in an explosion of energy from below the Circle, through the silicate molecules of rock and into his body. Sparks shot from his outstretched fingertips and his hair stirred with a crackling charge. Yul shuddered violently as he received the energy bestowed upon him by the aligned magnetic fields of the earth and sun. He stood several minutes longer as the sun glittered brighter and brighter, rising in the pink sky. Then with a respectful bow he jumped lightly from the rock, as if gravity had been altered just for him.

Magus was overwhelmed at what he'd witnessed. Such power! And it wasn't even a festival; even in his early days he'd never been so powerfully blessed. He stepped forward into the arena of the Stone Circle. Yul turned to him, his eyes burning like stars, and Magus felt the confidence and magic surging within the boy.

'I want to speak to you, Yul.'

Yul merely raised his eyebrows.

'Come and sit with me on the stone.'

'It's a sacred altar, not a seat. I'll stand.'

'Very well. I want to speak to you about the future of Stonewylde. I know you have some notion about taking over from me at the Winter Solstice, but let's be frank here – we both know that could never happen. But I want to see if we can work something out together, some kind of partnership which will benefit the whole community. I see just how very strongly the Earth Goddess loves you.'

'And no longer loves you,' retorted Yul, looking his father straight in the eye, 'which is why you want to share my power. You're a stealer of energy – Sylvie's moon magic and my Earth Magic. If the Goddess wanted you she'd still be blessing you, and not me. But the energy has stopped coming to you and now you're finished.'

Magus watched the boy in bemusement. Yul had blossomed; metamorphosed from a simple Village boy into a powerful young magician. As Magus had seen yesterday in the Galleried Hall, his son was no push-over.

'Yul, you have no concept of what it is to be magus of Stonewylde. It's more than just standing on a rock as the sun rises and feeling a tingle in your fingertips. It's about leadership of the people, stewardship of the land, guardianship of the magic. Yes, I'll grant you, the Goddess loves you and you've been abundantly blessed with the magic, but that's not enough on its own to make you magus.'

Yul shrugged and Magus gesticulated impatiently.

'Listen to me, Yul! You need wisdom and experience. You can't even read and write and you haven't the remotest idea how much organisation and paperwork's involved in running this place. You must've heard tales of how bad it was in the days of my father, my uncle and their father too, when Stonewylde was falling apart and the people were starving. That was due to poor management and lack of organisation and I've spent my life putting that right. I'm very good at it now and I have a wealth of experience and knowledge. I'm also a very rich man, thanks to my business interests in London, and I use much of my personal wealth to subsidise the community. How could you do all this? You wouldn't know where to start – you don't even know what money is! But together, Yul, we could run Stonewylde perfectly.'

Yul looked at his father and knew that what he said was true – he had no idea how to run Stonewylde. But he also knew this was a man unable to compromise, a man who'd allowed his darkness of spirit to overrule his sense of decency and morality, and certainly a man who couldn't be trusted, however honeyed his words now. Yul shook his head.

'I don't know how to run a community, but there are many people here to help me and I'll learn. Being magus doesn't have to mean managing the community alone just because you've done it that way. The magus is the magician, the wise one, the one blessed with the Earth Magic, and that's me, as you must've just seen. I didn't choose or ask for this honour but it's come to me and I accept the responsibility that goes with the power. So save your breath – whatever you say, you can't change what's going to happen.'

Magus regarded him steadily, keeping his temper reined in.

'Are you angry because I lied to you about Sylvie?'

'I'm angry about everything you've ever done to Sylvie.'

'Can you understand why I pretended she was your sister? I'm sure you can – and remember, by doing that I was also denying myself.'

Yul shrugged again.

'You don't really want Sylvie, not for herself and all that she is. You only want to steal her gift of moon magic.'

'It's true I want to share her gift, but only because it benefits the community. When I've tasted her magic, I'm full of energy. Have you felt the power in those moon eggs? I have some left up at Mooncliffe – we'll go up there now and you can feel just how strong they are. It's different from the Earth Magic, more exciting and wild somehow.'

'I'd never take the moon magic and it isn't for you either – it's for Stonewylde. Sylvie must channel it into the hill at Hare Stone, where the spirals are strong. But you make her feed it into the moon rocks and you've become evil and greedy, thinking only of your own needs and not those of Stonewylde. And that's why you're finished.'

Magus sighed, turning so that he stood face to face with Yul, who was only very slightly shorter than him now. It seemed only a few months ago that he'd been looking down at a boy – a tousle-haired, surly boy who defied him with his smouldering eyes and curled lip. And now he faced a young man who pulsed with power and confidence.

'Yul, together we could run this place like it's never been run before! I have the wisdom and experience, the money and the knowledge. You have the Earth Magic, the energy, the youth and the power. Think of it – father and son, ruling together in harmony. The day after tomorrow you'll be an adult and you can have any woman you choose for your Rite of Adulthood. I'd even let you have Sylvie, though she's a little young. A moongazy girl is special and to be prized above any other woman. She's unique and magical, but I'd be prepared to give her to you to prove just how much I'm willing to sacrifice for the good of Stonewylde.'

The sun had risen well above the horizon now and shone into

297

the Circle, its glittering mid-winter light gilding everything it touched. As Magus watched, the sunlight turned Yul's skin to gold, his dark curls to glossy sable. The boy laughed, his eyes flashing sparks as he looked at the shadowed face of the great man before him.

'Do you really think I'd let you be part of my life and my future? All you've ever wanted is my death and suffering – you hate me and you've always hated me. And as for offering me Sylvie – she's not yours to give away. You can't use her as a bribe to get what you want. *She* has chosen *me* and y*ou* don't come into it at all!'

His grey eyes flicked over his father with contempt.

'Two more days, Magus of Stonewylde.'

Yul turned and left the Stone Circle, heading for the Village.

Magus walked up to Mooncliffe and gazed out to sea, still struggling to curb his anger. It was cold and breezy, the wind whipping the sea into sparkling waves that danced in the sunlight. He was furious at the cavalier way that Yul had rejected his offer of partnership, but as he calmed down he decided that maybe it was just as well. It'd been a stupid, spur of the moment decision to spare the boy's life and suggest a joint rule. It could never have worked, and nor could he ever have let Yul have his moongazy girl. Sylvie might think she loved Yul but he'd enjoy showing her the error of her ways.

Magus climbed onto the great moon rock and felt only a slight flicker of the moon magic, for it was almost two months since Sylvie had danced here for him. He thrilled at the thought of the Moon Fullness the night after this, on the eve of the Winter Solstice. It would be particularly strong, a mixture of moon energy and solstice power, and he'd drain every drop of magic from the girl. He'd bring her to heel and break her spirit, whatever it took. Once he'd disposed of Yul it would be so much easier, and he'd savour every moment of her misery.

Magus jumped off the moon rock and went over to the two wooden chests where the used eggs were heaped all around in a great pile of sparkling white stone. There were six moon eggs left, locked away safely in one of the chests. After last month's fiasco he'd been rationing them carefully and hadn't touched one for ages. He knew how crucial it was that he had power for the Winter Solstice, if he meant to kill Yul. If by some terrible misfortune he didn't manage to get Sylvie up here first to energise the moon rock and all the eggs, at least with the power from these remaining six eggs he'd still be able to defeat the boy. Yul had such an unfair advantage, he thought angrily, with all that stolen Earth Magic inside him.

Magus pulled the padlock key from his pocket. One chest was empty, and he opened the other one. Yes, six moon eggs remained, nestling together in a glorious white heap of pure moon magic. He decided to treat himself as he was feeling so low. He needed a boost; he was tired and angry, drained from his unexpectedly humiliating experience yesterday in front of all the Hallfolk, and livid with that damned boy and his arrogance in the Stone Circle.

Sylvie was waiting for him up in his apartments, probably awake by now and crying pathetically in a corner. He'd been a little harsh with her since the incident in the Galleried Hall; it was Clip and Yul he'd really like to get his hands on, but she was a captive target. He must get himself under control and not break her completely before the full moon tomorrow. Martin could help tomorrow night with all the eggs and there'd be no trouble getting Sylvie up here, weakened as she was. And should that jumped-up brat of his try to rescue her, he'd be in for a nasty shock. Magus smiled grimly – he had that covered.

He reached into the chest for an egg, bracing himself for the jolt of quicksilver that would flood through his body and continue for hours while he held the egg. There was no other sensation like it on Earth. His long fingers curled around the white, sparkly rock– nothing happened. He frowned in disbelief and snatched up the egg. No magic at all! He tossed it down onto the pile outside the chest; he must've put a used one back in the chest by mistake and now he only had five.

Magus picked up another one and yelled in dismay for this too was dead. In dread, he touched the remaining four eggs one by one. With a scream of pure rage he stumbled backwards, unable to believe it. Somebody had switched the eggs! What if something went wrong tomorrow night? There was no back-up now. His vision dimmed as wave after wave of fury pounded from his head down into his abdomen. Somebody had dared to steal from him, to trick him, and it had to be Yul.

Sylvie looked around the beautiful room that had been a living hell since yesterday morning when they'd returned from the revelation in the Galleried Hall. Magus had been terrifying and the very sight of her seemed to fuel his anger further. Clip had tried to come in but Magus had yelled at him and locked the door, pacing the floor like a caged beast and roaring his fury at her all day and evening. Sylvie had been cooped up alone with him all that time, entirely at his mercy, and had for once been grateful for the mead which allowed her to slip from reality.

She hoped today would be better – perhaps after a ride or whatever he was doing now, he'd have calmed down. She got up from the sofa and hurried through the chain of rooms to her bedroom hoping that Cherry had left her something to eat – she was so desperately hungry. She knelt down and peered under the four-poster bed and her heart jumped at the sight of the tray waiting there for her. Delighted, for she'd eaten virtually nothing the day before nor the one before that, she tucked ravenously into the food. As she crammed cold chicken and ham pie into her mouth, chewing as fast as she could, Sylvie wondered as ever how she'd have managed over the past few days without Cherry's help.

After brushing her teeth and making sure her breath was fresh, for she knew just how astute Magus could be, Sylvie returned to the sitting room and flung the windows open. The cold air made her shiver but was better than the stifling stuffiness and a welcome relief from the roaring heat that made her so drowsy and weak. She was living a nightmare and her only consolation was that tomorrow night was the Moon Fullness, when she could finally escape. She could survive anything knowing that the end was now in sight.

Sylvie looked out of the window at the blue sky, cold and crisp in the December sunshine. Wood pigeons called softly from the delicate pattern of the trees' bare branches and she suddenly thought of Professor Siskin up in Oxford. She had an image of a large, comfortable room, as ancient as this one, and the old man sitting at a desk in an oriel window gazing out at the cloistered green below. She felt, in one of her occasional flashes of intuitive empathy, his infinite sadness and longing. In that moment she understood just how passionately the professor loved Stonewylde and how very much he missed being here. In the autumn she'd decided to invite him back to Stonewylde as soon as Magus was gone, but why not invite him home for the Solstice? Then he could see Yul become the new magus and be a part of the transition himself. She remembered how taken he'd been with Yul, and his preoccupation with both the ancient Green Man of Stonewylde and the wood henge of the Village Green.

Magus must have been gone for some time, but if she were quick she might be able to e-mail the professor before her captor returned. Sylvie raced through the chambers to her bedroom and looked around frantically for her computer, brought here when she thought she could do some school work. She found the bag and hurried all the way back to the sitting room where she could access the Internet, knowing it may not work well further down the long wing. Sylvie furiously typed an e-mail to the professor, briefly explaining the new turn of events. She suggested that he travel to Stonewylde tomorrow on Solstice Eve, so he'd be ready for the sunrise celebrations the day after at the Winter Solstice itself. She also mentioned her original idea that he move to Stonewylde permanently once Yul had become the new magus. Her fingers trembled as they flew across the keyboard, making stupid spelling mistakes in her nervousness. She sent the message the second she was finished and took a deep breath of relief.

Sylvie stuffed the computer back in its bag, not daring to wait for a reply, and then remembered what she'd hidden in the side pocket. She unzipped it and carefully drew out her precious photo of Yul, just what she needed to give her heart now. She sat down on the window seat and gazed longingly at that beloved face smiling dreamily out at her from a halo of leaves. Yul's deep grey eyes stared into hers and she felt a great surge of love for him, so powerful and overwhelming that tears came to her eyes. If anything were to happen to him tomorrow night at the Moon Fullness ... If anything were to go wrong ...

She heard the key turning in the lock of the great oak door and hastily slid the photo between the pages of a book lying on the cushions. She held the book in trembling hands and pretended to read, the weak midwinter sun washing her face. The heavy door was flung open and Magus crashed in. She'd never seen him so angry and her heart leapt frantically in her chest. His lips were a thin white line in a face dark and mottled with fury. He strode over as she shrank back in the seat trying to curl up small, cowering before his wrath. Grabbing her wrist, he yanked her roughly to her feet. The book fell to the floor and he kicked it right across the room.

'WHERE ARE MY MOON EGGS?' he roared into her face.

Cherry returned to the kitchens pale and shaken. She banged the tray onto the enormous scrubbed table and looked around the crowded room for her sister. The vast area was filled with Villagers scurrying about preparing the next meal for the Hallfolk, whose numbers were hugely swollen by all the extra visitors arrived for the Winter Solstice and Yule celebrations. The white-aproned servants worked diligently at their tasks, with a flushed and sweating Marigold bellowing orders and chivvying everyone in sight.

'Oh dear Goddess, I don't like the turn o' things,' said Cherry, shaking her head.

'What? What's ado, sister? Clover, do NOT put the egg whites in that bowl! What are you thinking of? And hurry along with them parsnips, April. They should be in the stove by now!'

''Tis the master. I never seen him like this afore – he's gone barking mad!'

'Why? What's happened? No, Clover, not *that* one! Cherry, I don't have time now – you see how rushed 'tis in here. Tell me later, my dear.'

'Aye, I will, but I'm that worried for the little maiden. I didn't use the dumb waiter and took the tray up myself so as I could see what's going on in there – and 'tis worse than I'd ever thought.'

'Is she alright? She looked starved yesterday – never seen a girl so thin and pale.'

'No, she seems even worse today and he wouldn't let her have any o' these sandwiches, not one! But she's still knocking back the mead at his say so, and he's shouting and ranting at her. She looks more poorly than when she came here a nine-month ago. And he's got that glint in his eye – you know what I mean, Marigold. The man's gone dog-demented, almost foaming at the mouth and I fear for that poor girl trapped all alone in there with him. 'Tain't right.'

'We'll feed up the poor maid when it's over, and 'tis not for much longer.'

'Aye, and just as well. Don't reckon she'd last much longer, way she looks now. He's a wicked man and he deserves what's coming.'

'True enough. And at least we won't have to cook all that fancy stuff them bloody Hallfolk clamour for at Yule. 'Twill be plain, wholesome Stonewylde fayre and nought else, after Solstice Eve. About time too!'

Old Greenbough yelled grumpily across the Circle at the men finishing off the great Solstice Bonfire. Like the one in the summer, it was built towards the edge of the Circle, on the opposite side to the Altar Stone. There was a platform with a beacon to be lit, and a ladder in the centre with a tiny entrance. The woodsmen were filling in the gaps between the large branches that formed the outer framework, and Greenbough stomped around issuing orders and muttering complaints.

'I miss Yul, I really do,' he said to nobody in particular. 'Like a squirrel he used to be as a lad, racing up and down the bonfire so agile. Nobody else comes close.'

'Aye, well, he won't be building no more o' these, will he, sir? Not when he's our new magus,' mumbled a huge man, chopping up extra wood for padding out the fire.

'Ssh!' hissed Greenbough, glancing at the Hallfolk who were with Merewen and a group of Villagers putting the finishing touches to the paintings on the stones. Fennel looked up sharply and glanced at his sister, Rainbow. They raised their eyebrows at each other, feeling the strange atmosphere in the Circle – suppressed excitement, anticipation, but also fear.

They continued their painting: mistletoe, holly and ivy, and the rising sun picked out in gleaming gold. The Altar Stone was decorated with evergreens around the base, and there were torches and braziers all surrounding the great Stone Circle. The entire Winter Solstice festival was a celebration of the return of light, the coming of the sun.

'Do you reckon what they've been saying at the Hall is true?' whispered Rainbow. 'That Yul will become the new magus tomorrow night?'

'I don't know,' muttered Fennel, 'but I bloody well hope not. Village bastard! I wish Buzz was still here so we could give him a good thrashing like we used to.'

'But what will happen to Magus? I don't understand; how can Yul just take over? Magus would never let that happen – we all know how powerful and fierce he is.'

'I don't know, Rainbow. It's a load of stupid Village talk I expect. We'll be celebrating the Solstice as usual from tomorrow evening, and Yule for the twelve days, and then off to Switzerland. Don't worry about it – Yul's just a Village peasant and nothing will come of all this bloody daft gossip.'

They fell silent as Merewen approached, filthy in her paint-stained overalls, curly hair springing in profusion around her no-nonsense face.

'Good, nice work. Rainbow, come and help me over at the big stone behind the altar – I need your fine hand.'

Rainbow glanced in surprise at her teacher as they surveyed the largest of the stones where the key image for the festival was being painted. Merewen had outlined something totally out of place at the Winter Solstice.

'I don't understand! Why on earth are we painting a Green Man?'

But Merewen merely smiled and handed her a paintbrush.

Down in the Village there was a great deal of activity in preparation for the feasting and dancing that would begin the following night and continue for twelve days, with dances, dramas, singing, musical events and games. The Great Barn was decorated with evergreens and many candles and the Yule Log already lay in the enormous fireplace, ready to be lit. Every cottage in the Village had an evergreen wreath on its front door, representing the wheel of the year, and Yule candles stood in parlour windows to welcome the return of the sun. The trees around the Village Green had been hung with small lanterns to be lit each night. There was an air of anticipation trembling amongst the bare branches and trunks of the trees that formed the circle. The children ran wildly around the Green in their warm homespun jackets and pointed felt hats. They spoke excitedly of the Yule elves, dressed in green leaves, who'd visit their homes tomorrow night and leave little gifts in the knitted socks hanging over every hearth; honeyed cobnuts and creamy fudge, and carved animals or bead necklaces.

In the cottages and at the Village bakers and butchers, people were busy cooking and preparing food for the feasts. Every household was filled with the fragrance of herbs and spices, the mouthwatering aroma of baking. Tomorrow was the Frost Moon and every Villager was aware of its significance and what would take place before the sun rose the following morning. In the cottage down the lane, Maizie tried to concentrate on her baking but when Sweyn and Gefrin, the two youngest boys, came tearing into the kitchen for the umpteenth time and knocked Leveret flying, she finally snapped.

'Get out, you little brats!' she shrieked. 'Get out of here and don't come back till I've finished the baking!'

Rosie was busy polishing everyone's festival boots in the parlour and came hurrying in, alarmed at the note of hysteria in her mother's voice. She found Maizie crying into the bowl of flour while Leveret howled on the floor.

'Oh Mother, don't cry! Geoffrey! Gregory! Take the boys down to the Green to play, and keep them there.'

She scooped up Leveret and put an arm round her mother's shaking shoulders.

'He'll be alright, Mother. Don't cry – our Yul will be alright.'

'We don't know that, Rosie! Magus is strong and clever, and Yul's only a boy, for all his new power. I can't bear it!'

'Think o' the prophecy, Mother. You know what Edward and Tom and everyone's been saying, about this being the right way. How 'twas destined to be since Yul's birth.'

'Aye, Rosie, that damn prophecy's been ringing in my ears for sixteen years! Don't mean it'll come to pass though. Old Heggy was a Wise Woman, but where are her powers now? She can't help our Yul and he's on his own.'

'No, Mother, he has the folk behind him, just like the prophecy foretold. He's got lots o' help.'

'You're wrong there, my girl. Oh aye, I know the folk are behind him and they want Magus gone as much as we do. I know they've all been meeting and planning and hatching, and all that talk about what will be, when Magus is gone – all the dreams about a Stonewylde run by the Villagers. But in the end 'tis Yul who must face Magus alone; 'tis my boy who must bring this all about. That's what's going round and round in my head like a ferret in a trap – my poor son, only a lad, up against that strong and desperate man. I don't think Yul stands a chance.'

Preparations for Yule were also taking place at the Hall. As in the Barn, evergreens hung everywhere and the Galleried Hall was particularly beautiful. The ancient vaulted roof and the gallery balustrade were woven with ivy and holly, and great bunches of mistletoe hung in white-berried magical splendour over every arched doorway. There were myriad pale beeswax candles on massive wrought-iron candle-trees standing in the corners. A huge evergreen tree had been decorated with tiny carved birds and animals and woven straw fairies and elves, all hanging from the tree with scarlet ribbons. The silver, twinkling lights were the only concession to the twenty-first century, sparkling amongst the branches. Another great Yule Log lay in the long hearth, decorated like the one in the Village with skeins of ivy and straw birds.

The Hallfolk went to the Great Barn for many of the entertainments, dances and feasting, but they also held their own private celebrations here. Galloping around the Barn with the Villagers and quaffing cider and hearty food was all very well, but there was much to be said for the more refined pleasures of the Hall. Trying to play charades and other more cerebral party games with illiterate Villagers was no fun at all. The Hallfolk, whose sophisticated palates craved more subtle pleasures, enjoyed fine champagne and exotic delicacies throughout the Twelve Days of Yule.

The atmosphere in the Hall was expectant, but also uneasy. Somehow the servants' gossip had become common knowledge and there was much speculation about the so-called prophecy of long ago. Most Hallfolk were outwardly loyal to Magus, but privately, many had recently become rather disillusioned. He'd been harsh and uncaring towards some, and seemed irrational and even a little unhinged at times, when he could be bothered to show his face at all. The sinister events of Samhain were known to all, even though Magus had tried to gloss over what had really happened. The incident at the Dark Moon when he'd terrified some Hallfolk girls and slapped Holly hard was discussed at length, and the sight of Sylvie in the Galleried Hall, clearly underfed and ill, had really worried people. The revelations of that morning had shocked many as Magus had told them outright lies for no apparent reason, and hadn't either apologised or explained himself since.

His behaviour was becoming increasingly erratic, and many now thought it was time for a new magus. But they feared they'd lose their privileges and lives of ease if a young Villager were to take over the reins of leadership. Yul may be Hallfolk by blood but he certainly wasn't one of them, as he himself had insisted so vehemently the other day. Below stairs there was a fever of excitement amongst the servants, and a fervent hope that the Hallfolk *would* lose their privileges and lives of ease.

'Might I have a quick word please, sir?'

Magus glanced up as Martin slid silently into his office. The man was so deferential and Magus acknowledged ruefully that he needed something to help calm him down; Martin was probably the best antidote for his rage. He'd spent it on Sylvie, of course, but every time he thought about the missing eggs he felt his fury rise up again. He'd left her locked in his apartments whilst he worked down here for an hour, trying to bring himself under control.

'Yes, Martin. What can I do for you?'

'Please forgive me being personal, sir, but I been wondering ... Yesterday Master Clip told us he were Miss Sylvie's father and I wondered if that was really true?'

Magus frowned, not wishing to be reminded of the debacle in the Galleried Hall and the awful humiliation as his lies were unmasked in public.

'I imagine so. It seems probable, and he and Miranda are agreed on it. Why do you ask, Martin?'

'Well, sir. I always understood that although Master Clip owns Stonewylde, passed on by his father Basil, as he had no children himself 'twould pass on to you one day. But if he has a child, then I suppose she'd be the heir to Stonewylde?'

'Yes, you're right. Whatever made you think of that, Martin?'

'My mother, sir – I visited her last night and she and my Aunt Vetchling were talking about it and wondering.'

'I see. And how is Old Violet?'

Martin's nose wrinkled with distaste at the memory of the filthy cottage shared by his mother Violet and her sister. Vetchling's daughter Starling also lived there, with her own little boy and her nephew, Jackdaw's son. The cottage was a little way out of the Village and the family were generally ostracised by the Villagers. The three women were not popular and the two little boys were dirty and unsociable.

'She's well enough, sir. Busy baking ceremony cakes for the Solstice o' course.'

'Good. And tell me, Martin ... what's the general feeling amongst the Villagers about this coming Solstice? I mean this business about Yul and the ridiculous prophecy that's been raked up again. Are people talking much about it?'

Martin eyed Magus carefully. He knew he was treading on eggshells here, for the master was touchy at the moment.

'I don't get to hear much of the tittle-tattle, sir, not in my position. The servants always whisper in corners, o' course, but they stop when they see me coming.'

'What about Violet and Vetchling, and Starling for that matter? Have they heard anything?'

Martin shook his head firmly.

'Not really, sir. But they have some scheme afoot for tomorrow night, some dark magic, and they'll do their bit to help out as ever.'

'So they haven't heard any rumours or gossip about Yul and his plans?'

'No, sir. My mother's family are treated shockingly, and that's a fact. Folk cross the road to avoid them. 'Tis on account of Jackdaw, o' course, but 'tis not right. Not for a woman of my mother's position. She should be respected, not insulted.'

'I promise you, Martin, that once this Solstice is over, things will change at Stonewylde. Loyalty will be rewarded ... and betrayal will be dealt with severely.'

'Have you seen what is to come? What will unfold?' asked Mother Heggy, peering almost sightlessly at the blond man in the chair opposite her. He shook his head, eyeing the crow on the table warily. He knew what that crow had done at Mooncliffe during the last full moon.

'I've seen very little lately,' he replied. 'My gift, such as it is, seems to have deserted me in recent months.'

The crone nodded and creakily bent forward to take his hands in hers. He flinched – all his life he'd been terrified of this woman. He knew she hated him and had done so since his moment of conception. She gazed at him with milky eyes and crooned softly as she rocked.

'Your father were a bad man,' she mumbled eventually. 'He took what he shouldn't have and he violated what were forbidden. And you, born under the eclipse – you should've been truly gifted. But you too took what you shouldn't have and you've suffered for that, right enough.'

Clip nodded and sat silently, reflecting on his plight. Mother Heggy sighed.

'But now you have another chance – you must protect your daughter and do what is right.'

'Yes I will! To discover I have a daughter, after all this time ... I want so much to do what's right. And I've never wanted to hurt anyone.'

'Aye, you speak the truth. You have the gentleness of my Raven in you, I see it clear. What you did under that Harvest Moon – 'twas destiny, for the silver girl had to be conceived. The moon-gazy maiden had to return to Stonewylde to dance the spirals. But she's in great danger, the bright one, caged as she is. I feel it strong, yet 'tis not clear. My power has all but gone. The binding spell is almost over, its magic spent, and tomorrow my dark one will stand alone. Oh how I fear for him!'

It was silent save for the crackling of the meagre fire in the hearth and the creaking of the rocking chair. Clip felt himself drawn to the ancient Wise Woman and wished that he'd visited

310

her before. He'd always been too scared to approach her knowing how she cursed him and his brother, and when Yul had said Mother Heggy wanted to see him he'd been terrified of the encounter. But now he felt the old magic in her, the knowledge and wisdom of a true witch. He could've learnt so much from her over the years, if he'd only had the courage to seek her out. He resolved to forge a bond with her and visit regularly from now on. He'd make the tumble-down cottage more comfortable for her too; it was in a terrible state of repair.

'Beware o' your brother,' she whispered suddenly, her grip on his hand tightening. 'He has evil in his heart. He's the serpent that creeps.'

'I've always been wary of my brother,' he replied sadly. 'I know he's evil and I long for his reign to be over.'

'No,' she said. 'I speak not of him. 'Tis the *other* brother who's a danger to you.'

Clip frowned at her, but then she began to moan softly, a strange noise that made his skin horripilate. The old woman was peering under the table, and he bent to see what she stared at. The scraggy black cat was under there, growling low, its mangy tail lashing. Laid out carefully in a neat row were five dead rats, their throats torn. The cat glared malignantly, daring anyone to touch his trophies.

'Five! Always five!' croaked Mother Heggy. She clutched at her dirty shawl in fear, her gnarled fingers scrabbling on the worn fabric. 'Five deaths at the Solstice! Five souls for the Dark Angel, and I know not whose!'

18

The day of Solstice Eve finally dawned. Yul received the earth energy not on the Altar Stone as usual, but in the dolmen up in the hills by the woods. He sat in the ancient temple feeling the power spiral up from beneath him as the sun rose above the horizon. This was the energy of the earth dragon of old, the serpent lines of green magic that lay deep in the ground, waiting to be drawn upon by those wise ones with special ability. He'd spent the night in the dolmen, not trusting Magus to leave him alone. There could have been a midnight raid on his cottage or a surprise visit to the Stone Circle at sunrise, as Magus had done the day before.

Yul sat for a while, deep in thought. Tonight was the brightness in the darkness, the Moon Fullness at the Winter Solstice. As from sunset today, Yul would be unprotected by Mother Heggy's spell and Magus would be out to hunt him down. By sunrise tomorrow morning at the Solstice, the prophecy would've come about if it were to happen as foretold. And if not, Yul would be dead. Whilst he wasn't trying to kill his father, he knew without doubt that his father intended to kill him. Yesterday Magus had offered him partnership and Yul had instinctively refused, knowing his father wasn't honourable and couldn't be trusted. Regardless of what Magus might promise, he and Sylvie would always be in danger from him, and so he'd refused the compromise.

Tonight he must rise up against his father to overthrow him.

He had no choice, for those words had greeted his birth and blighted his life. Tonight, when the moon was full, was the time for fulfilment of the prophecy. Yul had to face his father one to one at the Place of Bones and Death. All that remained unclear was the outcome; what would happen there tonight was out of his hands, and all he could do was be there to let destiny take its course.

Yul's clear grey eyes roamed across the body of the woman before him, clothed in her winter robe. Trees sprang from her head, and the hills formed her shoulder and hip as she lay on her side. The curve of her waist was the valley, and the ancient tumuli her breasts. The Goddess in the landscape lay silent and still before him as he looked out from his vantage point on the hill. This was the woman who held the gift of life in her womb, latent now in the depths of winter but ready to be born again as the returning sun bestowed his warm caress in the spring. This woman, this sentient landscape, was Stonewylde; he must guard her with his life and cherish her until his death, for he was the chosen one, the magus.

Yul thought then of Sylvie, the other woman he must protect. She too was part of the synergy of Stonewylde and linked to the landscape as strongly as he. As ever, just thinking about her made his bones melt. He loved her more than life itself and tonight he was prepared to die for her. Should everything go wrong and she be put in danger, he'd give his life to save her from Magus.

'Bring hand guns, yes. You shouldn't need them, but ... yes, exactly. Remember the element of surprise will be crucial and it'll all take place outside. Definitely camouflage gear, and cuffs and rope too. When you arrive you'll be stopped at the Gate House. They'll ring me and I'll come to get you, and brief you fully ... Yes ... I see, but absolutely no later than three p.m. You have to be in position before sunset at four ... Yes, and the other half on completion. Fine, see you at three.'

Sylvie shut her eyes and pretended to be asleep as Magus came over to the sofa. Her heart clutched with terror at what she'd overheard – a hired man to help him tonight with guns, cam-ouflage gear and rope? Yul wouldn't stand a chance; she had to get warning to him. She quaked with fear but tried to keep still as Magus looked down at her. He ran his fingers delicately over her cheekbone and she stirred slightly.

'Wake up, sleepy head,' he said gently. 'Breakfast will be coming soon and I'm sure you're hungry.'

He knelt and stroked the hair away from her face, then leant forward and softly kissed her cheek. She was enveloped in the exotic smell of him, and remembered with shame how there'd been a time when that scent had thrilled her. She opened her eyes quickly to prevent any further intimacy and gazed at him in trepidation. He'd been so very cruel to her yesterday. Was he still playing cat and mouse? But Magus was kindness itself this morning; a different person from the man of the previous night who'd shouted at her and threatened her with torture on the rock at Mooncliffe. He went off to run a bath for her as they waited for breakfast to arrive.

Immediately Sylvie ran to his desk and grabbed a pen and a scrap of paper. Her hands shook badly and the heavy diamond cuffs weighed her wrists down and caught on everything on his desk, restricting her movements. She had to get a message to Yul and warn him, particularly as Magus had said the element of surprise was crucial. Fingers trembling, she scribbled a note to Clip and crumpled it small in her hand. Her black silk pyjamas had no pockets where she could hide it and she thought fran-tically – would a servant bring the food or would it come in the dumb waiter? She usually missed breakfast and had no idea, but decided on the latter.

Her hands shook uncontrollably as she yanked open the con-cealed panel. She saw with relief that the small lift was up here and not downstairs. She put the note inside, knowing that the servants would find it. She hoped against hope that they'd pass it on to Clip, who'd make sure Yul was warned.

'What are you doing?'

'I . . . I thought I heard the food coming, but it wasn't.'

'Are you very hungry?'

'Yes, I am.'

'Come here.'

She padded reluctantly to him as he stood by the window. The sun had risen and was sparkling the melting frost into dew on the lawn to the south-east. He pulled her to him and wrapped his arms around her, feeling her thin shoulders and arms as he cradled her head against his chest.

'I'm sorry, Sylvie. I've treated you cruelly and I'm truly sorry. Something inside me – it takes over sometimes and I can't stop. It's not your fault, any of this, but you've borne the brunt of my anger and frustration over the past month. Look at the state of you! I've starved you deliberately and now you're far too thin, and your poor arms with these horrific black bruises ... You're beautiful and delicate like a rare butterfly and I've damaged you with my rough, careless handling. I hope you'll be able to forgive me – I fully intend to put everything right, believe me.'

She stood perfectly still, her skin crawling wherever he touched her. His fingers gently but insistently caressed her back, feeling her bones through the flesh, tracing her shoulder blades and the vertebrae in her spine. He sighed and squeezed her tightly for a moment, then held her away a little and tipped her face up to his. His gaze was soft and he groaned.

'Oh Sylvie, I'm so sorry for mistreating you, my lovely girl. I've been brutal – Clip always says I go too far and he's right. But I'm not a bad person, not deep down inside. You must help me develop my better nature and overcome my darkness.'

To her horror he bent to kiss her lips. She jerked back, every muscle in her body screaming resistance, but he held her firmly. He put one hand behind her head, bringing her face inexorably towards his. The thick diamond collar dug deeper into her throat and neck, cutting into her skin so she couldn't twist her head away. Magus' eyes gleamed as he closed in and then she felt his mouth move on hers, his lips firm and insistent, his tongue adamant. She struggled, trying to pull away from his hungry, invasive kiss. Relief flooded through her as the buzz of the dumb

315

waiter signalled the arrival of breakfast. With another groan he pulled back and smiled ruefully, his eyes heavy-lidded and glazed.

'We'll continue that later on. I've held back for far too long and Goddess knows why – you're clearly a beautiful woman now and no longer a girl. But you're hungry, my darling, and I must feed you. Go and sit down and I'll bring breakfast over.'

He served her at the table, waiting on her hand and foot, piling food onto her plate from the silver serving dishes. Sylvie enjoyed her cooked breakfast, the first proper meal she'd had for a long time, all thoughts of the kiss pushed to the back of her mind. She sat in her black silk pyjamas, blond hair everywhere and diamonds sparkling, and tucked in to her food hungrily. Then she soaked in the bath he'd run and felt a great deal better than she had for ages.

As she lay in the bubbling black marble tub, the truth dawned. Of course – it was the Moon Fullness tonight and Magus wanted her able to cope with the ordeal that awaited her on the moon rock. All this thoughtfulness and attention was just to make her a little stronger, which negated any apparent kindness; he was simply being his usual calculating self. But Sylvie knew it wasn't for much longer, and that thought gave her courage – just a few more hours to endure and then she'd be free.

Professor Siskin watched the countryside roll past the window of his first-class carriage. A modest suitcase and precious computer bag were his only luggage and the latter now sat on his knees as he gazed out of the window, unable to concentrate on his work. Since receiving the e-mail from Sylvie yesterday, he'd been desperately excited. He hadn't spent the Winter Solstice at Stonewylde since Sol became magus many years ago.

He muttered to himself and received odd looks from other passengers, but the old professor was oblivious. He was going home! Sylvie was such a lovely girl, kind and caring and passionate in her love of Stonewylde. Of course she was Clip's daughter – it was so obvious once you knew. Who'd have thought Clip would ever father a child and produce an heir? As for Yul

... Siskin pulled out his photo of the boy and felt that thrill of recognition all over again. He knew he was looking at the Green Man, whose return to Stonewylde would ensure that all would be well and all would prosper. The magus and the moongazy girl, the Green Man and the May Queen, the Earth Magic and the moon magic, Yul and Sylvie. Stonewylde hadn't had anything like this for a long time, not for centuries, in fact. The good times were about to begin and Siskin smiled joyfully in the knowledge that he'd be there, in his beloved home, to herald the dawn of the new magus and the return of the sun.

When Sylvie returned to the sitting room from her bath, she found the fire had been re-laid and was now blazing in the great hearth. The room had been cleaned too; she smelt the beeswax polish and the carpet looked freshly vacuumed. Magus was at his desk working as usual, and looked up as she entered.

'Refreshing bath? Sit down and I'll dry your hair for you.'

Her heart sank. This involved him fiddling about with her hair and her neck, and after the attempted kiss this morning she was scared of him. She could tell he was unstable at the moment, balancing on a knife-edge of normality but capable of going completely over with minimal provocation. He was terrifying today, with a desperation in his eyes she hadn't seen before. He must know that tonight he could be finished – so today he may feel he'd nothing to lose.

Sylvie found her large comb and sat on a cushion in front of the sofa, the fire's heat blasting at her. She crossed her legs, tucking her bare feet beneath her, and straightened her back. Magus came and sat on the sofa behind her, teasing out the long strands of hair that fell down her back like a jumble of wet string. His fingers were gentle and he seemed calm enough, and Sylvie started to relax. The fire made her cheeks flush but it was also drying her hair quickly, so he'd have to release her soon.

She was just beginning to feel safe when she noticed her book. The servant who'd cleaned the room must've picked it up, after Magus had kicked it across the room yesterday, and it now lay on a small table in direct view of the sofa. Where was the photo? Given Magus' present volatility, the sight of Yul might tip him over. She realised he was talking to her and dragged her attention back to him.

'I'd like to buy you a horse in the spring,' he was saying. 'I'll teach you to ride, and then we can travel all over Stonewylde together. You said you liked horses, didn't you?'

'Yes,' she said quickly, thinking of her strange ride with Yul on the milk-white horse through the misty woods full of red toadstools. 'I've always wanted to learn to ride.'

'I'll buy you a beautiful horse,' he said. 'A really gentle, but intelligent, mare. I suspect you'll be a natural.'

His fingers raked through her hair onto her scalp, massaging her with a confident touch.

'And we'll go abroad too, as I promised, wherever you want to go. You can swim in the clearest, warmest waters and I'll enjoy showing you the wonders and beauties of the world.'

She didn't know how to respond to this, so kept quiet. He scooped up all her hair into one handful and raised it from her neck. He touched the heavy diamond choker, and gently traced where it chafed her skin.

'Is this sore? Does it rub?'

'Yes, all the time. It cuts into me and hurts when I'm trying to sleep.'

'Oh well, I'm sure you'll get used to it. It's like a new saddle or bridle on a horse – always rubs a bit at first while it's being broken in.'

His long fingers slid around the choker, caressing her neck and throat. She held her breath, desperately hoping he'd be distracted by something and stop. His thumbs began to massage the back of her neck, moving to her shoulders. Sylvie knew she must get out of this situation fast. She pulled away slightly and pretended to cough. He stopped and waited until she'd finished, then reached forward and cupped a hand under her chin.

Magus tipped her head right back against the sofa so that she was looking backwards, her throat arched and fully extended, right into his upside down face. He looked almost demonic. His dark eyes gleamed with that black light and his smile was strange. He traced her feathery eyebrows and stroked her jaw line, and she noticed the muscle in his cheek twitching.

'You're mine,' he said thickly. 'My own moongazy girl, so special and magical. Nobody else will ever have you, Sylvie – you belong to me.'

His fingers slid to the choker on her arched throat, now biting into her windpipe. He caressed the delicate skin, tenderly feeling the chafing.

'Sylvie,' he groaned, 'what've you done to me? I've never felt like this before – it's so much deeper than simply wanting you. You're the only woman in the world who can give me what I need and you've no idea the torment I'm going through. Today ... today it's more powerful than ever, maybe because of the full moon tonight. I'm on fire today.'

With a swift movement Magus rose from the sofa and stood before her on the hearth. He bent and took her hands in his, pulling her upright. The diamond cuffs glittered on her wrists, and her hair, now dry and silky, cascaded over her shoulders in a wild silver mass. He stood in front of her, holding her hands loosely in his, gazing at her. Her cheeks were flushed from the fire and her eyes bright as she watched him fearfully, petrified of what was coming next. His breathing was heavy and she recognised that expression in his eyes; she'd seen it in Yul too. Magus started to close in and she edged backwards, trying to get away. He tugged and she pulled back, shaking her head, her eyes wide with fear.

'Sylvie, please ...'

'No!'

'I love you, Sylvie. I never thought I'd say those words, but I do.'

'You don't love me! If you loved me you wouldn't treat me like this. You've been so cruel to me!'

'I've only been cruel *because* I love you. It's so strong it hurts, and it makes me want to hurt you in return. You torture me with your coldness and indifference ... if you'd just show me some warmth, some gratitude for everything I've given you. Look at you! You're dripping with my diamonds; they're worth thousands of pounds. Any other girl would die for those diamonds.'

'I hate them! They're cold, and they cut into me and hurt me, like you do. I don't want your love, Magus. Your love is selfish and cruel, and—'

'Come here, Sylvie, and let me kiss you properly. You're so innocent; you don't know anything and I know all there is to know. Wait until I've shown you what making love is all about. When you've flown and touched the stars, then tell me you don't want my love. Come here, Sylvie!'

He tugged so sharply she stumbled into him, and he wrapped his arms fiercely around her, crushing her attempts to struggle from his grasp. She closed her eyes, praying desperately for a miracle to save her. She knew his steely determination to have his own way, and she also knew of his legendary passion, his need for women. He'd hardly left the room for days and he must be ready to explode. Nothing she said or did would make any difference. She could feel just how he craved her, trembling as he held her close. He bent his head to kiss her, his eyes boring into hers.

The intercom buzzed sharply once and then again, insistently. Sylvie felt him tense like a coil.

'Bloody hell!'

Magus strode over to the phone on his desk, practically ripping it from the connection.

'This had better be bloody important!' he snarled, face scarlet with anger. 'What? Oh, yes, we'll be down, Martin – I'd forgotten. Give them all some more mead and wait for us – we'll be ten minutes.'

He slammed down the receiver and glared at Sylvie as if it were her fault.

'We're eating lunch downstairs today. I hadn't realised it was so late so go and get dressed quickly. And put make-up on too – I want you to look especially beautiful today. Be quick, girl!'

320

Gratefully, Sylvie slipped past him and through all the rooms to get to her bedroom. A dress of midnight-blue crêpe de Chine lay on the bed and a pair of elegant high-heeled shoes had been put out too – Sylvie knew she was to be displayed again in front of the Hallfolk, exactly as he'd tried to do in the Galleried Hall. He'd even chosen underwear for her and she felt resentment boiling up inside. How did he think anyone could bear to live like this, with every detail controlled by him? But no time for rebellion now – and none of this would matter soon anyway. Tugging off her black pyjamas she slipped into the ivory silk underwear, quickly rolled the fine stockings up her long legs, and then stepped into the beautiful dress. She could hear Magus coming through the connecting chambers and struggled frantically with the zipper to fasten it before he came in. She quickly moved away from the untouched bed and sat on the stool before the dressing table, snatching up her mascara with a shaking hand.

'Hurry up, Sylvie!' he said. 'They're all waiting for us in the Dining Hall.'

He stood behind her as she caught up her mass of hair in a pretty clasp at the back of her head. Then she applied some make-up and he watched her movements as if mesmerised, his eyes meeting hers in the mirror. She rose and slipped her feet into the high-heeled shoes, transforming instantly into an elegant young woman whose eyes were almost level with his. His gaze swept down the length of her, noting the skin tight fit of the dress and the way it accentuated her model's figure, the hemline brushing her slim calves. The diamonds at her throat and wrists glittered, and with her hair up, she looked every inch the sophisticated ingénue. He smiled, his eyes still burning with desire, and ran his hand down the side of her ribs and into the hollow of her tiny waist.

'Perfect! Now come on – we're very late.'

He took her hand and led her down the wide staircase to the great Dining Hall where all the Hallfolk were gathered for lunch. The huge room was packed full with extra visitors but the noisy chatter fell silent when they entered. Sylvie held his arm as she'd been ordered as they swept in together, and Magus smiled graciously around him, greeting people and nodding. Sylvie remained silent and impassive, keeping her eyes fixed ahead; she wasn't going to pretend she was enjoying this.

Magus led her up the long length of the room to the head of the high table, where an extra place had been laid next to his. He seated her attentively, fussing over her, his message to the Hallfolk very clear. Sylvie refused wine or mead and he couldn't force her to drink in front of everyone. When lunch was served she ate each course hungrily, uncaring of people's surprised stares as she wolfed down the food. She felt all eyes on her; the people she knew, and many visitors who hadn't seen her before, or barely recognised her as the young newcomer from earlier in the year. Of her mother and Clip, there was no sign at all.

Sylvie's peer group watched her the whole time with undis-guised envy. They were too far away on other tables to make conversation with her but they followed her every move, staring at the expensive couture dress and the heavy diamond choker and wristbands that glittered as she moved. They commented to each other on her thinness and beauty and her air of complete detachment from everyone, even Magus. Each of them would've loved to have been in her place wearing those clothes and jewels, sitting alongside a man so clearly obsessed. Magus watched her closely as well, frowning as she accepted a second helping of the main course.

'Don't overdo it, Sylvie,' he said quietly. 'I've just told you that you're perfect.'

'I'm hungry!' she retorted, feeling safe from his bullying with so many people about. 'You've been starving me and I need food.'

'Yes, and I want you to eat today, but you'll make yourself sick if you have too much.'

'That's a change from you making me sick with all that mead. Leave me alone, Magus – I'll eat what I want.'

'Don't speak to me like that, Sylvie,' he said very softly. 'You might get away with it here, in front of all these people, but you know I'll make you pay for it later when I've got you alone.'

She glared at him and continued eating, knowing it was annoying him and feeling glad. When this was all over, she vowed that she'd never miss a meal again.

Yul raced up the track to Mother Heggy's cottage. He was very busy today but knew he must see her. It was turning colder, he noted, although the sun shone brightly. There'd be a hard frost tonight, he was sure, for the December Frost Moon. He knocked at the battered and rotten door and went in.

Mother Heggy was crouched in a corner poking at something on the floor. She peered up at him and rose creakily to her feet, her back still bent almost double. She shuffled towards him and, to his surprise, embraced him. She felt like a tiny bird. Beneath the layers of grimy, ancient clothing, there was barely anything left of her.

'The time is here,' she wheezed. 'The brightness in the darkness. 'Tis all up to you now, Yul – are you ready for it?'

He nodded. 'I am, and everything's in place. Will you come to the sunrise ceremony tomorrow morning, Mother Heggy? I'd love to have you there and it'd be fitting too – full circle.'

She shook her grizzled head.

'I can't be out in the cold and dark with my old bones, Yul. Maybe the Summer Solstice, when Sylvie's sixteen. 'Twill be warmer then.'

'Alright, but we'll both come and see you tomorrow. You'll be looking at the new magus then!'

She felt the excitement and certainty flowing in him, but shook her head again.

'I need your help, Yul. Will you drag the table over to the wall?'

'Yes ... but why?'

He pulled the heavy oak table, scraping it over the uneven flagstone floor. She picked up an ancient besom and began to brush feebly at the debris that littered the floor.

'That's why,' she said breathlessly, pointing to the floor. 'You do it for me, Yul. I feel so weary today.'

She sank into the rocking chair whilst he swept the floor, with the crow crouched on the table watching. Yul saw marks scratched into the flagstones and gradually a large pentangle within a circle was revealed. He automatically made the sign in the air, touching his heart to signify that his spirit and the elements were as one, bound by the same laws and the same love of the Goddess.

'There, Mother Heggy. Anything else?'

She pointed to the things she needed, her breathing laboured in the dust raised by Yul's sweeping, and he set up the magic circle ready for her. He placed a small candle in a green glass jar at each point of the pentangle, and a bowl of salt in the centre. He knew that before she started her ceremony, she'd sprinkle it carefully around the perimeter from within, to keep the dark forces at bay and protect herself inside her circle. He placed her special symbolic objects at each point of the star, next to the candles. There was one each for the four elements – earth, air, fire and water – and one for the spirit, the fifth element. He placed matches and a taper next to the salt, ready for her to light the candles. Finally he added a cushion for her, placing it within the pentagon formed at the heart of the pentangle.

Yul surveyed the magical space marked on the floor and respectfully stepped out of it. He didn't cast the circle or call upon the elements; he didn't need to. Yul felt the power of nature everywhere; the Earth Goddess spoke to him directly through the green magic at the special places all over Stonewylde. Clip needed the dragon lines within the dolmen and the ridgeway. Sylvie needed the full moon and the magical spirals in the hill marked by the Hare Stone. Many people simply needed a wood, a beach, a hill top, or just blue sky on a sunny day. And others, like Mother Heggy, cast their circles with salt and flame and called upon the powers to visit them and bless them. Yul respected each way of communing with the force of nature, the magic of creation, the life energy that throbbed and snaked and sparkled everywhere all over the earth. Each to their own – there were many paths to the same destination.

'Blessings, Yul. You're a good lad and I'm proud of you. I'll be within my circle tonight as the sun sets and the moon rises and I'll do all I can for you. No! Don't say you need none o' my help! We all want that man gone and if I can call upon any of the forces, then I will. Don't imagine tonight will be easy, Yul. Don't think that because I made that prophecy sixteen years ago, 'twill all come to pass as you hope.'

Mother Heggy sighed heavily and the crow hopped onto her lap. She stroked its glossy plumage with a twisted finger.

'Your father is still very powerful. That man has dark elements on his side that only he can use. And there are ancient echoes of energy and ancient story patterns at Stonewylde still in play. Nought is set in stone. Anything could happen once my spell of protection comes to an end. You could fail tonight, my dark one, and Sylvie could be taken. Did you give her the charm bag? My Raven's magical things?'

'Yes, Mother Heggy, she has them and she'll wear them tonight for protection.'

'Well enough – let's hope they do protect her. Didn't help my girl in the end, mind you.' She hung her shrivelled head, her breathing obstreperous. 'And you, my boy, glowing there with the green magic all sparkling about you – don't make the mistake of thinking all will go to plan just because Stonewylde loves you. Stonewylde has had her dark times afore, terrible times when all seemed lost and gone. 'Tis possible we'll enter those dark times again.'

Yul stared at her, worry creasing his face. He knelt before her as she crouched in the rocking chair and took her withered hands in his young, strong ones. He looked into her milky eyes, his fierce spirit blazing from within.

'Thank you for your wisdom, Mother Heggy. I heed what you say and I'll do my best and fight my hardest. I don't know how this will end but I must trust that the Goddess will watch over me, just as you've watched over me my whole life. And if ... if I should fail tonight, please help Sylvie. She'll need you.'

The old crone nodded.

325

'Go, Yul – I must sleep for a while. I feel so tired and 'twill be a difficult night. I'll look out for the bright one, just as I've always looked out for you, the dark one. Bright blessings, young magus.'

She made the sign of the pentangle over his head and prayed silently to the Goddess to keep him safe. After he'd gone she dozed for a while and when she felt a little stronger, she rose slowly, muttering to herself, and began to prepare everything she needed for the night ahead. She was very frightened; earlier that morning she'd found five black feathers lying on her doorstep. The scrying glass still wouldn't show her what would happen that evening at sunset, when her binding spell was finally unravelled. Despite a lifetime of magic and practising the craft, the Wise Woman was now as much in the dark as the next person. Except for the message of five – that was as clear as spring water.

'This is all my fault,' said Hazel sadly as she removed the cuff from Miranda's upper arm. 'Your blood pressure's a little high, which is hardly surprising.'

Miranda rolled down her sleeve and patted Hazel's hand.

'It's *not* your fault. Don't even think it.'

'But I brought you here! It was my idea.'

'And what was the alternative? Leave Sylvie to die in London? Come on, Hazel, you did what you thought best and despite everything, I'm pleased you did.'

She looked down at her enormous pregnant bump and sighed. The baby was kicking again and had been agitated all day. She and Hazel had shared lunch in the hospital wing whilst she had her check-up, unable to face the clamour of the Dining Hall and the oblivious Hallfolk.

'Try to get some rest, Miranda. You look exhausted.'

'Tomorrow, when this whole nightmare is over, I'll rest. Clip's coming to fetch me in a minute and you know where we're going.'

She stood up and held out her arms to Hazel, who bent in an awkward hug over Miranda's belly. Unexpectedly the young doctor began to sob silently, the strain of the past weeks released at Miranda's unexpected show of affection.

'I'm so sorry,' Hazel mumbled through her tears. 'So very sorry it all turned out like this. I was completely fooled by him. I was *horrible* to poor Sylvie and I blamed her for everything. All the time he'd been making her suffer terribly at the Moon Fullness and I didn't believe her.'

'We're all guilty of that, Hazel, me more than anyone. I'm her mother and I should've been protecting her. Do you think she's alright? I'm still so worried about her up being there alone with him. Clip is sure Magus won't harm her, but . . .'

Hazel pulled away and found a tissue.

'I'm sure she's fine. Just a few hours more and she'll be safe for ever.'

'But what if it goes wrong this evening? Why won't Yul do what we all wanted? He should've agreed – how can he possibly deal with Magus alone?'

Hazel shook her head.

'That boy – that young man – is as determined and iron-willed as his father and he insists that he alone must challenge Magus. He says it's part of the prophecy and although he has the folk behind him, the conflict itself has to be resolved one to one. What can we do?'

'He'll make a good magus, I'm sure,' said Miranda, 'despite his lack of education. We're all here to help run Stonewylde, but he's got what it takes to lead the community. There's something very special and powerful about Yul.'

'Green magic,' said the doctor. 'Yul has the green magic now and that's why he's so adamant about what must happen tonight. With the Goddess on his side, how could he fail?'

As soon as the long lunch was over, Magus dragged Sylvie back upstairs. Once they were in his rooms with the door shut, he turned on her furiously, jabbing his finger at her aggressively.

'You need to learn how to behave, young lady! When I allow you downstairs to mix with the Hallfolk, you'll be sociable and gracious, both to them and to me. You're *never* to speak to me in that disrespectful way in front of them. And you're never to be so greedy either, stuffing food down your throat as fast as you can. Where's your sense of refinement and decorum? If you behave like that when I let you out, then you won't go out at all. You'll stay locked in these rooms until your manners improve. Do you understand?'

She nodded, her defiance gone now they were alone again. She looked out of the window; it was still bright and sunny but the wind looked cold.

'I'd like to go out for a walk,' she said. 'You haven't let me outside for ages and I need some fresh air.'

'Well you can't. You'll get plenty of fresh air tonight.'

'Then I'll change. This dress is too tight and it's cutting into me.'

'That's because you ate too much. No, keep it on – if it's uncomfortable it serves you right, and maybe it'll teach you not to be so greedy. I want you to rest for the afternoon, so sit down and read your book.'

He picked up her book where it lay on the table and handed it to her. Sylvie took it carefully, unsure if the photo was still inside. She went over to the window seat and he followed, unable to leave her alone.

There was a discreet knock at the door and Martin appeared. He stood respectfully before Magus, paying no attention to Sylvie.

'You said you wanted to speak to me after lunch, sir.'

'Yes, it's about Mooncliffe tonight.'

Martin's glance flicked to Sylvie.

'I'd be glad to assist you, sir.'

'Of course. I want you to go up there now and stack all the eggs around the rock.'

'Yes, sir. Will that be all?'

'No – take a couple of blankets too, and put up the little pavilion ready for us, and the brazier and wood for a fire. I'll need to keep my moongazy girl warm as she's going to be there most of the night.' Magus patted her knee, smooth under the crêpe de Chine. 'I did warn you, Sylvie – it's going to be a heavy night.'

She turned her head away pointedly and gazed out of the window. Magus smiled and looked at Martin, standing so impassive and cold-eyed.

'Oh, and one more thing, Martin.'

'Yes, sir?'

'Take the other things up there too.'

'The usual, sir?'

'Yes, the usual. Silk cushions, candles, champagne . . . you know what's required.'

The stony-faced man nodded and gave a small smile.

'I know what's required. And if I might say so sir – about time too.'

When he'd gone, Magus turned to Sylvie. The blood had drained from her face and he chuckled.

'I see you understood that.'

She nodded, unable to believe what he was planning for her.

'I simply can't wait any longer, Sylvie,' he said. 'I'm burning up for you – it's like a fire inside me and it hurts. I've heard my father was the same with my mother and I guess it's the moongaziness. You just don't understand the effect you have on me.'

She sat very still, her heart thumping with fear. What if everything went wrong tonight? She had faith in Yul but things had gone wrong before. And she remembered Magus' phone call – he had help coming soon which would give him such an advantage. What if they overpowered Yul? She'd be weak from the moongazing, unable to fight Magus off, and he was so much bigger and stronger than her anyway. She'd never be able to stop him. Sylvie started to cry softly, the tears rolling down her cheeks and smudging her make-up.

'Don't cry, my darling. I'll be so gentle, I promise. I love you, Sylvie, and after tonight, you'll love me too. I can guarantee that.'

'How can you do this to me if you love me?' she choked,

wiping the tears away impatiently. 'I don't want you and I'm too young – I'm not ready for this. There are so many others here and you can have anyone you want at Stonewylde.'

'But I don't want anyone else. It's *you* I crave. You're the only one who can feed the stones and give me the moon magic I need, and you're the only one I want to make love to. You're so beautiful and spirited and there's something so magical about you … nobody else will do when I can get everything I want and need from you. I won't wait another six months, Sylvie. I thought I could but I can't.'

He pulled out his handkerchief and gently wiped away her tears and mascara. He smiled at her ruefully.

'I've certainly never had this reaction before, when I tell a girl she's been chosen for the Moon Fullness! Please don't cry, Sylvie – you'll learn to love me, I promise. Let me get you some mead to help you relax.'

She groaned as he went over to the cabinet and found her crystal goblet. Still clutching the book, she gazed at the garden through the diamond paned glass, like a bird imprisoned in a cage. Here she sat, passive and confined, awaiting her fate. Sylvie hated being the victim and wanted more than anything to take control of her own life and destiny. She knew the whole community was busy preparing for the Solstice and that Yul would be preparing to implement his plan for her rescue. Everyone knew what was going on except for her. She was completely in the dark, unable to do anything to help herself, yet what happened tonight would determine the rest of her life.

If Yul failed, she'd never escape Magus' clutches. He'd keep her prisoner, starved into submission whenever he felt like it, every detail of her life controlled. He'd shower her with gifts, dress her in expensive clothes and jewels, parade her as a prized possession, but he'd never allow her any freedom. He'd dominate her every minute, binding her with his love and his hatred. For despite his protestations of love, Sylvie knew he hated her for her coldness towards him. She'd slowly wither under his obsessive captivity, like a wild bird trapped in a gilded cage.

Magus returned with her mead, moving across the floor like a great panther. She looked up into his face, so attractive with those strong features and dark eyes, his silvery-blond hair emphasising the perfection of his chiselled cheekbones and jaw. He was tall and muscular, every woman's dream of a desirable man, and yet he filled her with loathing and dread. He smiled at her as he held out the crystal goblet, his eyes bright with admiration and desire.

'Here you are, my moongazy girl. You look beautiful sitting there like that against the light. I feel—'

At that moment the photo, still between the pages of the book in Sylvie's hands, slipped out and fell to the floor. She gasped and quickly tried to cover it up with her foot. Magus frowned and placed the glass very deliberately on a side table.

'Magus, can we—'

She stopped, having no idea what she could say to distract him. Her mind was paralysed and her heart pounded with dread in the heavy silence. He looked her in the eye and something within him uncoiled itself, slowly and carefully.

'What are you trying to hide from me, Sylvie?' he asked quietly. 'What's this you're attempting to conceal?'

He bent and slid the white rectangle from under her shoe. Straightening up, he turned it over and stared full into the face of the Green Man. He saw the foliage in an aura around the head, the thick dark curls full of vegetation, and those clear, grey eyes, slanted and long-lashed, gazing out from the green-smeared face with such clarity. Sylvie froze in absolute terror and Magus raised his eyes to meet hers. He finally realised then, in that moment, that Sylvie would never love him. This boy was the one she wanted, the only one she'd ever love. He, Magus of Stonewylde, was nothing to her and never could be. With a roar of pure animal rage, he ripped the photo in two.

'*Why?*' he bellowed. '*Why him? Why not me?*'

He ripped the photo in half again, and then again, throwing the pieces to the floor and grinding them under his boot in a paroxysm of fury. He snatched up the goblet and flung it violently across the room. It hit the wall and smashed in an explosion of crystal shards and amber liquid. His chest heaved with anger as he glared down at Sylvie, his hands clenching and unclenching, his breathing loud. She curled up as small and tight as her skin-tight dress allowed, burrowing into the corner of the window seat, her face white and eyes enormous with terror. He fell to his knees before her, taking her shoulders in his hands and gripping her tightly. His eyes were wild in his hollow face. His voice was low and trembling, nothing like his normal smooth tone.

'You cut me to the bone, Sylvie. I've told you how I feel about you and I laid myself open to you. I offered you something I've never offered anyone before, not even the girl I once cared for so many years ago. All I ask for is your love. Why's that so difficult to give? Every woman I've ever noticed has fallen at my feet and been mine for the taking. Nobody's ever turned their back on me, not wanted me. Why are you so different? How can you love that boy and not me?'

His voice cracked in anguish and for a terrible moment she thought he was going to cry. She stared at him, mute with fear, and he felt her trembling beneath his hands. Suddenly a white hot rage welled up inside him and with it an overpowering urge to hurt her really badly. To hit her and hit her until she was nothing but a piece of battered debris, her beauty ruined and her spirit smashed. His hands flexed on her shoulders as the desire to destroy her flooded through him. He could do it so easily. Then he saw a pulse beating frantically in her white throat above the diamond choker, like a small trapped bird.

With a groan he let her go, pushing her violently away from him. She fell back hard against the window. His face was dark with unspent rage and pain. He looked down at the fragments of photo beneath his feet for a long moment and took a deep breath. Then he looked up at Sylvie, his face now under control, his voice like steel.

'Yul will die tonight at my hand and at my pleasure. Because you love him, I shall kill him slowly and his death will not be easy. And then, on that rock, I'll make you pay. No gentleness and no love in it. You'll pay every day for the rest of your life for hurting me like this. You'll wish that you'd loved me while you had the chance, before you turned love into hate. You'll wish it with all your heart.'

Siskin climbed into a taxi at the station and tipped the porter who'd helped with his suitcase. The porter looked askance at the dapper little man, something from a bygone era with his patent leather shoes, brushed overcoat and hat.

'Stonewylde please,' said Siskin, closing the car door.

'Where's that to then, sir?' asked the taxi driver, clearly a Dorset man.

Siskin sighed, but in his heart was glad that somewhere the size of Stonewylde had managed to remain unknown even to locals, cloaked in mystery and invisible to the Outside World.

'Take the main road out of town and I'll direct you,' replied Siskin. 'It's about an hour away.'

He sat back in the taxi and smiled to himself. Not long now, and he'd be back home where he belonged.

19

The intercom on Magus' desk buzzed. He covered the room in a few long strides and jabbed the switch, picking up the receiver.

'Yes? . . . Good. No, keep them there. I'll be with you in fifteen minutes or so to collect them myself.'

Sylvie looked away quickly as he came over to her. The hired men must have arrived at the Gate House, and once again she desperately hoped her message had got through to Yul. The alternative, so vividly explained by Magus, was too awful to contemplate.

'I have to go out for a while,' he said neutrally, standing over her as she huddled in the window seat. 'I'll be gone for less than an hour and while I'm away, you must lie down and rest.'

He reached across and smoothed down her hair, and despite his earlier cruel words there was gentleness once again in his touch. He took her chin in one hand and looked into her eyes. She was so very beautiful and so very vulnerable, and he felt the desire to protect her and to violate her in equal measures. He smiled tightly and patted her cheek.

'After this Solstice, Sylvie, that boy will be gone and you'll forget him. You'll live by my side day and night and you'll learn to love me. I know the Earth Magic will return to me and together you and I will be so powerful; a partnership such as Stonewylde has never known before.'

He sighed and taking her hand, guided her over to the sofa and pushed her down gently onto the soft leather.

'Try to get a little sleep, Sylvie – you've a long night ahead of you. I'll be back to collect you before sunset.'

He perched on the edge of the sofa and took one of her hands in his, examining her bitten nails.

'You're an unpolished jewel, Sylvie, but under my guidance you'll glitter and sparkle. I'll enjoy working on you, polishing and refining you until you reach perfection. I'll devote myself to you.'

He raised her hand, heavy with the diamonds locked around her wrist, and held it to his cheek, closing his eyes momentarily. He sighed deeply and looked into her eyes. The black fire blazed as he scoured her soul.

'A moongazy girl is hard to find and I shall never, ever let you go. Remember that, Sylvie. I'll be with you always – for ever.'

He bent and kissed her on the lips. His scent filled her nostrils as he lingered, seeming loathe to leave her. Then he rose and his gaze swept her one last time.

'I'll be back for you, Sylvie.'

'Goodbye, Magus,' she whispered.

She heard the key turn in the lock and her heart thumped wildly with anticipation.

Three cloaked figures left the woods and laboriously climbed the hill. Wheezing and panting, they lugged themselves up the slope, skirting around the litter of boulders that rose out of the rough grass.

'Sacred Mother, I hope we're not going right to the top!' gasped the youngest but heaviest of the three.

'Aye, we'll be casting up there round that stone, but there's another spot hereabouts that I have a mind to search out first,' replied Violet. 'Not sure where 'tis exactly but I'll know it when I find it.'

'Aye, sister, you did talk about this place afore, I recall,' said Vetchling, her breathing harsh with the exertion. 'That day we was harvesting our Fly.'

In the soft golden light, the three women paused to catch their breath. Beneath them spread fields, dark and fallow at this time of year, the brown woods lapping at the edges. Above them stood Hare Stone, jutting out against the pale blue sky and catching the long, low rays of the dying sun.

'I don't see why we're doing this,' grumbled Starling. ''Tis known that Magus is taking her up to Mooncliffe for the Frost Moon. She won't be coming here.'

'Aye, right enough. My Martin will be up there a-helping him, the right-hand man as ever he was. But here 'tis the place she always favours, as did that Raven afore her.'

'So why are we here if they're at Mooncliffe? 'Tis a waste of time, if you ask me,' whined Starling. 'I could be home snug by the fire with a bag o' chestnuts.'

'We must do what we can, daughter,' said Vetchling. 'Tonight is the time, and that old crow Heggy has been waitin' a long time for this, Dark Goddess rot her bones. All will be decided tonight.'

'Aye, sister. We must add our own magic and we must spoil this ground, where them moongazy maidens love to dance. 'Tis not the place that Magus favours for there's no snake stone here to drink the power. So stop your moaning, Starling – any fool knows we need three for a charm o' powerful trouble. And we must hasten!'

As soon as Magus had left, Sylvie jumped up and raced over to the dumb waiter, wrenching open the panelling. The note had gone! Yul would know the danger he was in – so long as the message had reached Clip and been passed to him. She hurried down through the chambers to her bedroom. She must get changed into warm clothes and find the charm pouch Mother Heggy had sent for her to wear tonight. She wished she knew what the plan was. There wasn't much time till sunset and Magus wouldn't take long to drive up to the Gate House and back. The sky was still bright but she was getting twitchy with the familiar sensation beginning to prickle under her skin. With shaking fingers she pulled the tiny bag's dirty thong over her head, wondering what was inside the fastened pouch.

Sylvie heard the intercom buzzing back down in the sitting

room and hesitated, for she wasn't allowed to answer the phone or intercom. But then she realised it might be for her, something to do with her rescue, so she raced back through all the rooms, hair flying, and reached the phone before it stopped buzzing.

'Magus, sir?'

'No, it's Sylvie.'

'What? I need to speak to Magus.'

'He's not here – he's gone out.'

'He can't have! No, no he can't have!'

The line went dead. She guessed the Villager on the other end didn't use the phone much. It buzzed again.

'I'm sorry, miss. 'Tis Tom here, Tom from the stables. I need to speak to Magus to tell him that Yul's been here.'

'Tom, is this part of the plan? Yul's plan?'

'Aye, miss, you could say that. But if Magus ain't there, I don't know what to do. Where is he?'

'He's gone up to the Gate House, Tom. There are men coming with guns and he's gone to collect them. I sent a note about it to Clip this morning and I thought you'd all know by now.'

'No, miss, we ain't heard nothing. With guns? That's bad.' He paused, and Sylvie's heart sank. 'Well, I don't know what to do now, miss. We thought the master'd be with you so I don't know what to say. You just be ready to leave very soon.'

Greenbough surveyed his band of trusted woodsmen gathered around the little hut deep in the woods. Many carried their axes, the younger ones their staves, and all stood quiet but restless. Greenbough took a final swig from his mug of tea and threw the dregs to the ground.

'I know 'tis the custom to gather in the Stone Circle for the sunset,' he began, his face grim. ''Tis strange times and we all know what's afoot tonight. And us men, the woodsmen of Stonewylde – we have a job to do tonight. So we'll be missing the sunset ceremony and we'll be doing our bit to help young Yul.'

There was a growl of approval at these words.

'Yul needs the folk behind him if he's to take his rightful place. Are we all behind him, men?'

There rose a mighty roar of confirmation.

'Right then, gather in and listen close.'

Sylvie felt sick with fear and her agitation increased as the hour of sunset drew nearer. She collected her cloak from the wardrobe and as she passed through the chambers again, she glanced outside. The sun was low in the sky and the shadows very long. Her heart beat fast and her hands trembled. Where was Yul? Magus would be back soon with these men. She was terribly scared, especially now she knew what else he had planned for her at Mooncliffe tonight.

When she returned to the sitting room, she didn't at first notice the tall figure standing in the shadows. Her heart jumped as the blond head turned at the sound of her approach. It was Martin! He stared at her and she felt uncomfortable, as always, under his expressionless scrutiny.

'Hello, Martin. I ... what are you doing here?'

'I've completed the preparations at Mooncliffe and all is in place for the night ahead.'

'So why are you here? I don't need babysitting. Go back downstairs, please.'

He shook his head, pulling a scrap of paper from his pocket. With a plunge of despair Sylvie recognised her note.

'You think to escape! You're the moongazy maiden and you should be honoured to serve, yet you've been scheming and plotting with those who stand against our Magus. You who owe him your life! But I'll make sure you're ready and waiting for the master.'

He smiled and Sylvie shivered. How would Yul rescue her now? She went over to the window and looked out. The sky was tinged with pink and sunset wouldn't be long.

'Martin, you really don't need to stay here. You've got the wrong idea entirely – I'm happy to go up to Mooncliffe with

Magus and I'm ready, as you can see. I've changed into my warm clothes.'

Martin chuckled at her words, and the sinister sound made her flesh creep.

Downstairs, Cherry and Marigold were hurriedly pulling on their cloaks.

'We'll be late for the ceremony, sister! Those blessed cakes took so long and everyone's left already.'

'Aye, well won't be as normal anyway, will it my dear? Magus won't be there, nor Clip neither.'

'But we need to go all the same. Oh Goddess, I'm afeared for tonight! What if it doesn't go to the plan? So much depends on everything falling in place just right. I do hope Tom's done his bit.'

'Course he has, Marigold. Magus will've got Tom's message about Yul and soon he'll be on his way.'

But just as they were hurrying out of the great kitchen door into the courtyard, Harold came running up.

'You're as late as us, my lad! Come on, fetch your cloak and we'll get to the Stone Circle together,' said Cherry.

'Something's wrong!' said Harold, his eyes darting about nervously. 'Ivy just said she saw Magus leave earlier, before Tom called. So Magus can't have had the message that Tom was meant to give.'

'No! That's can't be right? And where's that old weasel Martin? I saw him skulking about not so long ago. Ain't he meant to be out o' the way up at Mooncliffe?'

Marigold clutched her sister's arm. Both women looked at each other fearfully, knowing only too well how much was at stake tonight, and the consequences if the finely-tuned plan failed.

'I'll stay here,' said Harold quickly. 'I may be able to help if aught has gone wrong. May I use your keys, Cherry? I could take a peek in all the rooms and see what's going on.'

'Aye, lad, 'tis a good idea. You're a quick-witted boy and no mistake – do what you can. We'd best get off to the Circle afore that sun disappears and join our voices in the ceremony. Never missed a Solstice Eve sunset yet.'

'Where's Jack Daw then? Are we gonna see him tonight?' asked the hard-faced man in the front seat of the Land Rover next to Magus. Both thugs reeked of the Outside World, with their shaven heads, harsh speech and stench of tobacco.

'No, he's not here,' replied Magus evenly. 'That's why I've had to call on your services for this job – he'd given me your number and recommended you. Now remember, stay away from the girl – you mustn't approach her. All you need do is patrol the area around the cliff-top and grab the boy when he makes an appearance. He'll be trying to get to the girl and he won't be expecting you there. Capture him, cuff him and keep him out of my way.'

'So you don't want the target done over at all?' said the man, frowning. 'We thought you wanted him taken out. Why bring this kit then?'

'I want him caught and held securely. If you really think he's about to injure me or get the girl then yes, deal with him. But only if it's strictly necessary – I'd hoped to have that pleasure myself. When I've finished at the cliff-top, we'll move the boy up to the Stone Circle, which is where I want to take his life. I'll need you two along in case he has any misguided followers with him. Feel free to eliminate them by all means.'

'Right you are. You got that, mate?'

He turned around to the other thug in the back seat, who nodded grimly but remained silent. Both were controlled and tense, the strangeness of their mission not their concern.

Silently a dark figure appeared in the doorway of the connecting room. Sylvie looked away from Martin, her heart jolting again. Not Magus but Clip! He wore his black birds' feather cloak and held his ash staff, the one that had transformed into the Rainbow Snake all those months ago. Dressed like a shaman he looked out of place here in Magus' domain, a strange man with his long, wispy hair and pale grey eyes. Eyes just like her own. He smiled at her and held out his hand.

'Come, Sylvie, my lovely daughter. I've come to take you moondancing.'

'No!' cried Martin, stepping out from the shadows. 'She's for Magus! All is prepared.'

Clip jumped at his voice and spun round to stare at the tall blond man so very similar to himself.

'No, Martin, she's not for Magus.'

'Yes! She must be taken tonight, at the brightness in the darkness! The magic is strong and powerful and Magus must take his fill tonight on the stone of snakes at Mooncliffe. Then she'll be bound to him and she'll never break free. Her magic will be his for evermore!'

Clip frowned.

'Those are your mother's words, Martin. What evil is Old Violet up to now? Come here.'

Reluctantly Martin stepped forward until he and Clip were level with each other. Sylvie gasped – she'd never seen them so close together before. Clip stared at Martin.

'Look at me! Martin, you will sit down, and—'

'Oh no! You won't catch me like that!' he cried, looking away and holding a hand up to block Clip's view of him. 'Keep away and don't try your tricks on me!'

He rushed over to Sylvie and grabbed her roughly, all semblance of servility now vanished.

'Stay with me, girl,' he hissed. 'Don't defy the master or it'll be worse for you.'

'Let her go!' commanded Clip, striding towards them. 'How *dare* you do this, Martin!'

'I don't take my orders from you!' he said contemptuously. 'You're not the master! You're a poor thin shadow not even worthy to walk behind him. He'll be back any minute and then we'll see how you cower when he raises his voice to you, just as you've always done since we were lads. You keep away from this girl! 'Tis her destiny to be bound by the snakes in the rock. 'Tis

341

her destiny to feed their hunger and give the master what he craves.'

Clip looked hard at him and then began to hum, a low, strange sound that gathered force. Slowly he raised his ash staff as the humming grew in intensity and twisted it round and round in his hands like a screw. The staff seemed to waver, the solid wood softening and losing definition. Sylvie was as transfixed as Martin, unable to tear her eyes away although she knew she should.

Clip took a few steps back and tilted the nebulous wood on its side, gripping the end. He'd changed too, no longer wispy but dark and menacing, a huge black bird with plumage of the night. He began to spin the staff around him. Round and round it whirled, losing all shape and becoming part of the deep whirring noise. The black-feathered cloak flew out in a vast circular wing of darkness, enveloping and overpowering.

Martin gazed spell-bound, his grip on Sylvie loosening. She stepped back, terrified, but Martin remained rooted, unable to look away and his eyes bulging. The shaman swung his staff in a great blurred arc and, with a mighty crack, caught Martin full on the side of the head. He fell like a tree, straight down and almost in slow motion. Sylvie cried out in horror.

'No time for that!' barked Clip. 'Come on! Magus could be back any minute!'

Together they hurried down through the connecting chambers until they came to her bedroom. The door was already open and they rushed out into the long corridor towards the back stairs.

'Where are we going?' cried Sylvie, clasping the cloak around her to stop it tangling.

'To Woodland Cottage,' he replied as they clattered down the narrow wooden stairs. 'Your mother's already there and she's desperate to see you.'

'Will Yul be there?'

'No, he's away dealing with Magus. He wants you safe whatever the outcome of their conflict and it's me who'll be taking care of you tonight, Sylvie. It's about time I looked out for your welfare.'

She smiled at this, proud of her magical father, and hurried to keep up with his long strides.

At the Gate House, the two Villagers on duty were surprised when a taxi pulled up outside the enormous iron gates and Professor Siskin emerged. They recognised him but had no idea he was due to visit.

'All the Hallfolk visiting for the Solstice have already arrived, sir,' said one of them, carrying his case into the Gate House. 'We weren't expecting you. There ain't no car here to take you down to the Hall, and you've just missed Magus. He were here hisself a few minutes ago.'

'No matter!' said Siskin brightly, breathing the late afternoon air deeply and beaming with happiness. 'Ah, but it's good to be home! I'll come in and have a cup of tea with you two chaps, if you don't mind.'

'Course, sir. I'll phone down to the Hall and get someone to drive up and collect you soon as they can, but I reckon you'll miss the sunset ceremony in the Stone Circle.'

'No hurry – I wasn't planning to attend that one anyway. The sunrise tomorrow is what I'm here for.'

'Right you are, sir. Well, if there's no rush to get to the ceremony, I'll put the kettle on.'

'Splendid! And I'm just as happy to travel in horse and cart if necessary. I want to go to the Village first anyway and have a glass or two of cider in the Jack in the Green.'

'Very wise, sir. Wouldn't mind one myself.'

Mother Heggy took a jar from her dresser and poured some of the thick liquid into a heavy goblet. She added another thinner liquid and stirred in a sprinkle of desiccated herbs, then carefully hobbled over to place the goblet inside the pentangle, next to the salt and matches. She took a small cake wrapped in a piece of linen, and her clay pipe and herbal tobacco, and put these inside the magic circle as well. The light was fading fast. She stoked up the fire with extra logs, knowing that the chill would be bad later on, and once the circle was cast she wouldn't be able to break it until the rituals were finished.

Finally she opened a little black box and removed the figure, taking it into the circle with her. She pursed her lips and summoned the crow, who hopped delicately inside with her, sitting at the head of the star. Mother Heggy picked up the bowl of salt and, muttering her incantations, carefully sprinkled it in an unbroken circle onto the circumference marked out on the flagstones. She was now protected within the circle from any malignant forces abroad tonight, anyone who might wish to harm her with Dark Magic. Then, with great difficulty, she sat down on the cushion in the centre, feeling her ancient joints and ligaments crack in protest. She lit the taper and reached to light the five candles in the points of the pentangle. Now she could summon the elements. Now the ceremony could begin.

'We're approaching the Hall now,' said Magus. 'We'll collect the girl and go straight up to the cliff-top.'

'Nice pile,' muttered the heavier man in the back seat of the Land Rover, eyeing the grand stately home. 'Very nice.'

Magus pulled up and led them inside, heading straight upstairs. The two shaven men in full combat gear were incongruous in the mediaeval setting of the Hall, but the place was deserted with everyone at the Stone Circle for the sunset ritual to mark Winter Solstice Eve. Magus imagined Clip there now, ready to lead the chanting and ceremony as the sun descended behind the stones. Magus hurried up the stairs, unlocked the door to his apartments and ushered the men inside. He was annoyed to find Sylvie wasn't on the sofa where she should be, and called her angrily.

Then he tripped over Martin's unconscious body lying in the shadows, and switching on a lamp, he saw the great lump on the side of the man's head. He cried out in fury and ran through the rooms shouting for Sylvie. When he realised she wasn't there and saw the door from her bedroom to the outside corridor standing open, he paled and let out a bellow of pure rage. As he raced back through to the sitting room where the men were waiting, the intercom began to buzz.

'YES?' he yelled.

'Sir, Magus, 'tis the boy Yul!' began Tom, relieved that at last the master had returned so he could put his part of the plan into motion.

'What about him?' shouted Magus. 'Is this Tom? Have you seen him?'

'Aye sir, he's been here in the stables and he's took Nightwing. He—'

'WHAT? Why did you let him do that, you bloody fool?'

'He said you gave permission, sir. I weren't sure and I tried to phone you to check, sir, but you been away. I kept trying.'

Magus slammed his fist on the desk, white with fury. He took a deep breath.

'Alright, Tom, he's taken Nightwing. Did you see Sylvie? The young girl?'

'Aye, sir,' said Tom quickly, adjusting the plan to cope with the new train of events. 'She were with him. He took her on the horse too.'

'I don't believe I'm hearing this! And you didn't think to stop them?'

'He told me he had your permission, sir. And seeing as how he's your son, and she's Master Clip's daughter, I didn't think 'twas my place to say—'

'I'll deal with you tomorrow, Tom, when this is all over. Saddle another horse for me! I'm on my way down now. I'll find them at the Hill Stone, no doubt.'

'Well, sir, I were just about to say, I think I know where they've gone.'

'Why the hell didn't you say so? Where?'

'Well, they was arguing, sir. Miss Sylvie said she wanted to go to Hare Stone, wherever that is. Maybe she meant Hill Stone? But young Yul, he weren't having none of it. He said they were going to Quarrycleave.'

'Quarrycleave?'

'Aye, sir, he definitely said Quarrycleave. I were standing right with them while they was talking. Felt awkward, I did, listening in. He told her there was a special stone up there that she could dance on just for him. They argued a bit and she cried and he shouted at her. Quite harsh he was with her, and she were very upset. Then she said alright, she'd do it for him as 'twas his birthday, just the once. Those were her very words, sir'

'The sly, cunning, little *bastard*! All that crap he gave me yesterday and he wants her moon magic too! Don't worry, Tom, I won't need a horse. I'll drive up there in the Land Rover.'

Quivering with anger, he smashed the phone down. His eyes flashed dangerously as he spoke to the two men.

'Change of plan! We're driving up to the quarry. The boy's on horseback and he's got the girl, and he'll take her to a tall stone at the head of the quarry. Under absolutely no circumstances are you to approach that stone or touch the girl. Do you understand? I want the boy captured as we discussed before but more than ever now I want to kill him myself, so don't shoot at him or anything like that. Your job is to catch him and restrain him. Now come on, let's get a move on – the moon will be rising soon.'

Edward surveyed the crowds gathering for the ceremony. Still they poured into the arena from the Long Walk, Villagers and Hallfolk mingling, their numbers swelled by the many extra visitors. Wearing his best ceremony robes, Edward took a deep breath and tried to calm himself. His heart pounded with anxiety, not only at the prospect of leading the sunset ritual tonight as Clip had requested, but also at what would happen at moonrise.

Everything was at stake now. Should Yul fail, the future of all those who'd supported him would be bleak. Although, thought Edward grimly, that meant almost every Villager on the estate and Magus would have a hard job punishing them all. But he put those thoughts aside; of course Yul would triumph tonight just as the prophecy had foretold. So why, he wondered, was he so very scared? Why did he feel this terrible draught of fear breathing down his neck?

Old Violet crouched amongst an outcrop of boulders on the hill. A thin plume of acrid smoke rose into the clear pink sky as she muttered under her breath. The black horn-handled athame she clutched in her dirty hand swept through the air as she directed the elements to witness her intent. Vetchling assisted her in the invocation and Starling looked on crabbily, her belly rumbling.

'There,' said Violet finally, ''tis done.'

'And this is the place, sister?'

'Aye, and now 'tis marked. We must get up to the stone at the top now to cast our circle there. That moongazy maiden will find her path blocked, should aught go wrong at Mooncliffe with Magus and my dear son. 'Twas ever the women as put things right, and we done a fine job here.'

'Will it take long?' asked Starling. Violet eyed her niece balefully, gathering her bits and pieces and stuffing them into an ancient bag. She left the small fire smouldering and rose creakily.

''Twill take as long as it takes, so no fussing and fretting from you, woman. You know well what's afoot tonight. Magus will take the maiden on the snake stone, and with all that moon magic inside him he'll kill the dark brat. Old Heggy's spell ends tonight and that's been a long time a-coming. 'Tis our task to blight this place, mark it as ours, and if that maid does break loose and somehow get here, we'll be waiting for her!'

'Aye, sister,' cackled Vetchling. 'She'll be ours for the taking. We'll blight her an' all and that'll be the end o' these moongazy maidens.'

'Waste o' time,' muttered Starling under her breath as she trailed higher up the hill behind them. 'She'll be on that snake stone tonight and giving our Magus what's his by rights. Don't know why we're messing about up here alone.'

At Woodland Cottage Miranda sat, hugely pregnant, in an armchair by the fire watching her daughter pace the room. She and Clip had discussed Sylvie's terrible revelation about the hired men, but realised there was nothing they could do as it was now impossible to get in touch with Yul. They had to trust in his strength and ability to take care of himself. Both wanted to help the boy and they considered sending reinforcements, but rejected the idea. They knew how adamant he'd been about engaging with Magus fairly, one to one; unfortunately his father didn't share his scruples. Clip looked out of the window.

'Sun's going down,' he announced. 'We'll go up there soon, Sylvie.'

She nodded, the tension becoming unbearable. She tingled and prickled and her feet moved of their own accord. She wanted to get out, to go up high and dance with the hares.

I must spread my wings and fly, fly round the spirals, feel the moon magic in my soul and dance for Stonewylde!

She rushed to the door and tried to wrench it open.

'Steady, my dear,' said Clip, taking her arm. 'You need to wrap up warm first.'

She turned her face to him but her eyes were completely blank, the pale grey irises with their dark rings suddenly looking unworldly. She was listening, but not to him, and tried to push past him. Miranda heaved herself out of the chair and put the scarlet cloak around Sylvie, fastening the clasp. She tried to put gloves on her but Sylvie pulled them off angrily.

'Go, go, go! I must go!'

'Is she normally like this?' asked Clip. He'd only ever seen her up at Mooncliffe which was somewhat different, especially when she'd been hypnotised.

'Yes, she is,' replied Miranda, remembering all the incidents in the London flat when Sylvie had been frantic to get out onto the balcony and she'd feared for her daughter's life. 'She loses all reason just before the full moon rises.'

'Come on then,' said Clip, taking Sylvie's hand in his and lifting the door latch. 'I have no idea what time we'll be back, Miranda.' He paused and looked down at the red-haired woman and the blond-haired girl. 'It's a pity we can't take her together, isn't it? It'd be fitting, given the circumstances. Still ... I'm honoured to be entrusted with her, after all I inflicted on the poor girl before.'

'You know you've been forgiven for that,' said Miranda, peering out into the darkness and shivering. Clip patted her arm as he led his daughter outside.

'Remember there'll be several Villagers outside keeping an eye on you, Miranda. Edward will be back after the sunset ritual, and Greenbough and his men are patrolling the area so you're not alone. Don't worry, everything will be fine, I promise.'

They walked rapidly up the path towards the woods, Sylvie tugging impatiently at Clip's hand.

'Quick, quick, quick! The hares are gathering. Hurry!'

Up at Quarrycleave, Yul was alone and more scared than he'd ever been in his life. He'd ridden up here very fast. Earlier, at the stables, he'd whispered to Nightwing and without protest the great stallion had allowed the boy to mount. They'd flown to the quarry like the wind, pounding swiftly along the miles and miles of ridgeway. Silhouetted as the sun sank lower in the sky, the dark boy and the dark horse were as one; sweat and muscles flowing and stretching, hearts pounding in unison. Yul had glanced down at one point and seen the impossibly long and magical shadows of horse and boy racing along beside them; it was the stuff of his dreams.

Yul dismounted at the quarry mouth, landing on light feet, his thighs trembling from the exhilarating ride. He tethered Nightwing loosely to a stunted elder tree and glanced around. They were close to the caravans where Jackdaw had taken such pleasure in humiliating him. He smiled grimly; that all seemed so long ago now. Yul caressed the horse's long head, his hand gentle on the velvety nose. He whispered into Nightwing's flickering ears and the great black horse dipped his head in compliance. He'd crop the grass and wait quietly here.

The quarry was a place of brooding and menace in the day time; at twilight it took on an even darker atmosphere. The stone was pale and seemed to glow slightly in the half-light. It was impossible to see from one side of the horse-shoe shaped quarry to the other, for the rock had not been blasted out entirely. There were channels and walls, cliffs and mounds, great boulders lying tumbled everywhere. The place was a massive labyrinth ripped and gouged into the land, a wild jumble of fossil-encrusted rocks and half dressed blocks of stone. Great twisting ropes of ivy snaked up the cliff faces, the glossy leaves covering cracks and crevices and hidden recesses. Yul remembered climbing up those faces in the summer and hacking away at the sinuous ivy.

Debris from the stone work done under Jackdaw's command lay everywhere. Yul knew, through the Village grapevine, of the deaths that had occurred just after he'd left Quarrycleave. Somewhere under tons of fallen rock lay the men's bodies, the same men who'd thrown their empty beer cans at him and laughed as Jackdaw forced him to further degradation with each new day. He shivered at the thought of those recent corpses.

Yul looked up at the hill above the quarry and took a shuddering breath as a sudden breeze chilled his sweating skin. The sun was dropping rapidly towards the horizon and Yul felt a strange tug inside. He thought of the tiny Wise Woman and the immense power she must once have wielded, to protect him from a man as determined and ruthless as Magus. Without her Yul would've died – he knew he owed her his life – and sending her a message of love, strong and heartfelt, he vowed that her sacrifice wouldn't be in vain. Tonight he'd do what had to be done and rid Stonewylde of its bad master.

The golden ball slipped down below the horizon in molten glory and it was finally sunset on the eve of the Winter Solstice, the moment Yul had waited for all his life. And now, for the first time since his birth, the binding spell was broken and Mother Heggy's magic no longer cloaked him in protection. He truly was alone. Yul peered into the shadowy labyrinth ahead and remembered the creeping, deadly lure of the quarry. Standing at the mouth of the Place of Bones and Death, he knew with certainty that Quarrycleave's terrible hunger would soon be fed. Here, tonight, somebody would die.

20

The drums had quietened to a soft throbbing heartbeat as the Stonewylde folk gazed silently at the darkening skies. The sun had set on the Stone Circle leaving only a pale pink whisper. The Winter Solstice Eve ceremony had been subdued, led ably enough by Edward but somehow lacking its normal thrill. It had been replaced by a dreadful sense of anticipation, as if the whole community, Villager and Hallfolk, held its breath.

'Bloody typical,' Holly muttered bitterly as she looked around the shadowy Circle. 'At this rate I think all of us due for our Rite of Adulthood tomorrow will have to postpone it. This should be one of the most important occasions of my life and it's not fair to have it ruined like this!'

'Don't worry, darling, we'll speak to Magus later on and arrange everything,' said her mother, immaculately turned out and wearing a smart cloak. 'We can't let this silly business with that dreadful girl spoil your special day. William's told us all about her, ghastly creature. Clip's daughter indeed! And I can't believe that Magus was so harsh with you just because you pointed out a few home truths to her. Is there something wrong with him, do you think? I've heard some rumours and one does wonder . . .'

'Well they're saying lots of things, but mostly that Magus may not even be the magus by tomorrow,' said Holly. 'And really, maybe it'd be better if he weren't, now he's so cruel and peculiar.'

'Ridiculous nonsense all that gossip!' growled her father. 'As if

351

some bloody Village peasant could oust Magus! I don't know –
Stonewylde isn't what it used to be. Some damn fool's even got
the Altar Stone image wrong for the Solstice festival. I don't
like being led in a ceremony by a Villager and I don't like the
atmosphere here tonight. There's no respect and no deference.
Magus will have to deal with this swiftly if he wants to maintain
the status quo.'

Holly's parents linked arms and joined the masses leaving
the Circle. Holly trailed behind with her friends, who crowded
around her in support.

'So Yul won't be your partner tomorrow night, then?' said
Rainbow innocently.

'For Goddess' sake, don't wind her up!' groaned July.

'It won't be any of the three I'd originally have liked, now that
Buzz is gone and Magus has disappeared,' said Holly. 'Not that
I'd want *him* any more. Where is he tonight anyway? He can't
just disappear like this.'

'He announced at lunch that he'd be elsewhere tonight, didn't
he?' said Dawn. 'Though what's happened to Clip I don't know –
he was meant to be leading the ceremony. Doesn't it feel weird
this evening? There's a horrible brooding feel, like something
dreadful's about to happen.'

'I think it is,' said Rainbow. 'I think everything they're gossiping about really will happen. We all know how Magus has
completely lost it. I think Yul's going to kill him and take over
and we'll all be chucked out.'

'Rainbow! Don't even think it!' said Wren in horror.

'Wouldn't surprise me,' said Holly. 'Ever since that little cow
turned up things have gone wrong. She's ruined Stonewylde –
it's all *her* fault.'

'Nonsense!' said Hazel briskly, coming up behind them. 'If
there's anything wrong at Stonewylde it certainly isn't Sylvie's
fault. You need to look to the top to find the cause.'

'Yeah? With loyalty like that I'm not surprised Magus is having
a hard time,' said Fennel belligerently. 'Have you switched sides,
Hazel? Fancy yourself as a rough Villager now? Pity your hair's

the wrong colour and you've got a brain in your skull then.'

'And it's youngsters like you who prove just how flawed this whole feudal system is,' retorted Hazel. 'It's about time other qualities were recognised and rewarded at Stonewylde. You may well find your blond hair a bit of a curse after tomorrow, young man!'

As the light thickened and the first stars began to peep, Yul ran lightly along the paths of the steep-sided labyrinth. He twisted his way from the shallow end at the mouth where the quarry was only just below ground level, to the far end of the vast horseshoe where the sheer cliff face led straight up to the top of the hill. His journey through the canyons of stone may have seemed random, but like most aspects of the landscape at Stonewylde, nothing was without significance. This was not a structured, seven-coiled labyrinth but nevertheless, the journey through its paths was ritualistic. Yul's feet trod the ancient passageway as so many others had before, and in doing so the spell was woven, the summons completed, and the beast animated into voracious life. Yul was heading for the Snake Stone.

This special stone was a column of white, sparkling rock, many metres high, standing inside the far end of the quarry like a great chimney. It stood apart from the high cliff face, and the dangerous chasm between them was a precarious mess of jagged, smashed rock and great unstable chunks of stone debris. The top of this giant pillar of stone had been flattened into a platform but it was difficult, though not impossible, to go directly from the hill to the platform, even though they were of similar heights. The best and slightly safer way to reach the top of the Snake Stone was by travelling through the quarry itself and then climbing a steep and treacherous path upwards, over tumbled rocks and boulders which formed rough steps, to the summit.

Rising from its bed of jumbled stone like a fist thrusting up from the grave, the Snake Stone was no natural phenomenon. It had been hewn into its smooth pillar shape and snakes were carved all over it, massive coiling serpents that writhed and twisted themselves up the sides of the rock to the very top. The entire column was formed of the same glittering stone as the disc of rock at Mooncliffe, and it was where Magus had sourced the stone for his eggs.

As Yul came closer to the quarry face at the end, he gazed upwards and shuddered. If Quarrycleave was a natural temple of death, the Snake Stone was the altar. And it was on this altar, so very different to the one in the Stone Circle where he received his Earth Magic, that Yul felt he should confront Magus. Somehow that felt right; all he had guiding him tonight was his instinct. In the rapidly fading light he began to climb the winding path leading up over the boulders towards the summit. It was a sharp and dangerous climb but at last he reached the platform on top of the pillar of Snake Stone and he stood there, still and silent, surveying the darkening scene below.

The quarry was a vast stone-scape of shadows far below him. The pathways between the rocks were channels of blackness and anything could be lurking down there in the maze of stone. Yul felt the menacing atmosphere pressing on his soul and recalled the awful compulsion he'd succumbed to last summer when he'd wanted to sacrifice his life to feed the maw. He'd only been prevented from suicide by Sylvie and the two creatures summoned to save him. Tonight, once again, he experienced that growing dread, that same feeling of pain, terror and death, although this time he had everything to live for.

Yul sensed something of the ritual slaughter performed in this hollow place over the ages. But he knew nothing of the remains of many bodies concealed beneath him; the bones, skulls and sad fragments of things once held precious by the ancestors of Stonewylde. He knew nothing of the past sacrifices of blood and flesh, the torture and murders committed in the name of appeasement and supplication to ancient gods, out of greed and man's eternal lust for power. Quarrycleave was where the darkest and most dangerous aspects of Stonewylde were focused, and a fitting arena for the fulfilment of the prophecy which had overshadowed his whole life. Yul knew the quarry was the Place of Bones and Death, the place where tonight he must face his father for the final time.

The Land Rover bumped up the track to the quarry, pot-holed and gullied by years of winter rains and neglect. His two passengers held on tightly as they bounced in their seats. Magus drove like the devil, swerving violently to avoid the worst potholes but never slowing his breakneck pace. His face was grim and he swore softly under his breath, a continuous stream of invective against Yul, the boy who threatened his very existence as Magus of Stonewylde. He'd counted on feeding on Sylvie's moon magic at Mooncliffe tonight, for strong and fit though he was, without that special energy he was no more than an ordinary man. Magus thought again what a good job it was that he had two of Jackdaw's brutish mates at his side. He'd noted the sunset with glee; finally the binding spell was broken and he was free to rid himself of the brat.

He seethed at Yul's duplicity and greed, knowing how much power the boy had literally at his fingertips. Only yesterday Magus had seen him glow with it, the energy crackling around him. How could he be so greedy as to want the moon magic as well? Magus cursed him again, and that ungrateful little bitch. He'd laid his heart open to her, offered her the world, yet she'd only willingly share her gift with his bastard son who didn't even need it. When he got hold of them tonight, nothing would stop him exacting his revenge. With the two thugs to help, he'd kill the boy slowly. And then he'd turn his attention to Sylvie and her punishment. He wasn't sure which he looked forward to the most.

As they reached the field at the foot of the hill, Sylvie broke free from Clip's grasp. She ran through the cold grass and around the boulders, up towards the dark stone silhouetted against the pale blue sky at the top. The sun was gone; a peachy glow marked its point of departure and a single bright star twinkled in the clear sky. The temperature was dropping rapidly as Sylvie raced up the hill, followed more slowly by her long-legged father.

She paused when she reached a small fire smouldering in the half-light and Clip caught up, staring down at the remains of Violet's handiwork. Sylvie turned unseeing eyes to him, cocking her head as if listening to something.

Something bad here, something not right. Where are my hares to honour the Bright Lady? My feet are heavy and all is wrong.

Harold slid one of the keys dangling from the heavy iron ring into the lock, turning it slowly. He really didn't want to be here but had the strangest feeling that something was amiss. He'd been racing around the Hall, empty of Hallfolk and servants, trying to locate the source of his foreboding. He'd hoped to discover what was wrong before he came to Magus' apartments; creeping into these private chambers was petrifying, even though Magus had been sighted going off in the Land Rover earlier. It was Sylvie that Harold was really concerned about, and whether she'd been safely spirited away. Pushing the great door open a little, he tiptoed into the huge, darkening room, terrified of what he might find. But all seemed silent and still and Sylvie was nowhere in sight. Breathing a huge sigh of relief, Harold stepped forward into the shadows.

A strange noise halted him and he froze in terror, every hair on his body bristling. Something was stirring in the corner; a long dark shape that sighed and moaned. Harold's mouth clamped shut over his dry tongue and his eyes darted wildly about. What dark magic was this? What terrible creature was lurking in Magus' rooms? He knew where the light switch was and twisted to find it, his hand scrabbling in the darkness that deepened by the second. In his fear he couldn't locate the switch and a sob escaped him.

He sensed movement in the shadows and just as his fingers found the switch, something grabbed hold of his ankle like the jaws of a trap. Harold screamed as the light burst on. And there, latched onto his leg, lay Martin. Spread full length on the floor and pale as death, the man looked up at the boy, his face twisted and strange. Harold saw the great purple swelling on his temple and the way his mouth was working, eyes rolling up into his skull at the effort of moving and trying to speak.

'Martin! What happened?' Harold cried in alarm. 'Oh ... your head!'

'We must stop them! We must find the moongazy girl and take her to Mooncliffe to the master.'

Martin's speech was horribly slurred and Harold tried to shake him off but Martin's grip was solid. The tall man began to pull himself to his feet and Harold nearly lost his balance.

'Help me, boy! The girl must be captured – the master's waiting for her and *everything* depends on this.'

Harold hesitated, a lifetime of training and obedience battling with his desire to help Yul. Martin had struggled to all fours and started to push himself up into a standing position. Staggering, he grabbed Harold's shoulder, almost pulling him down.

'No! I won't help you. Sylvie can't go to Magus. She's with Yul—'

'So – another viper in the nest!' Martin hissed, reeling alarmingly and fixing his bloodshot eyes on the boy. He made a lunge for Harold who leapt backwards trying to avoid the long grasp. The keys jangled and Harold realised what he must do.

He flicked the light switch so the room was plunged once more into shadows, flung the heavy door open and escaped into the dark corridor outside, slamming it shut behind him. Fumbling desperately, he tried to get the key into the lock. He could hear Martin bellowing with rage on the other side, crashing into something as he tried to reach the door in time. Harold's hands shook violently as he managed to slide the key in the lock, exactly at the moment he saw the handle begin to turn. With a cry he twisted the key and felt it catch, the handle rattling uselessly from the other side.

Sobbing with relief, he crumpled against the door jamb.

'I'm sorry, sir! I can't let you help Magus. He's turned bad and we must help Yul now. Yul's the one to lead us.'

From the other side of the door he heard Martin's wave of vitriol as the man pounded on the heavy wood.

'You'll suffer for this! You'll be whipped, Harold! Yul will never lead us and you'll rue the day you turned against our master!'

Then, chillingly, all went quiet. Harold listened intently, heart thudding, wondering if Martin had collapsed again. It took him a moment to realise why and, with another cry, he yanked the key from the lock and ran down the corridor to the next door. Martin mustn't escape to aid Magus.

He raced down the shadowy corridor and checked each door leading out from Magus' long suite of chambers. Martin, doing the same inside the rooms, was much slower, having to negotiate furniture and staggering from his head injury. One by one Harold tried the doors and found each one locked – until he came to the last one, Sylvie's room. This was where she and Clip had made their escape. As Harold ran down the almost black corridor he could see it stood ajar where Magus had flung it open in his fury at discovering Sylvie gone.

Harold shook so much he dropped the heavy ring of keys. Snatching them up again in panic, he couldn't find the keyhole. His heart pounded as he tried to shove the old iron key into the lock. It was the wrong one, and frantically he tried another and then another. Martin came crashing through the room just as Harold wrestled the right key into place and locked the door. The tirade of abuse that poured from Martin's lips was shocking, and even with the solid door between them Harold backed off quickly, not wanting to hear any more of the dreadful fate which now awaited him. Martin's mother was a force to be reckoned with and not known for her good magic.

Rosie held her mother protectively as they made their way back up the Long Walk, cloaks wrapped tightly against the chill December night. Maizie's steps were slow and she stumbled; every so often a sob burst from her.

'Come now, Mother, 'twill be alright. Yul will do it – we must have faith.'

'Sixteen years I've waited for this terrible night,' cried Maizie. 'Sixteen years of standing by and watching my boy being cruelly treated at every turn. And now 'tis almost over.'

''Tis not over, Mother! You wait – our Yul will win.'

'And his lovely new robes I made him, with his own Green Man sewn all over – my poor boy will never wear them, never reach adulthood. All thanks to that meddling old biddy!'

'Don't talk like this, Mother – Yul needs all the folk behind him, including you. You'll see – he'll beat Magus tonight, and then tomorrow—'

Another woman came up behind them, heavily pregnant and stumbling in her haste to reach them. She shoved Rosie hard in the back almost knocking her over, and the girl spun round in surprise.

'No he will *not*! Don't you dare speak o' such a thing! Magus is our master and always will be.'

Maizie and her daughter glared at the young woman, squaring up for a confrontation.

'Not after tonight he won't!' said Maizie, her lip curled. 'That man is finished and 'tis my boy that'll do the deed. Your child will be fatherless, Rowan, and best thing for it.'

'No!' the laundry maid screamed, trying to claw at Maizie's face. 'Magus will always rule here and he'll love our child!'

'He's no better at loving his children than he is at loving his women,' spat Maizie. 'And I should know! He's spent my son's life trying to destroy him and that man deserves what's a-coming to him tonight. Yul is worth ten o' him and all the folk think so too. You'll have to change your tune tomorrow, my girl, when Yul becomes our new magus!'

Up high on the hill, three women huddled around the great standing stone, their hands joined to form an unholy circle. They shuffled widdershins, chanting an incantation to the darkening sky. They'd marked a rough outline on the ground around them, and placed objects at various spots on it – strange and sinister things that had no place at such a sacred site.

Violet broke off from her crooning and paused, listening.

'The moongazy maiden is a-coming! Now, sisters, we must trap her in our circle and let the Dark Magic do its work afore the Frost Moon rises.'

'Aye! The trap awaits and you was right, dear sister, all along. She escaped from Magus but she won't get away from us three.'

'Should we hide ourselves?' asked Starling a little incongruously, as there was no cover other than the stone itself.

'Aye, we shall become the land itself. Sink down, my dears. Crouch low as rocks.'

With an agility defying their size and creakiness the three women melted down, forming dark huddles on the ground under their cloaks. In the deepening twilight they'd became low boulders surrounding the tall Hare Stone. Three silent mounds waiting for their victim.

Siskin sat back in the deep oak settle, the noise of the Villagers in the Jack in the Green all around him as he sipped his glass of cider with closed eyes. He was perfectly happy. The couple of very elderly men, sitting in the pub by the warm fire, had fallen silent when he'd arrived a little earlier, driven down finally in a car. Siskin had been served a drink and then eyed suspiciously as he lowered himself onto a hard stool at a little table. When a great throng of noisy men had burst in soon after, the Stone Circle ceremony completed, they too had fallen quiet at the sight of him. The last thing the Village men wanted tonight was a member of the Hallfolk in the pub.

But Siskin suddenly had understood their hostility and anxiety, and had produced the photo of Yul from his bag. He'd held it up proudly, inviting all to see.

'*This* is why I've come!' he said excitedly. 'To see this young man take his rightful place as our new magus, as our own Green Man. I'm on your side, chaps! Sylvie invited me here for the Solstice sunrise ceremony tomorrow. I can't go up to the Hall yet because Magus doesn't know I've returned. I'd be grateful if you'd let me spend the evening in here with you good folk, keeping out of the way while Yul does battle.'

This had earned him much hearty back-slapping and toasting, and the Village men were delighted to welcome him. They found the professor some food and settled him comfortably in a cosy corner by the fire with a fresh glass of cider. Siskin was happier than he'd been in years, and increasingly excited about the sunrise ceremony in the morning.

Unseen, Greenbough and the woodsmen stepped silently from the wood, their axes and staves in hand. They'd waited for Sylvie and Clip to pass by on their way to the top of Hare Stone and now they could take their places around the hill, forming a ring of protection for the magical girl in her scarlet cloak. Should anyone arrive and attempt to abduct her or disturb her moon-dancing, the woodsmen would intervene and keep her safe.

'What if Magus comes though?' muttered a burly man. 'I'm a-willing to do my bit to help, but I don't know as I could fell the master hisself.'

''Tis unlikely, ain't it? Our Yul's the one to rise up against Magus, like the prophecy foretold. I tip my hat to that young man, I really do!'

'Aye, I ain't scared of aught, but *I'd* never do it. He's a brave lad and no mistake.'

'Stop your chit-chat and keep quiet,' growled Greenbough. 'We'll climb up the hill a bit and make sure the maiden is alright. Master Clip said we must protect her and 'tis a vital job we got here. Miss Sylvie is Yul's sweetheart, and he needs us to take care o' her while he takes on Magus tonight. Hush now, and follow me.'

At his feet, Yul could just make out the six stolen moon eggs that Edward had brought up earlier. They nestled snugly in cup-like hollows on the platform of the Snake Stone. The top of the stone was encircled with several such hollows and Yul believed they'd once all held similar stone eggs, for the size and shape was too close for coincidence. He'd heard how Magus loved to come here as a youngster – perhaps those empty sockets had inspired him with the idea to make moon eggs. Yul remembered Tom up on Dragon's Back, driving the cart back from Quarrycleave all those months ago, and Sylvie's reaction when she'd touched the sparkling white chunks of stone.

The hollows looked very old, as if they'd been carved out a long, long time ago. Maybe there'd always been a moongazy girl at Stonewylde, who could be forced to charge the rock here and at Mooncliffe with her powerful moon magic. Maybe there'd always been a magus who received the Earth Magic from the Stone Circle, but stole the girl's magic when his own was gone. Perhaps there was eternal conflict; patterns and stories that came and went, repeated endlessly in the circle of time.

Yul didn't know and didn't care. All he hoped was that Sylvie was safely at Hare Stone within her ring of protection, and that Magus would soon be here to meet his son, and his destiny.

It was dark and shadowy in the cottage on the hill. The light was almost gone from the sky and the longest night of the year was about to begin. The Frost Moon had not yet risen as Mother Heggy sat, silent and still, in the centre of her circle. The fire crackled in the hearth sending crazy shadows chasing around the ancient walls. The Wise Woman's home had seen many a drama over its long years, but tonight was something special.

Grizzled head bowed, she channelled her mind into a tight stream of concentration, focusing on the two she knew could be the saviours of Stonewylde. The brightness in the darkness – this was their night. All hung on the outcome of this conflict and she must do everything in her feeble power keep them safe. They must be allowed to fulfil their destiny.

Muttering softly, Mother Heggy took a sip from her goblet and a toothless bite of the small cake. Her furrowed face creased further as she concentrated intently on an image of her magical girl from long ago. Calling, calling, Mother Heggy summoned Raven into the battle.

Harold sat at the top of the great staircase near the main door to Magus' apartments. All around him the Hall creaked and settled in the darkness. The sky, visible through the enormous windows overlooking the stairs, was just a shade lighter than the gloom inside. Harold's hands shook violently as he huddled on the top stair, crying silently. He'd never been more terrified in his life.

He could hear Martin through the locked door. The man seemed to have lost his mind, calling on every dark force to help him escape. Harold sat, too frightened to move, seemingly alone in the vast Hall save for Martin who still pounded on the door. The boy had done his bit to help, preventing Martin from leaving the Hall to help Magus, and he could do no more. Harold longed for everyone to return from the Stone Circle and fill the place with light and noise. The shadows loomed larger and larger all around him as he crouched paralysed on the top stair. The corridor stretched away around like a black tunnel on either side, whilst below, the hall was a pool of deepening, unfathomed darkness He couldn't even begin to imagine the terrors that Yul faced tonight; this was more than enough for him.

Leaving the strange fire behind, Sylvie continued up the hill on light feet, her cloak billowing behind her. Senses tingling, Clip followed her closely. He too felt something was wrong, and as they approached the summit his sense of foreboding increased. He knew this spot of old, recognising it as one of the very magical places of Stonewylde, one of the places where the energy was most powerful. But there was something else here tonight – something dark and menacing. Was Magus hidden behind the standing stone? Had Yul's plan to lure him to Quarrycleave failed? He tried to hold on to Sylvie but she eluded him at every step, desperate to reach the spirals before moonrise.

As she climbed the last few metres, instinctively avoiding the stones that littered the cold, dewy grass, she slowed. Again she cocked her head, listening. Stepping fearfully now, she approached the huge rock that reared up towards the sky, her hand outstretched.

Where are my hares and my owl? Why do the spirals not draw me in tonight? What evil cuckoo squats in my moon nest?

Her foot brushed one of the mounds that had no place on this hill. Clip had a sudden flash of understanding and tried to save her – but too late. In a flurry of movement and screams, the three shapes unfurled from the ground into solid, flailing figures that surrounded the girl and enfolded her in a wall of stinking flesh and musty cloth. She cried out, struggling as their talons dug into her, and Clip yelled in dismay. He tried to grab one of them but she turned on him with a snarl, her face a mask of rotten teeth and wrinkles in the near darkness.

'Stand at bay!' she cried. 'You will not touch us, nor will you take another step. We are protected and you cannot move!'

To his horror, Clip found himself rooted to the spot and unable to move at all. Fear clutched his heart at the strange sensation of being turned to stone. This was the power of the crones and their dark magic, held in abeyance for so many years ready, at this moment, to rear up in dreadful triumph.

Old Violet cackled horribly and the other two joined in, their voices shrill and hoarse. Clip tried to call out, knowing there should be a group of men in the vicinity to protect them. Surely they must've heard the terrible noise? He couldn't open his mouth to warn them but he heard voices and then the band of woodsmen arrived, spread out around the approach to the summit.

'Stay!' cried Violet, sweeping her raised arm and staff towards them all. 'You will come no further! Old Violet commands this and you are bound by my spell. Stand where you are!'

Sylvie was becoming frantic, for the moonrise was imminent. The binding spell that paralysed every man seemed to have no effect on her as the Frost Moon drew closer and her agitation grew. She fought the crones, flinging her arms about and trying to break free. But there were three of them and their grip was strong and powerful as they capered, prodding her and pulling at her hair.

'Oh aye, moongazy maiden! Can't wriggle out now, can you? Where's your moon magic now?' cried Starling in delight.

'Get her down on the ground!' shrieked Violet. 'Pull her off her feet, sisters, and then we can hold her down flat ready for the Moon Fullness moment. That's when we'll cut her! That's when we'll mark her and spoil her!'

'Aye, pull her down!' shouted Vetchling, wrenching at Sylvie's arms, yanking at her hair. With vicious fingers the three crones snatched at Sylvie who, outnumbered and overmatched, still struggled violently.

'Get her down!' screamed Violet again. 'Starling, you pin her down – you're the biggest and strongest!'

Their attack grew more vicious and Sylvie's struggles became more frenzied, but she was caught in the snare of moongaziness and unable to think or act straight. Starling used her massive weight and size to bludgeon her down, and as Sylvie fell to the ground, threw herself on top.

My Bright Lady comes and I must dance! Let me free!

'Eh? What's she saying? What tongue is that?' gasped Starling, heaving herself forward on hands and knees.

'No matter – we'll cut it out and Magus won't care if she's forever silent!' screeched Violet. 'Keep her down, Starling – she's still thrashing about!'

The huge woman let her whole weight fall across Sylvie, her rolls and mounds of solid, heavy flesh settling, crushing her to the earth. Sylvie couldn't move beneath her, and Clip and the woodsmen looked on helplessly, rigid as a ring of standing stones circling the hill, unable to move a muscle to protect the magical girl. Whilst Sylvie lay squashed on the ground with Starling spread bulkily over her torso and Vetchling holding down her legs, Violet was busy in her old bag rummaging for the things she needed. Triumphantly she produced her sharp knife, bone handled and sheathed in a worn leather case, and cackled again gleefully.

'Aye, now I have it! Now we can mark the maiden and spill her blood on this ground. No more moongazing here, once we've done! Starling, hold her down hard now and use all your weight – I don't want no wriggling from her at all. As the Frost Moon rises I shall draw her blood and then we'll have her tongue out!'

'Magus'll thank us for that!' cried Vetchling. 'She don't need a voice to give him what he wants on the stone at Mooncliffe!'

Sylvie tried to squirm, frantic to greet the moonrise, but the huge weight spread across her was overwhelming and she could barely breathe. Feebly she moved her head but Violet grasped her chin in a claw-like grip and hissed at her to keep still or she'd be cut badly, and even in Sylvie's moongazy state this warning penetrated.

''Twon't be too long now till moonrise,' said Starling comfortably.

Violet released Sylvie's chin and began to scrabble at the little part of her upper body that emerged from beneath the enormous woman, trying to release the clasp of the cloak round her neck so she could reach skin.

'Shift yourself a little, Starling,' she muttered. 'I need to get to her flesh . . .'

But as she clawed at Sylvie, her long broken nails catching on the rows and rows of diamonds, Violet's fingers closed around the old leather pouch around the girl's neck. The thong snapped and the bag came away in her hand. She let out a piercing scream and the air filled with a sharp smell of burning flesh. The crone flung the pouch away from her, clutching her blackened hand and howling with pain.

'What's ado, sister?' cried Vetchling, releasing Sylvie's legs and twisting round. 'Why do you scream?'

Starling too had rolled aside and half lay on the ground like a great seal, struggling to get up.

''Tis a toad bag!' screeched Violet in agony. 'The maid wears a toad bag! Look – my hand is burnt!'

The other two women managed to scramble to their feet hastily and stepped back from Sylvie in horror.

'What?' said Starling. 'A toad bag? Who's gave her that?'

''Tis that old hag Heggy,' moaned Violet, trying to blow on her seared flesh. ''Tis her doing, as ever. I smell Raven here when I never thought to again in this world. There's things of her in that toad bag, powerful things as I can't o'erpower with my magic. The girl is encharmed, sisters, and there's aught we can do to touch her tonight.'

The three of them spat in unison on the ground, and suddenly the spell was broken. Clip almost fell forward and quickly knelt over Sylvie, who still lay dazed and crushed on the cold ground, her eyes vacant and her hair spread out around her. The group of woodsmen charged up, grabbing the three women roughly.

'Get off!' screamed Violet. 'Don't touch us with your filthy hands! Be warned – we three are protected and you'll all suffer.'

The men backed off fearfully, many making the sign of the pentangle in the air.

'Go back to your cottage, then,' said Clip, gently helping Sylvie to her feet and adjusting her cloak around her. 'You and your dark magic have no place here.'

'We have our place everywhere,' hissed Violet. 'And who are you to be ordering us about, Son o' Raven? You're the one who has no place here, nor this skinny spawn of yours! She don't belong here nor ever will.'

'Aye, she has no place here. Never the crone! You'd do well to heed my sister, Raven-whelp!'

'My daughter belongs at Stonewylde and you'll curb your tongues and wicked ways or be sent away, all three of you,' he said firmly. 'Go home or these men will drag you there.'

'They know better'n to spite us,' spat Violet. 'They know better'n to cross our paths. You wait, you runt o' the litter. Your end will come soon enough, and I know the one that'll take you there too. A proper man, he is, not like you, ever the lame gelding.'

'Come, let's get back to our warm cottage,' said Starling. 'We done our work here tonight.'

'Aye, you speak true, daughter. This place is tainted now and we marked it proper. We know, us three. We know what'll come about in time.'

Muttering spiteful threats, the women hobbled away down the hill escorted from a safe distance by the woodsmen. They all took up their positions in the fields below, shaken by the encounter with the crones but anxious to protect Sylvie from further threat.

Clip stood beside the great stone with his daughter waiting for the moonrise. She faced the north-east where the full moon rose at the Winter Solstice; exactly the same place as the Summer Solstice sunrise. Her scarlet cloak was flung back as she raised her arms to the heavens. Early stars glittered in the cold night air. The sky was clear and bright, perfect for the Moon Fullness. Sylvie's mass of silver hair flowed around her, cascading onto the scarlet velvet as she stood with her wings held high.

She began to sing the strange moondance music. The hares, crouching and hidden further down the hill, raised their long, velvet ears and sat up on their hind legs. The first sliver of bright buttery yellow appeared on the horizon far out to sea. The girl's wild voice soared in glory and the hares turned towards the water to gaze with glinting eyes.

Yul felt the strange spirals of moon magic in the eggs at his feet and tried to keep his distance from them. Their magic was cold and liquid, like quicksilver threading around him. It was different to the deep, hot magic of the earth and he didn't want any of Sylvie's gift. He needed the earth spirals and the sun brushing his face, not this silver and black energy. But the eggs were key to luring Magus onto the platform.

Just as he thought this, Yul heard an engine approaching in the distance, the sound echoing off the stone around him. His heart lurched – at last! The plan had worked and Magus had fallen for his ruse. The lights tilted in and out of sight as the Land Rover jolted up the track, and then the noise and lights cut out. Yul heard a car door slam – no – he heard three car doors slam! His heart began to thump very slowly and very hard. Magus had arrived and he hadn't come alone.

21

'Remember,' said Magus softly, 'catch him but don't kill him unless you really have to. And don't touch the girl. We'll split up and meet at the head of the quarry. I want the two of you to keep out of the quarry itself for now – you'd probably get lost down there in the dark.'

'No torches?'

'No! No torches – we must surprise him. The moon'll be up soon anyway. You can both skirt around the quarry, up on the hill, and head up to the summit. Split up and go separately, one to each side, and watch out for the boulders up there. There's a chance he may be on the hill rather than in the quarry, though I doubt it. Don't get too close to the edge – it's a steep drop. I'll make my way through the quarry itself and meet you up there.'

'So we wait up there for you?'

'Yes, and keep very quiet until we know where he is – though I imagine he's got her on the Snake Stone by now. He'll have heard the Land Rover so he'll know we've arrived, but won't know our exact whereabouts. We'll take him by surprise.'

Yul stood on the rock considering the consequences of three people arriving. How could he fight them all? This should be one to one, as he'd insisted to all those who'd wanted to help him. He should've realised Magus would never play fair. Suddenly a black shape appeared in the gathering gloom and brushed past. It uttered a loud caw and circled him. Yul smiled; now he had reinforcements too. The crow landed in a flurry on his shoulder, sidestepping and pecking gently at his ear. He murmured to it, grateful to Mother Heggy for sending her emissary. He looked down but could see nothing below in the dark.

But then slowly, silently a huge yellow disc emerged from the purple haze on the horizon. Peering over the ridgeway was the moon, and he thought of his beloved Sylvie. He imagined her at this moment raising her arms and transforming into a moon angel, dancing the spirals at Hare Stone. Yul sighed, wishing he could be with her now . . . The crow croaked in his ear and took off, sailing down into the huge black pit below and Yul knew he must follow.

The two men, on opposite sides of the great quarry, were finding it hard going. Both were tough and completely ruthless, but their experience was all in city gangland. This terrain was very different and there was no street lighting; the darkness at Stonewylde was absolute and the moon was still too low to give any light. They trod carefully, wary of the quarry edge and unsure of where the paths lay. Both were wondering what they'd got themselves into, but they were professionals and would see the job out. Stealthily, they continued to pick their way up the hillside to the top of the quarry as instructed.

Magus stepped down into the shallow mouth of the quarry and took a deep breath. Memories flooded in – not from recent visits but from long back, when he was a lad of about Yul's age. He'd always loved Quarrycleave, savouring its darkness and danger. Something within him responded to the deadly lure of this place, revelling in the malignance that lurked in the stone labyrinth. He knew most people feared the place but that only added to his sense of belonging.

And now, on the eve of the Winter Solstice with everything at stake, Magus found himself empowered by the menace within the quarry. He felt a dark energy feeding him, fuelling his thirst for blood to be spilled. This was another kind of Stonewylde magic, and one which the three crones would understand. His fingertips tingled with it, every hair on his body alive and quivering with alertness. He knew the beast lurking in the ancient labyrinth was on his side.

He trod carefully as he moved along the dark corridors of stone, sometimes brushing against the ivy-clad walls and occasionally stumbling on small rocks in his path. His earlier anger had turned to an icy resolve; first he'd hunt the boy down and finish him once and for all. And Sylvie would watch as a prelude to her own ordeal. He smiled to himself in the darkness and shivered with a sudden rush of bloodlust. Sixteen years he'd waited for this chance, for the binding spell to expire, and now he longed to get his hands on the boy and slowly, carefully, extinguish his life.

Yul climbed carefully back down the huge, rough steps and boulders into the quarry, feeling his way in the thick darkness. His feet remembered the path and he was soon down in the black depths, the moon not yet visible here as it still hung low and golden in the sky. As soon as he lost sight of it he felt cut off from Sylvie and her brightness, and terror clutched at his heart as he entered the maze of stone passages. All his fears about Quarrycleave, instilled during his exile here six months ago, came back in a rush. Something monstrous waited for him just around the corner, stalking him as prey, craving his blood.

Magus was here too, hidden somewhere in the stone web, and Yul was sure that the two others were up on the hillside outside the quarry. He'd heard noises from both sides and wondered who Magus had brought with him. Hallfolk, surely – no Villager would've helped Magus against him. Yul moved silently and stealthily through the high canyons of stone, heart beating loud in his ears as he searched for Magus. The crow had disappeared. Yul heard a sound and froze, knowing that Magus was close by. The ivy was thick here, swarming up the stone walls, and Yul melted into a crack in the rock shielded by the leaves.

Magus approached quietly but Yul heard his breathing, deep and heavy, and his feet made small noises on the loose stones.

Yul could smell him too, the exotic scent he wore mingling with something more primeval; the fresh sweat of a strong, fit man hunting his prey. Yul picked up a small stone and threw it far ahead and Magus paused, then hurried forward. Yul grinned, feeling the thrill of outwitting his hunter. He still had no idea how he was to overthrow his father, now that he'd lured him here, but at present simply keeping him away from Sylvie at the moonrise was enough. Time for the conflict later, when all danger to his moongazy girl had passed.

Rocking back and forth and clutching her shawl around her, Mother Heggy moaned and muttered in the centre of her circle, calling on every power to help the boy tonight. She'd sent her crow some time ago, knowing Yul would need all the help she could give. She hoped that somehow Raven had heard the summons and responded, as she'd done at Samhain when Yul was paralysed in the Stone Circle. Mother Heggy knew only too well Magus' strength, intelligence and utter ruthlessness. Tonight he'd be fighting for his existence at Stonewylde and would stop at nothing to remove the threat that had haunted him for so long.

She hoped desperately that Sylvie was safe up at Hare Stone. She couldn't send Raven to both her precious ones, and figured that Yul was in the most danger of the two. But Sylvie had the charm pouch for protection and Mother Heggy knew the power this afforded. That magical set of seven sacred objects, all collected by Raven so long ago, should ward off any evil forces. Tonight Mother Heggy could see nothing; her second sight had deserted her completely. She thought again of the five deaths. They were the only thing of which she was sure; the outcome of the battle still eluded her. She shivered and stared hard at the five green points of light about her. All the candles in the pentangle still burned steadily; nobody yet had died.

Up at Hare Stone, harmony had been re-established now the three crones and all visible traces of their dark practice were gone.

Their presence at Sylvie's sacred site, the place where she must draw down the moon magic into this hill, the womb of Stone-wylde, had tainted her moongaziness and kept her creatures at bay. The three women's malignant intent and physical attack had blocked her true moondancing just as effectively as Magus did, when he forced her to stand on the stone at Mooncliffe.

But Raven, through the power of her charm-bag, had proved herself stronger than the three evil hags and Sylvie was now released from their contaminating influence. The ache where Starling's enormous bulk had crushed her lungs and ribcage, and the stings from the women's poking and pinching were forgotten as Sylvie felt again the thrill of dancing for the Bright Lady. This was why she'd been brought to Stonewylde; this was what she must do.

Sylvie danced in the moonlight, her feet brushing the freezing wet grass as she leapt gracefully in spirals around the stone. The hares had crept up the hill and now they raced with her, ears back and long hind legs pounding. The barn owl had also arrived on silent wings and circled overhead. Clip watched in awe at his magical, beautiful daughter in her wild moondance. The brilliant golden moon was higher now, glowing brightly in the cold night air. Sylvie spun around, her cloak and silver hair flying out about her, the diamonds at her throat and wrists sparkling as they caught the moonbeams. Below the brow of the hill the woods-men stood, silently gazing up at the enchanted figure dancing in the moonlight. Strangely, they all believed they heard the proud, primeval howl of a wolf echoing from the hill top out into the starry night.

The two men finally met up at the head of the quarry, glad to find each other in the silvery darkness. The moon had risen fully and now they saw more clearly what they were up against. The quarry glowed below them in the moonlight, its walls a sheer precipice in places and a tumble of boulders in others. Somewhere down there amongst the piles of rock and deep channels of shadow was their intended prey. And the man who'd hired them.

He should've been up here to meet them and now they had no instructions. Fingering their guns, they stared uneasily into the blackness below. Both were hard and experienced and neither had any qualms about their role here, yet something made them feel very uneasy. Neither would admit it was fear.

They waited for a while, unsure how to get down into the quarry from this great height and not prepared to risk their lives trying. With their employer nowhere in sight and all silent below, they had a whispered conference and agreed to go back down the hill together to the mouth of the quarry and see if he was there. Both were becoming edgy, despite their experience. There was something going on here that they didn't understand; something otherworldly and unreal that was beyond their knowledge of violence and death.

The two men dodged the boulders that lay strewn everywhere as they made their way back down the hill. They were beginning to feel hunted, as if something were stalking them. Both felt the menace of the place, the brooding atmosphere of terror and bloodshed. They looked back repeatedly over their shoulders and glanced down into the hungry shadows below. They knew that something was watching them – watching and waiting. They sped up, trying to lose whatever was on their tail, keeping their guns ready in case of attack. Their pace quickened and they began to hurry, clumsy in their haste as they swore continuously under their breath, stumbling and losing their footing. Both men had broken into a sweat, prickly beneath the heavy camouflage gear, and panic started to squeeze infectiously at their pumping hearts. They skirted a clump of stunted trees and boulders that blocked their path, forcing them to go even closer to the quarry edge.

Just as they were rushing past a twisted elder tree there was a loud caw, slicing through the absolute silence. They jumped, hearts leaping in shock as a huge black bird launched out of the branches towards them. The heavier man lurched to one side to avoid the wing-flapping nightmare flying straight at his face. He lost his balance but there was nothing to seize to save himself. Almost in slow motion, he started to fall, trying desperately to twist himself back to safety. But too late; with a cry of disbelief he tumbled over the drop into the void. A second later his companion heard the heavy thud as he hit the rock below, whilst the crow continued to circle overhead and call loudly. Down in the quarry, the bird's cries echoed and bounced eerily off the stone and both Yul and Magus understood their significance; Yul nodded grimly and Magus cursed softly.

The remaining man scrambled away from the cliff edge in total blind panic. He'd been in tough situations before and was no coward, but there was something here that scared him witless. He knew that had been no accident – the bird had intended to kill. His breath rasping in his chest, he reached another clump of trees. Sweat poured into his eyes as he ran, tripping and falling over stones and pushing himself up again to stumble on madly. It couldn't be far to the safety of the Land Rover. He glimpsed a large black shape in front and rushed towards the vehicle, only realising his mistake when it was too late.

With a startled whinny Nightwing reared up, eyes rolling madly in the bright moonlight. The man cried out in terror, shielding his head with his arms. His gun clattered to the ground as the great hooves fell down on him with fracturing force. He was hammered to the earth, then trampled again and again as the agitated stallion tried to rid himself of the aggravating mound beneath his feet. Yul heard Nightwing's mad distress through the darkness and the abrupt silencing of the man's screams. He took a deep breath; now it was just the two of them, father and son. Now it could begin.

Inside her pentangle, Mother Heggy caught her breath as two of the green candles snuffed out almost simultaneously. Two had died! Two deaths on the eve of the Solstice, and still she had no idea whose.

The moonlight threw everything into monochrome, bleaching out all colour and tone. Black and white, darkness and brightness, the white of skin and hair and stone: the black of eye and shadow and fear. The magus and the boy, stalking each other in the place of bones and death. And now something else was here, something that prowled freely amongst the boulders and passages, something raised by the spilling of blood. The two thugs had sacrificed their lives, tempted by the cash stashed uselessly in their pockets. Now their bodies lay broken on the stone, killed by the black creatures of the night. The crow and the dark horse had been summoned by the boy's magic and he felt powerful knowing that two were fallen. But he wasn't invincible.

Yul had lost track of Magus as they prowled around the canyons of the quarry. The man had been ahead of him until Yul took a detour, creeping down a narrow alleyway of stone. The moonlight failed to reach the shadows in this dark corridor and suddenly Yul felt a lurch of pure terror. Something was rustling close by, making a snuffling, shuffling noise that he couldn't place. His eyes darted about wildly trying to locate it, straining in the deep darkness. He felt as if the ground beneath his feet had suddenly become less solid, as if there was a pit looming and he stood on the crumbling brink. Frantically he spun around to retrace his steps and there was Magus, right behind him and so close that his breath fanned Yul's face. Yul's legs tensed for flight but too late – Magus' hand shot out and grabbed his jacket in an iron grip. He laughed in triumph and the noise was strange in the enclosed space.

Magus slammed Yul into the stone wall, knocking the air from his lungs with a grunt. Yul couldn't get his breath and taking advantage of his incapacity, Magus punched him hard in the stomach. As Yul doubled over in pain, the fist slammed into him again, into the side of his face. His head jerked back into the cushion of ivy.

'No escape now, you little bastard!' hissed Magus, pinning Yul by the throat to the stone wall. 'Where's Sylvie?'

'She's hidden,' spluttered Yul. 'You won't find her.'

With a roar of anger, Magus let him drop and spun him around. He grabbed Yul's arm and twisted it up behind his back, then pushed him hard into the wall again. He shoved his full weight into the boy, feeling the crunch and give of skin and bone against solid stone. The noise was sickening, as if ribs at least had been broken

'*Where is she?*'

'She's hiding!' gasped Yul, barely able to breathe but knowing at all costs he must keep Magus here, at Quarrycleave. 'I left her so I could find you. She's in one of the caves.'

'Why did you bring her here? This is a dangerous place.'

'She wanted to dance on the Snake Stone for me and give me her moon magic.'

Magus felt the stab of jealousy deep inside.

'I shall kill you tonight,' he hissed, lips next to Yul's ear. 'I shall kill you very slowly in front of Sylvie. And then I'll begin *her* punishment.'

The moon shone silver-white, now high in the sky and blindingly bright, and Sylvie came at last to rest. She gasped with exertion having danced and sung for some time, and knelt down in the freezing grass to gaze up in silence. The beautiful Frost Moon was surrounded with a bright halo of silver light, formed by ice crystals high in the cold night air. The hares were now moon-gazing too, sitting up on their great hind legs. The barn owl had swooped down on silver-feathered wings and now perched on the standing stone, its moon face glowing round and white.

I've danced the spirals for you, my Bright Lady, and brought down the magic to Stonewylde. Together with your creatures, I've honoured you tonight at this special place.

Clip saw the dew turn to frost, the diamond drops freezing to silver crystals. His hands and feet were numb as he gazed down at his magical, diamond-studded girl, knowing deep in his soul that this was why she was here and this was why she'd been conceived. Stonewylde needed her and he'd created her, a moon-gazy maiden to bring down the silver moon magic from the Moon Goddess to her sister, the Earth Goddess. Clip sighed; his heart was glad and brimming with pride.

*

In the pub Professor Siskin stood up a little unsteadily. He'd had a few glasses of cider and made his way to the privy out the back. But afterwards he decided to take a stroll on the Village Green instead of returning to the warm pub. A minute or two in the cold night air would clear his head. The Green, with its ancient history and magic, was his favourite part of Stonewylde. He tottered onto the grass, stiff now with a rime of frost, and looked up. He saw the stars glittering incredibly brightly. Hundreds, thousands, millions of them, so clear at Stonewylde where there was no light pollution. He saw the great face of the full moon shining down, haloed with brightness, and the pale grey hare visible as a shadow on the silver disc.

He wandered right into the middle of the Village Green remembering the cricket matches he'd watched here over recent years and all the other Midsummer and Lammas celebrations he'd been permitted to join. And before that, before Sol had become magus, he remembered other festivals; the maypole dancing at Beltane, the labyrinth at Samhain, the archery at Imbolc. The Green held many happy memories for him stretching back to his early childhood so many years ago.

As he began to think back further, strange images crowded into his head, jostling for attention. People in different clothes dancing, feasting, singing and competing here. He could see and hear them clearly, and as a scholar he recognised their language; it was very old. Then further back still, to a moment in time when woods surrounded this clearing for miles and miles, covering all the land. He saw a great wooden structure built to enclose the sacred grove. This was the heart of the woodland, the vitality and fertility almost tangible in such a magical place. The trees had been consecrated and he saw the yew, much smaller and younger that it had been in its later glory but the same tree nevertheless. He saw too a great lime tree, much like the one Yul had been resting under when he'd taken his photo.

And then – the Green Man himself! Surely? A young man with dark hair, clad in green and brown. His skin was mottled with lichen and leaves formed a halo around his head. The green magic chased and danced about him as he walked from the circle of trees, smiling at Siskin, leaves sprouting from his mouth and nostrils. The old professor felt a strange flutter in his chest, like a bird flexing its wings before it flew away. He sank down to the frosty ground and curled himself up like a child, cradled in the loving bosom of Mother Earth.

The Green Man came close and smiled down at him, his bright eyes flashing warmth and merriment. He held out a hand in invitation and the young Siskin stood up easily, joints now strong and supple, following him into the sacred grove to become one with the ancestors of Stonewylde. Siskin had finally returned from exile back to the magical place he loved so dearly, just as Sylvie had promised. The spirit of the young man rejoiced in its freedom and release, whilst the old man's body remained in the frosty grass beneath the cold, starry sky.

In the pentangle a third candle guttered and suddenly extinguished itself. Mother Heggy muttered her incantations and continued to rock backwards and forwards in the shadowy hovel. She had no idea who the Dark Angel had taken, but she believed in her heart she'd know if it were Magus or either of her special ones. The room was still warm; the wood she'd banked up on the fire had caught hold and was burning brightly. Firelight flickered around the tiny cottage, chasing the darkness from the corners as Mother Heggy raised the goblet and sipped at the drink slowly, then nibbled at the cake with her bony gums. Two of the green flames still burnt steadily. Two who must die tonight were still living – she begged the Goddess once more that Yul and Sylvie were not the two.

The Hallfolk and servants had returned to the Hall and lights blazed from every window. Adults sipped mulled wine in the drawing room, library and Galleried Hall, while the servants scurried about in the kitchens preparing dinner for them. Hallfolk children raced all over the stately home in a state of high excitement, whilst the teenagers gathered in knots, discussing what would happen the following day with the Rite of Adulthood. None of the normal preparations had been made and Magus, having been more or less absent for the past few weeks, was still nowhere to be found. Confusion and dissatisfaction reigned amongst the Hallfolk, whilst the servants tried to go about their business as if nothing were amiss.

Nobody questioned Martin's absence. The servants knew that he'd intended to assist Magus at the Moon Fullness and some did wonder where he could be now. If Magus had been successfully lured to Quarrycleave, there'd be little for Martin to do at Mooncliffe. But it was so hectic coping with the disgruntled Hallfolk that no one thought to search the Hall for him.

So Martin, lying injured on the floor in Magus' rooms, went unnoticed. Harold had long since abandoned his spot on the stairs and was now busy stoking fires in the rooms downstairs, grateful for a return to normality. He thought every so often of the man lying upstairs, locked in Magus' apartments, but tried to put him to the back of his mind as he traipsed around with log baskets.

In the darkness Martin had collapsed again, exhausted by his attempts to escape the rooms. The huge purple oedema on his temple pulsed as he lay sprawled in a heap, his breathing shallow and his pulse thready. The temperature in the vast room dropped steadily, for the fire remained unlit, and Martin grew colder by the minute.

Magus shoved Yul through the twisting corridors, his arm forced so far up behind his back that his bones creaked, making for the caves at the head of the quarry. Yul had tried struggling but feared for his arm, which Magus wrenched even more brutally at any suggestion of resistance. It was difficult to see anything, deep in the stone canyons where the moonlight failed to reach. As they neared a great pile of broken rock, Magus paused, yanking Yul to a stop.

'Do you know what's under there?' he asked, his voice hard and cruel. 'No? Let me tell you then – six men. Six of the men you worked with in the summer – well-rotted by now I should imagine, if the air's got anywhere near the corpses. Death, Yul – death is what Quarrycleave is all about. Can you feel it, just around the corner waiting for you? Here, tonight, you will die.'

'I will not die tonight,' said Yul quietly. 'Tonight I'll take my place as the new magus.'

Magus' laughter pealed out, its volume shocking in the silence. With one hand he held Yul tight, and with the other pulled a vicious hunting knife from its sheath at his waist. He waved it before Yul's eyes, the blade gleaming wickedly. He pricked the tip into Yul's side and Yul gasped, having no idea of the depth of the stab wound but feeling a sharp pain.

'You're a joke, boy. New magus! How are you going to achieve that, exactly? Do you have any weapons on you? No, of course you don't. I could kill you now and throw your body on that pile of rock for the rats and carrion crows to dispose of. The only reason I haven't is because I need to find Sylvie. We can't abandon her here all alone in the darkness, can we? And I want to witness the touching farewell scene as the star-crossed lovers take leave of each other.'

'That won't happen.'

'You're not in a position to argue. Which cave is she in? Show me, boy!'

'Never.'

'Where is she? You *will* tell me!'

He jabbed the knife again into Yul's side and this time the pain was very sharp. Yul felt a hot wetness inside his shirt which terrified him – he couldn't die now, not like this.

He looked around desperately. They were right at the head of the quarry, near the bed of jumbled rock that surrounded the base of the Snake Stone. Massive boulders and huge chunks of stone surrounded them, blasted long ago from the hillside itself, eating into the green land that rose much higher above. The moonlight penetrated this more open area, silvering the rock and creating deep pools of blackness in the recesses. Yul heard another strange noise, a kind of sigh, and felt something evil stirring in the black depths of the maze behind them. His hackles rose.

But then ahead, over to one side, he suddenly noticed a raven, huge and dark, strutting along a rock. It seemed to have materialised from out of nowhere and he started and stiffened, wincing with the pain in his side. Magus sensed this, loosening his grip as he swung round to see what had caught the boy's attention. With a rapid twist Yul yanked his arm free and leapt onto a rock, scrambling upwards as fast as injury allowed. Magus followed rapidly but Yul turned and kicked him full in the face. Blood sprayed onto the white stone, shockingly dark. Magus roared and fell back, trying to stem the flow, and Yul seized his advantage.

He leaped up the rocks like someone possessed, fear giving him strength and speed. He slipped many times, each time regaining his balance and climbing upwards. The pain in his side from the double puncture wounds became stronger and he knew he bled badly. He could hear Magus below, giving chase but far less agile than him, and gradually losing ground. At last Yul reached the place where the boulders formed a rocky path up to the top of the Snake Stone. He saw the great raven above him and knew he'd been guided here – he must go back up to the very top, on the platform of rock. His instinct had been to hide and dodge, but now, to be magus, he must flush out his hunter and confront him in the open. It was time.

Magus paused, panting for breath, on a boulder below the Snake Stone. He wiped the blood from his face again and could see Yul clearly up above. The figure stood tall on the stone, his head thrown back, face washed in moonlight. His dark hair hung down to his shoulders and the bright moonlight chiselled his face into strong planes and deep hollows. Magus realised with a shock that he was looking no longer at a boy but at a man – a man who seemed to glow in the moonlight. For the first time, Magus felt a genuine tingle of fear. Yul pulsed with power and strength. He stood with his legs apart and his face turned to the moon. And despite everything, despite his injuries, he wasn't scared; he wanted this confrontation.

Magus could just make out Sylvie standing behind him. The moonlight shone full onto Yul and in comparison she was faint and shadowy. Magus saw her wild silver hair and her white skin, her thin arms and legs bare in the cold winter's night. He felt a shiver of excitement at the sight of her, his moongazy girl. And she belonged to him – not that upstart son of his. He clambered up the last rocks, breathing heavily with exertion despite his fitness.

By the time Magus reached the top of the Snake Stone, Yul stood there alone. Magus climbed onto the platform and the two men faced each other, almost the same height. They could see each other clearly in the moonlight which shone as brightly as the sun, but silver not gold. Glittering black eyes locked into smouldering grey ones.

'Boys and girls come out to play! Where's she gone?'

'Sylvie's not here – she's at Hare Stone.'

'Of course she's here. You said she was.'

'I lied. I'd never put Sylvie in danger.'

'Yes, you *are* a liar! I saw her here, right next to you, just now. I know you're planning to take her moon magic, but it belongs to me! You have no right to—'

'I don't need her magic – I have my own.'

Yul held out a hand, identical to Magus', and they both saw the tiny sparks coursing from his square finger-tips. Yul reached out to touch him but Magus stepped back, drawing his knife again. He teetered at the edge of the platform and his eyes rolled in alarm, but then his foot brushed something and he looked down.

'My moon eggs!' he cried, bending and picking one up. 'I knew you'd stolen them!'

He closed his eyes as the energy coursed through him, quicksilver in his veins. Nothing came close to this ecstasy, this pulsing explosion of power that filled him with silver magic. He smiled and opened his eyes to glare at Yul, the icy venom strengthening his bloodlust. Sylvie had returned and once again stood in Yul's shadow, staring at Magus with moon-filled eyes. He raised his hand clenched around the heavy stone egg and showed her.

'See? I got my eggs back after all and it was pointless trying to fight me, Sylvie. I always win in the end. And now I have my magic back and you'll both suffer. Yul will die slowly. But for *you*, Sylvie, death will be an impossible dream.'

'What are you talking about?' demanded Yul. 'You're mad!'

'Get out of my way! Sylvie's mine – move aside, boy!'

He brandished the knife at Yul, the blade glinting in the moonlight.

'You're imagining things – Sylvie *isn't* here,' said Yul firmly. 'You and I are here to resolve this conflict, as the prophecy predicted at my birth. I've risen up against you and I have the folk behind me – nearly all the Villagers, and even a few Hallfolk, want me to replace you as magus. You've had your day and you're finished. I'm overthrowing you but I'm giving you a choice. I've no wish to kill you although believe me, I will if I have to. So you choose – exile or death. Which is it to be?

Magus laughed, the sounds bouncing around the stone arena and echoing back in manic amplification.

'Yul, my son, I will *never* leave Stonewylde. Nor will I ever concede to you. Why on earth would I? I'll fight you to the death, for Sylvie and for Stonewylde.'

He stood, tall and magnificent, on the platform of stone, a moon egg in one hand and the long hunting knife in the other. His blond hair gleamed silver and his eyes flashed like pools of blackness.

'I am Stonewylde and Stonewylde is me! My life is here in this place where I was born, this place that I love. I've given my life to Stonewylde and she loves me. You can never win, Yul.'

Yul looked at his father in the moonlight, looked deep into those dark eyes which shone with tiny reflected moons. All his life he'd feared this man, and for much of his life he'd hated this man. And yet, looking at that face, so familiar and hated, he suddenly saw himself. He saw someone else who'd fought back at the world and never given in; someone else who'd stop at nothing to protect and nurture Stonewylde, this beautiful magical woman of the landscape. And Sylvie was the essence of Stonewylde, part of the same magic. No wonder Magus wanted her as well.

In that instant, Yul saw Magus and recognised himself as a man. And he recalled Sylvie begging him to promise he wouldn't kill Magus. Suddenly he knew that despite everything, he couldn't commit murder.

'Magus, you're my father and . . . maybe the time has come for us to put this hatred aside? Forget about the prophecy – I don't want to kill you and I understand you can't give up Stonewylde. Can we talk about this?'

He felt the terrible creature stirring below in the darkness, craving and howling for more blood. But it could still be cheated!

'Yesterday you spoke of a partnership,' Yul continued, 'of you and I leading Stonewylde together. That's the answer! If we could—'

'No!' cried Magus. 'I'll *never* share with you! You're dead, Yul, and Sylvie's mine.'

The knife's long, vicious blade caught the moonlight, creating a moonbeam of silver, as Magus suddenly lunged forward aiming for his son's heart. Yul sidestepped quickly and behind him Sylvie laughed, shaking her head, taunting him. She dared to defy him, thinking Yul would protect her. With a growl of anger he swung really hard at Yul with the stone egg in his other hand, trying to smash his son's skull. Yul stumbled as once again he dodged the blow, grabbing Magus' arm to right himself. As he touched him, the Earth Magic blazed in a great electric charge and a bolt of pure energy hit Magus, lighting him up like a torch. His silver hair stood out on end, his heart leapt in his chest and his eyeballs sizzled as if they'd explode with the heat and pain.

Magus cried out in agony and staggered backwards, the heavy egg in his hand giving his movement momentum. He teetered as if frozen on the brink of the enormous stone. He gaped in horror, knowing that he'd fall, knowing in a flash of understanding that this was his childhood nightmare finally come to pass. *He would lie in agony, alone and cold in the silver darkness, with a terrible pulsing in his head as the life-blood spurted out of him and the creeping blackness closed in.*

His terrified eyes met Sylvie's and she threw back her head and laughed. He saw her small, pointy teeth and Magus knew he'd been wrong – this moongazy girl wasn't Sylvie at all. And he realised, in that split second, that the Dark Angel comes in many guises and was here now to lead him from this stone to that cold, lonely haemorrhaging in the darkness.

'Yul!' he howled as he hung in the silver brightness, the name echoing again and again around the stone graveyard in the cold night. 'Yul! Yul!'

There was nothing to stop him from falling from this platform where so long ago a cruel and violent man had hurt a young, helpless girl, and in doing so had caused his conception. There was nothing to hold on to and save himself from death.

Yul leapt forward across the stone and his hand shot out to save his father' life. But it was too late; he caught nothing but thin air, where Magus had stood a second earlier. It was a long way down from the Snake Stone, at the head of the moonlit quarry. A long way down, still falling, to the jagged rocks that waited like sharp pointed teeth at the bottom.

Blood had been spilled – the blood of three men, an appeasement to the dark evil that stalked this ancient arena of death and bloodlust. Three lives had been taken to satisfy the hunger that prowled the labyrinth in the Place of Bones and Death. And now the young magus stood on the ancient Snake Stone, the place of sacrifice, with a raven by his side. Her eyes and feathers glinted silver in the moonlight. The young man gazed out across the white moonscape of the quarry with a heavy heart and eyes full of tears; a strong and brave man had died here tonight.

The stars twinkled in the cold midwinter air and frost dusted the land with sparkling glitter as the moon, clothed in silver, walked the night. The time of the Winter Solstice was approaching. The great Wheel of the Year turned, and the earth turned, and the centuries came around, and time almost stood still, like the sun in the sky at this point in the calendar. Time stood still, but the ancient patterns played themselves out. The ancient stories clamoured to be retold, again and again . . .

Stonewylde had her new magus, the darkness had been satisfied and the dance could go on.

As the fourth green light was suddenly extinguished, Mother Heggy peered at the mangled remains in her clawed hands. It was a tiny wax figure and bore a lock of soft, silver hair taken long ago from a child's head. She nodded, knowing that the prophecy she'd given, all those years past, had been fulfilled.

Under blue and red, the fruit of your passion
Will rise up against you with the folk behind
At the time of brightness in darkness,
And will overthrow you
In the place of bones and death.

She cackled toothlessly and raised the goblet again, drinking deeply this time, toasting the new magus. She threw the tiny mommet out of her circle and into the blazing fire. It hissed and melted, the lock of blond hair sizzling and giving out a foul stench as it burnt.

She gazed at the one green light still burning. Only one left – who could it be? If Magus was dead, Yul should now be safe. But Sylvie – what of her? Old Mother Heggy felt the cold clutch of fear around her heart in a sharp squeeze. Not her little bright one – she couldn't bear to lose Sylvie. The girl was so precious, just as her Raven had been. So whose was the fifth death?

There was a soft knock at the door, making her jump in her old, wrinkled skin. Who could be knocking on her door at this time, in the darkness, up here at the cottage on the hill? It couldn't be Yul yet, for he was miles away. Perhaps some kind soul to check that she was alright? Maybe to see if she'd come to the sunrise ceremony after all? She shook her wizened head – it was warm in this room but she knew how cold it was outside, and she was far too old and feeble to risk exposure to the freezing night air.

The knock came again, louder and more insistent – impatient almost.

'Lift the latch and come in!' she croaked, looking up.

Her milky eyes widened in surprise at the sight of her unexpected visitor.

'Oh, 'tis you! Aye, right enough, 'tis time. I should've known.'

Moonlight silhouetted the robed, hooded figure standing tall and silent on the threshold, the darkness around him just a little blacker than it should be. She nodded – now she understood. With a sigh, Mother Heggy gazed deep into his fathomless eyes and then her head fell to her chest. The fifth green light faltered, flickered and died.

Full Circle

In the darkness before dawn, the folk of Stonewylde packed into the Stone Circle, their breath forming white clouds around their heads. The sun had not yet risen on the shortest day of the year, but the longest night was over. The great Solstice Bonfire stood at one edge of the circle, its boughs dusted with frost. A boy shivered up on the platform at the summit, by the brazier, waiting to herald the dawn. Below him the folk shifted restlessly with anticipation.

The drummers played their rhythms softly and Clip chanted with quiet assurance at the Altar Stone. Tall and thin, he looked resplendent in white robes with a headdress of mistletoe and ivy on his wispy blond hair. His movements and voice were soothing but his grey eyes danced with excitement. As the sun approached the horizon the tension rose and the drumming picked up speed and insistency.

People's hearts beat faster, the drumbeats reverberating in their chests, and their heartbeats became as one, a great pulsing rhythm of sunrise and hope. The boy on the platform cried out and lit the flame. The brazier flared brightly and the people chanted, welcoming the return of the sun and the return of longer days. The boy climbed down the ladder inside the fire, clutching the torch he'd lit in the brazier. But every face was turned towards the Long Walk where two figures approached.

Yul and Sylvie stepped into the Stone Circle hand in hand. He wore a golden Solstice robe and a great headdress of mistletoe, ivy and holly. The woven winter foliage seemed to sprout from his dark curls in a riot of greenery and berries and his beautiful face was solemn but joyful. Next to him Sylvie was tall and slender in dark green Yule robes. The evergreen material was embroidered with a pattern of leaves and the white mistletoe berries, red holly berries, and black ivy berries. Her glorious silver hair cascaded down her back, topped by a filigree circlet bearing a silver crescent to signify the Maiden. Her moonstone eyes danced with quiet delight to be united at last with Yul.

As they came level with the bonfire, the boy emerged from the concealed exit. With a bow he passed the flaming torch to Yul, who held it aloft as he and Sylvie continued their procession to the Altar Stone. Sylvie took her place next to her father whilst Yul climbed the step and stood upon the stone, outstretched arm holding the Sacred Flame high. He stood there for a heartbeat and then the first beams of the sun flashed through the gap in the aligned stones. The golden rays hit Yul and his robe seemed to light up, the embroidery of radiant suns glittering and reflecting the beams of light.

As sunlight illuminated him, Yul felt the earth energy beneath him start to spiral up through the stone and into his body. But this was stronger, much stronger, than ever before. The very earth seemed to sing, a strange music of rock and soil, the voice of the Goddess in the Landscape.

A deep shuddering rumbled beneath the Stone Circle, almost like an earthquake, making the ground tremble and the people shake. It lasted only a brief heart-lurching moment. Reaching a terrifying crescendo, the spiral of Earth Magic shot out of the Altar Stone and swirled around Yul in a whirlwind, encasing him in an aura of pure energy. He radiated light, his robed body and wreathed head were haloed with green brightness. The torch in his hand flared brilliant green and his eyes burned like stars as he stood tall, doused in Earth Magic that seemed to set him on fire.

'Folk of Stonewylde,' cried Clip, 'behold our new magus! The

Green Man has returned to Stonewylde! All will be well! All will prosper! We greet him and offer him our loyalty!'

'MAGUS OF STONEWYLDE!' roared hundreds of voices.

The energy flew around the Circle touching the hearts of every person there. The drums rolled triumphantly and the community burst into song, an ancient song whose words were remembered but no longer understood. The ceremony continued in the crisp morning air, brilliant with sparkling sunlight and a new atmosphere of liberty and joy.

Yul and Sylvie caught each other's eye and smiled, unable to believe that this day had finally dawned. Sylvie looked around the packed Circle, wondering if Professor Siskin had managed to return to Stonewylde. She hadn't seen him yet, but as the light glowed brighter by the minute she scanned the faces expectantly. She hoped that he'd seen the amazing moment when the Green Man returned to Stonewylde, just as he'd foretold. She knew the professor's soul belonged here, as did hers, and with his long exile finally over the elderly man could now find contentment in the place he loved so dearly.

Yul thought of Mother Heggy and his intended visit to her today with Sylvie. She'd be so happy to see the pair of them together, the grandchildren of her Raven. The man she'd hated since his brutal conception on the Snake Stone was gone and her prophecy had come true. As he thought of Mother Heggy and the part she'd played in this, there was a flapping and a flurry. The great black crow appeared, flying slowly into the sacred Circle cawing loudly. Yul noticed many people make the sign of the pentangle, remembering old Mother Heggy and her natural magic. The crow circled overhead, his wings splayed, and then alighted in a tumble of feathers onto Sylvie's shoulder. People around the Stone Circle nodded. The Wise Woman's crow had spoken – Sylvie truly belonged by Yul's side.

When it was time for the customary sharing of cakes and mead, the people came forward as usual in lines towards the altar. But there was also an exodus, by silent consent, of many Hallfolk. They left quietly, streaming back up the Long Walk towards the

Hall and their suitcases, understanding that Stonewylde was now a different place. Visiting adults took their children, and soon there were few blond heads to be seen amongst the vast crowd of Villagers.

The folk who stayed were surprised to find the cakes delicious but not spiced with strange herbs. The mead was heady but not laced with anything stronger. Instead they received something infinitely more enthralling. One by one they stood on the step before Yul, reaching up to him on the Altar Stone. Glorious in golden Solstice robes and evergreen winter headdress, he bent and clasped their hands in his. Grey eyes blazing with energy and light, he looked deep into each person's eyes and gave them a taste of green magic. For this was the true but long forgotten role of the magus, the magician, the wise one. The energy at Stonewylde was everyone's – not a privilege to be hoarded by one, but a gift to be shared by all.

Maizie and Miranda came up together, both glowing with pride at their children's bravery and triumph. Clip too received the energy from Yul, full of respect for the young man. When he looked up at the handsome dark face before him he knew Yul would succeed as magus. He was too much his father's son to do otherwise.

Finally, when every person had been blessed one by one, Sylvie came from her place beside the stone. She stood before Yul, the black crow on her shoulder. He guided her up from the step to stand next to him on the Altar Stone. Holding hands they faced each other, and the energy flowed in both directions. Green magic and quicksilver. Their eyes locked together as they gazed into each other's souls. The fear, pain and suffering of the past months melted away to nothing, like frost in the sun. Their passion and adoration glimmered around them in an aura for all to see. The crow took off and flew to the stone behind them, where the image of the Green Man smiled amidst the traditional symbols of the Winter Solstice.

The sun blessed them both, gilding them like bright angels. They looked deep into each other's eyes and time seemed to stand still for a moment. Then, moving as one, they fell into a fierce embrace. The folk cheered as they held each other tightly, two hearts beating wildly in unison.

Sylvie and Yul felt the cogs of time falling into place. They felt the wheels of fate revolving and knew this was their rightful destiny. The ancient story was told again. The pattern was repeated as it had been throughout the ages in this enchanted place. The Green Man and the moongazy girl, the darkness and the brightness, together as one.

The true guardians of the magic of Stonewylde.

Acknowledgements

My acknowledgements written for the original, self-published edition of this book still stand. So continued and deepest thanks to:

Clare Pearson, my first agent – you were right all along!

My three sons George, Oliver and William for putting up with my obsession.

My family and friends, many in Dorset, for your love and support.

Rob Walster of Big Blu Design for the original cover.

Mr B – for giving me the freedom to pursue my dream.

Now that Stonewylde has been taken on by Gollancz and this new edition published, I must add further heartfelt thanks to:

My readers – the thousands of you who've stuck with me, encouraged me and loved Stonewylde, and especially the lovely people in the Stonewylde Community.

My wonderful family and friends again – for your enthusiasm and kindness.

Piers Russell-Cobb, my literary agent, for being so clever.

Gillian Redfearn, my editor, for your excellence and patience.

My sister Claire of Helixtree and Rob Walster of Big Blu Design for the beautiful Stonewylde logo.

Mr B, my own personal magus.